THE CATHEDRAL OF KNOWN THINGS

D0770901

Also by Edward Cox from Gollancz:

The Relic Guild

THE CATHEDRAL OF KNOWN THINGS

Book Two of The Relic Guild

EDWARD COX

The right of Edward Cox to be identified as the author of
this work has been asserted by him in accordance with the
Copyright, Designs and Patents Act 1988.

First published in Great Britain in 2015
by Gollancz
An imprint of the Orion Publishing Group
Carmelite House, 50 Victoria Embankment,
London EC4Y 0DZ
An Hachette UK Company

This edition published in Great Britain in 2016 by Gollancz

1 3 5 7 9 10 8 6 4 2

A CIP catalogue record for this book is available
from the British Library

ISBN 978 1 473 20034 0

Printed in Great Britain by Clays Ltd, St Ives plc

MIX
Paper from
responsible sources
FSC® C104740

www.edwardcox.net
www.orionbooks.co.uk
www.gollancz.co.uk

For my daughter Marney, who is still too young to read about the adventures of her namesake. You were no help whatsoever while I was writing this book, but please don't ever change …

TIME MECHANIC

At times, he played the long game in the strangest of places.

Above, the primordial mists of the Nothing of Far and Deep roiled beneath an angry sky yet to warm its cold days with the fire of a sun; a monumental dome of liquid slate devoid of nights filled with the ruby and silver glares of its moons. Below, unused time congealed into slabs of pulsing colour to create a landscape of blues and reds hued so variedly as to fill the spectrum between dusk and dawn. Raw thaumaturgy dashed the air like static, whipping, dancing, as free and wild as windborne snow. A hum, low enough to be felt rather than heard, vibrated and churned the volatile atmosphere, coaxing shape from shapelessness.

Hovering between the angry sky and the landscape in flux, Fabian Moor was exhilarated by the flakes of higher magic swirling around him, stinging his face, singing to his blood. An age had passed since he had last been able to enjoy the moment.

Defeat at the hands of the Relic Guild was far in the future, yet a distant memory now. Those petty, interfering magickers might have proved much more intelligent, problematic – even more powerful – than Moor had been prepared for, but ultimately their meddling had achieved nothing that hindered Lord Spiral's greater strategy. Yes, details had been compromised, planning required adjustment, new pathways needed to be found; but all the Relic Guild had really achieved was to buy themselves a little extra time. Just a few more years.

With a feeling of satisfaction, Moor looked to the northern horizon, and stared with wonder upon a column of energy that connected unstable land to swirling sky like an umbilical cord of liquid fire. Droning with a mournful song, blazing, spitting bolts of purple at the ground, the column snaked and twisted through the air like a whirlwind. The

First and Greatest Spell, that energy was called, and it bore a legend. It had been cast by the only creature of higher magic worshipped by all lower races: the Timewatcher.

The First and Greatest Spell would one day be contained within a building named the Nightshade. But now, in its raw state, the spell was an immense and untamed formation of thaumaturgy that inflated an ever expanding bubble within the Nothing of Far and Deep. It held aloft the sky while solidifying time into the founding stones of an intrinsic House that would come to be known as Labrys Town, a human haven surrounded by the alleyways of an endless maze called the Great Labyrinth. The creation of this House would prove to be the Timewatcher's grandest achievement, and her biggest mistake.

Among all the Thaumaturgists, only Spiral, the Lord of the Genii, had been able to match the Timewatcher's power; only his command of higher magic had been able to smuggle Moor back to this time, a thousand years before the Genii War, to when the Timewatcher's fabled First and Greatest Spell birthed the most significant epoch in the history of the Houses.

Moor's sense of wonder grew. In this time frame, the Aelfir were warring against each other, out among the plethora of realms, fighting in perpetual, bloody battles that never heralded a victor – a cycle of pointlessness that was already centuries old. When the Great Labyrinth was completed, The Timewatcher would use it to break that cycle, and spell the end of what the Aelfir would come to call the Old Ways. Moor understood what a privilege it was to be chosen to bear witness to such an important beginning, to such … *creation*. Labrys Town might give the Aelfir a common ground, give them peace, but that peace would not last.

And to think, in only a millennium, the Great Labyrinth would become the catalyst that caused The Timewatcher to lose so many of her children. Lord Spiral and his Genii were coming, and nothing would be the same again.

An itch crawled across his skin.

Hollowness gnawed inside him.

Fabian Moor sighed.

From the satchel which hung from his shoulder, he took a phial of blood and popped the cork with his thumb. He paused before drinking, staring at the phial and its contents.

A part of Moor had hoped that being present at this primitive stage of the Labyrinth's creation might ease his cravings; that the flakes of raw thaumaturgy, hissing in the air like a storm of static, might substitute the need for sustenance that ached in his core. He wondered: was this chronic need to feed on blood a weakness? Perhaps the virus that he carried meant he had become nothing more than vermin. Or did his condition make him greater even than the Thaumaturgists?

In the overall scheme of things, did it matter?

Lifting the phial to his lips, Moor drained the blood in one go. He was repulsed by how willingly he savoured the rusty tang as it slipped thickly down his throat, quenching his hunger, filling the void inside him. The phial fell from his grasp, and he watched it tumble down, end over end, until it disappeared into the fluxing landscape. There was no time left for musing and marvelling. Slowly, Moor descended. His eyes ever watchful, his instincts alert, almost fearful.

The purple fire of the First and Greatest Spell might have been providing the highest of thaumaturgy by which this House was achieving existence, but the Timewatcher's spell would not sculpt the final design. For that, the Great Labyrinth and its town required labourers … of a kind.

Moor could see them as he neared the ground, hundreds, thousands of them, scurrying and lumbering and sliding over slabs and boulders that glowed blue and red. Radiating a vague violet sheen, the workers burrowed and dug, carved and built. Labouring tirelessly, in perfect unison, they hardened time to the black stone foundations of this House. Sculptors, creators, the builders of realms, these things were the Timewatcher's loyal pets. They were the Time Engineers.

Some of them appeared humanoid, hefting stone and laying brickwork; others appeared as giant slugs that devoured everything in their path to then excrete lines of dull purple jelly like icing squeezed from tubes. The last of them were arachnids, and they scooped up the jelly upon flat backs and carried it to the humanoids to use as mortar in their work. The Time Engineers needed no sustenance, no rest, and were unconcerned by the hostile environment. They would not stop building until this House was finished.

Moor spied an area of completed ground beside a wide chasm, and headed towards it. Landing near the edge of the chasm, he froze, tense and ready, as an arachnid scuttled towards him, back laden with purple mortar.

For the most part, Time Engineers were apathetic creatures, harbouring no prejudices, incapable of distinguishing between friend and foe. They understood only order and purpose. However, whether Moor be Genii, vermin, or a new and brilliant form of life, he remained fundamentally a creature of higher magic. If the Engineers detected his thaumaturgy, they would regard him simply as raw material to be mashed and ground into the foundations of Labrys Town.

The single arachnid didn't pose much of a threat. But if the one approaching detected Moor, it would summon its fellow Engineers, and one Genii could not stand against the thousands that would answer that call. Should he attempt to fight, they would alert the Timewatcher to the discrepancy, and Moor would have to flee before his lord and master's orders could be carried out. There would be no second chance. Subtlety was his best friend in this place.

Thankfully, the lone Engineer was focused on its current task. It did not pursue the Genii who had broken into this timeframe, but scurried up to the chasm and disappeared down into it. Relieved, Moor peered over the edge.

The fissure was shallower than he had expected, though it still sank into the ground a fair way. Its mouth might have been crude and ragged, but the further down the chasm reached, the neater and squarer its walls became. Moor could see Time Engineers working tirelessly, their violet glow lighting the depths. Some clung to the walls, smoothing and shaping; others worked at the very bottom, constructing what Moor supposed would be the partitions of interconnecting rooms.

Glancing nervously around at the forming landscape, ensuring no other Time Engineers were close by, Moor dipped a hand into his satchel again, this time producing a small terracotta jar. He ran a pale hand over the smooth and plain surface, feeling the charge of higher magic held inside.

The last of the Genii.

The other jars containing the essences of Moor's fellow Genii were already in place. Viktor Gadreel, Hagi Tabet and Yves Harrow now lay waiting among the bones of Labrys Town. This final terracotta jar contained the essence of Mo Asajad.

In Moor's natural time period, the war against the Timewatcher was over, and Lord Spiral had lost – or so his enemies believed. The rest of the Genii faced imminent execution, and the last of their allies among the Houses of the Aelfir had been vanquished. Every one of the secret strongholds Spiral had created within the Nothing of Far and Deep was being searched out and destroyed. There were no safe havens left for the only remaining Genii.

Moor could not take the other Genii to where he was headed; a tomb of his own awaited him, and his immediate future was too unpredictable to play minder to his comrades. The passage of time, while they lay hidden beneath the noses of their enemies, was the best weapon they had now. The higher magic that contained Asajad, Gadreel, Tabet and Harrow inside the terracotta jars was unstable; but with the energy of the First and Greatest Spell wrapped around them, they would be kept safe, kept strong, waiting for the day that Moor could return to reanimate them.

It was Lord Spiral himself who had taught Moor the forbidden thaumaturgy that had preserved the essences of his colleagues. Moor remembered the tortures it had inflicted upon them. He could not rid himself of the images and sounds of their suffering. Only Mo Asajad had refrained from screaming when Moor had reduced her physical form to ashes. She had glared at him throughout the process, gritting her teeth against the agony, and she had not stopped glaring until she no longer had eyes to glare with.

Moor studied the terracotta jar in his hands, struggling to understand why Lord Spiral had chosen Lady Asajad for the task. Her devotion to the Genii cause was pure, but Spiral was the only person Asajad would obey without question. When her essence was reanimated she would resent following Moor's orders. She would not function well within a group not under Lord Spiral's personal command. Mo Asajad lived to dominate, she craved control. She was an unhinged creature of higher magic, and Moor could foresee problems.

He circled a finger around the jar's wax seal.

It was not beyond the realms of temptation that he might compromise Asajad's containment device. He could hurl it down into the chasm, to the very bottom, where the terracotta would shatter and release the thaumaturgy it contained. And when Asajad's essence began its ravenous search for meat and blood and reanimation, the Time Engineers could have their way with her. They could recycle her thaumaturgy and grind it into the fabric of the Labyrinth. Getting rid of her now might cause fewer problems in the long run, Moor reasoned. And who would know what he had done?

No. Spiral had chosen Asajad, and Moor could not defy his lord and master.

Holding the jar securely in both hands, Moor stepped off the edge of the chasm and floated down.

Careful to keep himself away from the arachnids clinging to the sheer faces surrounding him, he continued descending until he neared the bottom. His earlier suspicions had proved correct; the Engineers were indeed segmenting the wide and long floor into rooms. The walls they had built thus far were incomplete, appearing as ruins. Moor wondered what manner of building would eventually rise from this great pit.

He landed in a half-finished room where a single humanoid Time Engineer, its glowing skin fractured by black lines like a network of veins, laboured away. The Engineer did not react to the Genii's arrival. It continued to build its wall higher.

Taking a steadying breath, Moor latched onto the thaumaturgy with which the First and Greatest Spell had saturated this land and flashed a quick command to the humanoid.

The Engineer ceased working and turned to face the source of the irregularity.

It had no features as such, just a swirl of black-veined violet where its face should have been. The glow of its body brightened and dimmed as though it was unsure how to proceed. Once again Moor touched the First and Greatest Spell. He didn't dare delve too deeply lest its power absorb his own entirely. He barely skimmed the surface, scratched down just enough to send the Time Engineer a simple but firm command which it could not refuse.

Moor placed the terracotta jar on the newly formed floor and stepped back. The Engineer stepped forward to kneel beside the jar. And then, just as the other Engineers had done for Gadreel, Tabet and Harrow, it proceeded to bury the essence of Mo Asajad.

It punched the floor, its fist sinking effortlessly into hardened time with a sound oddly poised between breaking glass and splashing water. The Engineer plunged its arm down to the shoulder before withdrawing it, leaving behind a perfectly circular hole. Moor held his breath as the Timewatcher's labourer picked up the terracotta jar and lowered it into the opening. The worker then began rubbing flat palms over the floor in circles as if washing it. Faster and faster it rubbed until, with subtle pulses of red and blue, the hole was filled and smoothed to black stone.

Moor relinquished his command of the creature. The Engineer turned away from him to continue working on the wall. Only then did the Genii sever his connection to the First and Greatest Spell; only then did he rise at speed, up past the arachnids clinging to the walls, out of the chasm and high into the blizzard of thaumaturgy.

Fast and silent, Moor continued to ascend, soaring towards the roiling slate-grey sky. To the north, the fire of the Timewatcher's mighty spell continued to drone and spit; below, the violet glow of the Time Engineers dotted the landscape. He did not stop rising until he came within several yards of the thick and churning primordial mists of the Nothing of Far and Deep. For a final time, he pushed a hand into his satchel and removed the last item, a simple wooden scroll case.

Moor slid out the scroll and unrolled it carefully, letting the case fall from his grasp. Upon clean white parchment were glyphs and symbols, swirls and shapes, strange configurations, written in black ink by a hand that Moor knew all too well. It was a complicated formula that decorated the page, more complicated than any other Thaumaturgist could create. These were the words of Lord Spiral himself, the language of higher magic, and they were for Moor's eyes only.

This scroll was one of two that Spiral had left Moor before his defeat at the hands of the Timewatcher. The first had allowed Moor to travel back to this early stage in the Labyrinth's creation. But the second …

In this time period, Moor was as a single bee in a forest, a grain of sand in a desert, an unnoticed interloper, but he could only remain for a short while. He was not shielded from the raw elements as the essences of his comrades were in their terracotta jars. He was whole, alive, and if he lingered too long, the mighty thaumaturgy that had delivered him to this time would cease protecting him. The First and Greatest Spell would drain the higher magic from his body until only dust remained. Fortunately, Lord Spiral had given him a way out.

Moor began reading aloud from the scroll, the language of the Thaumaturgists hissing and sighing from his lips as quick and fleeting as the flakes of higher magic whipping around him. He intoned the words of his lord and master, his voice growing in intensity, barely able to contain his urgency.

As Moor recited, a grey churning disc appeared in the Nothing of Far and Deep directly above him. Growing darker and smoother, it swirled faster and faster until Moor read the last word and the disc collapsed into a portal, a black hole punched into the sky.

The scroll burst into flame, burning in a flash to ashes that blew from Moor's hand to be lost in the blizzard.

With his work done, the Genii gave a final glance below him to the landscape birthing a House. The Relic Guild would see Fabian Moor again, and at a time when they were not prepared to deal with him. Moor would return to wake his fellow Genii, and together they would search for Spiral. They would find the hidden prison that the Timewatcher would come to create for the Lord of the Genii.

All things were known in the end.

Moor rushed up towards the portal. Without hesitating, he flew into the black hole and disappeared from the Labyrinth. For now …

CHAPTER ONE

HOUSE OF DEAD TIME

Samuel couldn't breathe. He couldn't see. He couldn't hear.

As soon as he stepped into the portal, the cellar beneath the warehouse in the southern district of Labrys Town had swirled away, the police officers and their guns blinked out of sight, and it was as if the old bounty hunter had jumped into a huge, suffocating blanket. Blackness engulfed him, pressed against his eyelids like the thumbs of a murderer; filled his mouth and nostrils like thick poison searching for the passage of his throat. And it was cold.

In vain, Samuel tried to shout his defiance; to thrash and struggle against the darkness that refused him air and light and sound. His body was unresponsive, numb. With an unfeeling finger, he tried to squeeze the trigger of his revolver, to shoot blindly, madly, into the void. But his deadened nerves had relaxed his hand to a listless thing, and the revolver had already slipped from his grasp to be lost forever in nothingness.

The suffocating blanket seemed to stretch under his weight, until finally it ripped open and spilled him into freefall.

No sooner had Samuel sucked in a great gulp of air than it was stolen from his mouth by rushing wind. His vision was assaulted by streaks of purple lightning. The echo of a bestial scream reached his ears, full of rage and pain. Samuel felt that he would fall forever, down, ever down, until age withered his body, addled his mind, and his life would crumble to dust amidst a starless sky.

Just as he had embraced this notion silver light dazzled his eyes, and the darkness spat him out onto hard, solid stone with a bone-jarring thud.

Sprawled face down on damp cobbles, Samuel groaned and then rose to his hands and knees. He looked up. The portal's glassy surface rippled within a rectangle on a wall of black bricks before him.

With a nudge from his prescient awareness, Samuel jumped to his feet and drew the rifle from the holster on his back. He ejected the empty magazine, slapped a new one into place, and took aim at the portal. The power stone behind the barrel gave a small whine and glowed with violet light as he thumbed it. He might have run out of fire-bullets, but the four metal slugs in the magazine would still kill anyone who dared to follow him.

'I do not think the police will be brave enough to come after us, Samuel.'

The old bounty hunter looked over his shoulder. Van Bam stood behind him, his hands atop his green glass cane.

The illusionist added, 'And I suspect the portal closed once we left the warehouse.'

As if to confirm Van Bam's words, the portal shrank with a low drone. With a sigh and a puff of dust, it disappeared, leaving behind black bricks and no sign that it had ever been there.

Samuel lowered his aim and turned around.

Van Bam's smoothly-shaved head was tilted to one side. The black, loose-fitting shirt and trousers he wore looked dishevelled. The tip of his glass cane touched the cobbled ground between his bare feet, and the metal plates covering the illusionist's eyes glinted with reflected light.

Samuel looked up: Silver Moon shone in the night sky. He looked to his right: a long, wide alleyway stretched away into the gloom. Its walls were supported by buttresses positioned every fifteen paces.

Samuel's features fell. 'The portal led us out into the *Great Labrynth*?'

Van Bam nodded gravely.

Samuel was aghast.

When Fabian Moor and his fellow Genii had taken control of the Nightshade, they had claimed total dominion over Labrys Town, and Samuel had thought everything lost. Yet the Relic Guild had found an unlikely ally in the form of a blue ghost, an avatar which had offered aid, albeit in a strange and dangerous way. It had led them to a secret portal hidden in the cellar of an abandoned ore warehouse. But the portal was meant to be the Labyrinth's backdoor, an emergency exit, an escape route that would lead the Relic Guild to those who could save the denizens from the machinations of the Genii. Instead, it had led them out into the endless twists and turns of the giant maze that surrounded Labrys Town? People disappeared in the Great Labyrinth.

'How does *this* help us?' Samuel demanded of Van Bam.

They could have been anywhere in the Great Labyrinth. The only place of civilisation was Labrys Town, at the centre of the maze. And even if returning there was an option, it could take hours or days, weeks, months or years of walking through never-ending alleyways to find it.

'It would seem the portal has only delivered us to the midway point in our journey,' Van Bam replied solemnly. His face was turned toward a slim stone pedestal that had risen from the alley floor, a few paces ahead.

Closely followed by Van Bam, Samuel stepped over to the pedestal. Its top had been fashioned into a square box, which was filled with a colourless, gelatinous substance. Before the pedestal, a section of the cobbled ground had been smoothed to form a large disc of grey.

'A shadow carriage?' Samuel said.

Van Bam nodded. 'It is a sure sign that the doorway to the House we need is in the Great Labyrinth. But to summon a shadow carriage to take us to it, we must first know the symbol for that House.'

Samuel frowned. 'Where's Clara?'

Van Bam gestured with his head, and Samuel looked to his left. The alleyway stopped at a dead end. Against the wall, Clara's small figure lay crumpled. Moonlight glinted from the blood that pumped from the bullet wound in her side, which she had sustained back at the warehouse. Her blood formed a puddle on the cobbles around her. She wasn't moving.

'No,' Samuel said.

He took a step towards her, but was checked by Van Bam's voice.

'We have another problem, Samuel.'

The ex-Resident was facing down the long alley. Samuel could see something moving down there. Although the sky was clear, it was as though a veil of cloud was being drawn over the light of Silver Moon. In the near distance, darkness deeper than the night gloom slithered over brickwork and cobbles, making oily, fluid progress along the alley towards the agents of the Relic Guild.

A light breeze brought strange scents to Samuel's nose. Age. Corruption. Hopelessness. The temperature dropped, became icier than the fresh chill of Silver Moon.

'Shit,' Samuel spat, his breath frosting before his face.

The Retrospective … that House of dead time, of corrosion, perversion, where all the monsters dwelt … it had sensed the Relic Guild. Its doorway was opening.

'I lost my revolver,' Samuel stated, gripping his rifle tightly. 'And I've only got four bullets left.'

With gritted teeth, Van Bam stabbed his glass cane down onto the ground. To a musical chime, bolts of illusionist magic sped from the cane, hurtling down the alleyway to merge and form a hard barrier of transparent green that stretched from wall to wall. When the slithering doorway met it, a low creaking filled the freezing air. But the barrier held. It had halted the Retrospective.

'It will not last long,' Van Bam warned.

Samuel's magic refused to help him. The prescient awareness that had served him well throughout his life, that had saved his skin on innumerable occasions, told the old bounty hunter that this was his last stand. There was nowhere else to turn, and soon the wild demons of the Retrospective would come hunting his flesh.

Samuel looked at the pedestal and the stone box, with a searing sense of frustration. All he needed to do was draw the right House symbol into the gelatinous contents, and a shadow carriage would appear to whisk them away to safety.

'We need that damned House symbol right *now*, Van Bam!'

'If the avatar knew it, then Clara is the only person it gave it to.'

Clara's small form remained unmoving against the dead end wall.

'Clara!' Samuel bellowed. He felt a small pang of relief as her face twitched, and she stirred. 'Did the avatar give you a symbol? Quickly!'

The changeling struggled but failed to open her eyes. She released a moan of pain.

Samuel made to approach her again, but this time Van Bam grabbed his arm.

'Do not touch her,' he hissed.

Samuel froze. He had never heard such fear in Van Bam's voice before.

'It is her colours, Samuel,' the illusionist added. 'I can see—'

A loud snap shattered the air. A jagged crack had appeared in Van Bam's magical barrier. The crack continued to spread and groan as the weight of the Retrospective pushed against it.

Clara moaned again. Or was it a growl?

She seemed to be trying to open her medicine tin. The lid gave, but the tin slipped from her grasp, spilling tiny white tablets into the puddle of her blood. She looked up at the night sky, opened her mouth and gave a growl of frustration. Her canine teeth had lengthened to sharp points. She glared at Samuel and Van Bam, her eyes shining with yellow light.

'It's coming,' she whispered hoarsely.

And Clara howled like a wolf.

CHAPTER TWO

THE SECRETS OF FLOWERS

Fabian Moor stood inside his sterile cube of silver metal.

The cube had been constructed by thaumaturgy, and it had been Moor's safe haven since the end of what the humans called the Genii War. For forty years, he had sheltered inside it, hidden from those who did not know that a handful of Genii had survived the war against the Timewatcher. In any other place, Moor was compelled to feed on blood to preserve his life. But the cube's magic had suppressed this maddening need. Still, the long decades of isolation had at times threatened to drive Moor insane, but he had resisted, retained his sanity by never losing sight of the day when his undoubting faith and unwavering patience would be rewarded.

Now that reward was at hand. The purpose of the sterile cube of thaumaturgic metal was almost served.

Behind Moor, Mo Asajad focused her attention on the empath who was slowly dying in the clutches of the serpentine tree that grew at the centre of the cube's silver floor. Lady Asajad, tall and stick-thin beneath a priest's cassock, long, straight black hair flowing down her back – she stood still, frozen, tense, watching the empath as keenly as a carrion bird hovering over a battlefield, searching for bloody spoils.

It wasn't that Moor didn't share his fellow Genii's fervent eagerness – high expectations had been placed on this human magicker called Marney. She was to reveal her secrets and fulfil the desires of the Genii. But if the isolation of the last four decades had taught Moor anything, it was the virtue of patience. Occasionally, one could do nothing but wait for events to happen as and when they were ready.

Leaving Asajad to her crow-like observations, Moor cleared a wall of the silver cube to shimmering air. He gazed out on a silent House of nightmare.

The Retrospective was a huge and violent realm, home to countless monsters fighting each other in never-ending battles that raged across a scorched landscape beneath a hateful sky filled with poison and lightning. It had been the Timewatcher – a being supposedly the embodiment of benevolence and equality – who had created this place at the end of the Genii War. The monsters roaming this House of damnation had at one time been Aelfirian soldiers who had fought bravely alongside Lord Spiral and his Genii. The Retrospective was punishment for their choice, for their *treachery*, a prison in which dead time perverted their bodies and minds with ceaseless fury and blood-lust.

Moor had to wonder if the Timewatcher, while serving her brand of vengeful justice upon Spiral's armies, had ever paused to consider the true implications of creating the Retrospective. Across the scarred and beaten landscape, Moor could see innumerable beasts of every shade of nightmare fighting and killing, hacking and maiming, stabbing, slicing, biting and feeding upon each other. Lust, raw animal lust, revelling in lawless pandemonium. But if the wild demons could be tamed and united into one mighty army, they would form such an unbeatable force that even the Timewatcher's Thaumaturgists would tremble before them.

Moor quelled a surge of impatience.

The power to tame the wild demons was beyond the likes of Fabian Moor and Mo Asajad. Only Lord Spiral could achieve this. Only his mastery of thaumaturgy, which rivalled the power of the Timewatcher Herself, could command true unification within the Retrospective. But Lord Spiral was lost. At the end of the Genii War, the Timewatcher had banished him to his very own prison realm, a House called Oldest Place, where he was to face his every act of betrayal in endless, repetitive waves of torture. It was said that only the Timewatcher knew where She had hidden Oldest Place, but Fabian Moor knew better…

He looked over his shoulder at the empath held aloft by the serpentine branches of the tree-like creature. Soon she would reveal the secret location of Oldest Place, and Lord Spiral would be freed. He would lead an unstoppable army of wild demons through the Houses of the Aelfir like a tempest of eternal fire that would blaze and grow, spreading to realms and dimensions far beyond the comprehension of lowly minds like that of this magicker. And the Timewatcher would come to learn how blind She had been in creating the Retrospective.

Moor's eye was caught by an anomaly outside, within the violent panorama. A lone demon stood mere paces away from the other side of the cube's wall of shimmering air. Apparently uninterested in the bestial warfare raging behind it, the monster was staring back at the Genii.

Broad, muscular, standing at least seven feet tall, this wild demon didn't seem quite so … *wild*. Oh, it looked vicious enough: skin the colour of corpses, arms and legs covered in gashes crudely stitched with thick twine and puckered into angry red lips. It wore a leather kilt, studded with sharp and rusty spikes, and a leather jerkin whose pointed hood covered the beast's head and face. On its feet it wore calf-length boots made from skin fresh enough to be still greasy with sweat and blood. And in its huge hands – hands with sinewy fingers tipped with cracked, black nails – it held a woodcutter's axe, a weapon that might have seemed mundane if not for the sheer size of its wickedly sharpened head.

Despite its appearance, Moor detected a consciousness within this demon's madness, buried and calculating.

In truth, this was not the first time Moor had observed the creature. Genii and demon had stared at each other in this way once before. On that occasion, the demon had attacked. It had run towards Moor, its huge woodcutter's axe raised and ready to cleave. Moor had easily repelled the attack with a simple burst of thaumaturgy that punched the demon to its back. When it jumped to its feet again, Moor had expected a second assault. But the demon had hesitated and seemed to think twice about its actions. It had raised the axe above its head, performing a series of threatening gestures, as if to retain its pride in the face of a fight it recognised it couldn't win.

That act of pride had piqued Moor's curiosity. He had probed the demon's mind, wondering if there was more than just a spark of intelligence within its mindlessness. The Genii had been surprised to discover a strong awareness that bordered on personality. But the intrusion into its mind had confused the demon, shattering its resolve, and it had fled in fear.

Now the demon didn't run, didn't seem frightened, and made no threatening gestures. Moor gained the impression that this thing had been waiting for him to return. Did the demon remember the Aelf that it used to be? Did it recognise Moor as a Genii, one of Spiral's generals who had led the Aelfirian rebels in the war against the Timewatcher?

Intrigued, Moor reached out with his thaumaturgy, sent it through the wall of shimmering air to stroke the demon's senses. At first, he felt nothing but hate and rage, and the beast flinched, raising its axe defensively. Concerned the monster would again flee, Moor quickly latched onto the intelligence that was buried beneath layers of madness. He whispered to it.

Slowly, the demon lowered its axe. Moor was pleased to sense a pulse of inquisitiveness. He posed a question to the demon: was it still loyal to the Genii?

In answer, the demon dropped to one knee, heavily, clumsily. It laid its axe down upon the scorched earth and bowed its hooded head.

Moor's satisfaction came as a grim smile.

'Fabian!'

Asajad's voice carried its usual tone of disrespect, and Moor's smile of triumph quickly changed to a grimace of irritation.

'What?' he snapped.

'Stop playing with the monsters and look at this.'

The serpentine tree was stirring.

Looking back into the Retrospective, Moor saw the demon had remained on its knee, head bowed. He let the beast know that he was pleased and pulsed a command into its being – *look for me*. He broke his connection with the demon and returned the wall of the cube to its solid silver state. As the Retrospective disappeared, Moor turned and moved to stand beside Asajad.

The strange, treelike creature was shuddering, which in turn caused its captive's body to spasm. Leathery branches coiled tighter around Marney's arms and legs, hoisting her higher into the air. The empath's eyes remained closed and not one sigh of distress escaped her dry and cracked lips.

Marney's head snapped back, her neck muscles straining, her mouth working silently as if trying to articulate her agony. Moor knew that the tip of the leathery limb that had punctured the empath's lower back and coiled up around her spine was now drinking memories from Marney's mind, absorbing her life, draining her of everything she had ever been, of everything she knew.

The expression on Asajad's small, porcelain face was eager, her breathing was quick and hard, exhilarated.

The tree became more agitated.

Its roots writhed and twisted on the floor like a nest of snakes; its highest branches stabbed and slapped the silver ceiling. Marney began shaking, her entire body tense and vibrating. Her eyes fluttered open and rolled to white. A small gasp escaped Asajad; a single limb of the serpentine tree had stretched towards the Genii, pointing at them accusingly. Its tip swelled like an abscess, changing the leathery brown-green bark to a taut and angry red. But when the abscess burst, it was not with blood and pus. Instead, a thing of beauty was revealed.

A flower. Crimson petals unfurled like a hand reaching for salvation. Delicate florets in a vibrant yellow centre lay matted and heavy with clear nectar sugared sweet with the memories of an empath.

From the sleeve of her cassock, Asajad produced a small scalpel and offered it to Moor. He took it from her and stepped forwards. The flower quivered before him. He hooked it between his fingers, gently pulling the petals forward to expose the stem. With one careful but deft motion, Moor cut the flower free. The stub bled a brownish sludge.

Moor stepped back with his prize nestled in his hand.

The outreaching branch dropped to the silver floor with a slap. The tree ceased all movement, and Marney hung limp in its grasp. The tree gave a sudden judder. With a wet sucking the branch that had coiled around the empath's spine slid out of her back, and hung flaccid, blood-smeared and glistening. And then the strange, serpentine tree entered its death throes.

A creaking filled the air before quickly turning into a multitude of dull pops and cracks. The tree began steaming as every drop of moisture within it was superheated. The greens and browns of its bark turned a sun-baked, clay-like grey. Finally, the strange creature began to crack and crumble. As it collapsed into a pile of broken stone, its purpose served, the empath fell heavily to the floor, where she lay face down and motionless.

Moor stared at the ugly red hole in Marney's lower back, and then let the scalpel clatter down beside her. He cradled the crimson and yellow flower to his chest, and turned to his fellow Genii.

'The memories of an empath,' Asajad whispered.

'In which lies the location of Oldest Place,' Moor added.

Neither of them could hide their euphoria.

The moment was interrupted by the wall behind the Genii changing from solid silver to pearlescent liquid and finally to shimmering air. A view into a room within the Nightshade was revealed, along with the considerable form of Viktor Gadreel.

Unlike the thin and bird-like Asajad, Gadreel was thick and wide of shoulders, obese in body, beneath his cassock. Bald-headed and heavy-jowelled he had only smooth skin where his left eye should have been; his right eye glinted with intolerance. Gadreel stepped into the silver cube, his footfalls heavy. The hulking Genii was not pleased.

'Hamir is still unreachable,' he announced, his voice a rumble. 'For the life of me, Fabian, I cannot break through to him.'

The shine of Moor's elation dulled.

Hamir, the Resident's aide, the necromancer – he had gone into hiding when the Genii had taken control of Labrys Town. He had locked himself away in the very bowels of the Nightshade, in a room with a door that first Asajad, and now Gadreel, could not open.

'And now Hagi tells me that the denizens have failed us,' Gadreel continued. His eye was full of hate. 'The *police* that she sent after the Relic Guild were useless.'

Moor's jaw clenched. To have this moment spoiled by mention of those petty magickers drove him to thoughts of murder. 'The Relic Guild survived?'

Gadreel nodded, once. 'They escaped the warehouse. Reports say they just disappeared. Perhaps they found a doorway out of the Labyrinth, Fabian.'

Moor drew a calming breath. 'Impossible. No human could reverse the Timewatcher's prerogative. And those *magickers* are certainly not skilled enough to create a portal themselves. The Relic Guild is still in Labrys Town, and they will be found—'

'Fabian …' Asajad's irritated whisper also carried an air of pleading which was not often heard from the Genii. 'Forget the Relic Guild. Forget Hamir. We have what we need.'

Gadreel's one eye narrowed as he considered the empath lying crumpled amidst the ruins of the serpentine tree. He then looked at Moor's hands held protectively to his chest.

'It is done?' he asked.

Moor answered by allowing him a glimpse of the crimson and yellow flower.

Gadreel licked his fat lips. 'We are ready to free Lord Spiral?'

'Almost.' The ghost of a smile returned to Moor's face. 'The time is close, my friends. Come.'

Moor strode away from Asajad, past Gadreel, heading toward the room in the Nightshade on the other side of the silver cube.

'Wait,' said Asajad. 'What about her?'

Moor looked back at Marney. Her skin was grey and scarred; the wound on her lower back angry and weeping. Whether she breathed or not, he could not tell. The empath, the filthy human lying naked and stripped of all dignity – she too had served her purpose.

'Her mind has been erased,' Moor said. 'Her body is only a shell now.'

'And we leave the shell here to die?' Asajad said hopefully.

'If it isn't dead already.' Moor gave a nod and gazed around at the silver walls that had served as his sanctuary for forty years, at the ruins of the strange tree-creature that had given the Genii everything they needed, and finally at the faces of Asajad and Gadreel.

'There is nothing left here that we require,' Moor told them, still holding the flower protectively. 'And the Resident is waiting.'

CHAPTER THREE

CHANGELING

It was agony worse than anyone should have to endure.

The bullet had shattered Clara's hipbone; but it felt as if half her body had been ripped away too. She searched inside herself for a sign that Marney was still with her. She asked for guidance to calm the panic, begged for soothing medicine to ease the pain. What she found was the empath's box of secrets, alive and vibrating at the back of her mind. It told the changeling to let go, to submit to the inevitable, to accept that this was a *good* thing …

Clara recoiled from the advice like it was counsel offered with a poisonous sting.

Alone, bathed in silver light, slumped upon the hard and wet cobbles of a foul-smelling alleyway, she was finding it too hard to recall who she was, to remember all she had learned. Hot blood slicked her skin; her heart thumped a fiery tempo. The pain had sapped her strength and she couldn't open her eyes, let alone move. And in this state, lost and incapacitated, Clara decided she would die.

That was when the first growl came to her throat.

'Clara! Did the avatar give you a symbol? Quickly!'

She recognised the voice, but could not remember the man who spoke. She wanted to reply, but the blood in her veins had turned to molten metal, and only a groan passed her lips. Her temples pounded, her muscles cramped, her skin felt too tight for her skeleton.

'Do not touch her,' another man hissed.

Clara growled as her magic gathered momentum. Broken bones began to knit; torn flesh began regenerating. An ache pulsed in her jaw; her teeth felt long, her tongue a fat slug in her mouth. Skin burning as hairs sprouted from follicles like thick, hot needles, Clara made a supreme effort of will to pull from her pocket a tin filled with tablets of monkshood, the medicine she had taken for most of her life to keep her inner monster buried.

Greasy fingers struggled to open the medicine tin, but she had no real control over her actions. When the lid gave, the tin slipped from her grasp, and her medicine spilled in a cascade of tiny white pills. With another growl, she looked up and forced open her eyes to meet the glaring silver disc of the moon, high and cold in the sky.

Vision painfully sharp, Clara faced the two men in the alleyway. They stood either side of a slim pedestal. One of them, metal plates covering his eyes and dressed in simple black garb, held a cane made from glass so deeply green its facets seemed to ripple in the moonlight like emerald waters. The other man seemed older, his short hair and goatee practically white, his face lined with age. He wore a long brown coat, and held a rifle in his hands, its glowing power stone reeking of thaumaturgy.

Both men were covered in grime, and Clara could hear them breathing. She could taste their fear. Didn't they know they should be running from her?

'It's coming,' Clara warned them.

She tried to scream in anguish, but the slow-burning fuse of her magic touched the explosive, and it was a howl of triumph that escaped her mouth.

A series of dull creaks and pops filled Clara's head as bone and cartilage shifted, broke, grew, and the brutal reorganisation of her skeletal structure began. Clara's face stretched forward, cracking loudly as it snapped into its new elongated shape. With each white-hot break and pop inside her, a cough-like bark escaped from her constricted throat. She thrashed on the floor as muscle and sinew morphed, expanded, ripping clothes at the seams. For a moment, her boots refused to give, but then the leather split and buckles bounced off the alley walls like a spray of bullets. She scrambled forward onto all fours: her arms were now powerful forelegs, covered in thick silver hair; hands were now meaty paws, tipped with nails, long and sharp.

She waited for that moment when the monster strangled her humanity, that moment when animal rage drowned all memory of who she was. But, within Clara, Marney's box of secrets opened just a little more. When the agony and suffering subsided, the usual moment of forgetfulness did not come.

She was the wolf.

Yet with a slap of recognition, she remembered the men before her, and remembered them well. They seemed puny now.

Van Bam stood with his back to Clara, looking down the alleyway that stretched ahead. Samuel didn't seem to know where to look, and the aim of his rifle swung between Clara and what his friend was watching. He directed his desperate eyes to the stone box that sat atop the pedestal.

'What's the damned symbol?' he hissed.

A sharp crack filled the air, followed by several more, like ice breaking under pressure. Ahead of the two men, a barrier of green magic blocked the alleyway from wall to wall. The barrier was already fractured by a series of jagged lines. It groaned as it bulged outward, and then the magic shattered into a hundred pieces that swirled away like smoke on the breeze. A blackness was revealed, scratchy and darker than shadows, its surface uneven and studded by sharp objects like shards of night. The clamour of distant violence reached Clara's erect ears; the already cold air turned to bitter winter. A stench of age and corrosion filled her nostrils ... along with the reek of wild demons.

Samuel had decided exactly where to point his rifle now. With a degree of disgust, Clara noted the old bounty hunter's hands shook as he took aim at the doorway to the Retrospective. Van Bam stood beside his fellow agent, clutching his green glass cane, facing the danger with courage that Clara sensed he did not truly feel.

With the way ahead blocked, and a dead end behind, the sole option left was to stand and fight. This did not displease the wolf.

'Here they come,' Samuel whispered.

The Retrospective opened its door. The jagged studs parted and the fluid blackness clung to a crippled form that pushed its way through. When the Retrospective finally released its denizen, the monster stumbled into the alleyway with a low belch, as if it had emerged from a burst bubble of viscous liquid.

Spindly and hunched, the wild demon paused to taste the air with a fat, lolling tongue, dripping grey saliva. With a round mouth opened wide and full of sharp teeth, it turned its elongated head one way and then the other. Insectile eyes, as large and smooth as the metal plates covering Van Bam's sockets, settled on the Relic Guild agents. The demon stepped forward, dragging clubbed feet over wet cobbles, and raised its long arms, displaying sharp horns for hands, like monstrous rose thorns.

Clara growled.

The demon screeched.

Samuel's rifle flashed and spat.

The bullet smashed through the creature's gaping maw, and the hairless bulb of the back of its head burst with a steaming spray of oily blood. Its scream abruptly silenced, the demon dropped to its knees and fell backwards. The doorway to the Retrospective boiled, reaching out with tentacles that wrapped around the corpse and dragged it back into the depths. No sooner had the body disappeared than the doorway opened again. Three more demons stepped into the alleyway. They differed in shape and size from the first, but each of them had monstrous horns for hands, and faces mostly comprised of gaping fang-filled mouths and large, insectile eyes.

Two more followed them.

Van Bam stabbed his cane down against the floor. With a high, discordant chime, three fist-sized globes of green sped down the alley and punched three of the demons onto their backs.

Clara barked and bounded forward to meet the two still standing.

With a screech, the first demon struck at the wolf with its horned hand, swinging the sharp point in a wide, clumsy arc. Clara easily dodged the blow, and the creature stumbled. She set about the second, leaping into it and bowling it over to the floor. She felt its cold rancid breath as she trapped its head between her huge jaws. She growled and crushed and shook and tore the monster's head from its neck. The demon's flesh and bone had a damp, pulpy texture, and filled Clara's mouth with the taste of rot.

Spitting out the mauled mass, Clara launched into the second demon. Rising on her hind legs, she used her forepaws to shove the monster back against the wall. Its head cracked black brickwork, and it sank to the ground. Clara again used her powerful jaws to rip its head loose.

The other three demons had recovered from Van Bam's assault. They clambered to their feet, shrieking with quick, stuttering voices, and converged on the wolf.

Samuel's rifle flashed and downed two in quick succession. Clara disembowelled the third with the sharp nails of one paw, and tore away its chest with the other. The corpses quickly melted to thick oil that ran along the cobbles to be sucked back into the Retrospective.

The wolf howled to Silver Moon in victory.

'Stand clear,' Van Bam shouted.

The illusionist tried to cast another protective barrier. He failed. As soon as his magic spread across the liquid doorway it fractured, shattered, and blew away on the cold air. Slurping like feet pulled from mud, the surface of the Retrospective began lapping in folds, excited, agitated, preparing to unleash its next monstrosity.

Had she been able, Clara would have smiled.

Legend said there were an infinite number of wild demons within the Retrospective, a never-ending horde of merciless beasts whose passion for violence and blood knew no limits. Clara wanted them to come; she was ready to fight them all, and she faced the doorway with battle-lust raging in her ears.

Behind her, Samuel and Van Bam were arguing about a House symbol. The weakness in their voices angered the wolf, the desperation that searched for some way out when it was obvious that all options led to the fight. Her tail, pointing to the ground, was rigid as a rod of iron; her front quarters lowered, hackles raised, Clara – huge and fierce – bared her teeth with a series of barks. Once again, the Retrospective opened and sent forth its warrior to meet the wolf's challenge.

The sickly green colour of disease, a monstrous worm slumped onto the cobbles like a flaccid limb. Its blubber splayed across the alley, pressing against the walls, blocking the doorway. Patches of thick hair grew from its glistening skin like tufts of wild grass. Slowly, as though yawning, the worm opened its mouth: a gaping hole filled with row upon row of finger-sized teeth. A putrid stench invaded Clara's nostrils as she gazed into the filthy maw. The worm hunched the segments of its body and slid towards the wolf with the greasy sound of slimy flesh over stone.

Clara stood her ground.

With half its body still buried in the Retrospective, the worm raised its mouth high, preparing to descend and swallow its enemy whole. Muscles bunching, the wolf prepared to pounce.

'Clara, no!' Van Bam shouted.

Clara ignored the illusionist, but her assault was checked by a glare of blue light.

It appeared suddenly, blazingly, filling the space between Clara and the demonic worm. The wolf recoiled from its glare. The worm hissed putrid breath, its body contracting and shying away. The light coalesced into the vague shape of a human surrounded by an aura of sky blue. It waved limb-like tendrils that spread from wall to wall, separating the combatants.

Clara backed off a few paces. The vision tugged at her memory, its aura and shape, the black eyes that leaked tears of smoke …

'The avatar,' she heard Van Bam whisper with awe.

Clara knew that was important, but she didn't care; she only wanted to stand her ground, to face this *avatar* and show it her full might. But energy radiated from the spectre, a force that raised the hairs on the wolf's body and frightened the worm. This energy pushed Clara into further retreat, and she hated her weakness in the face of it.

A pale tendril of light waved towards the wolf, snaking in the air as it passed over her. Clara followed its path, watching as it engulfed the stone box atop the pedestal in a blue glow.

Van Bam and Samuel stood transfixed as the avatar's light intensified around the stone box. Both men flinched as a crackle of energy filled the air. It was followed by a low hum. A few paces behind the pedestal, a large disc of shadow had appeared on the floor. The men flinched again and wheeled around as, with a wrenching of stone and a rush of air, a circle of brickwork on the dead end wall crumbled and swirled away into the glassy surface of a circular portal.

Around the pedestal, the aura of blue light sputtered. The avatar blinked in and out of existence a few times. And then it disappeared.

Clara's ears were filled with a hissing, and rancid breath assailed her nostrils. The worm's fear of the avatar had not caused it to flee back into the Retrospective. It slid forwards once more, mouth open and eager to devour the wolf.

'Clara, we are leaving,' Van Bam bellowed.

Clara scorned the idea of backing down from this fight. She showed the worm her teeth.

'Clara!'

'Leave her, Van Bam,' Samuel shouted. 'We can't control her.'

'Clara, listen to me!' Van Bam begged. 'Come with us now, or you die here!'

Flashing her teeth and spitting saliva, Clara began barking at her foe as it pushed its blubbery body ever closer.

The idiot's quite right, you know, a voice said in the wolf's mind.

Confused, Clara skipped back, feeling as though she had been slapped on the snout by an invisible hand.

This really isn't a fight you can win, Clara.

The voice felt harsh and intrusive in her head, and it brought images of a man's gaunt face, his expression hard, his brown eyes maniacal.

Don't get me wrong, child, the voice continued, *I admire your courage, but it truly is time for flight, not fight.*

With the worm still pushing towards her, Clara looked back at Van Bam and Samuel. They stood upon the disc of shadow on the alley floor. Van Bam's expression was pleading as he reached out to her.

'Please ... you cannot survive this.'

Clara faced the worm again, and saw that it was within four paces of her. Some of the fight had left her, but she still bared her teeth and stood her ground. If she used the alley wall as leverage, she could jump up onto the demon's back and bite and slash until it was slaughtered—

And then what will you do about the hordes of wild demons waiting to follow this ugly brute, Clara? The voice drew a breath and shouted at her. *Just run, you idiot!*

Compelled into action, Clara gave a final growl, turned from the worm, and ran to the Relic Guild agents.

The instant she joined them, the edges of the shadow disc furled. Wire-thin strands of shadow arced and criss-crossed overhead to encase the three of them in a mesh-like sphere. The lines began spinning, issuing a whine that slowly rose in pitch. Clara felt tingling in her stomach, and then she and the two men lifted from the ground to float within the sphere.

Outside, the worm gave itself a mighty push. It slithered over the cobbles, crushing the pedestal and the stone box atop it beneath its blubbery body, and reached the sphere.

Clara barked at the demon.

Samuel aimed his rifle.

But as the worm's lipless mouth descended, the thin, spinning lines of shadows began shredding flesh and breaking teeth. Spraying black blood and broken teeth, the worm recoiled with a savage hissing. The whining of the sphere reached a crescendo and it shot away from the Retrospective and its minion. In the instant before the strange carriage entered the portal swirling on the dead end wall, Clara saw the worm's remains lying limp and steaming.

The sphere passed through brickwork as easily as a stone dropping into water. With a *whump* the bright light of Silver Moon returned. The world was streaked, blurred, as they travelled through the alleyways of the Great Labyrinth. Without heeding the twists and turns or the solid brickwork, the shadow carriage continued at a speed Clara couldn't comprehend. Though she floated calmly inside the sphere, her stomach was nauseated by the sense of movement beyond the spinning lines. Floating to her right, Van Bam seemed unconcerned by the journey; on her left, Samuel's teeth were gritted, his face a mask of anger and fear.

The sphere disappeared suddenly, ending the journey abruptly. Clara was sent skidding along slick cobbles. She rolled over to her feet, bristling immediately in a defensive stance, ready for any attack.

Van Bam and Samuel exhibited no ill effects from the jaunt through the Great Labyrinth, and stood facing the wolf. Samuel had trained his rifle on her. There was deadly intent in his eyes, shining as clearly as the power stone set into his weapon. Clara showed him her teeth.

'Clara?' It was Van Bam who had spoken. He raised a hand to keep Samuel's trigger finger at bay, and then took a step towards the wolf. 'I know you can understand me.'

Her yellow eyes glared at him.

'This is a waste of time, Van Bam,' Samuel said dangerously.

'Samuel, just *wait*!' The illusionist took another step towards the wolf. 'Clara, you are either with us or against us. Which is it to be?'

There was no expression on his face, no inflection in his voice. The question had come as a cold statement: life or death – choose one. By what right this man presumed to hold command over her, Clara didn't know. But he had a rude awakening coming if he thought she would ever be subservient to him.

'Nod your head if you are with us, Clara,' Van Bam added.

I'd do as he says if I were you. The man's voice again, coldly amused inside her head. *Van Bam is prepared to give you a chance, Clara, but Samuel is a delicate little princess, and I'm fairly certain he has at least one bullet left.*

Inside Clara, the memory of words came back to her and she found a mental voice of her own.

I know you, she thought to the presence.

The man chuckled. It felt like having an itch inside her head that she could not scratch.

Perhaps you have dreamed of me, he said. *Or is it that you're remembering one of Marney's recollections?*

Gideon …

There will be plenty of time for proper introductions, Clara. First, please show your gentleman friends that you're in control of yourself.

Van Bam was now looking at Clara with a curious expression. Beside him, Samuel held his rifle with a sure and steady aim. Clara could feel the old bounty hunter's readiness to defend himself in any way necessary.

'Clara,' Van Bam snapped. 'Are you with us?'

Do let him know that you are, Gideon cajoled. *Samuel never misses, and it would be such a shame if you died before we became better acquainted.*

With a snort, Clara sat on the wet cobbles and bobbed her head.

Van Bam smiled. 'I think you can lower your weapon now, Samuel.'

The old bounty hunter did no such thing, but his body visibly relaxed.

Van Bam held out a hand to the wolf. The metal plates covering his eyes reflected moonlight with a soul-piercing glare. Clara felt a spark of anger. What was he expecting? That she would sniff him as if he was pack leader?

Of course he does, said Gideon. *You have never been in control of your magic before, Clara. The wolf has always been wild, as it were, and Van Bam knows that. He needs irrefutable proof that the girl is dominant. That you are indeed* with *him.*

I don't need to prove anything to anyone, she thought back angrily.

What, not even to yourself? Gideon's tone was bored. *It's your decision, of course. Personally I think they need you more than you need them.*

Why are you in my head?

Gideon chuckled. *Just show your loyalty, you idiot. Before Samuel remembers he lacks compassion on a grand level.*

With reluctance, Clara edged forward and sniffed Van Bam's hand. His skin reeked of sweat and magic. She sat down, her head level with his chest, and allowed the illusionist to scratch her behind the ear.

'Thank you,' he whispered to her.

This act was enough to finally convince Samuel to lower his rifle. He deactivated the power stone and slid the weapon into the holster on his back. He then bent, placing his hands upon his thighs, and puffed his cheeks.

Play nicely, Clara, Gideon prompted.

The wolf padded up to the old bounty hunter. He raised his eyes to meet her yellow gaze, their faces only six inches apart. For a moment, Clara thought that Samuel might reach out and scratch her behind the ear too, but he seemed to think better of it. Instead, he gave the wolf a nod, didn't quite smile, and said, 'Good to know you're still in there.'

Clara snorted breath into his face.

Good girl, Gideon purred. *You might just live through this yet.*

'A strange day, wouldn't you agree, Samuel?' said Van Bam.

The illusionist was standing before an end wall, where a door was set into the brickwork – a simple, innocuous wooden door.

Van Bam continued. 'A House symbol and a shadow carriage just when we needed them? Surely you must now believe the avatar is on our side?'

'I don't know what to believe anymore,' Samuel grumbled. He skirted around the wolf and approached the wooden door. 'This shouldn't be here, Van Bam. All the doorways were removed after the Genii War.'

'As the avatar said, someone saw fit to leave the Labyrinth with an emergency exit.'

'Yes – but *who*?' Standing on tiptoes, Samuel peered up at the rusty metal plaque above the door. 'The symbol's rusted away,' he said, dropping down and facing Van Bam. 'There's no telling which House this doorway leads to.'

Van Bam seemed amused. 'Intriguing, is it not?'

'*Worrying* was the word I was thinking of. There's nothing to say it'll lead us to friends.'

'There is the word of the avatar.'

'Hmm.'

It's like listening to an old married couple, don't you think? Gideon said to the wolf.

Why are you in my head? Clara asked again.

Gideon didn't reply.

'Well, there's no point trying to get back to town,' Samuel said, and he rubbed his face. 'And we can't stay here. The Retrospective will find us again eventually –' he glanced quickly, nervously, at the wolf – 'or we'll starve to death.'

Gideon laughed in Clara's head.

With a nod of agreement, Van Bam grabbed the metal doorknob, and wrenched the door open. Clara couldn't help but issue a little growl. The doorway revealed a thick, swirling whiteness from which came the distant moaning of a lonely wind.

The Nothing of Far and Deep, Gideon said. *I'm sure you've heard of its legend, Clara. Only the pathways to the Labyrinth lead through its primordial mists—*

Why don't you just tell me why I can hear your voice? the wolf thought back angrily.

It's a long story, Clara, Gideon replied. *We'll talk about it later.* And then he fell so silent, Clara wondered if his voice had ever been there at all.

Van Bam stepped back from the doorway and stared intently into the swirling whiteness. Finally he looked back at his colleagues, a broad grin splitting his lips. 'Whichever House this leads to,' he said, 'the Aelfir on the other side will be able put us in touch with the Thaumaturgists once again.'

'And all our problems will be solved, just like that,' Samuel replied humourlessly. 'Since when was anything that simple for the Relic Guild?' He stepped up to the door and held it open. 'After you,' he said to the illusionist.

With a quirked smile on his lips, Van Bam nodded at Clara before stepping up to the threshold. 'See you on the other side,' he said, before disappearing into swirling whiteness.

Still holding the door open, Samuel looked at the wolf. His body language suggested he was now starkly aware of the fact they were alone together for the first time. His uncertainty pleased her.

Samuel swallowed. 'Ladies first,' he said.

With a snort, Clara walked forwards and fearlessly followed Van Bam into the mists of the Nothing of Far and Deep.

SPIDER WEBS

Air, humid and thick, coated the inside of Samuel's mouth with an oily film, sour with the taste of effluence. Sweating, leg muscles burning, he gulped lungful after lungful of the fetid atmosphere, following the directions of the spirit compass in his hand. In the dim light of wall-mounted glow-lamps, he ran as fast as he dared along the slippery walkways. Beside him, a river of rancid sewage water flowed. Behind him, Macy and Bryant, his fellow agents of the Relic Guild, kept up easily. With their endless reserves of strength, the twins were snapping at Samuel's heels, egging him on, pushing him to increase his speed as he led the group further into the sewers beneath the streets of Labrys Town.

According to the spirit compass, the automaton spider was moving steadily towards the eastern district. Invisible to the naked eye, the metal construct, with its melon-sized body, long, spindly legs and the head of a golem, had been climbing and jumping and scurrying its way across town ever since Hamir had released it from the warehouse in the southern district. And the Relic Guild had been shadowing its path from below.

Hamir had warned the group that the spider would move fast, relentless in its pursuit of Fabian Moor, and the agents would have a hard time keeping up with it. Samuel could not allow himself a moment's respite in which to catch his breath. All he could do was keep running and focus on the spirit compass as it tracked the magic of the Genii preserved in the spider's golem-head.

Attempting a sharp left off the walkway and into a tunnel, Samuel lost his footing on the slimy stone. He began skidding and stumbling towards the river of sewage. Just as it seemed inevitable that he would fall in, the strong hand of Macy gripped the back of his coat. She flung him into the tunnel, and Samuel ricocheted off the wall. Macy kept him upright and shoved him back into a run.

'Look lively, Samuel,' she called, clearly amused. 'There's a Genii to catch.'

Bryant laughed along with his sister.

The twins were enjoying the thrill of the hunt, but Samuel wished there was time to give them a splash of cold water. Their confidence should have bolstered his own, but for all their magical strength, Macy and Bryant did not carry the burden of knowledge Samuel did; they had yet to see what Fabian Moor's virus did to a person. They seemed to have forgotten that this mission was not only to hunt and capture a Genii, but also to rescue a fellow agent of the Relic Guild.

It had been more than a day since Fabian Moor had abducted a magical apothecary called Gene. An elderly agent, quiet in his ways, Gene had never been blessed with courage. Fabian Moor wanted to know the identities of the Relic Guild agents; he wanted to extract secrets from them that would show him how to enter the Nightshade. Gene certainly didn't have the defences to stop Moor taking what he wanted. He wouldn't last long under the interrogation of a Genii. Would any of them? Samuel prayed to the Timewatcher that the automaton spider did its work quickly enough to save Gene's life. And perhaps the lives of all of them.

At the end of the tunnel, he led the twins across a bridge that spanned the river, down another tunnel, and then along the walkway on the other side.

Samuel wore a pair of goggles that Hamir had given him. They were heavy, stifling. The faceted, green glass lenses looked like the eyes of an insect, and were imbued with magic. They had turned Samuel's world to shades of grey – not that there was much colour to see down in the sewers. Hamir had designed the goggles to see through illusions, to penetrate the spell of invisibility that had been cast upon the automaton spider; but Samuel had to marvel at how the lenses also gave his pencil-etched world such depth and detail.

The mortar between brickwork, the glow lamps fixed to the walls, the rough texture of the walkway, the mammoth stone rafters high above – everything came to Samuel in its own unique shade of grey.

But the goggles made the way through the sewers clear and stark, all dimness and shadow banished. Clear though the route was, the trek was pushing Samuel to the limits of his endurance.

After an hour of hard running, the spirit compass became confused, its needle spinning undecidedly around its face, and it was with immense relief that Samuel drew the group to a halt. He bent double – one hand clutching the compass, the other on his knee – and gulped down breaths of bitter air.

Macy walked up to him. Tall and broad, her blonde, shoulder-length hair pulled back into a tail, there was a frown on her not-quite masculine face. Bryant stood next to her. His hair was the same colour as his sister's, but close-cropped; his face was almost identical – apart from a scar that slashed down his cheek from the corner of his left eye.

There was not one bead of sweat on the brow of either sibling, and they were barely out of breath. At that moment, Samuel considered their magical gift of strength and fitness much preferable to his prescient awareness.

'Why have we stopped?' Macy asked.

'The Spider,' Samuel said between breaths. 'We must be ... standing directly ... below it.'

She looked up at the sewer ceiling, high above. 'It's found Moor?'

'Likely ... but its path ... might be blocked.'

'How can we tell?'

'Give it a minute.' Samuel took a huge breath, and showed Macy the spinning needle on the compass. 'Let's see ... if it starts moving again.'

'We must be well into the eastern district by now,' Bryant said. He looked around. 'I'll go and find a way out, just in case.' And he set off along the walkway.

Samuel stood upright, shifted the goggles onto his forehead, and wiped sweat from his eyes. The gloom of the sewers returned. He thought about removing his coat, but he didn't suppose the humid atmosphere would be any more forgiving on his damp skin.

Macy raised an eyebrow at him. 'Are you all right?'

Samuel nodded and steadied his breathing.

Like her brother, Macy wore a thick cloak over her clothes, the hood of which was made from charmed material that would steep her identity in shadows. She also wore gauntlets and a gorget made of black leather stuffed with chain mail. When Fabian Moor's hiding place was discovered, the three agents would likely be facing victims of the Genii's virus – a virus that drove a person mad with a savage thirst for blood before eventually converting all their organic matter into animated stone, and creating a simple-minded golem. The twins had taken every precaution against getting bitten and infected, but only on Samuel's insistence.

'I've found the way out,' Bryant called from a little way down the walkway.

Samuel checked the spirit compass – the needle still spun around the face. He nodded to Macy.

She gave a crooked smile. 'Your power stones are charged, right?'

Samuel pulled the goggles down over his eyes. 'Let's go.'

Bryant led the way up a caged ladder fixed to the sewer wall to a metal grille platform and a set of narrow stairs ascending to a hatchway in the sewer ceiling. Samuel put on his wide-brimmed hat made from charmed Aelfirian material, and his face became hidden in shadows. Macy and Bryant hitched up the hoods of their cloaks, and the three agents climbed out into fresher air and the clear morning sky over the eastern district.

The alleyway they entered was deserted; it was narrow and the walls were high. The sun didn't shine in the alley, and the shadows retained the chill of night. The hatchway was imbued with magic and became indistinguishable from the cobbled ground when Bryant closed it. The spirit compass' needle fixed onto a direction and led Samuel to the end of the alley. He smelled wood smoke and drew the twins to a halt.

Peeking around the corner, Samuel saw two vagrants – a man and a woman – sitting in an overgrown communal garden before a small fire made from broken packing crates. On the other side of the garden, a shabby apartment block rose three storeys. It was a squat and ugly building, rickety, somehow looking like a crooked old man. Through the lenses of the goggles, the grey shades of its brickwork seemed scorched and pockmarked, its windows cracked and thickly grimed. And halfway up, the automaton spider clung to its face.

Though the spider was invisible to the naked eye, the magic in the goggles revealed it as a huge eight pointed star shape made from wispy, purple smoke. It wasn't moving.

Hamir had said that if Fabian Moor detected the spider closing in on him, he could destroy it easily. The necromancer needed Samuel and the twins to divert Moor's attention – which was a polite way of saying the agents needed to be bait – and keep the Genii unaware of the spider's mission. Did the arachnid construct understand the situation? It had been created from a thaumaturgic metal that was supposedly sentient. Did that mean it could know to wait for the Relic Guild's diversion?

'What's going on?' Bryant asked.

'I can see the spider,' Samuel said.

'What's it doing?'

'Waiting for us, I think. I hope.'

'I know that place,' Macy said, indicating the building. 'They call it a shelter.' There was a bitter edge to her voice. 'But really, it's where the infirm and homeless get dumped and forgotten.'

'Perfect place for Moor to hide,' Samuel said. He slipped the spirit compass into his coat pocket. 'Don't forget what I told you,' he warned the twins.

The three agents stepped from the alley and made their way across the garden. The vagrants ceased their conversation and stared at them. The old woman began cackling as they neared; the man grinned, revealing crooked and stained teeth.

'Well, look at this,' he said, gesturing to the hidden faces. 'A visit from the Resident's men.'

'And woman,' said the woman. She seemed pleased with herself and jabbed a finger at the man beside her. 'Told you something strange was going on. Didn't I tell you?'

Macy was the first to reach the pair. She crouched before the fire, slipped off her gauntlets, and warmed her hands while Samuel and Bryant stood watching.

'And what are you two doing out here?' she said genially. 'Why aren't you inside that place?'

'It's not from lack of trying,' the old woman said, looking at the shelter building behind her. 'The doors are locked, and no one's gone in or out for two days.'

'You're right,' said Macy, 'that is strange.'

'But don't think that's the end of it,' the old man chipped in. He too glanced at the building, and he shivered. 'The noises that come out of that place ain't right. Sounds like someone's in a bad way.'

'More than just someone, I reckon,' the woman added. She leant forward and gave Macy a gummy smile. 'Let's just say we're not surprised the Resident sent the Relic Guild, dear.'

The man agreed with a wide-eyed nod.

Macy looked quickly at Samuel and her brother, then turned back to the vagrants. 'I'll tell you what,' she said, reaching under her cloak to fish out a folded wad of money. 'While we go and do our job, why don't you two catch a tram to another part of town?' She flicked off forty Labyrinth pounds and held the notes out to the woman. 'Go and find a better shelter and get some food. Sound good?'

Encouraged by a quick, affirming nod from her fellow vagrant, the old woman snatched the money from Macy's hand. 'Sounds brilliant,' she said. 'Thanks very much, dear.'

'My pleasure.'

They got to their feet and shuffled away from the fire. By the sly smiles on their faces, Samuel knew the last thing they would spend Macy's money on was food and a tram ticket. But at least it got them out of the way.

As Macy slipped her gauntlets back on, Samuel drew his revolver and thumbed the power stone set behind the chamber. It gave a brief whine and glowed with violet light. Bryant led the way to the entrance of the crooked and decaying shelter building.

Samuel crossed the garden and passed through a patch of warm sunlight. He gave an involuntary shudder when he stepped out of it and into the chill of the building's shadow. The automaton spider was still clinging motionless to the wall. Samuel followed the twins up the steps to entrance doors which were firmly locked. Through a slim gap, a rusty chain could be seen looped around the inside door handles.

'I've got a phial of acid in my belt,' Samuel said.

Bryant scoffed at his idea, leant back, and kicked the doors. They burst inwards with the ping of snapping metal.

Bryant shrugged at Samuel's irritated look. 'Hamir said to distract Moor. We might as well make some noise.'

Macy clapped Samuel's shoulder and pushed him after her twin into the building. 'Bet you wish you'd gone with Van Bam and Angel, don't you?' she chuckled.

High above a shimmering desert, the sun burned so fiercely that the sky was bleached to the palest shade of pink imaginable. Dunes rolled into the distance like frozen swells on a sea of copper, casting weak shadows upon golden-red sands. The horizon was a jagged line of broken teeth, a mountain range of mystery and foreboding. Nothing disturbed the silence, no breeze shifted the stillness. Harsh and unforgiving, the desert of Mirage was not the most welcoming realm among the Houses of the Aelfir.

Amidst this barren, lifeless landscape, a huge monument of rock protruded from the desert. It was named the Giant's Hand, for it resembled the wrist and hand bones of a long-ago buried behemoth. It rose from the desert as if offering its palm to the sky. The ledge of its fingertips was thirty feet above the hot sands.

Two frames stood in the palm of the Giant's Hand. The first held a bell made from red glass lined with veins of gold that reflected the sun with dazzling sparkles. Bulbous and heavy, the bell hung from a rope dangling from the sturdy stone frame. The second frame, also made of red glass, held a simple wooden door. Set high on the door was a metal plate which had been engraved with three concentric squares: the House symbol of the Labyrinth.

A hum filled the air. The wooden door opened to reveal a sheet of viscous whiteness, churning and moaning. When the whiteness parted, the desert plains of House Mirage greeted a tall human with dark brown skin, holding a cane of green glass.

Van Bam stepped from the doorway and shielded his eyes against the glare of the sun. The heat took his breath away. Squinting, he looked out across the golden-red landscape that stretched all the way to the mountains. The shimmering sands and copper dunes made for a majestic view, but the illusionist was immediately struck by how empty, how lonely the desert seemed.

He looked down at his sandals. They protected the soles of his feet from the burning stone of the Giant's Hand, but he didn't much like wearing them. Van Bam always preferred to feel what was real against his skin, and they said that everything was hidden in Mirage.

Twirling his green glass cane in his hand, he watched Angel emerge. The healer was dressed similarly to Van Bam, in a loose fitting shirt and trousers of white cotton. Her long black and grey hair was pulled back into a tail, and she had prepared for the journey by bringing along a lace sun-umbrella.

Angel gasped and fanned her face with her free hand. 'Timewatcher's arse!' she said. 'I'd forgotten how bloody hot this place is.'

Van Bam shrugged. 'It is not too bad.' He wiped away the beads of sweat that had already formed on his bald head. 'Certainly not as hot as the Floating Stones of Up and Down.'

'Hardly a fair comparison, Van Bam, seeing as the Floating Stones are volcanoes.'

'Ah, yes, there is that.'

Angel puffed her cheeks and flapped the collar of her shirt. 'I'm really not made for this kind of heat, you know.'

'Perhaps it is your age.' Van Bam grinned. 'I have heard that it is the province of the elderly to find complaint in all things, including such a pleasant change of climate.'

'I'm forty-four, you cheeky bastard.'

Van Bam gave her a mock bow. 'Of course, my lady. Perhaps it is time for your nap, yes?'

Beneath the shadow of her umbrella, Angel's smile was lopsided. 'Why are you in such a playful mood?'

It wasn't as if Van Bam didn't appreciate the seriousness of the situation. He and Angel were following the trail of a delegate of House Mirage, a dead Aelf by the name of Ursa who had been complicit in bringing Fabian Moor into the Labyrinth. Who knew what dangers they would encounter in this desert realm? Yet Van Bam's mood was indeed light, and there were a couple of answers he could've given to the healer's question.

After two years of isolation, Van Bam felt great relief at having swapped the squalid streets of Labrys Town for the open wonder of an Aelfirian House – a House he had never visited before. It would also be true if he said that he still felt the warmth from the previous night when he and Marney had admitted their true feelings for each other.

'Oh, I get it,' Angel said. 'Is being in love agreeing with you, Van Bam?'

The illusionist chuckled. 'It is that obvious?'

Angel rolled her eyes. 'I've been around long enough to recognise the *look*.' She sighed, fluttered her eyelids, and her voice became wistful. 'The eyes become glazed, and a sort of dumb, vacant expression appears on the face. And everything in the world is sugar-coated with dreamy romance ...' She gave a pitying pout. 'The young are masters of looking stupid in love, even illusionists. It's a little bit irritating, to be honest.'

Van Bam gave a twirl of his cane. 'I will take your jealousy as a compliment.'

Angel scoffed. 'I'm happy for you, Van Bam, but you need to be careful.'

'Angel, if you are worried about Marney ...' He shook his head, smiling at fond memories of his lover. 'Believe me, she can look after herself. Honestly, have you ever tried to hide your feelings from an empath?'

'Oh, I've no doubt Marney knows how to handle you,' Angel said. 'But that's not what I'm talking about, Van Bam.' She paused for a moment. 'It's the Gideon factor that should be worrying you.'

At the mention of the Resident's name, Van Bam's good mood ebbed a little. From the open palm of the Giant's Hand, he surveyed the barren desert and the shimmering waves of heat rising from the copper dunes.

'Gideon is not in favour of our relationship, this much I have come to learn,' he told Angel. 'But Marney and I understand our commitment to the Relic Guild. We will work hard to ensure our relationship never hinders our duties.'

'No, you *don't* understand,' Angel said, her voice sad, expression serious. 'Gideon doesn't care if your relationship never causes problems to the Relic Guild. He just doesn't like his agents being romantically involved, full stop. Trust me, Van Bam. I know that from personal experience.'

Van Bam frowned at Angel, waiting for an explanation. But before she could speak further, the Nothing of Far and Deep began churning, and a hum vibrated the rock beneath their feet.

'We'll talk later,' Angel said, and the portal opened to release the rest of their travelling companions.

The first to arrive was an elderly and portly Aelf, dressed in desert robes with his head wrapped in scarves that concealed the points of his ears. His nose and mouth were small, but his eyes were twice the size of any human's, and his face carried the odd triangular shape that was typical of the Aelfir. Ebril, Ambassador to House Mirage, shielded his large eyes from the sun, and a toothy grin split his impressive grey beard.

'The Giant's Hand,' he whispered, and then bellowed at the pink sky. 'Home at last!'

He dropped to his knees and kissed the rock.

The rest of Ambassador Ebril's entourage emerged from the doorway: five younger Aelfir, three women and two men, all dressed desert-fashion. The last and youngest of them was Ebril's daughter Namji. A petite Aelf, her face had more of a subtle heart shape than the typical triangular appearance. The long plait of her black hair hung over her shoulder like a snake. As Namji breathed in the desert air, her soft green eyes gazed at Van Bam for a moment. They filled with tears and she mouthed the words 'thank you'. She then laughed happily at the sight of her father kneeling upon the floor, lips pressed to the Giant's Hand, before sharing excited hugs with the rest of the Aelfir.

Ebril and his entourage had been conducting diplomatic business in Labrys Town when the war against Spiral began, and the use of the portals leading in and out of the Great Labyrinth had been revoked for all. Two years they had lived in exile from their House, refugees of the war, and their joy at returning home was infectious.

'You should be careful,' Angel whispered to Van Bam. 'I think Namji has a thing for you.'

Van Bam nodded distantly as he watched the celebrations. Namji was a young Aelf – only fifteen, sixteen at the most – but the illusionist had already been warned that she was a slippery customer who was not to be trusted.

With a groan, Ebril got to his feet and bowed to the Relic Guild agents. 'My friends, we are in your debt,' he said, and then turned to his entourage. 'Come, let us announce our return.'

From around his neck, Ebril removed a thin chain connected to a small gold pendant that had been cast in the shape of a teardrop. Van Bam and Angel stepped aside to allow Ebril through as he marched up to the bell of red glass. He pushed his hand up into the bell, and began running the pendant around its interior. The bell emitted a tinkling that seemed to *spread* rather than grow in volume. It continued after Ebril had stepped back.

Van Bam gained the impression that the bell was calling out to the desert.

The air shifted and wavered.

'You might want to catch this show,' Angel said, nudging Van Bam forward.

He stepped closer to the edge of the Giant's Hand and gazed down onto the desert.

Fifty yards from the rock sentinel a wall began to form, like a great veil of water that glistened beneath the scorching sun. Beyond it, dunes began to collapse, one by one, their sand running away to lie flat on the desert floor. Blocky shapes formed, shadowy movements whispered across the levelling landscape; all of which was soon hidden as the veil thickened into the hard golden-red stone blocks of a high wall. Beneath the bleached sky, a mighty citadel revealed itself.

'Behold,' Ebril said proudly. 'The House of Mirage.'

It was said this citadel was home to more than one hundred thousand Aelfir, and Van Bam could well believe it. To the left and right, the wall stretched away into waves of heat. He gazed up at the turrets and crenellated ramparts. Armed guards, looking small at that distance, stood sentry, gazing down at the new arrivals, their rifles in hand. Flags struggled to flutter in the weak breeze, each bearing the House symbol of Mirage: a simple castle shape beneath the circle of a desert moon. There were no window slits cut into the mighty wall of the citadel, but almost directly opposite the Giant's Hand, across a gulf of hot air, huge wooden gates had appeared.

'Impressive, is it not?' Ebril said, standing alongside Van Bam.

Van Bam agreed. Even his skill with illusions had not enabled him to see through the magic that had kept this House invisible. He looked at Angel; she didn't seem any less impressed for having witnessed this spectacle before.

They said, in Mirage everything was hidden.

Finally, a stone bridge materialised between the citadel's gates and the fingertips of the Giant's Hand. Once the bridge had fully formed, the gates swung open and an Aelf marched out with eight armed guards following him.

The lead Aelf was dressed in crimson robes. His head was swathed in scarves, and his hand rested on the hilt of a decorative sword sheathed at his hip. Each of the eight guards, marching in sync behind the leader, wore robes of light blue but no headdress. They held their rifles diagonally to their bodies. Despite the searing glare of the desert sky, the violet thaumaturgic glow of power stones could still be seen. These weapons were primed and ready for use.

'Trusting lot, aren't they?' Angel muttered, as the militia marched closer.

'Living in a desert as harsh as Mirage, it is in our nature to be cautious,' Ebril said with a smile. 'Please, do not take offence.'

He stepped ahead of the two magickers and his entourage, stopping where the bridge began, to meet the armed welcoming party. Van Bam felt a presence standing close on his left. Namji had taken the space her father had vacated beside him. She gave the illusionist a dazzling smile; she appeared young and innocent. Beautiful. Van Bam moved his hand away as hers brushed against it.

The leader of the guards came to a halt a few paces from the end of the bridge. His face was clean-shaven, old and weathered. He scrutinised the group behind Ebril whilst his guards stood stiffly to attention.

'Ambassador Ebril,' the leader said with a nod. 'Mirage welcomes you home.'

'Thank you, Captain,' Ebril answered brightly. 'It is very good to be back.'

The Captain then nodded to Van Bam and Angel, and said, 'High Governor Obanai also welcomes the delegates of the Nightshade to his House,' in a humourless sort of way.

Van Bam and Angel shared a look.

The captain addressed Ebril again. 'The High Governor has asked me to relay his apologies. He wished to greet you personally, but affairs of state have tied his hands. The days in Mirage are never without duty, I'm sure you'll remember, Ambassador.'

'Of course,' Ebril replied.

'Rooms have been prepared at the High Governor's house for our human guests.'

'That is most kind.'

Although Van Bam couldn't decipher details, he caught a definite intent, a hidden meaning, behind the exchange between the two. Denton had taught him long ago that Aelfirian politicians were clever, devious, and never to be fully trusted. Van Bam wondered if High Governor Obanai had just relayed a coded message to his Ambassador via the captain.

'Your families are eager to see you,' the captain said to the rest of the entourage, who stirred excitedly. 'Please, allow me to escort you into the citadel.'

Half the guards followed their captain as he made his way back across the bridge; the remaining half waited for the entourage to pass before bringing up the rear.

The bridge was easily wide enough to walk three abreast. Van Bam followed the ambassador, with Angel on his right. She seemed highly amused that Namji had decided to stay close to the illusionist's left.

'I can't wait for you to see my home,' Namji said, staring ahead at the open gates. 'Mirage is a beautiful House.'

She linked her arm in Van Bam's, and then looked behind to share a childish giggle with one of the entourage.

Angel leant into the illusionist. 'When we get home,' she whispered into his ear, 'I'm telling Marney.'

'Shut up,' he whispered back.

'You must understand that not even Gideon knows the details of our mission,' Denton said. 'We are working in secret for Lady Amilee alone. It is vital that you never tell anyone about where we have been and what we have done. And that includes Van Bam, Marney ... Marney? Are you listening to me?'

Marney supposed she was, in a vague sort of way, but Denton's words could not cut through the awe she was feeling for her surroundings.

She had read about forests; she had heard the other agents talk about them, and had seen artistic representations. But no book, no words, no painting could ever do justice to the world that now filled her sight.

The Trees of the Many Queen, this House was called. Marney and Denton stood side-by-side with their backs to the portal – a wooden doorway framed by two trees – that had delivered them there from the Great Labyrinth. She stared down a bare dirt road that cut through the forest. The air was humid, and the breeze that sighed and whispered through the dense and verdant leaves was damp against Marney's face. The earthy scents that filled her nostrils were somehow clean and wholesome. The buzzing of insects and the occasional flapping of wings were the sounds of freedom.

Marney's breath caught as a distant tapping echoed through the forest, a fast knocking on wood, almost like drilling. It stopped and then started again, repeating several times before the echoes faded away.

'What was that?' she asked in wonder.

A bird called a woodpecker, Denton's voice said in her mind. *Now, sorry to interrupt your daydreams, but can I ask if you've been paying attention to me?*

Marney frowned at him.

Denton, tall and overweight, pushing eighty and nearly always with a cheery expression on his ruddy face, was now giving his protégée a reproachful look.

Usually favouring crumpled three-piece suits, the old empath was dressed in heavy fatigues, a jumper that struggled to confine his generous paunch, and a travelling cloak of green wool that covered the rucksack on his back. He carried no weapons – unlike Marney, who wore a baldric of twelve slim, silver throwing daggers beneath her cloak – and his footwear was a sturdy and sensible pair of hiking boots. However, his headwear gave him a slightly ridiculous look: a floppy, wide-brimmed hat that had seen better days, but one that Denton refused to be seen without.

Well? his voice urged in Marney's head.

Oh! Right. Marney shook herself and spoke aloud. 'Yes, Denton, I was listening. No one knows what we're doing. Say nothing about the mission, not even to Gideon.'

'*Or* Van Bam,' Denton stressed knowingly.

'Okay. I get it.'

'I hope so, Marney, because the House we're travelling to is … well, a little *fabled*, to say the least.'

Denton impressed an emotion upon Marney then, a light sense of anxiety that was enough to lessen her awe of the Trees of the Many Queen.

She swallowed. 'The Library of Glass and Mirrors,' she whispered.

'Exactly,' Denton said. 'And I hope that you appreciate just what a perilous place it is, Marney.'

She did. The Library of Glass and Mirrors was indeed a fabled House, a myth, a fairy tale, or so most humans and Aelfir would claim. The legends said its librarians kept the records of what was, what is, and what would be. The complete histories of the past, present and future – how could such a library exist?

Yet it did – somewhere out there, its dangerous doorway hidden among the Houses of the Aelfir. The Thaumaturgists knew it was real, had always known, but they feared the Library of Glass and Mirrors and the impossible histories it kept. The Thaumaturgists encouraged the myths and disbelief in its existence. Yet now Lady Amilee had sent the two empaths on a secret mission to find the Library. But to reach it, Marney and Denton first had to cross many Houses, many of which were embroiled in the war against Spiral and the Genii.

'Ah, here comes our liaison,' Denton said, and he pointed into the trees to Marney's left.

Marney struggled to see her at first. She began as a shadow of movement that emerged from the treeline, and only then did Marney realise that the stranger's cloak must have been charmed to blend in with the colours of the forest. The stranger carried a quiver of arrows on her back and an unstrung bow in her hand. She stopped on the dirt road and pulled back her hood, revealing unruly brown hair and a grubby Aelfirian face with large, keen eyes.

'Greetings,' Denton called. *Remember, Marney, say nothing of our mission*, he added mentally.

The Aelf approached them. Her clothes matched the design of her cloak, and there was a curved dagger tucked into her belt. Instinctively, Marney reached out with her empathic magic, reading the Aelf's persona. What returned were the emotions of a trustworthy woman, stern yet kind, but nobody's fool.

'And greetings to you,' she said. Her voice was gruff, it seemed to belong in a forest. She appeared to size up Marney, and then Denton. 'Can I be of assistance?'

Denton smiled. 'We're looking to procure passage through your wonderful House. Perhaps you've been expecting us?'

'Perhaps I have. Do you carry proper permission for this passage, sir?'

'Indeed I do.' Denton pulled out a black leather wallet, which he flipped open to show the Aelf a square plate of a strange grey metal that seemed both solid and liquid.

The Aelf stared at the plate for a moment, and then reached out to press a finger against it. Immediately, the strange metal began to change, bubbling and sinking into grooves that quickly depicted the shape of a diamond set within a circle – the sigil of Lady Amilee the Skywatcher.

With a satisfied nod, the Aelf gestured to the treeline on both sides of the dirt road. Marney heard undergrowth rustling and twigs snapping, and she caught the shadowy movements of the Aelfir who had just been ordered to withdraw from the human visitors. But she had sensed no emotions, detected no other presences in the vicinity. How many arrows had there been aimed at the empaths?

'It's wise to remain cautious at such times,' the Aelf said, giving

Marney a relaxed smile. 'Welcome to the Trees of the Many Queen. I'm to be your guide. I've been ordered to lead you to your next destination.'

'That is gracious of you,' said Denton, sliding the wallet back into a leg-pocket of his fatigues.

'My pleasure.' The Aelf raised a hand as Marney made to introduce herself. 'Forgive me, miss – best not speak of names. I've been told to ask nothing of you or your plans.' She nodded meaningfully at each empath in turn. 'Now, there's a fair way to go, and nightfall's not far off. We should be leaving.'

Without further word, she turned and led the empaths from the dirt road and into the forest.

Nightfall? Marney thought to Denton. *It was morning when we left the Labyrinth.*

Denton smiled at her as they entered the trees. *Time doesn't run evenly through the Houses, Marney. I'd have thought your books would've taught you that.*

Marney smiled back at him. *Well, a wise old man once told me there's a big difference between knowing a thing and experiencing it.*

Ah! Denton's chuckle was light in her head. *That must've been a very wise old man indeed.*

Conversation was limited as the group headed deeper into the forest, the Aelfirian guide speaking least of all. Leading the way, she kept the pace of their progress slow for Denton, who grumbled now and then about his old legs and aching joints.

Marney opened herself to her surroundings, dropped her emotive defences, and allowed the sights and sensations to wash over her. She chuckled to herself as she waved away curious insects, and savoured the texture of the bark beneath her hand, and the smell of dirt and moss that stained her skin. Sturdy roots weaved in and out of the forest floor like dead tentacles. Above, through the thick green canopy that whispered in the damp breeze, sunlight winked between gaps in grey clouds. The Trees of the Many Queen was a good House, a peaceful forest, and it seemed far from the troubles that might be waiting ahead for Marney and her mentor.

The terracotta jar that had contained the essence of Fabian Moor had been found in a mysterious House called the Icicle Forest. Van Bam and Angel were on a mission to Mirage, to investigate an Aelf called Ursa, the one responsible for transporting the jar to the Labyrinth and reanimating Moor's essence. Marney and Denton's mission was to learn more about the Icicle Forest.

Even Lady Amilee had no information about that place. It was thought to be a Genii stronghold, a secret House hiding in the Nothing of Far and Deep, where Spiral plotted and planned against the Timewatcher. If the location of the Icicle Forest was to be revealed, if any information on this enigmatic House existed, then Lady Amilee believed it would be found at the Library of Glass and Mirrors.

The task ahead of Marney suddenly seemed so daunting that the beauty of her location became as dull as the sky.

After an hour of walking, the humidity broke and the temperature dropped. A fine drizzle misted the air and collected on leaves, dripping down on the travellers. After another hour, the light began to dim and the drizzle turned to hard rain. When Denton asked for a rest, the Aelf led the empaths to a log shelter with one exposed side, standing beside a forest stream. A ring of stones had been laid with dry wood on the shelter floor, and the Aelf set it ablaze with tinder and flint. She then took a black iron kettle from a hook on the wall, filled it with water from the stream, and hung it over the flames to boil.

The Aelf left the empaths alone, saying that she needed to scout the area. Marney suspected that in truth, she just didn't want to overhear anything they might discuss of their mission. Alone and soaked to the skin, the empaths sipped green tea and feasted on hard oatcakes.

'I'm really not cut out for this kind of lark, anymore,' Denton grumbled as he rubbed his knees. 'Not sure that I ever really was, to be honest.'

Marney said nothing and stared into the flames.

'I wonder how the others are getting on,' Denton said after a while. 'I've been thinking about them. You?'

Marney looked at him. 'Hmm?'

'The others,' Denton said. 'I wonder if Samuel and the twins have located Fabian Moor yet.' He lowered his eyes at her. 'I wonder how things are going in *Mirage?*'

Marney smiled sheepishly. 'Yes, all right, I was thinking about Van Bam.'

Denton squinted at her. 'What's that you've got?'

It was a small, open tin that Marney held in her hands. She had taken it from her backpack, and it was filled with light brown crystals that carried an aroma not out of place in the forest.

'Bath salts,' she told her mentor in a quiet voice.

Denton chuckled. 'You brought *bath salts* with you? On a trip like this?'

'Yes – no – I mean, I wanted to bring them because …' She felt too embarrassed to finish the sentence.

'Ah,' said Denton. 'They were a gift from Van Bam?'

'I know it's stupid, Denton, but I'm comforted by the smell. It reminds me of him.'

'Nonsense – I think it's very sweet,' Denton replied. 'What do they smell of?'

'Sandalwood.'

'Your favourite scent, if I'm not mistaken.'

Marney lifted the open tin to her face and sniffed. 'I can't quite explain it, but the smell of sandalwood reminds me of good things – nothing specific, it's just … like smelling happy memories. Does that make sense?'

'Perfectly,' Denton said with a smile. 'Smells very often become associated with memories. And emotions. Perhaps most especially for empaths.'

Marney nodded. 'I like to think that one day someone might smell sandalwood and remember *me*.'

'And I'm sure they will.'

Marney closed the tin and returned it to her backpack. 'It seems strange, don't you think? I mean – that we have to keep secrets from the others, that we can't tell them about this mission? We're fighting on the same side in this war.'

Denton paused before picking up his wooden cup and draining it of tea. He poured himself another, and then set it aside to cool.

'I have something for you,' he said. 'Nothing as charming as Van Bam's gift, I'm afraid.' He undid the straps of his rucksack, dipped his hand inside, and produced a fat envelope. 'This must be kept safe,' he said, holding it out to Marney. His eyes were intense, ensuring that he had her full attention.

Marney couldn't explain why, but she was reluctant to take the envelope, and kept her hands in her lap. She could see that the wax seal had been stamped without a symbol.

'There are often good reasons for secrets.' Denton's expression was sympathetic but firm. 'We are heading into the war, and it would be ignorant for us to believe that our lives are not under threat, yes?'

Marney nodded.

'There are certain aspects to what *we* are doing that I cannot tell you about,' Denton continued. 'However, this envelope contains *every* detail of our mission. But there is only one occasion on which you must open it. Do you understand what I am saying?'

Marney looked away, unable to hold her mentor's gaze, not wanting to hear where she very much understood this conversation was leading.

'If I should be killed—'

Marney recoiled from his words.

'Listen to me, Marney,' Denton said sternly. 'If I should be killed, it will fall to you to complete this mission. In this envelope you will find coded instructions on how to find the Library of Glass and Mirrors, and what to do once you get there.' He jabbed the envelope toward her more forcefully. 'You are an agent of the Relic Guild, and I need to know you will do what is necessary, no matter what.'

'Of course I will,' Marney said, more angrily than she meant to.

'Then take the bloody envelope, Marney.' Denton was almost pleading. 'If it comes to it, you decipher the instructions, memorise them, destroy the evidence, and report everything that you discover *only* to Lady Amilee.'

Marney sealed up her emotions. To any other person she would have disappeared from perception. It was an act of self-preservation, a desperate bid to stop herself admitting that what she feared more than this mission was to be alone. She was terrified of the day when Denton was no longer around and she would have to face the world without his tutelage and guidance.

Without meeting his eyes, she took the envelope.

Denton sent her a wave of hopeful and affectionate emotions. 'This is only a backup plan, Marney. I sincerely pray to the Timewatcher that you'll never have to open that envelope.'

She looked at him and saw his eyes had become distant.

'Trust me,' he whispered. 'Not all Houses are Aelfirian, and there is a reason those Houses are not connected to the Labyrinth. There are places out there that you really don't want to know about.'

She frowned and made to stuff the envelope into her rucksack.

'No,' Denton said. 'Put it on your person – safe and close.'

Marney slipped the envelope into a leg-pocket on her travelling fatigues, and buttoned it up tight. She patted the pocket and gave Denton a nod to affirm that she understood her instructions.

'Always be mindful that you have it, Marney,' Denton said seriously. 'It's said that anything that can be known *is* known by the librarians at the Library of Glass and Mirrors. You don't need me to tell you how much the information in that envelope would be worth to the wrong type of people.'

'You can trust me,' Marney said, and sent her mentor a wave of emotion, letting him feel her sincerity.

'That's my girl.' Denton smiled. 'Here, have more tea.'

He poured green tea into Marney's wooden cup, and then picked up his own.

Glad the conversation was over, Marney looked out of the shelter into the rain beating down onto the forest.

'It's hard to imagine there's a war going on,' she said. 'This is such a beautiful House. So peaceful.'

'Ah, but don't be fooled by its beauty, Marney,' said Denton. 'The Trees of the Many Queen is not a House you want to cross. There is old, powerful magic here. The souls of the dead do not journey on to Mother Earth, you see – they stay and nourish the trees, keep this forest strong and young.' He sipped his tea and winked at Marney. 'The Genii's armies would have no easy time fighting the spirits of this House, no matter what weaponry and monstrous technologies they brought with them.'

'I hate the idea of the war coming here,' she said, watching the rain. 'I can't believe Spiral could find anything he needs in this forest.'

'Don't be quick to assume such things,' said the Aelfirian guide.

Startled, Marney looked around to see her standing in the opening of the shelter, no more than four feet away, carrying an armful of firewood. How had she moved that silently? Marney hadn't detected the approach of her emotions.

'We've got one thing Spiral wants,' the Aelf continued, 'and that's a doorway leading straight to you and your House. The Great Labyrinth is high treasure to the Genii Lord.'

That was indisputable, Marney decided. If Spiral gained control of the Labyrinth, his cruel fist could punch out at all the Houses that still opposed him. Before the war with Spiral, the Labyrinth had been the one realm that was connected to every Aelfirian House via doorways leading to portals that cut through the Nothing of Far and Deep. But the Houses that had fallen to Spiral had had their doorways removed, severing their connection to the Nothing of Far and Deep, and the Timewatcher ensured that no creature of higher magic could use the doorways that remained. However, that did not prevent the army of Aelfir who followed Spiral from using them. Gaining control of a doorway to the Great Labyrinth was high treasure indeed.

The guide dumped the wood on the floor of the shelter and crouched before the fire, warming her hands. 'And then, of course, there's *us*.'

She looked from one empath to the other, her large eyes narrowed and calculating. 'I've no interest in what you're doing, but I trust to the Thaumaturgists, and I choose to believe it's for a good cause.' She took a breath and exhaled heavily. 'If you don't mind me telling you, we let messengers come through our House from time to time, carrying news of the war. I've heard terrible things about what's going on out there. About where you two are headed.'

Marney felt a chill.

Denton leant forward. 'Really? We receive little news in the Labyrinth.'

The Aelf's eyes glazed as she stared into the flames. 'If Spiral leads his army to the Trees of the Many Queen – oh, we'd fight them, we'd fight them to the death. But I've heard you don't get a choice. The Genii, they have ways of making you want to join them. They have ways of ...

turning your thoughts, driving you mad, making you hate your fellow kind.' She sniffed. 'That's what I've heard, anyway.'

Marney could sense that the Aelf believed the rumours. She was a brave woman, truthful, and her words were meant as a warning to the agents of the Relic Guild. There was fear inside her, a fear that the Genii would one day come and subjugate her House as they had subjugated many others in this war.

Marney looked at Denton, hoping to find reassurance in his cheery face, but the old empath was lost in thought, staring out into the rain, his emotions closed.

'Right then,' the Aelf said, rising to her feet. 'The portal's not far now, and we should be moving before the light's gone altogether.' She looked at Marney, saw the worry on her face, and gave her a friendly smile. 'Can't very well let the old man go tripping up in the dark now, can we?'

Denton snapped out of his reverie and scoffed. 'That's a fair point.' He got to his feet with a groan. 'As much as it pains me to admit it. Shall we?'

As Marney and Denton slung on their rucksacks and damp travelling cloaks, the Aelf extinguished the fire and then laid it with fresh wood as a courtesy to the next traveller. Once again, she led the empaths out into the rain and the depths of the Trees of the Many Queen.

By the time they reached their destination, it was twilight and the rain had stopped. The forest smelled fresher and earthier than ever, and was shrouded in a thickening mist.

The portal was an archway formed from two bent and twisted trees, ancient and leafless. Fixed to the apex of the archway, a bronze plate had turned green over time. The symbol engraved into it depicted two rectangles standing upright and connected by a straight line.

I don't recognise the House symbol, Marney thought to Denton.

The Union of Twins, Denton replied.

Marney had never heard of it.

It's a very different House to the Trees of the Many Queen, Marney.

'You should know,' the Aelfirian guide said, standing before the archway, 'that the only thing standing between the Genii and this House is the Timewatcher's army. The war is being fought in the Union of Twins.'

Marney's gut twisted as the Aelf pressed a knot on the old and twisted tree-frame. With a low hum, a dark, liquid portal began churning within the archway.

Denton laid a reassuring hand on Marney's shoulder.

'Good luck to you both,' the Aelf said. 'And take the blessings of the Many Queen with you.'

Giving thanks to their guide, Denton took Marney's hand and led her forward. Together they entered the portal.

Marney expected to find herself in a ghostly tunnel that cut a path through primordial mists to their destination. But this was no doorway, and the portal did not snake and twist through the Nothing of Far and Deep connecting an Aelfirian House to the Great Labyrinth; it was an inter-House portal, and it delivered Marney to the Union of Twins instantly.

A flash of light blinded her eyes, a roar like thunder deafened her ears, and a shockwave punched Marney from her feet. Before she could call for Denton, or make sense of her surroundings, she was sent spiralling down into unconsciousness.

Inside the decrepit building on the east side of Labrys Town, Samuel was a few steps ahead of Bryant and Macy.

He faced a hallway, long and wide, home to twelve apartments, six on each side. The door of every apartment was open or smashed from its hinges. Above, light prisms ran in a straight line down the centre of the ceiling, every one broken and useless. From the doorways to the left, ghostly shafts of pale sunshine penetrated into the hallway. Dust drifted and twinkled. The shafts of sunlight dimly lit the way ahead, down to the end and the closed door of the stairwell. Everything appeared dreary grey through the lenses of Samuel's magically enhanced goggles.

'What's your magic telling you?' said Macy.

Samuel's prescient awareness was warm inside him, as though it had one eye open, drowsy but not asleep. The noise of Bryant breaking open the entrance doors had not alerted anyone in the building. All was still and quiet, but ... 'There's something here,' Samuel said.

'What's that smell?' Bryant asked.

The building reeked of decay.

'Fabian Moor's virus,' Samuel said, his gut knotting. 'It's the smell of his victims.'

Bryant scoffed, unimpressed. 'Golems smell like rotting vegetables?'

'No.' Samuel's voice was low and sombre. 'But the infected do.' Gripping his revolver tightly, he turned to the twins. 'When they come for us – and they *will* come – be ready. The infected have no fear of what you can do to them. They'll only be interested in your blood. If you get bitten, there's no cure for Fabian Moor's virus. Remember that, and put them down quickly.'

'Okay then,' Macy said offhandedly, and she gestured to the hallway. 'I guess you're up.'

Samuel bristled. He could sense that Macy and Bryant's faces, hidden within the shadows of their charmed hoods, still carried arrogantly confident expressions, despite the warning.

'Stay behind me,' he said. 'Don't get in my way.'

Guided by the warmth of his magic, Samuel slowly moved down the hallway, revolver in hand.

The agents' footsteps rustled upon the threadbare carpet, kicking up puffs of dust as though they walked upon sun-baked dirt. The dingy grey paint on the walls was peeling into brittle flakes, and the plaster beneath looked ready to disintegrate into fine powder at the slightest touch. There was an unnatural ambience in the apartment block, a distant white noise that seemed to absorb sound into a lifeless hum, as if the building itself was dying. Dry and crumbling, it was as if this place had been abandoned for years.

When he stepped in line with the first set of opposing apartment doors, Samuel stopped and waited for his prescient awareness to detect any danger in the immediate future. It remained dull and drowsy within him. He gestured for the twins to check the apartment on his right, while he investigated the left.

He was greeted by a miserable one-room dwelling, small and cramped and scarcely habitable. There were no ornaments or personal flourishes, and the only furniture was a single bed and a rickety looking table. Both had been broken, and the mattress had been shredded. Dried blood spattered the carpet and a tangle of stained sheets. A thin layer of dust coated everything.

Samuel frowned when he turned to the tiny kitchen in one corner of the room. The oven had been vandalised. Its door lay on the floor. Its parts and internal workings had been ripped out. On closer inspection, Samuel saw the metal insulation box which held the oven's small power stone had been cracked open, and the stone itself was missing.

Back out in the Hallway, Bryant informed Samuel that he and his sister had found the same aftermath of violence in the other apartment, but no denizens, dead or otherwise.

'Is the oven broken?' Samuel said, and Bryant nodded. 'Is the power stone missing?'

Macy ducked back inside to check, and confirmed it was gone.

'What does that mean?'

Without reply, Samuel led the group to the next set of apartments, and then the next, and the next. In each, furniture had been smashed, blood had been split, and the power stones had been removed from vandalised ovens.

Three-quarters of the way down the corridor, Samuel looked up through a hole that had been cut into the ceiling. It was neat and circular, leading to the next floor, and large enough for him to pass through.

'Quicker than using the stairs, I suppose,' Macy half-joked.

'What's that noise?' Bryant said.

Samuel was aware of it too. A tapping – no, *patting,* dull and fleshy. His magic grew a little warmer.

Leading with his revolver, Samuel stepped away from the hole in the ceiling and checked the next set of apartments. They were the same as the others, as was the last room on the right; but the last door on the left was closed. The stench of rotting vegetables was stronger, the patting louder.

Samuel pushed the door open with the barrel of his gun. He looked into a communal bathroom and found two people inside.

One, an old man lying on the floor, was already dead, his clothes shredded. A woman crouched over him, so emaciated by the Genii virus her age could not be determined. Her head was bald, her skin clammy grey and streaked with black veins. With one hand, she reached into a gaping wound in the man's stomach, pulling out stringy lengths of innards and stuffing them into her mouth. With the other hand, she rhythmically smacked the man's broken and blood-smeared face as if her need for violence had formed a nervous tic.

Pat, pat, pat ...

Macy and Bryant moved up behind Samuel. Macy swore. Bryant gagged.

The infected woman stopped feeding upon the dead man and looked sharply at the doorway. Her jaundiced eyes were full of the purest hate. Blood and morsels of human flesh spattered from her mouth as she gave a series of shouts, a mixture of coughing and barking.

Samuel's revolver flashed and made a low and hollow spitting sound. The woman's head jerked back. The bathroom tiles cracked behind her in a spray of blood. She slumped forward over the old man's body, and Samuel lowered his gun. He closed the bathroom door and turned to the twins.

They stood uncertainly. Perhaps the message had finally sunk in; perhaps now they understood why Gideon had given them the order to show zero tolerance to any denizen carrying infection—

Time dulled ...

The environment pressed in on Samuel's senses like needles. The warmth of his prescient awareness flared to a fiery scream carried on his blood, drawing his eyes and the aim of his weapon to the hole in the corridor ceiling. He felt shifts in the atmosphere, imperceptible to the others, and he knew what was coming before he heard the shuffling of quick footsteps from the floor above.

'Get ready,' he said, and the twins wheeled around, standing before their fellow agent.

There was a scuffle at the hole, and then two of the infected dropped through, together, tangled and fighting as they fell crashing to the floor. With a series of barked shrieks, they disentangled themselves and ran at the agents, faces full of rage, the stench of infection preceding them.

Bryant met the first with a straight right cross, punching the monster from its feet. It slammed to the ground on its back, its face crushed and neck broken. Macy grabbed the second by the throat, holding it off at arm's length as it kicked and punched the air wildly. Macy took a moment to study the monster, and then, with an almost casual twist of her hand, broke its neck with a dull crack.

'That's not all of them,' Samuel warned.

There was another scuffle at the hole in ceiling. Three more infected jumped down, one after the other, and rushed forward. Macy hurled the limp body still in her hand. It crashed into the virus victims, knocking them to the carpet. The twins advanced, and the infected died before they could get to their feet.

No more followed. The air reeked of decay.

'Shit,' Bryant said. He was staring at the blood covering his gauntlets. He seemed agitated, desperate to clean it away. 'Get it off me!'

'Stop panicking,' Macy snapped. 'The virus is magical. Hamir said it dies with the carrier—'

'Shut up,' Samuel said. His voice was low but sliced the air like a blade.

His magic was still active.

As he heard a hard *thump,* Samuel spun around, aiming the revolver at the stairwell door at the end of the hallway. When it didn't open, he moved forwards, gesturing to the twins to keep back and stay silent. Laying a hand upon the dry and rough wooden surface, he closed his eyes and listened to his magic. It told him the door was locked and sturdy. But it warned him the immediate future would be grave if he opened it.

Samuel snapped his hand away as there came another thump on the other side of the door. This time, it was followed by the muffled cough-barks of the infected. Samuel stepped back as a fight broke out in the stairwell. The door shook and several quick screams were followed by abrupt silence. The silence was replaced by wet and angry gnawing. From the crack beneath the door, blood began soaking into the edge of the dusty carpet, making it a curious shade of grey through the goggles.

'How many do you think there are through there?' Macy said.

Samuel shrugged. He looked at the dead bodies in the hallway, and then up through the hole in the ceiling. His magic told him it was the safe way to continue on.

With the help of Bryant's interlaced fingers, Samuel was hoisted through the hole, and he climbed out onto the next floor of the building. He immediately checked the stairwell door to ensure it was locked on this level too. It was, and he wondered whether Fabian Moor had trapped his victims in the stairwell to wait until they had changed into servile golems.

There was another hole cut into the ceiling, and Samuel stared up into the last floor of the building as Macy and Bryant jumped up from the floor below to join him. Silently, the agents checked all the apartments.

'Why are the power stones missing?' Macy muttered to herself.

Certain now that there were no survivors, Samuel removed his charmed hat, rolled it up, and stuffed it into the inside pocket of his coat. The twins pulled back their hoods. Bryant rubbed the scar on his cheek as he always did when he was troubled. Out of habit, Samuel checked that his revolver's power stone was glowing and replaced the spent bullet. He then checked the spirit compass. The needle was slowly turning around the face again. The automaton spider was still outside the building, waiting to make its move.

Samuel took a breath and stood beneath the hole leading to the final floor. 'If Moor's here, he'll probably have golems with him.'

The twins gave Samuel a look as if to say that after what they had just dealt with, a bunch of fragile, slow-moving servants were no particular menace.

Samuel glared at them. 'Golems can use guns.'

Having enlightened them, Samuel looked up at the hole in the ceiling. 'And if Gene's still alive, he'll probably be up there too.'

Things were very different on the final floor of the shelter. This part of the dry and crumbling building felt almost alive, suffused with a strange darkness. Through the green glass lenses of the goggles, the darkness filled Samuel's vision, black yet luminous. The shadows of the third floor had become solid, tangible, chipped into a thousand million pieces that scuttled over threadbare carpet and crumbling plaster like a swarm of black-shelled beetles.

By the expressions on Macy and Bryant's faces, Samuel knew they could see the effect without the use of the goggles; and by the way they shifted, it was clear the twins could also feel the crackle of magic in the air.

The flow of the shadow-insects was converging on a closed door halfway down the hallway. Samuel walked to it, followed by his fellow agents. Curiously, the swarm on the floor parted beneath their feet, revealing the dry and worn carpet. With Macy and Bryant standing on either side of him, Samuel confronted the door. It was not coated in the strange darkness; rather the shadows crawled and scurried through the gap around the frame into the room beyond. Samuel considered the door, his prescient awareness stirring. A moment passed and Macy opened her mouth to speak.

Samuel didn't give her the chance.

Shoving out with both hands as hard as he could, Samuel pushed the twins away from him in opposite directions. He dropped to one knee just as a hail of bullets ripped through the door with violet flashes of thaumaturgic bursts and flew over his head.

Samuel was sprayed with splinters of wood. The bullets made a thudding noise as they hit the scuttling shadows on the opposite wall. Samuel's deeper instincts guided him. Aiming up, his revolver spat four times. The hail of bullets ceased immediately.

Samuel sprang forward, kicking the door open and rolling into the room beyond. He came up shooting. Four more golems fell to the floor to join the two he had shot through the door. They thrashed and jerked upon hardened shadows, cracking and popping as their bodies began breaking into chunks of dry stone within their cassocks.

The revolver empty, Samuel holstered it, drew his rifle and primed the power stone. His magic took stock of the situation.

The apartment had been gutted. Door-shaped holes had been cut into the left and right walls, leading into the neighbouring apartments. Samuel's prescient awareness warned him that danger approached from the left side hole, into which all the shadows seemed to be crawling. He pressed his back to the wall next to the opening and waited.

Another golem stepped through, holding its pistol directly in front of it. Samuel drew his empty revolver and held the barrel to the golem's temple. Without a bullet to propel, the burst of thaumaturgy still punched a hole straight through the creature's head, and it crumbled to the floor. A second golem appeared, tripped over the ruins of the first and stumbled into the room.

Samuel's rifle spat a bullet into its face.

Wasting no time, not bothering to wait for the twins, Samuel darted through the hole in the wall into the apartment where the darkness congregated. He shot three more armed golems before they could fire, and smashed the head off a fourth with the butt of his rifle.

As Samuel quickly ejected the rifle's empty magazine and slapped a fresh one into place, he was vaguely aware of the twins entering the room he had just left. He heard Macy telling Bryant to check the other apartment through the hole on the right side wall before she stepped up beside Samuel. Her breath caught as she saw her fellow agent was now aiming his rifle at Fabian Moor.

The Genii sat cross-legged upon the floor, deep in a trance which the noise of fighting had not disturbed. Through the lenses of the goggles, he appeared to Samuel in perfect colour. His eyes were closed and face expressionless; his smooth, pale skin was only blemished by a patch of scarring upon his forehead. His long hair, white and straight, flowed over the shoulders of his black priest's cassock.

Samuel had wondered a hundred times what this creature of higher magic might look like. Never had he imagined that he would be facing someone so human-looking.

With his hands resting palm up upon his knees, Moor sat before a head-sized sphere of glass that floated two feet off the floor. The flow of swarming shadow-insects converged at the bottom of the sphere, where they were absorbed into the glass to fill it, thick and roiling. On the outside, the sphere was covered in a mesh of metal; and held by the mesh, at regular intervals, were a host of power stones, each as small as a little finger nail.

'Samuel,' Macy hissed, panicking. 'What are you waiting for? Just shoot the bastard!'

Fabian Moor's eyes snapped open. He gritted his teeth, and by the use of thaumaturgy propelled himself to his feet in a heartbeat.

Samuel squeezed the trigger. The power stone flashed and the rifle spat a thumb-sized metal slug. But the Genii had surrounded himself with a magical barrier. It melted the bullet to drops of molten lead that slapped to the floor, hissing and steaming. Samuel shot again but with the same results. His face grim, Fabian Moor raised a hand toward the agents of the Relic Guild. Macy bellowed and made to rush him.

She had taken no more than two steps when the window to the right exploded with a shower of shattered glass and broken framework. Samuel covered his face with an arm as the purple ghost of a giant spider crashed into the room.

'No!' Fabian Moor screeched.

Through the magically enhanced goggles, Samuel watched the automaton spider speed toward the Genii. Moor's hand glowed with thaumaturgy, but it was already too late. Before he could release whatever power he had summoned, the spider was upon him.

A dazzling blaze of energy filled the room as the spider cut through Moor's defensive barrier, burning so bright and magical through the lenses of the goggles that Samuel had to rip them from his face. He heard Macy swearing. When the slashes and streaks of thaumaturgy had cleared from his vision, Samuel saw that the spider had become visible.

The giant spider construct, with the head of a golem perched upon its melon-sized body, had coiled four of its long, thin legs around Fabian Moor's body, trapping his arms and squeezing his legs together in a cocoon of thaumaturgic metal. The tip of one leg had smoothed and flattened, moulding to the Genii's face, covering his mouth. Moor just had time to glare at Samuel, eyes full of hatred, before the automaton spider fizzed and became invisible once again, along with its captive. Glass shards cracked and jumped on the floor, plasterwork broke, as the spider clambered out of the window on its four remaining legs, spiriting the Genii away to his prison in the southern district.

Samuel dropped the goggles and shared a look of silent incredulity with Macy.

Incredulity turned to worry as the power stones surrounding the sphere of glass began to shine with bright, violet light. A sharp hissing filled the air, and the swarm of shadows fled the room as though being chased back to the places where sunlight could not reach. Abruptly, the hissing stopped. The power stones lost their light and became inert, clear crystals. The glass sphere dropped onto the threadbare carpet with a soft thump, nestling among the stony ruins of golems. No longer filled with oily blackness, it now contained an inert substance that looked much like murky water.

'Is … that it?' Macy said. 'We succeeded?'

Samuel suspected her expression of dubious astonishment only mirrored his own. 'We'd better get this thing back to Hamir,' he said, indicating the glass sphere.

Macy nodded uncertainly. She bent down, paused, and then tentatively picked it up. 'Bryant!' she shouted, studying the sphere. 'We got him!'

When Bryant replied, his voice was full of anguish. 'Macy, Samuel.' A pause. 'You'd better come here.'

With Macy carrying the sphere under one arm, the two agents rushed from the room, crossed the apartment where broken golems littered the carpet, and went through the hole in the wall to join Bryant.

They found him on his knees, tears in his eyes, leaning over a figure on the floor who was shaking and moaning. Bryant looked back at his sister and Samuel.

'I don't know what to do,' he said.

Samuel holstered his rifle, pushed Bryant out of the way, and crouched down beside the Relic Guild agent called Gene.

The frail apothecary was naked, stripped of clothes and dignity, and secured to the floor by chains connected to a metal brace around his neck. Gene's jaundiced eyes found Samuel's and he grabbed his hand.

'S-Samuel,' he said from between chattering teeth. 'I-I'm sorry. I tried to fight him … b-but he was too p-powerful.'

'It's all right, Gene,' Samuel said. 'You—'

'No, you don't … understand.' Gene was weeping now. 'I-I gave you up, S-Samuel. All of you. Moor knows … Moor knows who every a-agent of the Relic Guild is—'

Gene groaned in pain, and Samuel tightened his grip on his hand.

'Gene, listen to me. Did you tell Moor how to enter the Nightshade?'

'Don't … Don't know …'

The apothecary's skin was slimy, but not from sweat. His whole body was coated with a sticky excretion that emitted a sterile pungency. There was a bite wound on his neck, and it was obvious that Gene was using his magic, generating all manner of antidotes from the chemicals and minerals in his body, in a desperate attempt to fight the effects of Fabian Moor's virus – a fight he was losing.

'There's no cure,' Gene hissed, anger fuelling his normally gentle voice. 'I-I don't want to become a golem, Samuel. B-But I can't help myself. Please … stop me. I-I already want to kill you.'

A new tone was lacing Gene's weak voice now, like a distant scream. Black veins were trying to criss-cross his skin; they emerged and faded as they fought with Gene's chemical magic. Samuel's prescient awareness issued a warning: it was time to put distance between him and the apothecary.

As Gene began thrashing on the floor, choking and coughing, Samuel dropped his hand, and took several quick steps backwards. Macy and Bryant remained behind him. Samuel drew his rifle, but he couldn't bring himself to prime the power stone, to do what he knew was necessary.

Gene stopped thrashing and glared with yellow eyes filled with animal rage. He clenched long teeth set in receding gums. 'Do it, you bastard!' His words came as shrieks. 'Don't be a coward!'

Black veins began spreading over his skin.

Samuel thumbed the power stone and took aim. 'I'm so sorry, Gene,' he whispered.

The apothecary screamed, straining against his chains as he tried to rise, to attack, to feed on the blood of his fellow agents.

Samuel's rifle spat and the bullet burst Gene's head.

The fleeting moment of stillness was shattered when Bryant shouted with fury and punched a hole in the wall. Macy laid a hand on the barrel of Samuel's rifle, gently coaxing him to lower it. He was vaguely aware of her telling him he had done only what had to be done.

Zero tolerance.

'You'd better report to Gideon,' he heard himself tell the twins in an empty, cold voice.

'What about the infected locked in the stairwell?' Macy said. 'We can't leave them here.'

'I'll deal with them,' Samuel replied. He couldn't take his eyes off the corpse of the old apothecary. 'I'll meet you back at the Nightshade.'

The twins were silent and didn't move.

'I don't need your help to clear the stairwell,' Samuel said. There was no argument in his voice, no willingness to debate the matter; it was a simple statement. 'Just go.'

One of the twins, probably Macy, patted him on the shoulder, and they left without a further word.

Samuel didn't know how long he stood staring at Gene's body before he set fire to the dry and decaying homeless shelter, but by the time he stood outside, watching the building burn, the morning sun had passed its zenith in the sky and was descending into the afternoon.

CHAPTER FOUR

HOUSE OF THE AELFIR

Although this was the first time Samuel had seen Clara as the wolf, he had witnessed once before how powerful the changeling was. What now seemed a lifetime ago, Samuel had found the remains of a man Clara had killed. The man had been slaughtered, practically torn into bloody chunks. His limbs had been pulled from their sockets. His head had been ripped from his neck and left as a crushed pulp beside his savaged torso. Samuel remembered wondering at the time what size of monster could inflict such wanton carnage. And now the answer was before him.

Timewatcher have mercy, he thought. Clara was huge!

As the Relic Guild drifted along the circular tunnel that burrowed into the Nothing of Far and Deep, travelling to whatever destination resided on the other side, Samuel kept to the rear of the group, maintaining a very calculated and watchful distance between himself and the wolf. Clara stood next to Van Bam. Her head was at chest level to the illusionist, and she was easily big enough to carry him on her back. Her body was sleek and muscular beneath a thick, silvery pelt. Strong, sturdy legs ended with meaty paws, tipped with sharp, black nails.

The wolf looked back at Samuel, mouth open and tongue lolling as she panted. Samuel could see the very long and very sharp teeth set in a jaw big and powerful enough to crush a man's head. He resisted the urge to keep the coarse but reassuring feel of his rifle in his hands.

Van Bam casually reached out to scratch Clara behind the ear. The wolf looked at the illusionist, and they stared at each other for what seemed a suspiciously long time.

Samuel narrowed his eyes.

Van Bam had been willing to trust Clara from the very beginning. He kept complete faith that she would not pose a threat when she changed into the wolf, even though, by her own admission, Clara had never been in control of her magic. Samuel remained sceptical. His prescient awareness hadn't completely died away since entering the Nothing of Far and Deep; it radiated a low magical warmth in the pit of his stomach, uneasy like a nagging doubt. He couldn't be certain whether his magic was keeping him on his toes due to the unknown location he was heading towards, or because of the wolf.

Samuel's gut, the instincts of an old and seasoned bounty hunter, trusted Clara – for the most part. But he couldn't help wondering what she would have done had the wild demons not attacked the Relic Guild. In the moments after Clara's metamorphosis into the wolf, Samuel's magic had told him that the fury in her yellow eyes represented an overwhelming desire to fight that bordered on frenzy. If the Retrospective hadn't trapped the Relic Guild, if it hadn't opened its doorway and released its bloodthirsty monsters, would Clara have sated her rage upon her fellow agents?

The one remaining bullet in the rifle felt like insurance to Samuel.

A burst of light assaulted Samuel's vision. Beyond the tunnel's wispy, cloud-like wall, streaks of blue and red lightning crackled through the thick white of the Nothing of Far and Deep, as if the agents travelled through a gigantic storm cloud charged with monumental energy. It was an impressive sight, a revitalising sight, and one Samuel hadn't seen for many years.

A long time ago, before the Genii War, the Relic Guild had been a much stronger force. Throughout the centuries, every agent who had ever served the clandestine organisation had been born a magicker, touched by a gift. Magickers were the only humans permitted to use magic, but only if they served the Resident; only if they used their gifts to protect Labrys Town. *That* was the promise all Relic Guild agents had to make: to defend the denizens against sinister and mysterious forces.

A major part of the Relic Guild's duties had been to retrieve the magical relics and artefacts that treasure hunters liked to steal from the Houses of the Aelfir to sell on the black market. This very often meant that the agents had to travel to the Aelfirian realms – magical places filled with wonder and beauty. Long ago now, Samuel had relished those trips, considered them the best part of his duties. But then Spiral had tried to take control of the Labyrinth and conquer the Houses of the Aelfir.

Spiral and his hordes might have lost the Genii War, but at its conclusion, it was the Timewatcher who gave up on the denizens of Labrys Town. She severed all pathways that cut through the Nothing of Far and Deep and linked the Labyrinth to the Aelfirian Houses, abandoning one million humans, and leaving Labrys Town as a forbidden zone. No one got in and no one got out. During the forty years since the war's end, Samuel had often dreamed of escaping the Labyrinth and seeing the magical realms of the Aelfir again. But never once had he dreamed that he would have to flee as an outcast from the town he had promised to protect.

As he watched lightning crackle through the Nothing of Far and Deep, Samuel couldn't help but feel relieved to discover that at least one of the old pathways still existed; that for the first time in forty years he was travelling to an Aelfirian House – wherever that might be. Despite everything he had been through, despite the troubles behind him and the uncertainty ahead of him, a sense of liberation lifted the old bounty hunter's spirits.

'Samuel,' Van Bam called back. 'Our journey is almost over.'

Ahead of the illusionist and the wolf, the pathway came to an end at the black circle of a portal. It was only the size of Samuel's fist, but was growing larger, and he could see it devouring the wispy substance of the tunnel wall as it swirled.

The mystery House residing on the other side of the portal had been sending food and supplies to the denizens of Labrys Town for the past four decades. If not for those deliveries of essential goods, the denizens would have starved to death years ago. However, that did not necessarily mean that the Relic Guild was now heading toward friends; that did not mean the Relic Guild would be believed. It was no certain thing that the Aelfir on the other side of this tunnel would jump at the chance to help two humans and a wolf contact those powerful enough to end the reign of the Genii.

At that moment, Samuel felt he would settle for just a hot shower and a change of clothes. The journey to this point had included a trek through the sewers beneath Labrys Town which had left Samuel caked in dried waste and smelling foul.

The portal grew larger, drew closer. Out of instinct, Samuel reached over his shoulder to slide his rifle from its holster. As if sensing this action, Van Bam looked back and shook his head.

'In all probability, we are about to enter a scenario that will be tense at best,' he said, the strange acoustics in the wispy tunnel bringing his quiet voice close to Samuel's ears. 'Please, do not aggravate the situation further.'

Samuel scoffed. 'I really don't think my rifle is more threatening than a wolf the size of a pony – do you, Van Bam?'

Clara snorted.

A wry smile appeared on Van Bam's face. 'Nevertheless – no weapons.'

Samuel dropped his empty hand to his side, and Van Bam faced the swirling black circle again.

Samuel tried and failed to decide if he was moving towards the portal or if it was speeding towards him. It was a surreal sensation he had experienced a hundred times before when travelling these tunnels in his younger days. They rushed to meet each other nonetheless, and he felt a thrill as Van Bam and Clara disappeared into glassy darkness. Samuel held his breath the instant before the portal engulfed him too.

For a moment he felt choked, and then there was solid ground beneath his feet and light in his eyes.

He stumbled, feeling slightly nauseated, and took a moment to adjust to the transition of jumping from one realm to another.

Clara growled.

The portal had delivered the group into a warehouse of enormous size. Row upon row of violet glow spheres hung from the high ceiling on thick chains. The air was cold but cleaner than the air Samuel was used to. Directly ahead, a wide and clear section of stone floor stretched away like a valley between two long lines of platforms stacked high with packing crates, sacks and metal storage containers. The platforms were numerous, far more than Samuel had time to count before movement on the far side of the warehouse caught his eye.

The last of a sizeable group of people were fleeing the area. They scurried out of the warehouse, through the wide and high opening of its huge door. Clara made to chase after them, but Van Bam told her to stay put.

The illusionist stepped forward. 'Wait,' he shouted at the fleeing people.

The last person in line began barking orders at the others, telling them to not stop, to get out, to escape. He paused to look back at the two men and the wolf. Dressed in a bulky overcoat, he stared with round Aelfirian eyes, larger than any human's.

'We are denizens of the Labyrinth,' Van Bam told him. 'We mean you no harm.'

The Aelf turned and ran for the door. He paused before exiting, using his elbow to smash the glass cover of a big red box on the wall. He then thumped something hidden inside the box with the palm of his hand, and the air was shattered by the piercing wail of a klaxon. Clara began howling, and the glow spheres hanging from their chains above began flashing with a bright and warning orange light.

'Please,' Van Bam shouted, 'we need your help!' but his voice was drowned by the klaxon.

With a final glance at the group, the Aelf sprinted from the warehouse. A huge shutter door descended behind him and locked with a loud bang.

◙

In the Nightshade, the Genii Hagi Tabet hung from a web of leathery tentacles that had sprouted from her back and punctured the stone of the walls, floor and ceiling of what had once been an isolation room. Strong and taut, dividing the room into two halves, the tentacles not only kept the new Resident of Labrys Town suspended in the air, but also connected her to the ancient magic of the Nightshade, which gave her omnipresent sight and command over the lives of one million humans.

Fabian Moor stood below Tabet, looking up at her naked and withered form hanging from the leathery web. Her watery eyes were vaguely focused on her fellow Genii. There might have been a hint of intrigue in her absent expression, a mild interest to know what was hidden in the hands that Moor clutched protectively to his chest. But Hagi Tabet did not speak, did not enquire, and Moor did not show her the crimson and yellow flower he hid in his hands. Instead, he shifted his attention to the left side of the room and studied the human who stood there.

Moor didn't recognise the man. He was tall and slim, wearing a pristine police uniform. He stood to attention, back straight and hands clasped behind him. His hair was thinning and slicked back. The lenses of his spectacles were tinted enough to hide the colour of his eyes, but Moor could easily see the uncertainty in them. Fear and confusion etched into his gaunt face as he tried to process the strange company he was currently keeping.

Viktor Gadreel and Mo Asajad stood behind Moor. He turned and raised a questioning eyebrow at them.

'Don't look at me,' Asajad said. 'I've no idea who he is.'

Gadreel shrugged his meaty shoulders. 'Ask Hagi. She summoned him to the Nightshade.'

Hagi Tabet smiled dreamily at Moor. 'This is Captain Jeter,' she explained, her voice, like her expression, dancing precariously on the edge of insanity. 'He commands the Labrys Town Police Force for me. I have brought him to the Nightshade to hear him explain why he allowed the Relic Guild to escape.'

Moor looked at the human again. He knew the name Jeter. This man's loyalty to the Nightshade was without compromise, or so Tabet had said. He had blind faith in the Resident, and didn't question the change of regime that had occurred in his town. But his faith would crumble if he realised who he stood in the room with.

Jeter thought better of stepping forwards, and cleared his throat. 'As I was saying to our Resident,' he said, his voice more confident than his body language, 'the Relic Guild—'

'Shut up,' said Moor.

At first, it seemed that Jeter didn't know whether to be fearful or affronted at having his authority quashed by anyone other than the

Resident herself. To Moor's immense irritation, the police captain then decided to whine and plead his case directly to Tabet.

'Please, what chance did we have against magic? The Relic Guild murdered many of my officers. Only one of them escaped the warehouse alive ...'

He trailed off as Tabet began giggling. With confusion evident on his face, Jeter looked to Moor and opened his mouth to continue his defence.

'No, Captain,' Moor said. 'If you value your life, do not say another word.'

'But don't worry,' Asajad added. 'We will certainly *discuss* your incompetence soon enough.' To which Gadreel rumbled a chuckle.

Jeter's lips quivered. He looked from the cold intent of Moor to the calculating malevolence of Mo Asajad, to Gadreel's hulking promise of brutality, to the strange, almost loving smile of Hagi Tabet, and the police captain found the good sense to remain silent. He bowed his head and stepped back, taking care to distance himself from the fence of Tabet's tentacles that divided the room.

'Good,' said Moor.

Leaving the human to fester for the short time that remained to him, Moor gave the watery, semi-mad gaze of Tabet his full attention.

'Hagi,' he said, moving his hands away from his chest. 'I have a gift for you.'

It was hard to keep his cupped hands from shaking as he raised the yellow and crimson flower like an offering to the Resident. 'The time has come, my old comrade,' he whispered.

Tabet reached down with an expression of longing on her face. Asajad and Gadreel stepped forwards to stand shoulder to shoulder with Moor, sharing his anticipation. Tabet took the flower with gentle fingers and lifted it to her face. She closed her eyes and breathed the scents of an empath's memories. Her eyes remained closed as she opened her mouth wide, wider still, revealing a blood red tongue and long white teeth. With a little moan of childish pleasure, Tabet pushed the flower into her mouth.

She began to chew – slowly at first but then with determination. Her jaw muscles flexed, her lips smacked, and saliva dribbled down her chin. As soon as Tabet swallowed, her back arched, her arms splayed, and her legs opened wide, displaying herself to her fellow Genii. She moaned as though entering the throes of climax.

On the left side of the room, the human called Jeter had moved a hand to his sidearm – an unconscious action – and his fingers worried at the catch on the holster.

Moor's lips set into a grim line.

Hagi Tabet's body relaxed with an abruptness that left her limp upon the web of leathery tentacles. Her breathing was harsh, as though she had just completed a ten mile run. Almost as one, Moor, Asajad and Gadreel leaned forwards expectantly. Slowly, Tabet raised her head and glared triumphantly at her fellow Genii.

'I can see her,' she whispered hoarsely. 'The empath – she is in my head ...' She began swinging on her web, agitated, excited perhaps. 'Oh, Fabian, there is wonder here, wonder and awe ... Marney had faith. She knew love—'

'Hagi,' Moor said softly, though his teeth were clenched and his temples pounded. 'Focus on what we need to know.'

'It is hard to see, Fabian,' Tabet breathed. 'Everything is quick ... too quick ...' Her eyes flickered from side to side as if struggling to keep pace with the speed of memories flowing through her head. 'Marney led a full life ...'

Gadreel's patience was the first to crumble. 'Where is our lord and master?' he demanded.

'I-I'm trying ...' Tabet, up on her web, became frustrated, and her swinging motion increased. 'Oh, but the empath was clever. Memories have been hidden within memories. She has disrupted her timeline. There's no ... linear path to follow—'

'Try harder, Hagi!' Asajad's tolerance had broken. 'Tell us where he is,' she hissed.

Tears spilled onto Tabet's cheeks; her eyes flickered, blurs of vibration. 'Past and present ... I-I cannot tell the difference. All mixed, all jumbled ... the information we need is hidden within a lifetime of memories. It will take time.'

'We have already waited forty years,' Asajad retorted.

And Gadreel growled in agreement. 'Do better, Hagi!'

'Enough, both of you,' Moor said. He took a step towards Tabet, and then turned to face Asajad and Gadreel. 'Did I not tell you that the magic in Marney was strong for a human, that she was not to be underestimated?'

His fellow Genii stared angrily at him but held their tongues.

'Have patience,' Moor told them. 'A simple magicker, albeit a clever one, cannot hide her secrets from us for long. Am I right, Hagi?'

'Give me time,' Tabet whispered. 'I will find Oldest Place.'

'Of course you will,' Moor said. He allowed a smile to play out on his lips. 'Search in peace, Hagi. Bring Lord Spiral back to his Genii.'

In reply, Tabet closed her eyes and her body relaxed. Her breathing settled. Two tears ran down her pale cheeks and a beatific expression came to her face. Her eyes moved rapidly beneath the lids as she began searching the lifelong memories of the empath.

Moor gave Asajad and Gadreel a look, daring them to question his authority. Although Asajad gave her usual thin, concealing smile, Gadreel nodded, frustrated but content to follow.

A small and high-pitched whine cut through the air. Moor looked to the human called Jeter. He had drawn his pistol and primed its power stone.

'Genii?' the police captain said. His hand shook as his aim wavered between the three creatures of higher magic. 'Oldest Place? Spiral? I-I don't understand.'

'Forgive us,' Moor said. 'You must be terribly confused.' He gave a casual flick of a finger and sent out a small pulse of thaumaturgy.

Captain Jeter yelped as the power stone jumped from his pistol, sparking as it shattered upon the floor.

'Viktor,' Moor said pleasantly. 'Explain the situation to the captain, will you?'

In a blur of motion faster than any human eye could see, Gadreel jaunted across the room and gathered the human into a crushing embrace. Jeter's struggles were as weak as a child's in the hulking Genii's arms. He sucked in a great lungful of air as Gadreel pulled his head back by the hair and sank his long teeth into his neck. Blood gushed down his uniform.

'And Viktor,' said Moor, 'when you have finished, please return to the lowest region of the Nightshade and find a way to drag Hamir out of his hiding place.'

As he fed, Gadreel grunted an affirmation. Moor addressed Asajad.

'While we are waiting for Hagi, there is something I would like you to see.'

Asajad paused, wincing as Jeter released his breath in a piercing scream, and then said, 'So lead the way, my dear Lord Moor.'

A couple of hours had passed since the Relic Guild had been trapped inside the enormous warehouse. The giant shutter door remained closed and locked. Samuel had silenced the scream of the klaxon, and put a halt to the flashing orange lights by smashing the control box from the wall with a hammer he had found. He had then suggested breaking a window to escape the warehouse, grumbling, 'We haven't come this far just to be corralled.' But Van Bam had declined the offer. The Aelfir were obviously spooked enough by the sudden appearance of humans, and there was no point antagonising them further. 'We do nothing but wait for the Aelfir to make their next move,' the illusionist had decided.

Van Bam might not have been the Resident anymore, but he still led the Relic Guild.

Now, Van Bam sat on a metal storage container, twirling his green glass cane in his hand. He watched the wolf as she foraged for food among the multitude of crates and sacks stacked high upon a host of huge cargo platforms. Samuel stood upon the crates he had piled upon a workbench to the left of the shutter door. Arms folded across his chest, he kept vigil, watching the outside world through a window, frozen, silent, barely blinking. Though Samuel might have appeared calm and assured, Van Bam's inner vision detected the colours of Samuel's mood – the shades of frustration and hues of uncertainty that swirled within him.

As for Clara, she was content, happy to focus on nothing more than the present moment as she rummaged through a hunting ground of crates, sacks and metal containers.

Each of the platforms, piled high with cargo, was thirty foot long and fifteen wide. There were at least sixty – maybe seventy – of them, forming two lines in the warehouse; enough to comprise a full day of deliveries to Labrys Town.

Countless times Van Bam had witnessed these platforms arriving into Labrys Town, emerging from the portal outside the Nightshade, one after the other, from the first light of day to the dead of night. Always unaccompanied, always carrying food stocks and raw materials and medicines – every kind of supply that enabled a million denizens to survive. Each platform that came not only delivered essential cargo but also exuded mystery. Countless times Van Bam had wondered which Aelfirian House resided on the other side of the portal outside the Nightshade. Who was it that was keeping the people of the Labyrinth alive?

He was finding the reality somewhat uninspiring.

In truth, Van Bam didn't know what he had expected to find. Perhaps the glorious, mystical realms he had experienced in his younger days, or maybe one of the enormous Aelfirian cities that dwarfed Labrys Town. Certainly not this huge decrepit warehouse, cold and dimly-lit, with its high ceiling and greying walls, dull and unwelcoming, he was sure.

Clara gave a small yelp and skipped back as something sharp stabbed her snout. She shook her head and snorted before continuing to forage through the wooden crates stacked eight high on a platform, growling all the while.

With a sigh, Van Bam looked up at Samuel. 'Can you see anyone yet?'

'Nope.' The old bounty hunter didn't look away from the window.

'Any indication which House this is?'

He shook his head. 'I can't see beyond the loading bay, Van Bam. There's no one around. Maybe the Aelfir evacuated.'

'I do not think so, Samuel. They will be back, I am certain.' Because they had to come back, Van Bam told himself. The Aelfir had to return and they had to listen. They had to put the Relic Guild in touch with the Thaumaturgists again. Without them, there was no saving Labrys Town from Fabian Moor and the Genii. 'They will be back,' he repeated.

Samuel said nothing and continued watching through the window.

Close to the back wall of the warehouse, at the end of the stone floor between the platforms, two portals stood. They were inert, the space within their archways empty, giving a clear view of the grey wall behind them. Van Bam guessed that one was for export, the other for import.

Considering that the import portal had been closed since the end of the Genii War, that it had remained inactive for forty years, Van Bam couldn't blame the Aelfir for fleeing and trapping the Relic Guild in the warehouse. He imagined the panic when the portal suddenly activated after all this time, the shock and fear of seeing humans again, humans travelling with a huge wolf at their side. The agents of the Relic Guild were unwelcome strangers in this House, and their arrival had put a halt to the delivery of cargo that was essential to the people of Labrys Town.

Clara growled as she tussled with a crate, dragging it with her teeth from a platform, sending a pile of other crates crashing to the floor. The wolf dragged her crate clear, swiped at it with a mighty paw, and the wood cracked under her long and sharp nails. She tore a hole large enough to fit her muzzle inside, and she tugged a joint of dried beef free. Lying down, holding the joint between her forelegs, she proceeded to lick salt from the meat's surface and gnaw at its toughness.

Clara was magnificent as the wolf: large and powerful, yet sleek and fast. Back in the alleyways of the Great Labyrinth, Van Bam had experienced a curious sense of pride for the way she had fearlessly protected her fellow agents from the wild demons of the Retrospective, for the way she had retained control over her inner beast for the first time in her life. But he was inclined to wonder if that control had been encouraged by guidance of a spiritual kind.

Van Bam had been in tune with the Nightshade long enough for its magic to have felt like a sixth sense to him, and the voice of Gideon, the dead Resident, had been his constant companion and guide. But when the Genii had taken control of Labrys Town, Van Bam's connection to the Nightshade had been severed, its magic scooped out of him, and the voice of Gideon had fallen silent in his head. The illusionist had never felt that lost before. But now Gideon was back.

Van Bam could feel the familiar ghostly presence lurking in his mind, like a constant itch he could never scratch. He welcomed the sensation, recognised Gideon's return as a good thing, especially with the Relic Guild needing every ally it could find. But Gideon had thus far declined to speak with Van Bam; his interest had been piqued by someone else.

Somehow Van Bam knew that Gideon and the wolf were communicating – he could just *feel* it. Whether this was a good thing or not remained to be seen, but Van Bam hoped – desperately hoped – that Clara was strong-willed enough to cope with the pernicious voice of an unstable dead Resident in her head.

Are you truly concerned for Clara's sanity? Gideon drawled. *Or are you jealous?*

A wry smile touched Van Bam's lips. *I was growing bored of waiting for you to speak.*

Hello, my idiot. Did you miss me?

Not as much as you might like to think.

The voice chuckled.

Gideon, what in the Timewatcher's name is going on? How are you communicating with Clara?

I have absolutely no idea. Intriguing, isn't it?

Where have you been? What happened at the Nightshade?

The ghost was quiet for a moment. *I really don't know, to be truthful. One moment I was watching Hamir, and the next I was with you, fighting wild demons out in the Great Labyrinth.*

Do you know what became of Hamir?

No, and I wouldn't like to guess.

Van Bam cursed silently; he and Samuel had already decided that Hamir was most likely dead. *Then what of the Genii, Gideon? Did you see them enter the Nightshade?*

I saw nothing, Gideon replied. *It's strange, my idiot. I feel like there's a gap in my memory, yet the transition from one place to the other was seamless. As quick as blinking an eye.* His pause was thoughtful. *But I can tell you that my return seems to have coincided with the arrival of the avatar. Perhaps it had the power to call me back after the Genii took the Nightshade. Curious, isn't it?*

Van Bam nodded. Frustratingly, the mysterious avatar was shrouding itself in question after question while never revealing any answers.

Clara has told me all about the new Resident of Labrys Town, Gideon said. *Hagi Tabet. Do you know how many other Genii Moor has released?*

At least one other that we know of. Perhaps two.

And I assume you've worked out how they managed to enter the Nightshade?

There was no mockery or cruel edge in Gideon's voice, but Van Bam couldn't bring himself to answer the question. He had been trying hard not to think of Marney.

During the Genii War, when Fabian Moor had first come to Labrys Town, he had believed that the Nightshade had left a residue of its magic within the psyches of the Relic Guild agents; had unwittingly imparted a weak spot in its defences that Moor thought he could utilise to seize control of the Resident's home. Although Moor's belief had led to the deaths of Van Bam's friends, it was reckoned that Moor had been wrong; that the secrets he was willing to torture magickers to reveal simply didn't exist. But now it seemed it was the Relic Guild who had been mistaken.

Van Bam couldn't accept that it was Marney, of all the agents he had ever known, who had been the one to give Moor control of the Nightshade.

There is a lot to this situation that we do not know, Gideon said. Again, there was no cruelty in his words. *But I do know Marney would have fought Moor as hard as she could.*

Van Bam struggled to face the implication behind Gideon's words. He refused to believe that Marney, his old love, was just another victim to fall foul of the Genii's murderous nature. Yet if Moor had taken what he needed from Marney, then her usefulness was served. The Genii would never have allowed her to live.

It is time to accept reality, Gideon said. *Marney is gone.*

Van Bam cleared his throat and shifted in his seat.

The sly, amused lilt crept back into Gideon's voice. *Keep faith, my idiot – Marney might be gone, but remember that she left behind her legacy for us to decipher.*

Van Bam cocked his head to one side as he felt Gideon guide his attention back to the wolf, hungrily feeding on the joint of dried beef.

Before Marney had been captured by Moor, she had given Clara a message. With the use of her empathic magic and a simple kiss on the lips, Marney had planted information directly into the changeling's mind, information that the Relic Guild undoubtedly needed in these desperate times. The trouble was Clara could not recall what Marney had imparted.

Gideon said, *The information is hiding somewhere here in Clara's head, my idiot – I can sense the residue of empathic magic. But while Clara remains as the wolf, she has no interest in understanding Marney's little gift. Or letting me find it.*

Van Bam stared at the wolf licking and chewing the hunk of dried meat, and he frowned. *Why would Marney send us a message only to then hide it?*

The dead Resident's pause suggested a shrug. *Perhaps the message isn't intended for us at all, my idiot. Have you thought of that?*

Van Bam hadn't.

Either way, Gideon continued, *we might have to wait for Clara to take human form again before I can find out.*

Nonetheless, Van Bam said to his guide, his frustration growing, *keep searching Clara's mind. Discover anything you can.*

Oh, I intend to, my idiot. The wolf is very strong-willed, but I'm sure I can tame her.

Gideon, be kind to Clara. She is not—

'They're coming,' Samuel announced.

Forgetting Gideon, Van Bam jumped to his feet. Clara looked up from her meal, her ears pointed and alert.

Up on his makeshift perch, Samuel craned his neck for a better view through the window. 'I can see rifles … a *lot* of rifles. Police. They're bringing something with them.'

Clara padded over to stand next to Van Bam.

'What does your magic tell you, Samuel?'

He rocked his head from side to side, deciphering the message of his prescient awareness. 'There's no immediate danger,' he said, 'but keep on your toes. They're frightened.'

'As to be expected,' Van Bam said. 'At least for now the Aelfir wish us no harm.'

'Just as well,' Samuel said. 'I've only got one bullet left, and my power stones are losing their charge, for some reason – *Wait!*' The old bounty hunter peered closer through the window. 'The Aelf who locked us in here is out there. Looks like he's in charge.' He rubbed breath from the glass. 'I think he's going to speak—'

'Humans!' The voice was loud but muffled through the warehouse door. 'You are under arrest.' He spoke with an exaggerated confidence, proud almost. 'By leaving the Labyrinth, you have broken the Timewatcher's law. You will surrender to our custody peacefully. Lay down your weapons and control your *beast*.'

Clara growled. Van Bam laid a hand on her back, either to restrain her with his touch, or to find reassurance for himself in her strength. He couldn't decide which.

'Agree to our terms and you won't be harmed.'

Samuel was looking out of the window again. He swore and his colours became shaded with anger. 'Van Bam, remember those cages the Aelfir used to transport animals in?'

'I do.'

The old bounty hunter looked down at the illusionist with a sour expression. 'They've brought one for us.'

The metal plates covering Van Bam's eyes met the wolf's baleful yellow glare, and he heard Gideon chuckling in his head.

'Do you agree to these terms?' the voice bellowed.

'We agree,' Van Bam shouted. 'But please, give us a moment.'

He gave a nod to Samuel who jumped down from his perch and began unbuckling his utility belt. He threw it on the floor, and it was quickly followed by his rifle. Lastly, he unsheathed his knife and added it to the pile. As Van Bam laid down his green glass cane, the old bounty hunter sucked air over his teeth.

'You know, you could keep that with you. Make them think it's a walking stick. Might come in handy.'

Van Bam shook his head. 'We take no risks. Agreed?'

Samuel huffed. 'You're the boss.'

Van Bam looked at Clara. 'We do exactly as we are commanded, yes?'

The wolf looked away to stare at the warehouse door. Her tail was pointed to the ground, her body tense, and her colours were agitated.

'Clara?'

Don't worry, my idiot, Gideon assured him. *I'll keep Clara on a leash. For now.*

Van Bam turned to the shutter and drew a breath. 'We are ready,' he shouted.

'Keep your hands in the air,' replied the voice. 'Put the wolf in front of you.'

Sensible, said Gideon, clearly enjoying himself. *Keep the* beast *in clear sight of the rifles.*

As Van Bam and Samuel stepped behind Clara, raising their hands above their heads, there was a *clunk* followed by a hum, and the huge shutter door began to rise, clacking metallically, louder and louder, until it was fully open. Chill air stroked Van Bam's face as the loading bay was revealed. The illusionist counted ten rifles aimed at the Relic Guild, more than half of them trained on the wolf. The glow of the weapons' power stones filled Van Bam's inner vision with the violet glow of thaumaturgy, but the fear blooming in the bodies of the Aelfir came to him in subtle shades of grey.

Dressed in uniforms and wearing helmets that concealed their faces behind black glass visors, the police officers formed two lines of five on either side of a cage that was easily big enough to hold the agents. Made from thick metal bars, the cage sat upon the same kind of wooden platform used to deliver cargo to the Labyrinth, and its door was open.

Behind the line of police to the left stood the Aelf who had trapped the Relic Guild inside the warehouse. He wore a long and thick overcoat, and a woollen hat pulled down low enough to cover the points of his ears. There was a self-satisfied look on his oddly triangular face, menace in his large Aelfirian eyes.

'Get into the cage,' he ordered much louder than he needed to. '*Slowly.*'

Oh good, Gideon said dryly. *A megalomaniac.*

CHAPTER FIVE

UNINVITED GUESTS

To the east, a strange sun blazed. A gigantic ball of purple energy, surrounded by stars, licking out into space with snaking tongues of slow fire. It burned with such a purple radiance that only pure thaumaturgy could have formed it. Its light was too intense for Van Bam's inner vision. He turned his face from the glare, wondering to where in the realms he and his colleagues had been delivered. Neither the illusionist nor Gideon could recall an Aelfirian House that existed beneath a purple sun.

Held inside the animal cage, which sat upon a floating platform, the Relic Guild was being escorted through this strange House by the armed police officers. Samuel held to the bars of the cage, staring out, silent and contemplative; Clara, unfazed by the situation, had lain down on the floor, and was apparently asleep. The Aelf who had collected the magickers from the warehouse led the procession, and he seemed to be enjoying himself.

Despite the intensity of the burning, purple sun, the air was surprisingly cold.

From the warehouse, the journey progressed along a wide and cobbled road that cut through an open expanse of short, wild grass, heading towards buildings in the near distance. Eventually the road bent round to the left, and ran before the buildings: a long line of terraced shops and residential dwellings. Van Bam was glad the buildings hid the harsh glare of the strange purple sun. Myriad shades of grey filled his inner vision once more, but subtle colours remained in the air, hints, hues, that could only come from magic.

Van Bam noticed Aelfirian faces at the windows of the houses, furtively peering out through gaps in curtains, curious and eager to catch a glimpse of their human visitors. The Aelf in charge seemed to know he was being watched. His back straightened, his chest stuck out, and he raised his head a little higher. He wanted his fellow Aelfir to see him leading the police officers, for them to know that the humans in the cage were at his command. He acted as if this was a homecoming parade.

'I think we have wound up at the mercy of an idiot, Samuel,' Van Bam whispered, but his old friend didn't reply.

Samuel still clutched the bars of the cage, facing away from the buildings. He was frozen, looking out, and his emotional hues were as troubled as they were nostalgic. He was staring at where, a short distance from the road, the land ended abruptly. The area was marked by a sturdy-looking guardrail. And beyond the guardrail was nothing: no water that might signal the beginning of an ocean, no horizon – just … *emptiness*.

Van Bam gained the dizzying realisation that this House had been built upon a giant platform of rock that was free floating in space.

Interesting, Gideon purred.

The guardrail was broken at regular intervals by gates that led to wide rope and wood bridges. The bridges looped away, crossing the void, to connect to small, floating islands. Van Bam could see eight islands, each with a flat plateau that tapered down to jagged points like the roots of teeth. And standing on each plateau was the tall stone archway of a portal.

'Those portals,' Samuel said, his voice subdued, 'they lead to sub-Houses. Van Bam, I know where we are.' He looked back at the illusionist. 'This House is called Sunflower. It's the hub of the Aelfheim Archipelago.'

Van Bam knew of the Aelfheim Archipelago, though he had never had the chance to visit it. But it was supposed to be a collection of farming Houses, not a dismal realm with a strange purple sun that barely gave warmth.

'You are sure, Samuel?' Van Bam said dubiously.

'Without a doubt,' Samuel replied. 'The place has changed – I mean, something bad must've happened, but …' He looked out over the portals sitting upon drifting islands. 'I've been here before, Van Bam.'

The conversation was brought to a conclusion as the self-righteous Aelf ordered the procession to halt outside the House's large police station.

'Back it up!' he bellowed.

There was a broad grin on his face, as the police officers positioned the cage before the stone steps that led up to the station. Two more officers stood by the building's entrance, both carrying rifles, power stones primed.

'Come on, boys!' the Aelf in charge called happily. He smiled smugly at Van Bam. 'Let's get them into their cells.'

The wolf looked up at this, and Van Bam gave her a concerned frown.

Stop fretting, my idiot, Gideon chuckled. *Clara has promised to remain on her very best behaviour.*

With trepidation and twitchy trigger fingers, the police officers ushered the Relic Guild into a small jailhouse within the police station. There were only three cells, fronted by thick metal bars and divided by cold stone walls. The wolf was placed in a cell by herself, while Van Bam and Samuel occupied the cell next to her. Only when the cell doors were locked, and sturdy metal bars protected him from his prisoners, did the self-satisfied Aelf tell the officers to leave. And then he turned on an oily smugness that confirmed to Van Bam that he was not the person the Relic Guild needed to talk to.

'The name's Marca,' the Aelf said. He was facing the only window in the room, staring out onto the strange Aelfirian landscape. Beneath the window was a rickety table, upon which sat Samuel's rifle and utility belt, and Van Bam's green glass cane. 'I'm the supervisor of Sunflower.'

Marca turned from the window and rocked back on his heels, as if to allow his audience enough time to be suitably impressed by his declaration.

Really? Gideon said. *This fool has been keeping the denizens of Labrys Town alive all these years?* And he laughed heartily.

'Anything you've got to say, you're going to say to me,' Marca continued with an air of supreme authority. 'I'm the only one in charge around here.'

'I do not wish to appear rude, Supervisor,' said Van Bam, 'but I find that highly doubtful.'

Marca chuckled at Van Bam, and he slipped his woollen hat from his head, uncovering pointed ears filled with more greying hair than remained on his head. 'If I were you,' he said, 'I wouldn't be as smart with my mouth.' He rolled the hat up and smacked it against his palm. 'Wouldn't you agree, Hillem?'

Hillem was a young Aelf, early twenties, tall and slim, with a mop of brown, unruly hair, and watery eyes that gave him a sleepy appearance. Dim-witted, clearly the supervisor's lackey, he had been waiting in the jailhouse when the group arrived, and was the only other person to remain after the police left. And he had a fixation with the wolf.

Even though the adjacent cell held the first humans he had ever seen, Hillem hadn't stopped staring at Clara. Like Marca, he was wrapped up against the cold in a long, thick coat and a plain woollen scarf that hid the mouth and chin of his triangular face. He sniffed a lot, and repeatedly wiped his nose on the sleeve of his coat.

'Hillem?' said Marca.

The young Aelf's large, unblinking eyes didn't move from Clara's cell, but he worked his mouth free of the scarf. 'What?'

'I said wouldn't you agree?'

Hillem's eyes still didn't stray from the wolf. 'Agree with what?'

Marca sighed and shook his head. 'Never mind.' He addressed Van Bam. 'Now then. Would you like to tell me how you managed to escape from the Labyrinth?'

'I very much would not,' said Van Bam, his voice as calm as always. 'But I would appreciate the chance to speak with your superiors.'

Marca suddenly seemed a little unsure of himself. 'Why?'

'Because the news I bring needs to be heard by those with authority higher than yours. Please, fetch them.'

The supervisor made a show of going nowhere by folding his arms across his chest and giving the illusionist a deliberately provocative grin that was surprisingly wide for such a small mouth.

Clara thinks you're wasting time, my idiot, Gideon said unhelpfully. *She can't understand why you're not telling Marca about the Genii. I'll tell her you know what you're doing, shall I?*

Van Bam ignored him.

'Why does it keep looking at me?' Hillem said.

Van Bam heard Clara give a low growl as the young Aelf moved closer to her cell and wrinkled his nose.

'It stinks too, but not like them.' Hillem nodded towards Van Bam and Samuel, who still carried the reek of the sewers beneath Labrys Town. Hillem moved closer still to the bars. 'It smells … it smells like a zoo I went to. Saw a wolf there once, eating its own shit—'

Clara barked, once, hard. Hillem fell onto his rump with a cry and scuttled back.

'Careful, boy,' Marca said, eyeing the wolf. 'Given the chance, a beast like that would bite you in two and save one half for supper.'

Given the chance indeed, Gideon purred.

Hillem got to his feet, wide-eyed and slack-jawed. He was clearly gullible enough to believe anything he was told.

'Maybe we should have a word with the farmers,' Marca continued. 'I reckon they could do with another sheepdog.' He sneered cruelly. 'Farmers are hard bastards. They'd tame the bitch.'

'Leave her alone.'

To Van Bam's surprise, it was Samuel who had spoken.

Marca turned his sneer to the old bounty hunter. 'Was that a threat?'

'Most definitely,' Samuel growled.

Gideon laughed in Van Bam's head. *Why, my idiot, I believe Miss Clara has a new admirer.*

'So what are you?' Marca said. 'Criminals? Is that it? Are you on the run?'

'Yes and no.' Samuel's voice was as cold as Van Bam had ever heard it. 'Marca, you'd better do as my friend says before the shit storm we just escaped follows us here.'

Uncertain again, Marca glanced at Hillem, but the young Aelf was back to staring at the wolf while digging wax out of his pointed ear with a finger.

'You'd better start showing me respect,' Marca said to the humans. 'My *superiors* are a long way away from Sunflower. We're all alone out here.'

'That's not true,' Samuel told Van Bam. 'His superiors are through one of the portals we saw on the islands outside. It'd take him half an hour, tops, to go and fetch someone.'

'Is that right?' Van Bam said levelly.

Marca gritted his teeth. 'How do you know that?'

'Because I've been here before, Marca,' Samuel replied. 'And I know a bloody liar when I see one.'

The supervisor's face turned red. He drew himself up and pointed a finger. 'Now you just listen to me,' he said. 'If you know what's good for you, you'll start cooperating. I carry all kinds of authority, and not just in Sunflower. I have friends in the Panopticon of Houses, you know.' He said it like it was the ultimate threat.

'You are right, Samuel – he *is* a liar,' said Van Bam with a tired air. 'I have no idea what this Panopticon of Houses is, but this Aelf is no one of great importance. He is looking to use our capture as a means to gain himself a little glory. I rather think this conversation is over.'

Samuel scoffed. 'Did it ever begin?'

'Shut your mouths!' Marca was shouting now, and Hillem finally took notice, flinching and dragging his eyes away from Clara. 'No one gets in or out of the Labyrinth – that's the Timewatcher's law! You'd better start talking or things will get *very* uncomfortable for you.'

Van Bam sighed. 'You may leave now, Supervisor. And please do not come back unless you are bringing *real* authority with you.'

'Oh, I'll leave all right,' Marca shot back, 'but not because of your say so.' He gestured to Hillem with his head, and together they headed for the door. 'You've broken some big laws, *human* – you, your friend, and your wolf. And when I come back, you'll be lucky if it's not with an order for your deaths.'

As Marca shoved Hillem out of the room, he smacked a wall switch to extinguish the ceiling prism, plunging the room into darkness. He slammed the door behind him. The lock clicked.

What an imperious little bastard, Gideon said in the sudden silence.

Van Bam looked at Samuel.

'I hope you know what you're doing,' Samuel said miserably. He climbed onto one of the bunks in the cell and rolled over to face the wall. 'If we're getting executed, don't bother waking me up.'

A millennium ago, each and every Thaumaturgist had been taught that the source of the Nightshade's power was older and deeper than any of them could understand. The First and Greatest Spell, the Timewatcher told Her children, was far-reaching, stretching beyond the imagination of the mightiest creature of higher magic. The Thaumaturgists were warned to never question their Mother on this matter. But Fabian Moor questioned. He had witnessed the legendary First and Greatest Spell first-hand, back when the Labyrinth was new, and he decided it was high time to test the Timewatcher's warning, to see if the power of the Nightshade could easily shoulder aside the imagination of the Genii.

In the lower regions of the Nightshade, in an empty room that had probably not hosted a living being in centuries, Moor stood with his hands clenched into fists. Three of the walls still retained a bland cream colour, decorated with a repetitive pattern of hundreds of tiny square mazes, but the fourth wall had cleared to shimmering air. It was now a doorway, a portal into a House of dead time where nightmares roamed the land and soared through the sky.

'Fabian,' said Mo Asajad. 'I'm already bored. Please tell me why we are here.'

Moor didn't reply.

The implications of what Asajad was witnessing were wasted on her. Perhaps she couldn't understand the significance of it all; perhaps she could, but didn't care. In all ways, she disappointed Moor.

This view into the Retrospective – a view that came without sound or scent – it was a view into the future.

At one time there had been an unknown number of doorways scattered throughout the endless alleyways of the Great Labyrinth. Behind each of those doors had been a portal that led to the Houses of the Aelfir. The Timewatcher might have removed those doorways at the end of the war, but the power to create the portals had remained within the Nightshade: the First and Greatest Spell. And now the legendary magic that the Timewatcher had left behind was at the command of the Genii.

The portal that Moor faced was not a simple doorway that only opened onto the Retrospective; potentially, it could open onto any

Aelfirian House that existed. And that, Moor understood all too well, was the true depth of the Nightshade's power.

Soon, once Hagi Tabet had learned the location of Oldest Place and Lord Spiral was free, the Genii would announce their return to the Aelfir with legions of monsters behind them.

'Fabian?' Asajad urged restlessly. 'Why did you bring me here?'

'You will see,' Moor replied. 'Have patience.'

Moor found it fascinating that however often he gazed into the Retrospective he was never given the same view twice. He couldn't decide whether it was the doorway that moved location or if the landscape itself was ever-shifting. Perhaps it was both. But Lord Spiral would understand its design; he would be able to control the Retrospective's random movements, give it direction.

On this occasion, Moor was looking directly out of the mouth of a cave. The view beyond the cave was limited, but sufficient to confirm the pitiless and perpetual war being fought by untold numbers of wild demons. Moor could see them, revelling in violent lust out on the scorched landscape, too many to count. However, thus far the one particular demon that he sought had not yet answered the Genii's call. And Moor *had* called for it. He had sent his thaumaturgy out of the Nightshade to search the Retrospective, carrying a summons. The monster would come, given time.

'You know, it's curious,' Asajad said in a light voice. 'A thousand years have passed since the Labyrinth was created, and this is the first time that I've ever actually been here. It *is* an interesting place, in a repugnant sort of way.'

Moor looked back at Asajad. Her face was thoughtful.

'For example, that portal outside the Nightshade,' she said. 'It is the only one left to the humans anywhere in the Labyrinth?'

Moor was hesitant, wondering at the reason for this conversation. 'That is correct.'

'The Aelfir use that portal to send the humans food?'

'Yes, along with other supplies.'

'And then the humans collect those supplies as they arrive, for distribution among the townsfolk?' She chuckled into the back of her hand. 'It is similar to feeding time at a zoo, yes?'

Moor scowled at her. 'Lady Asajad, are you going to make a point, or are you merely trying to appease your boredom by irritating me?'

Asajad smirked. 'The portal outside the Nightshade connects to a House of the Aelfir, Fabian. Does it not seem reasonable that the magickers of the Relic Guild might have used it to escape the Labyrinth?'

'No,' Moor said, and he faced the Retrospective again. 'Nothing living can use that portal. And it only imports, Asajad. Nothing can pass out of it.'

'A one way portal? I've never heard of such a thing.' Asajad's tone was as suspicious as it was amused. 'Never mind,' she added brightly. 'Perhaps we should just destroy it, Fabian. Let the humans die. After all, we need relatively few of them alive to provide us with blood.'

Moor shook his head. 'And what of Hagi? She needs more than blood to sustain her life.'

'Ah, yes – there is that, of course.'

'We will not decide the fate of the humans – that will be for Lord Spiral to do.'

Asajad sighed. 'Then maybe I will entertain myself by seeing more of this town. I don't suppose it will be very interesting, but it has to be less boring than—'

She broke off with a noise of irritation. Two scrawny, leathery demons appeared out in the Retrospective. In a flurry of silent violence, they fought in the entrance to the cave, slashing and stabbing at each other with sharp, thorn-like hands; biting with gaping mouths filled with rows of hooked teeth.

'Honestly, Fabian,' Asajad said testily. 'Do these *things* never stop fighting?'

'You should take the time to understand what you are seeing, Asajad,' Moor replied. 'What I have learned from my observations is that each time one of these demons is slain, another rises in its place – sometimes two.'

One of the scrawny demons swiped a wicked gouge across the other's chest. The other paid no mind to its torn flesh, broken ribs and flowing blood, and focused on fixing its mouth to the side of the first demon's face. Hooked teeth tore away cheek meat.

'Fascinating,' Asajad said drolly.

The scrawny demons continued their eerily silent battle.

Moor continued, 'The Retrospective, I believe, uses all organic matter as raw material for creation. Perpetually rebuilding its denizens – maybe expanding its landmass. Can't you see? Our army will be self-replenishing.'

'Fabian, the Retrospective may provide everything that we need to conquer the Aelfir, but with just you, me, Viktor and Hagi – we are not strong enough to tame it. Until Lord Spiral has returned, the Retrospective is useless to us. I am bored and will leave unless you explain to me why we are wasting time watching this nonsense.'

A shadow fell across the fighting demons as a huge figure loomed behind them.

'Ah ...' A small smile curled Moor's lips. 'I think your interest is about to be engaged.'

Wholly focused on victory over each other, the scrawny demons did not seem to notice the newcomer. As they tore and ripped and bit, the new demon, larger and stronger than those before it, lofted its mighty woodcutter's axe. With surprising speed and agility, it chopped the scrawny demons into bloody chunks that hissed and steamed and melted into the ground. In a fleeting moment, they were reduced to nothing more than joints of raw material, which the Retrospective absorbed greedily to later create new abominations.

With its axe in hand, the huge and powerful demon stepped over the rapidly diminishing remains, and stooped to enter the cave.

Asajad stepped up alongside Moor. In his peripheral vision, he could see her intrigued expression.

With heavy footsteps, the demon approached the portal on the wall of the cave, its face hidden within the folds of its pointed leather hood. Stringy pieces of flesh still dangled from the wicked head of the woodcutter's axe which the demon laid down only a few paces from the Nightshade portal. The monster then knelt and bowed its head to the Genii.

'Oh my!' Asajad said after a sharp intake of breath. 'What is this, Fabian?'

'Hmm,' said Moor. 'Perhaps we should call it the Woodsman.'

'It … it is obedient?'

'*Now* do you see?'

Asajad took a few steps closer to the wall of shimmering air. She was obviously impressed with the demon's size and physique, or perhaps she found beauty in the grotesque gashes on its limbs, stitched together with twine.

She looked back at Moor. 'This *creature* remembers its loyalty to the Genii?'

'Perhaps also the Aelf it used to be,' Moor said. 'I have observed this specimen on a few occasions. It is surprisingly intelligent – for one of its kind.'

'I see.' Asajad studied the muscular hulk of the wild demon on its knees. 'The Woodsman,' she said, amusement in her voice. 'Congratulations, Fabian. You seem to have found our first ally in the Retrospective. But, remind me, how many other wild demons do you need to tame now?'

'I do not compare my power to that of Lord Spiral's, Lady Asajad, not even remotely,' Moor said warningly. 'But I think our master will be interested to know that some demons are more intelligent than others, don't you?'

Asajad sighed and looked back over her shoulder. 'This *thing* might have a modicum of intelligence, Fabian, but is it *enough*? Can it be controlled? Can it *learn*?'

'Let us find out.'

Moor flexed his thaumaturgy and sent it snaking out of the room in the Nightshade, into the cave within the Retrospective, where it latched onto the demon's bestial consciousness. He gave it a command, a simple order which it followed immediately, as if it had been waiting its entire life for this instruction.

Rising to its full, impressive height, the demon picked up its huge axe and strode towards the Genii with confident steps. Exhilarated, Mo Asajad quickly skipped back to stand behind Moor.

'What are you doing, Fabian?' she said excitedly, breathlessly, over his shoulder.

Moor stood resolute as the demon crossed the divide without hesitation. The wall of shimmering air parted with a quick tumult of rage and violence, along with the heavy stench of age and rot. The rip in the veil then sealed, and the demon stood in the Nightshade, towering over the Genii, wild and menacing.

'Bow!' Moor ordered.

The demon did so immediately, bending at the waist. It remained locked in that position, and Moor clasped his hands together, chuckling with pleasure.

'The Woodsman indeed,' Asajad said. She waved a hand before her face, trying to dispel the stench of the demon. 'What shall we do with it, Fabian?'

'Test the extent of its obedience, of course,' Moor replied, his smile growing. 'You said that you wanted to see more of this town, Lady Asajad. Perhaps you would like to show the denizens exactly who is governing them now.'

In the silence of the jailhouse, Samuel's slow, sleeping breaths filled the air. But Van Bam was awake.

Clara could sense the illusionist's proximity. She could feel him leaning against the other side of the wall that separated their cells. She could taste his concern in the air, mingled with the reek of stale sewage.

Van Bam wants to know if you're all right, Clara, Gideon said.

The wolf replied to such a frail and mawkish question with mental derision.

I thought as much, Gideon said happily. *I'll tell him you're not in the mood to talk, shall I?*

And while you're at it, ask him if he knows why you're in my head, Clara demanded.

I already have, and he agrees with me – it's something the avatar did to us.

Then why can't I hear Van Bam's voice too?

It's a mystery, to be sure, Clara. I'm certain the avatar had its reasons – though I really can't imagine what they might be. This little threesome isn't exactly fun for yours truly, either.

Clara snorted and began pacing the cell.

The edge of Sunflower's strange purple sun could be seen through the window, but its light barely lifted the shadows as it crawled weakly into the jailhouse. The sky outside was full of stars glinting above an alien landscape, but the narrow view did not impress the wolf. She felt constrained, restricted within these confines. With the bunks at either end of the cell, Clara could only take a few steps before having to turn around and pace the other way. Her frustration was building with every step. It hadn't been that long since Supervisor Marca had left with his dumb lackey, but to her it felt like a lifetime.

Clara, what are you doing? Gideon said.

Why do you care? she snapped back.

I don't. But I am curious. He was quiet for a moment. *Tell me, what purpose do you think the wolf serves in this situation?*

Clara was offended. *You think I'm useless, is that it?*

Oh no, far from it! You bravely fought the demons of the Retrospective, undoubtedly saving the lives of your colleagues in the process, and your control over the inner beast is admirable. You have done gloriously, Clara. But I am wondering if the wolf is steering your thoughts to ... to less important issues.

Less important? Clara could feel that Gideon's praise was only a brittle veneer beneath which malice reigned. *What are you—*

Just shut up and listen for a moment, Gideon interrupted. *You are eager to rage against your confinement, yet you find no wonder in the people who are keeping you confined. You long to escape this cell, but you don't think to appreciate exactly where this cell is.*

The Genii control the Labyrinth, Clara growled. *Stopping them, protecting the denizens – that's the only thing that matters.*

Of course it is, but I do wish your brains would match your brawn, child. Gideon sighed. *You are the first living thing to leave the Labyrinth in four decades. For a generation or more, no denizen has laid eyes on the Aelfir or visited an Aelfirian House. Yet here you are.*

So?

Really, this doesn't impress you at all?

It very much didn't, and Clara let Gideon know in no uncertain terms.

You know, he said slyly, *you could follow Samuel's example. You could lie down upon a comfy mattress, catch up on sleep. It might help you gain a little perspective. Of course, the wolf is much too big for these bunks, and you'd have to take human form first—*

Human, Clara retorted. *As if I'd ever allow myself to be that weak again.*

Gideon's laughter was harsh, and it rattled inside the wolf's head.

You really are a delight, Clara. As dumb as wood, but a delight all the same. You are a creature of two halves, and you should be celebrating both. Come, why not slip on your human skin?

Now it was Clara's turn to laugh back at the ghost, and it was full of scorn. *And why would I follow the advice of a psychopath?*

Psychopath? There was an edge of surprise in Gideon's tone. It felt genuine. *Have I offended you?*

No, but I'm sure you will. I know you, Gideon. I know your sort.

You know my sort?

Yes. And you can't intimidate me.

A brief silence.

I'm disappointed, Clara. The way the voice scratched the inside of her skull told Clara that he was telling the truth. *Have your colleagues taught you nothing about what it means to be an agent of the Relic Guild?*

They've taught me enough to know that they're better people than you could ever have been in life, Clara retorted.

Gideon clucked his tongue. *Don't you realise how childish this romanticised view of your fellow agents is? You have placed Van Bam, Samuel, and, most especially, Marney, up upon a glorified pedestal. And it is with this same romanticised view that you would now damn me as a villain.*

Understand me, Clara – long before you were born, when I was Resident, I taught those three idiots how to protect the denizens of Labrys Town. And I taught them well. You do not know the kind of things they have had to do in service of the Relic Guild.

Clara batted aside the ghost's provocation. *What about you?* She was full of heat now. *What kind of things did you do, Gideon?*

Oh my ... Gideon's tone became dark, his voice whispery. *You don't really want to know the answer to that, do you, Clara?*

The wolf stopped pacing. Her mind was filled with sudden images of razor sharp blades slicing tender, pink skin. Blood welled, seeped, poured, and words Clara did not understand imbued love with hatred and turned fearful whimpering to screaming agony.

You ... You were a blood-magicker, she said, disgusted.

I was much more than that! Gideon's voice was full of spite. *I was born touched by ancient magic, far more powerful than that of any other Relic Guild agent.*

You were a savage.

A laugh, hard and sharp. *I was descended from mighty ancestors, Clara, Houseless outcasts called the Nephilim.*

Never heard of them, Clara retorted.

Then let me tell you, child – the Nephilim were to be feared. They were giants, adepts of blood-magic. The Timewatcher turned her back on them.

Clara growled. *You can't intimidate me!*

Gideon's voice closed around the wolf's mind like a wicked claw. *Then perhaps I should tell you about your* heroes, *Clara. Did you know that Van Bam once drove a black marketeer insane by showing him illusions of his worst nightmares? Or maybe you'd like to hear how Samuel once tortured information from a treasure hunter by popping her eye out with a knife. But wait! I should tell you of the time that your beloved Marney used her empathic magic to convince a man it was a good idea to put the barrel of a pistol into his mouth and pull the trigger.*

The claw of Gideon's voice squeezed Clara's mind. Sharp talons stabbed into her memories, digging into her every thought and dream. It made her feel weak, and the wolf began to panic.

You and Marney aren't very different, Gideon hissed poisonously. *Whores, both of you, who liked to spread their legs for any man that came along. But where you liked to charge for your services, Clara, Marney gave it away for free!* He chuckled like hot wind rustling dead leaves. *Or is it better to not speak ill of the dead?*

Shut up! Clara spat.

But Gideon did no such thing. The wolf shuddered and whined as the ghost's grip on her mind tightened, draining her of courage and strength.

The Genii would have toyed with Marney before they killed her, you know. They would have made her screech like an animal. They would have taken the secrets of the Nightshade from her like they were ripping out her soul. And before she died, Marney would have known the true meaning of agony.

Stop it! The hate and lunacy of the blood-magicker who filled Clara's mind was too much to bear, and the wolf could only cower before it. *Please, I'm begging you – just stop!*

Don't ever presume to know my sort, *child!* Gideon bellowed. *And never forget that while I'm up here in your head, I can twist your every thought until they turn you mad!*

And Gideon released his grip.

Clara yelped. She turned in circles, her posture defensive, coiled, ready to strike, but there was no enemy in the cell with her. The silence in her head was sudden and complete, and she wondered if the ghost of the former Resident had blinked out of existence.

'Clara.'

Van Bam's voice coming from the neighbouring cell made her flinch. But it sounded familiar and reassuring.

'Gideon is a difficult presence to deal with at the best of times,' Van Bam said. 'Trust me. I know this.' He sighed. 'But you must remember to show him respect. Always. His advice should be listened to.'

Clara moved nearer to the bars of the cell, filled with the sudden urge to be closer to the illusionist, to hear more of his comforting words, to find protection from the madman in her head. But Van Bam said no more. Silence except Samuel's snoring. The atmosphere was uncannily still, and for the first time since changing into the wolf, Clara's confidence was blemished by doubt.

The incongruous presence of a dead Resident slowly returned inside her head. It was heavy with judgement.

I'm sorry, Clara thought to him quickly. *Marney – I never realised, I … I never stopped to think—*

Stop snivelling, Gideon retorted. *I don't need your apology, and Marney's death isn't relevant. But seeing as you're in the mood to rekindle our friendship, Clara, would you care to take some advice?*

Clara didn't reply with words. Instead she gave acquiescence with thoughts, respect with feelings. She did not want to give Gideon any reason to unleash the full force of his spite on her mind again.

Listen to me very carefully, child, Gideon said. *For the first time in your life you have control over the wolf. Yet here you are, doing your level best to not understand it. You revel in your power, consider yourself untouchable, slave to no one and master of all. You have become a bully, Clara.*

I ... What?

You're no better than that idiot Marca.

Wait—

No! You will listen to me. I've no time or patience to deal with the ignorance of the wolf. Marney has left a message in your mind, and it will be far simpler to discover what it is if I do not have to wade through all this pride and anger swirling around your mind.

She understood what Gideon was driving towards; she knew what lay at the end of his point. But she couldn't agree to it, despite her newfound fear of the ghost.

I don't have to change back, she said timidly, pleadingly. *I'll control myself.*

You're frightened of the change, Gideon said. *And I don't blame you. But this is for your own good, Clara.*

No. No, I'm not frightened, Clara lied. *I'm just better this way.*

Gideon snorted. *And you had the cheek to call me a psychopath.* There was a bored edge to his voice now. *I don't mean to disappoint you, Clara, but you are not the first changeling I've known, and certainly not the most impressive. You cannot deny the wolf any more than you can deny the human. If you continue to fight the process, your magic will ultimately make the decision for you, anyway. Only then, the metamorphosis into the girl will be agony beyond belief.*

A vision bloomed in Clara's mind. She saw a small girl, awkward in body, gawky of face, with short mousy hair streaked with red dye. She was frightened of herself, frightened of her world. She was bound by chains, staring back at the wolf with sad eyes.

I can't, she told Gideon desperately.

Then by all means continue fighting what you are, Gideon replied haughtily. *But if you carry on down this road, Clara, your magic will eventually drive you insane.* He broke off to chuckle. *It comes to this*

– to understand yourself is to accept that the human and the wolf are in symbiosis. Two creatures in one body. That is what it means to be a true changeling. Anything less serves no purpose to the Relic Guild.

To fully control your magic, Clara, you must learn to initiate the metamorphosis of your own volition. Chilly amusement had crept into Gideon's voice. *Now, I need to talk to the human about Marney's message. Lie down, please.*

It wasn't a request; and Gideon's order – the tone, the shape, the feel, the weight of it inside the wolf's head – could not be denied.

Although the cell's stone floor was cold against Clara's underside, she began to pant, her tongue lolling and hot breath steaming in the air. She could feel the frightened girl with sad eyes reaching out to the wolf.

I'm scared, she admitted, unashamed. *Stay with me.*

Gideon laughed. *Oh, don't worry. I wouldn't miss this for the world.*

CHAPTER SIX

TOWER OF THE NECROMANCER

If Hamir could claim to have been blindsided by discovering that in the bowels of the Nightshade there was a secret room called the Last and Lowest Chamber – a room that the Genii could not follow him into – and that the Last and Lowest Chamber hid not only the roots of the Timewatcher's mighty First and Greatest Spell, but also a portal leading out of the Labyrinth, then the necromancer supposed that some people would describe the location to which the portal delivered him as a masterstroke in the art of surprise.

All things considered, Hamir had to concede he was moved in the vaguest of ways by this last discovery. Although, he reasoned, had he only applied a little more logic to the situation, the oddly smooth and metallic-looking cave to which the portal had taken him would have merely served to confirm his suspicions.

The necromancer chided himself with a wry sort of smile.

The portal had gone. The thick, churning whiteness of the Nothing of Far and Deep was now covered by a wooden door on the back wall of the cave. A simple looking door that could have belonged to any house in Labrys Town. However, this door had locked tight after his arrival, and Hamir suspected that it would not unlock even if he applied his magic to the task. Not that he would make any attempt; returning to the Nightshade would only deliver him back into the mercy of the Genii.

Hamir walked away from the door, and out of the cave.

He didn't need to look back to know he had exited onto the lower quarter of a mountain just as unnaturally smooth and metallic-looking as the cave's interior. Before Hamir, a wide and grey path sloped down to a bridge that spanned a yawning chasm enclosed by the semi-circle of a great cliff face. In the near distance, at the end of the bridge, a tower rose from a gigantic disc of metal-rock, a mighty tower with a sleek black body, capped with a dome of grey metal.

The Tower of the Skywatcher.

Lady Amilee, Hamir thought in wonder. One of the most revered creatures of higher magic to ever serve the Timewatcher. Amilee the Skywatcher had, many years ago, been the patron of the Labyrinth's denizens, the liaison between the Relic Guild and the Thaumaturgists. And who else could be behind life's recent mysteries?

Hamir frowned. Before the Timewatcher had turned her back on the Labyrinth, Amilee's House, the Tower of the Skywatcher, had been famed for its beauty. The scene that now met the eyes of the necromancer was dreary at best.

Where roaring falls of emerald had cascaded from the high cliff to crash down into the yawning chasm and moisten the air with a fine, rejuvenating mist, pure and cleansing, no water fell now. The air was dry and gritty and still. Once, the stars and moons of an alien sky could be marvelled at through wispy clouds of many scintillating colours; now starlight and moonlight struggled to shine through dirty fog that drifted like smoke from forge chimneys. The metal dome capping the proud tower had been as bright as a mirror, sparkling with reflected light from the sky. The highly polished silver had become tarnished and dull grey.

The House of the Skywatcher was dead.

'Tragic,' Hamir murmured.

His footsteps ticked in the silence as he made his way down the path and onto the bridge. As he walked he kicked up dust. He wondered briefly about the fate of the Relic Guild. Had he warned them in time that the Genii had conquered the Nightshade? Were they trapped and hiding in Labrys Town, or had the avatar helped them to find a way out, as it had helped him? Were they dead? Did they think that *he* was dead?

Given the situation, the Relic Guild's survival seemed like it would be a good thing. On a personal level, Hamir had always found Van Bam a decent sort of fellow, if a little too internalised for his tastes. Samuel was just a miserable bore whose intellect couldn't stretch beyond the present moment. But Clara ... Clara was another matter.

There was something different about the young changeling, special perhaps. Hamir hoped she had survived, because he had rather enjoyed her company.

Why should that be? he wondered.

As Hamir made his way across the bridge, he pulled a phial from the inside pocket of his suit jacket. He held it up and shook the red contents. The phial was filled with blood – or more specifically, *Clara's* blood.

If one knew how to use it, the blood of a changeling was a powerful catalyst that could fuel the simplest of spells with the power of the highest of magics, if only for a short while. This was the second of two phials that the avatar had ordered Hamir to draw from Clara's veins. The first had helped the necromancer activate the portal in the Last and Lowest Chamber of the Nightshade, thus enabling his escape from the Labyrinth. The purpose of this second phial had yet to reveal itself.

Hamir reasoned he would recognise an occasion for its use when it arose, and slipped the phial back into his pocket.

Cresting the rise in the bridge, the necromancer headed towards the mammoth disc from which the Tower of the Skywatcher rose. He saw a figure standing sentinel at the end of the bridge. Hamir recognised the figure with a chilly pang and stopped in his tracks.

Tall and broad, still as a statue, comprised of thaumaturgic metal with exposed internal mechanisms like a giant clockwork toy, it was an automaton sentry which guarded the bridge.

Designed by the greatest metallurgists, the automatons had been the servants of the Thaumaturgists. If ordered to, this construct could wreak terrible violence upon foes, most especially upon unwanted guests. Hamir could not be confident that Lady Amilee would welcome him to her House. His magic would have little effect against automatons, and if this one decided to attack, the necromancer would be defenceless.

'Interesting,' he said sourly.

With little choice, Hamir advanced at a cautious pace. As he crept closer to the automaton, he was relieved to discover that it still did not react to his presence. He reached the end of the bridge, and the construct remained unmoving when he stood within touching distance of it.

Standing eight feet tall, the automaton's silver frame towered over the necromancer. The cogs and pistons of its exposed internal mechanisms did not turn or pump. A thick layer of dust coated the smooth, featureless metal plates covering its chest and face. Hamir reached up and placed a hand on its face plate. The metal was cold and inert, devoid of the warmth of magic. The thaumaturgy that animated this sentry was either dormant or dead. Either way, it was inactive.

'No more useful than a scarecrow,' Hamir muttered, and he walked around the automaton, continuing on his way across the giant disc of metal-stone.

The base of the Tower of the Skywatcher was easily large enough to match the Nightshade. Huge double doors were set into it, and they loomed before Hamir. Although they were at least fifteen feet tall, and as thick as a man's arm was long from wrist to elbow, the doors were surprisingly light and made not one creak or groan as Hamir pulled them open.

He paused before entering, gazing around at the dreary landscape, wondering if the Skywatcher was as dead as her House.

Inside the tower, the weak light crawling in from the entrance did little to banish the shadows in a cavernous reception hall. This was of no concern to Hamir, for his eyes needed no light to see.

Deadened glow lamps were fixed to the walls above a series of alcoves in which a host of inanimate automatons stood. There were at least fifty alcoves surrounding the hall, and Hamir remembered that the dusty and dysfunctional automatons inhabiting them were Amilee's private army; there had been a time when the Skywatcher had much to protect.

Lady Amilee. Her duty had once been to watch every pathway that led from the Houses of the Aelfir to the Great Labyrinth, to guard the denizens of Labrys Town. Hamir supposed that if one considered the aftermath of the Genii War, one could say that Amilee failed in her duty to protect the Labyrinth.

At the centre of the reception hall's hard, grey floor, two glass elevator shafts rose to disappear through the ceiling high above. The door to one was open, the elevator waiting inside.

Hamir made to step towards it, wondering dubiously if this tower still retained enough energy to activate the elevator. But as he approached the open door, he suddenly realised that he was not alone in this place.

His skin tingled. A presence hung in the air, palpable enough to feel – or perhaps *taste* was the better word – and Hamir gave a small smile. The necromancer had been keeping the company of ghosts long enough to recognise when one was close by.

'Let me take a guess,' he said, voice echoing around the hall. 'Alexander, is that you?'

Like a newly opened ancient crypt sucking a great breath of fresh air, a long, rattling sigh rushed at Hamir from all directions.

'What do you want?' the disembodied voice said.

It *was* Alexander, Lady Amilee's aide, an Aelf who had served the Skywatcher devotedly in life, and now, it seemed, in death.

'You're not welcome here, necromancer,' the ghost said.

'I really don't care what you think, to be honest,' Hamir replied with a raised eyebrow. 'Show yourself, please.'

'No. Go away.'

A twinge of boredom inflected Hamir's mood – or was it impatience? Difficult to tell these days. In all his long years of servitude to Lady Amilee, Alexander had always been an intolerant wretch, an Aelf in a perpetual bad mood without the grace of a single welcoming bone in his body.

'I see death hasn't mellowed you, Alexander,' Hamir said, and he shrugged. 'Show yourself, don't show yourself – by all means follow your wont. But, please, just answer me one question. Is Lady Amilee here?'

'Yes,' the disembodied reply was sibilant.

'Then be so good as to announce my arrival to her, would you?'

In reply, the ghost's laugh rattled around Hamir, full of sadness, full of bitterness.

Hamir cleared his throat. 'You know, I find myself in a situation that calls for at least a modicum of brevity, Alexander. Unless she is dead, I really must insist on an audience with her Ladyship.'

'Then you're going to have a long wait.' There was a cruel sneer to the disembodied voice. 'Go home, Hamir.'

'That wouldn't be a wise move – for me or the denizens of Labrys Town. The Genii have returned.'

A long moment of silence passed before the ghost replied. 'Lady Amilee no longer speaks to anyone.'

'Excuse me?' Hamir pursed his lips. 'Alexander, did you not hear what I told you? The Genii—'

'I heard what you said right enough. What you're asking for isn't possible.'

'Oh? Please explain.'

'No. Go and see for yourself.'

And with that, the ghost of the Skywatcher's aide fell silent, and Hamir felt the presence dissolve to nothing.

'Annoying,' he said, as he marched into the elevator.

With a low hum of thaumaturgy, the elevator rose to the highest part of the tower; its doors opened onto Lady Amilee's domed observatory.

Hamir was once again greeted by the air of dreary abandonment. It was cold in the observatory. Not the dead of winter kind of cold that caused water to freeze and breath to cloud; but a hopeless cold that Hamir felt, a soul-eating chill that he had come to know as the approach of death.

Where once the observatory's circular wall had held the dull sheen of thaumaturgy, there was now only grey, lifeless metal. The clear glass floor had once contained swirling, thaumaturgic mists, but now dirt and grime lay thickly upon it and nothing could be seen through the glass. Where the domed ceiling had glittered with the stars of a hundred thousand Houses, only the weak light of a single distant sun struggled to shine in starless space.

But sitting at the centre of the observatory were two isolation chambers. They sat side by side, stone bodies shaped like sarcophagi, their glass lids coated by a layer of dust just as thick as that on the floor.

Hamir stepped up to the first and wiped away the dust to peer inside. The chamber's interior was cushioned, stitched in the shape of a person, but no one lay inside. At the head, where a person's crown and temples would sit, three clear crystals had been placed. Inactive power stones, perhaps.

Moving to the second isolation chamber, Hamir was by no means surprised when he wiped away the dust and discovered it was occupied by a Thaumaturgist.

Lady Amilee could almost have been dead. Her eyes were closed, and the black diamond tattoo on her forehead stood out starkly against the pale skin of her otherwise flawless face, neither young nor old. Around her smoothly shaven head, three crystals shone with the light of thaumaturgy. Not one twitch disturbed Amilee's features. However, Hamir could see her chest rising and falling with the shallowest of breaths.

Sleep chambers, Hamir realised. These units were used for the art of oneiromancy, for the exploration of the dream realms. Lady Amilee's body might have been inside her tower, but her mind was very much elsewhere.

Hamir looked up at the single sun glinting weakly in the distant sky of the observatory's domed ceiling.

'Are you satisfied now?' said Alexander.

Hamir sensed the return of the ghost's presence a moment before it spoke. The necromancer felt his patience dissolving.

'Alexander,' he said, 'The Genii now control the Labyrinth. Does that mean nothing to you?'

'What do I care for *humans*?'

'I'm sure I don't know, and have little inclination to find out.' Hamir looked down at Amilee's peaceful face in the sleep chamber, and then gazed around the observatory. The ghost was close by, he could feel it. 'I'm warning you, Alexander. Either show yourself and explain to me what happened to this place, or leave me alone with my thoughts.'

The disembodied voice laughed bitterly again. 'You might be in love with death, *necromancer*, but I'm well beyond your reach now.'

Hamir sighed. 'I have been accused of being *in love* with death before, Alexander. It is a misconception, let me assure you. But if you're suggesting that a ghost cannot feel pain then, by all means, test my patience some more.'

Alexander's rattling laugh was cut short as Hamir's hand flashed out and grabbed something cold from the air.

The ghost materialised, the tie of its spectral suit gripped in the necromancer's fist. Details came like pencil etchings at first, drawing

Alexander in varying depths of grey, until he stood as visible as a spirit could be.

His sunken cheeks, small mouth and nose, eyes larger than any human's, gave his face the odd triangular shape that was a trait of the Aelfir. His iron-coloured hair was wispy with age, and also sprouted from the tops of his pointed ears. His mouth open, he looked in fear at the hand that gripped his tie.

Hamir's teeth gritted as his magic rose within him, darkening his green eyes with inky swirls. He pulled Alexander closer to him.

'I will ask you one last time, Alexander. What happened here?'

Alexander's small lips trembled. 'She tried to warn them, but they wouldn't listen.'

'Who?'

'Who do you think?' Tears of silver welled in Alexander's eyes and his gaze shifted to the sleep chambers. 'They abandoned her, Hamir. They imprisoned our Lady in her own tower ...'

With a piercing wail of despair that echoed around the observatory, the ghost swirled away into mist that Hamir couldn't hold onto. The mist dissipated, leaving Hamir clutching nothing but thin air. He decided not to force Alexander back. The ghost could go and sulk in whichever corner of this once great tower he chose to haunt.

With a sigh, Hamir dropped his hand to his side. The glass lid to the empty sleep chamber slid open with a hiss and a blast of dust. The three crystals inside began glowing with violet light, almost beckoning to the necromancer.

With a final glance up at the distant sun winking in the domed ceiling, Hamir turned a sour expression to the sleeping face of Lady Amilee. He half expected to see a smile appear on the Skywatcher's face.

'All right, my lady,' he whispered. 'Let's do this your way.'

Hamir climbed into the empty sleep chamber, lay down and closed his eyes. The lid slid shut above him, and the light of the crystals around his head dragged his mind into the realm of dream.

CHAPTER SEVEN

THE DECAY OF LABRYS TOWN

It rarely rained during the day in the Labyrinth. But it was raining on the day Captain Jeter was executed.

At the very centre of Labrys Town, in a plaza known as Watcher's Gallery, a crowd had congregated before the large square building that served as the police headquarters. The order for the gathering had gone out an hour before, a summons from the new Resident – Hagi Tabet.

Sergeant Ennis led crowd control – not that there was anything to control. He and his small group of officers stood within the crowd beneath a grey sky, surrounded by eerie stillness only broken by raindrops tapping upon hoods and umbrellas. Ennis ignored the cold drops that dribbled down the collar of his uniform, and scanned the crowd.

It was a select band of denizens who had been summoned by the Resident: members of the merchant guild and entertainment council, brewery officials and energy officers, delegates from the warehouse and labour unions, bankers ... a gathering of Labrys Town's elite. It was a miserable atmosphere, in which a sombre order had naturally formed.

Like most of the people there, Ennis had thought that the reason for the meeting was to address a problem that had arisen that very morning. The deliveries of the cargo essential to the denizens of Labrys Town were late. Thus far, not one platform of supplies had emerged from the portal outside the Nightshade. But now everyone seemed to understand that the topic of late deliveries was not the first concern on today's agenda.

On the lawn outside the police headquarters, four armed patrolmen guarded the emaciated form of Captain Jeter.

With raindrops bouncing and splashing off the black glass of their receptor helmets, with power stones primed on their rifles, each officer took aim at their prisoner. The congregation fidgeted and whispered worriedly as Jeter shattered the silence with series of quick shrieks, caught between harsh coughs and barks.

Naked, Jeter wore a metal brace around his neck that was connected to a short thick chain, which was secured by a heavy spike driven into the dirt. His body, limbs and face were clammy grey and lined with black veins like cracks in his rotting skin. What remained of his hair had been plastered to his head by the rain. Jeter strained against his chain, gnashing long teeth at the crowd, his jaundiced eyes bulging. He screamed his hunger and hate, and entered a frenzied fit of barking coughs.

As one, the denizens drew back from Jeter. Ennis unconsciously rested a hand on the pistol holstered to his hip. But Jeter's restraint held fast, and the crowd was kept safe from the magical virus that had beset the former police captain.

The main doors of the police building opened, and a tall, thin woman stepped out into the plaza. She wore a priest's cassock as black as her long straight hair. Even from a distance, Ennis could see her face was as pale and smooth as porcelain. He didn't recognise her.

Another figure, also dressed in a priest's cassock, walked alongside the woman, sheltering her with an umbrella. Ennis couldn't tell much about the figure due to the wide-brimmed hat covering the head and face, but this person was clearly deformed, and kept pace with the woman with lumbering steps. Following them was Moira, the new captain of the Labrys Town Police Force, who had attained the position only that morning. Moira's eyes were fixed on the ground, not daring to look at the crowd.

The woman with the porcelain face had no trouble, however. She stopped and gazed over the congregation almost happily; and when she spoke, her voice was soft – yet loud enough to be heard by all.

'You may call me Lady Asajad,' she said. 'I am … *chief aide* to your Resident Hagi Tabet. My friends, I'm sure you'll agree, today is a sad day.'

She didn't seem sad. In fact, to Ennis, Lady Asajad's tone was more concurrent with the best of days.

'But it is also a day for anger,' she continued, pointing to Jeter's ravaged form. 'This man was weak. He was infected by the vile temptations of the Relic Guild. He failed to uphold the law of the Nightshade. He failed in his duty to protect all of you.' Her finger swept the crowd.

'And look what has become of him, my friends. Look *very* hard.'

Although Jeter had ceased his shrieks and barks, he still pulled against the chain, this time trying to claw and gnash his way to the patrolmen surrounding him. Infection had reduced Jeter to an animal. The congregation observed him with deathly silence.

Each person present had heard how quickly the virus spread, how it threatened every denizen. But for most, they had never seen the virus in action before. This wasn't the first time for Ennis, however, and a grim thought told him it wouldn't be the last.

'There must be change,' Lady Asajad said. 'And change is not always an easy thing. Your Resident understands this, but she is brave enough to do what is necessary. For you.'

Ennis stared at the Resident's aide. There was something wrong with her forehead. Scarring, perhaps?

Asajad motioned to everyone present with splayed hands, as if ready to embrace them all. 'The Relic Guild may remain a danger to each and every one of you people, but the same mistakes will not be made twice!' She was obviously enjoying herself. 'Hagi Tabet demands strength and courage, and both can be found in your new police captain.'

Beside the Resident's aide, Captain Moira straightened her back as if standing to attention before the crowd; but her eyes drifted upwards to the grey sky, and she faced the rain with a sad expression, looking as though she would rather be anywhere else.

'My friends,' Asajad said with a fresh smile. 'Your Resident knows what is best for your town.'

Something began bothering Ennis, more than the incongruous nature of the day. It was a little detail out of place, tapping at the back of his mind. His eyes scoured the scene before him until it clicked, and Ennis realised there was a discrepancy in Lady Asajad's speech. The phrasing she was using – *your* Resident, *you* people, *your* town. This woman did not consider herself a denizen.

'The change begins today,' she was continuing. 'Weakness and fail-ure will be met with *intolerance*!'

Ennis braced himself – as did the rest of the crowd – suspecting that this was the moment Lady Asajad would give the order for the patrol-men to pull their triggers, to put Jeter out of his misery. But the order didn't come. Instead, the Resident's aide gestured with her hand. The hairs on the back of Ennis's neck stood on end as a rent appeared in the air behind Jeter. It began as a vertical line of shadow that widened to the size and shape of a doorway which was filled with a shiny blackness, rippling like water.

Gasps and murmurs of consternation stirred the crowd as a figure emerged.

Seven feet tall at least, wearing a pointed hood and a leather kilt studded with rusty spikes, the thing that stepped out onto the lawn was clearly nonhuman. Its exposed skin was deathly pale, covered in stitched gashes. In its hands it held an axe big enough to match its size.

The patrolmen forgot their duty and backed away from their captive. Jeter, too, while gripped by the madness of infection, seemed to recognise a greater might. He hunkered down on the grass, cowering and whimpering, as the creature loomed over him.

Denizens began covering their noses as a strange and powerful smell came from the creature, a reek of decay, of age, of hopelessness, which was immediately familiar to Ennis. He had smelled it before on the few occasions he had led search and destroy parties to rid the town of wild demons that had strayed from the Retrospective.

'Allow me to introduce you to the Woodsman,' Lady Asajad told the crowd. She looked vastly pleased with the monster standing over the former captain. 'The Relic Guild would tempt you to have faith in the worship of demons,' she continued. 'But let us be very clear about what it means to be at a demon's mercy.'

The Woodsman raised its axe. The first stroke cut vertically through Jeter's head and the metal brace around his neck. The second, the third, the fourth and the fifth – quick and fluid – dissected him into joints that could have been displayed in a butcher's window. Blood and offal steamed on the grass.

The demon stepped back, its body and axe spattered with gore. At a casual hand gesture from Lady Asajad, it turned and marched back into the liquid doorway, which collapsed and disappeared behind it.

Ennis heard the retching from within the crowd. People were looking at each other for explanations, whispering in horror.

'Some lessons have to be learned harshly,' Asajad said, 'Soon, on behalf of your Resident, I will meet with many of you to discuss how your laws and conduct must change.' Her smile was the coldest thing Ennis had ever witnessed. 'That is all, my friends. For today.'

Lady Asajad turned from the crowd and began heading back to the police building. As the person holding the umbrella turned with her, Ennis caught a glimpse of what was beneath the wide-brimmed hat: an eyeless, grotesque mask, deathly grey. Just like the faces of virus victims who survived to reach the end of infection – like those victims who turned to stone.

Captain Moira gave a nervous glance to the crowd before slowly making her way back inside.

Ennis shook himself and signalled to the other officers on crowd control duty. They began ushering the denizens out of the plaza. Slowly, as though moving through a dream, Labrys Town's elite began returning to their offices and bases. Ennis doubted they would accomplish much work today.

Ennis stared at the remains of Jeter on the lawn before the police headquarters.

'Sergeant Ennis,' a voice called.

Through the throng of people, a fresh-faced constable made her way over. Ennis recognised her, but didn't know her name.

'Captain Moira wants to see you, sir,' she said. She was clearly shocked and spoke a little breathlessly. 'After her meeting with the Resident's aide, sir.'

'What do you mean you can hear Gideon again?' Samuel demanded.

Van Bam sighed. The old bounty hunter had slept for less than an hour, and he had awoken in a sour mood.

'It occurred when the avatar came to our aid out in the Great Labyrinth,' Van Bam said. 'I do not understand by what magic the avatar could have brought him back to us, Samuel, but you should know that Clara can also hear Gideon's voice.'

Samuel's face dropped. '*What?*'

Van Bam held up a hand. 'Please, old friend. I have no explanations. Accept this as a good thing.'

'Oh really? You think a giant wolf with a lunatic in her head is a *good thing*?'

Van Bam cocked his head to one side as Gideon's laugh rattled in his mind. 'Samuel, how is it that you believe your arguments are a help at this time?'

Just as Samuel formed a choice retort on his lips, harsh panting came from the neighbouring cell, and he became instantly tense.

The wolf was having trouble breathing. Her panting was interspersed with small growls, as if she couldn't decide whether to whine or bark.

Gideon, Van Bam thought, *is Clara all right*?

The ghost of the ex-Resident didn't reply.

A dull crack filled the air. Van Bam shared a startled look with Samuel as the wolf howled, long and hard.

When the howl subsided, Clara began retching. More dull cracks were followed by pops and clicks, along with wet stretching, like limbs twisting in their sockets. Clara issued a series of whines so heartfelt that to Van Bam's ears they might as well have been coherent cries for help. The whines deepened, became more agitated, and then the sound of the wolf thrashing on the floor.

Samuel held onto the thick metal bars of the cell door with white-knuckled tightness.

'Clara is changing,' Van Bam said.

Samuel nodded. His face was downcast, his eyes closed.

In a position to do nothing but listen to the nerve-shredding noise of Clara's physiological reorganisation, Van Bam placed a hand on the wall separating their cells. He prayed for Clara to be brave, that the metamorphosis into human form would be swift for her, less violent and agonising than when she had changed into the wolf out in the alleyways of the Great Labyrinth.

Please, Gideon, the illusionist thought. *I beg of you – help Clara through this. Find no enjoyment in her suffering.*

Once more, the ghost remained silent.

The wolf howled again. Another protracted, bestial cry, this time rising in pitch until it became strangled, gargled, caught between human and animal, and finally the distinct scream of a young woman in the clutch of furious magic. The sickening noise of shifting joints, of shrinking flesh and creaking tendons, cracking bones and twisting limbs suddenly, thankfully, ended, and Clara's voice subsided into gentle and very human sobbing.

'Clara,' said Van Bam.

The sobbing increased.

'Please, Clara, speak to me.'

It was Gideon who replied. *I'm sorry, my idiot, but Miss Clara isn't receiving gentleman callers right now.*

His chuckling continued inside Van Bam's head until it was brought to a halt by a *clunk* that was quickly followed by the jailhouse door swinging open and the light prism glaring into life.

The simpleton Hillem was the first to enter the room, where he cowered with a sheepish expression. Angry voices followed him, and then Supervisor Marca appeared, wearing a face like thunder. Hot on his heels was an elderly Aelf with a stern expression, wrapped up against the cold in a thick cloak of fine blue material.

'I don't know how you heard about this, Tal,' Marca said angrily. 'I certainly never sent for you.'

'No, you didn't,' the elderly Aelf replied, his tone severe. 'You must remind me to ask you why that was, Supervisor.'

Before Marca could reply, Hillem began choking on his words and pointed at Clara's cell. His face bemused, Hillem's mouth worked silently for a moment before he said, 'What happened to it?'

Tal frowned and looked for himself. When he saw what it was the simpleton was pointing at, his large eyes narrowed dangerously and he became infuriated.

'What's the meaning of this, Marca?' he demanded hotly. 'I swear to the Timewatcher, if you've laid one finger on this girl—'

'I haven't touched her!' Marca said, outraged. He took a step closer to the cell, his expression as puzzled as Hillem's. 'She was a wolf the last time I saw her. Bloody big one too.'

'I think you'll find she is changeling,' Tal said with strained calm, and he rounded on Hillem. 'Give this girl some clothes.'

Hillem seemed confused. He looked about him for a moment, and then showed the elderly Aelf his empty hands. 'I ain't got any.'

'Then go and find some, you imbecile.'

When Hillem didn't move, merely turning his dumb, watery eyes to Marca for guidance, Tal lost all patience.

'Do as you're told!' he shouted, his face reddening. The anger in his voice sent Hillem scurrying from the room.

Tal rounded on Marca. 'You have a lot to learn about civility, Supervisor.'

Marca shrugged and looked into Van Bam's cell with a sneer.

Tal undid the gold clasp on his thick cloak and pushed it through the bars of Clara's cell. 'Here, child,' he said kindly. 'Cover yourself.'

Clara sniffed, and Van Bam heard her climb up onto a bunk. He shared a look with Samuel, whose pale blue eyes were glaring at Supervisor Marca.

Tal moved along and took stock of the two humans inhabiting the cell next to Clara's. The elderly Aelf's blue three-piece suit was as finely tailored as his cloak. He looked to be older than Van Bam and Samuel by at least a decade.

After a long moment of silent contemplation, Tal said, 'Marca, have you offered these people a change of clothes or a bath? Have you fed them?'

'No.' Marca's tone was defensive. 'They broke the Timewatcher's law.'

Still looking at Van Bam and Samuel, the elderly Aelf raised an eyebrow. 'So you thought you'd let them go hungry as punishment?'

'No point in feeding them. They'll probably get executed anyway.'

'Is that a fact? Have you bothered to ask them why they are here?'

'Wouldn't tell me. Makes no difference, anyway – they're *human*.'

'Meaning what, exactly? That they're animals?'

Tal's voice was calm, almost gentle, but it carried an unmistakable scalding undertone. Behind him, Marca's face flushed angrily.

'Look, *Councillor*,' Marca snapped. '*They* broke the Timewatcher's law. I'm not the one in the wrong here.'

'Aren't you?' Tal said. 'I rather think that as soon as these people set foot in Sunflower your first duty should have been to alert the Panopticon of Houses. Which I'm assuming you haven't done.'

'It's not my fault,' Marca said defensively. 'If they hadn't broken the law, this place wouldn't be at a standstill.'

Tal blinked several times, and then turned from the humans in the cell to face Marca. 'What exactly do you mean by *standstill*? Am I to understand the warehouse has stopped delivering cargo to the Labyrinth?'

'That's right.'

'On whose authority?'

'Mine.' Marca seemed proud of this. 'Don't see how we can carry on now.'

Tal drew an obviously calming breath. 'Supervisor, offering these people no food is bad enough, but what about the other million mouths that need feeding? Is it your wish to starve every denizen of Labrys Town to death?'

Marca remained silent.

'We must not live a day without sending the Labyrinth all that its denizens require,' the elderly Aelf continued. 'That is also the Timewatcher's law, Supervisor. Please, be so kind as to observe it.'

'But—'

'I want that warehouse back up and running within the hour. Is that clear?'

'You can't just—'

'Go and do your job!' the elderly Aelf bellowed. 'Before I employ someone else to do it.'

Marca tried and failed to hold Tal's hard glare.

'On your head be it,' Marca snapped, and he strode from the jail-house, slamming the door behind him.

The elderly Aelf watched after him for a moment, and then gave a sympathetic frown into Clara's cell before offering Van Bam and Samuel a friendly smile.

'Sorry about him,' he said. 'Marca always has been a little disagree-able, but he is surprisingly good at supervising Sunflower. Usually.' His smile faltered slightly. 'The last thing any of us expected was a visit from humans. Would you mind telling me how you managed to escape the Labyrinth?'

Samuel folded his arms across his chest, saying nothing, and Van

Bam watched as the elderly Aelf pulled a puzzled face and walked over to the table beneath the window.

He lifted up Samuel's utility belt and slid out Van Bam's cane from beneath it. He turned the length of green glass in his hands, giving it close scrutiny.

'Hmm,' he said. 'Aelfirian-made, if I'm not mistaken.' He looked pointedly at Van Bam. 'An illusionist's wand, am I right?'

Van Bam didn't reply. The elderly Aelf pursed his lips, placed the cane back onto the table, and approached the cell again.

'I can appreciate why you would be reluctant to speak after such a hostile reception, but you must realise that you will have to explain your presence to someone, eventually. And I'm rather hoping that someone could be me.'

His words were met by more silence.

'All right,' he said, 'let's begin with me, shall we? I am Councillor Tal. I represent the Aelfheim Archipelago within the Panopticon of Houses – an institution that was founded after the Genii War, so I can be fairly certain that you have not heard of it.'

Van Bam allowed him a small shake of his head.

Councillor Tal continued. 'As you can see, I'm enjoying my winter years – by which I mean that I'm old enough to remember the Great Labyrinth, the denizens of Labrys Town, and the magickers who served that noble administration called the Relic Guild.' His eyes shifted to Samuel. 'I recognise a changeling and an illusionist, but what are you, my friend?'

He sighed when Samuel replied with a glare as silent as it was hard.

'I don't know how you managed to get out of the Labyrinth,' Tal said. 'Perhaps it's not important for now. But I can say you've caused quite a stir in Sunflower, to put it mildly. Tongues wag, gentlemen, and I should think word of your arrival is already spreading through all the sub-Houses of the Aelfheim Archipelago. Please, help me to help you. You may consider me a friend.'

There's more to this Aelf than meets the eye, Gideon said in Van Bam's mind. *But I think he's telling the truth, my idiot.*

How is Clara? Van Bam said.

Exhausted and sleeping, Gideon replied testily. *Now stop fussing like an old nanny, and focus on the job at hand.*

Although Councillor Tal's smile and genial manner never faltered, his shades were fluxing to Van Bam's inner vision. As an Aelfirian politician, he had undoubtedly been trained to hide many things, but he could not hide everything from the scrutiny of an illusionist. Tal was not shocked or surprised by the humans who had suddenly appeared on his doorstep; he was more concerned with whatever news they might be carrying. And Van Bam's scrutiny agreed with Gideon's assumption; this Aelf could indeed be trusted, at least to put the Relic Guild in touch with the right people.

With a quick look at Samuel, Van Bam stepped closer to the cell bars. 'My name is Van Bam,' he said. 'This is Samuel, and the changeling in the next cell is named Clara.'

Tal nodded appreciatively. 'A pleasure to make your acquaintance.'

'We are indeed what remains of the Relic Guild,' Van Bam continued. 'And until very recently, I was the Resident of Labrys Town.'

'Forgive me,' Tal said with a frown, 'but don't the Residents remain in their position until death?'

'I was deposed from the Nightshade.'

'Deposed? My old memory might not be as sharp as it once was, but I remember well that only the magic of the Nightshade itself could decide who succeeded a Resident.'

'It is a long story, Councillor.'

'Well, we seem to have time for little else at present.'

'Don't be so sure,' Samuel said.

Tal stared at him.

'Councillor,' said Van Bam. 'It is imperative that I speak with the very highest authority.'

'Oh? And who would you consider the very highest?'

Van Bam paused. 'I need to contact the Thaumaturgists.'

Aelfirian eyes widened, and Tal's face became tinged with an unreadable hue. 'Why?'

'I will give my reasons to the Thaumaturgists alone.'

'Then you have a problem,' Tal said, not unkindly. He looked from one man to the other. 'Please understand – the Panopticon of Houses was established as a democratic union. Every Aelfirian House that survived the Genii War was given a seat within its structure. The Panopticon of Houses is the governing body that has ruled over the Aelfir ever since the Timewatcher and Her Thaumaturgists abandoned us.'

Van Bam felt Samuel stiffen beside him. He resisted the urge to step away from Tal, trying to deny his inner vision that was showing him that the elderly councillor was telling the open and honest truth.

That puts an interesting icing on the cake, Gideon sniffed.

'They abandoned you?' Van Bam said to Tal.

'As certainly as they abandoned the denizens of the Labyrinth,' Tal assured the illusionist almost apologetically.

'Why?' Samuel demanded, his tone accusing.

Tal shrugged. 'We were never given a definitive reason. Were you?'

Van Bam and Samuel shared a long look. Samuel swore under his breath.

Oh, grow some balls, Gideon said. *We've been in worse positions than this before … haven't we?*

'It seems that humans and Aelfir have a lot to catch up on,' Tal said. 'I'm sorry to be the one to give you this news, but the Houses haven't heard from the Thaumaturgists since the end of the Genii War. We have no way of contacting them, and I really don't think they're coming back.'

The elderly Aelf took a step closer to the cell, his expression stony. 'You should know that you have friends within the Panopticon of Houses, but not every House thinks of the Labyrinth favourably.' His voice was earnest. 'I beg you to trust me before you come to the attention of someone … less sympathetic. Now, if you were deposed, who is controlling the Nightshade?'

Samuel looked away from Van Bam, turning his heavy scowl toward the floor. 'Tell him,' he whispered.

Van Bam licked his lips. 'Councillor Tal, have you heard the name Fabian Moor?'

Tal didn't reply, but his expression became shrewd.

That's a resounding yes, Gideon drawled. *Can you see his shade of confirmation, my idiot? It's as if he was expecting you to mention Moor's name.*

Van Bam had to agree. 'Councillor?' he said curiously. 'What do you know of Fabian Moor?'

'I remember he was the most dangerous Genii under Spiral's command.' Tal drew a breath, seemed hesitant to speak further, but finally continued, albeit reluctantly. 'I heard a story that he managed to break into the Labyrinth during the war, but that the Relic Guild killed him.'

'We heard the same story,' Samuel muttered bitterly.

'Until very recently,' Van Bam explained, 'we indeed believed Fabian Moor to be dead.'

To Van Bam's inner vision, Tal's shades brightened with another flush of confirmation. 'He survived the war?'

'And he returned to Labrys Town, Councillor,' said Van Bam. 'He has gained control of the Nightshade.'

'And he brought friends with him, too,' Samuel added, 'The Labyrinth belongs to the Genii now.'

'Impossible,' Tal whispered. His large eyes glazed and stared into an unknown distance. 'No Genii survived the war. The Timewatcher destroyed them all.'

Listen to him! Gideon scoffed. *He doesn't believe his own words!*

But he believed the Relic Guild.

Van Bam wondered if Councillor Tal had been expecting their arrival for a long time, waiting for the day when they would bring this dire news to him.

'Please understand,' said Van Bam levelly. 'How Fabian Moor and his fellow Genii survived is academic. We can only guess what their future plans are for the Aelfirian Houses, but at present they threaten the lives of one million denizens.' He paused. 'Now, Councillor, I believe there is something you are not telling us, yes?'

When the elderly Aelf didn't reply, Samuel took a step forward. '*Councillor*!' he snapped.

Tal's eyes gained focus and he stared intently at Van Bam.

'It's complicated,' he said. He pulled a pocket watch from his waistcoat and checked the time. 'I'm afraid you'll have to remain locked in here for the time being,' he continued, his voice growing distant as he turned from the cell and made his way to the door. 'I-I have to make arrangements.'

'Councillor?' said Van Bam.

Tal paused to glance into Clara's cell, and then back at Van Bam and Samuel. He seemed to have aged.

'Gentlemen,' he said. 'I'm afraid I have to contact the Panopticon of Houses on this matter. But I will do all I can to rally those who are still your friends.'

And with that, he left.

Sergeant Ennis was twenty-six years of age. He had been born a generation too late to have known the Aelfir, to have known a time when the doorways of the Great Labyrinth had led to their fabled Houses. But he had heard the stories, and he knew well the history of his hometown. Never once, even in tales of the most ancient of times, could Ennis remember reading or hearing of public execution being condoned in the Labyrinth's society.

'... and to top it all off, today's cargo deliveries still haven't started arriving,' Captain Moira was saying. 'Troubling times, I'm sure you'll agree.'

Ennis nodded. 'Yes, Ma'am.'

Moira was in her office, at a desk upon which, Ennis noted, the remnants of Jeter's possessions still sat. She was in her middle years, her short hair greying. Lines of concern covered her face; wrinkles of worry surrounded her eyes. There was a second chair on the opposite side of the desk, which she hadn't invited her sergeant to use. He stood at attention before her.

'It might be difficult to stomach,' Moira continued, 'but Jeter's execution was just.' She was trying very hard to mean it. 'The example made of him will serve as a reminder to us all.'

A reminder of what? Ennis wondered, unable to stop thinking of the Woodsman. *That the new Resident is willing to abuse the use of magic and serve justice with wild demons?* He struggled to rid his mind of the images of a virus-ravaged Jeter being hacked to pieces.

Moira's gaze shifted to the eye device fixed to the wall behind Ennis.

The normally white fluid within the hemisphere of glass had turned a shade of pink – as it had in all the eyes of Labrys Town. The fluid was calm and not churning, suggesting that that the conversation was not being observed. 'We must not be weak. Understood, Sergeant?

When Ennis looked back to his new captain, Moira's eyes widened with a deliberate gesture, a silent warning: be careful with your words, she was saying, there was no telling who might decide to eavesdrop, or when. She was as frightened as he was.

'Yes, Ma'am.'

With a sigh, Moira rose from her chair and stared out of the window behind the desk. 'Hagi Tabet has promised to make many changes in Labrys Town. What they will be, I've not been told. But Lady Asajad has ... *impressed* upon me how important it is that I succeed in stopping the Relic Guild, and the virus they would use to destroy us all.' Her shoulders slumped almost imperceptibly. 'In this, *we* cannot fail.'

The truth was Ennis did not know how much he could trust Moira. She had been after the captain's position for years. A few people in the force called Moira Jeter's shadow because she was always there, watching and waiting for him to screw up, like a wasp eager to sting. But with the captaincy finally hers, Moira was as aware as Ennis that the position had become a poisoned chalice under Labrys Town's new regime. Was she the sort to take people down with her?

She turned from the window and sat upon the sill. She looked weary. 'Ennis, I have asked you here because your role in the Police Force is about to change.'

Ennis frowned. 'Ma'am?'

'For a long time now I've been noticing how Captain Jeter never really appreciated your efforts. In fact, I would go as far as to say that he took credit for much of your work. Am I wrong?'

Ennis averted his gaze. He couldn't argue with that. Jeter had always taken the credit for the good work of his officers; not so much for the bad.

'I've been watching you, Sergeant,' Moira said. 'You have a gift for police work. You think in ways that others don't. You see evidence and connections that others miss. Your instincts drive you to look in the unlikeliest places, and you have solved more cases than Jeter allowed the records to show.'

Ennis was looking at his feet. 'Just taking my job seriously, Ma'am,' he mumbled.

'Oh, don't be coy with me,' Moira said, lacking patience. 'You keep your head down, uninterested in praise, doing your job quietly, most proficiently, and criminals never see you coming. You are a credit to the force, Ennis.'

'Thank you, Ma'am.'

There was a long pause, and Ennis's gaze rose from his feet to the captain.

Moira was staring at the eye device again. 'I think it is high time I let you off the leash,' she said quietly.

Ennis gave her another frown.

'I'm taking you off regular duties,' Moira told him. 'And out of your uniform.' She paused, considered, and then: 'I'm ordering you to conduct a private investigation. Use those skills of yours and track down the Relic Guild for me. Find them so we can destroy them. Is that clear?'

Taken aback, Ennis nodded.

'Understand that I am giving you free licence to do whatever you think necessary, Sergeant. You are answerable only to me. Do not fail me.'

'Yes, Ma'am.'

'Good.' Moira returned to her desk. 'Then that is all. From this moment, you are working undercover.' Her expression darkened. 'We all need a quick resolution on this one.'

'Of course, Ma'am.'

Ennis headed for the door, his legs curiously light and shaky.

'And don't forget,' Moira added as Ennis placed his hand on the doorknob. 'You report directly to me. Tell no one else of your findings.'

CHAPTER EIGHT

FRIENDS AND FOES

All was quiet in the Aelfirian jailhouse.

Samuel didn't know how long it had been since Councillor Tal had left, but Van Bam seemed to have been asleep on the bunk in the cell for a long time. His face was peaceful, the smooth metal plates fused to his eye sockets looking up at the ceiling with a cold stare, dull grey and lifeless. In the neighbouring cell, Clara also slept – at least, Samuel hoped that was what she was doing. Her metamorphosis back into human form had been torturous to listen to, and he didn't want to imagine the kind of cruel agony it had inflicted upon the changeling's body. She hadn't woken since the change, and he prayed that Clara now slept because the experience had left her exhausted and not damaged – physically *or* mentally.

Clara, by a spiteful twist of magic, now had the voice of Gideon haunting her mind. Whatever motive the avatar had for doing this, Samuel thought that if he was in Clara's position, he would probably have shot himself already.

With a sigh, the old bounty hunter pressed his face between the cool metal bars of the cell, and stared out through the only window in the jailhouse. His weapons and utility belt lay upon the table beneath the window, maddeningly out of his reach.

The view outside was alien yet familiar. Samuel was certain that enough time had passed for the day to slip into night, yet the strange purple sun still shone above Sunflower. Samuel could see two of those wide wooden bridges that crossed to the tooth-shaped, free floating islands. And upon those islands were the portals that led to the sub-Houses of the Aelfheim Archipelago.

Samuel had visited Sunflower before, years ago; but the view through the window did not belong to the House he remembered. He wondered what had happened to this place, what had happened to all the Aelfirian Houses, during the last forty years.

The Houses haven't heard from the Thaumaturgists since the end of the Genii War, Councillor Tal had said. And it seemed like they weren't coming back.

Samuel didn't trust the elderly Aelf, but he trusted that Van Bam did. 'For certain, Tal knows more than he is presently able to tell us,' the illusionist had told Samuel earlier. 'It seems he has been waiting for the Relic Guild. I believe he knew we would tell him the Genii have returned. He wants to help us, Samuel.'

But if Tal's word could be trusted, if the Thaumaturgists, the overlords of human and Aelfir alike, had abandoned the Houses as coldly as they had abandoned the Labyrinth, how could the elderly Aelf help the Relic Guild? How could anyone? Who was left with the power to rid Labrys Town of creatures of higher magic?

With that daunting question hanging heavy and unanswered in his mind, his gaze still locked on the view through the window, it dawned on Samuel just how much distance had grown between humans and Aelfir. Four decades of separation, forty years of absence, enough time to forget, enough time for a new generation to grow with no memory of the old days. Samuel decided that the chill and unwelcoming landscape of Sunflower was a good representation of the cold divide that separated humans and Aelfir; and again he wondered – what had happened to this place?

More than fifty years had passed since Samuel had last visited the Aelfheim Archipelago. It had been a time before Van Bam and Marney had joined the Relic Guild, and Samuel had been painfully young, younger than Clara was now. An old and wise empath called Denton had chaperoned Samuel, but the trip had not been undertaken on official Nightshade business; its reason was to give a boy the experience to grow into manhood. It had been the first time Samuel had seen an Aelfirian House.

Denton had shown Samuel all the sub-Houses of the Aelfheim Archipelago, but it had been Sunflower that most impressed the boy. Back then, a great yellow sun had filled the days with brilliant light and welcoming warmth; the nights were fresh and clean and full of dreams, illuminated by three moons and a host of pinprick stars. Farmers had tended fields of golden crops that stretched as far as the eye could see; cattle wandered and fed upon sprawling plains of lush, green grass; animals roamed free and wild through forests of tall trees; and in giant greenhouses the size of the Nightshade, all manner of exotic fruits and plants were grown.

The two weeks Samuel had spent in Sunflower had become his most treasured memories. Some days he would help the farmers in the fields or collect chicken eggs or muck out the stables. Other days he might walk with Denton through a forest, learning about the Aelfir and what was expected of him as an agent of the Relic Guild. And sometimes Samuel would just walk alone, for miles and hours, across a natural landscape devoid of buildings – a vast change from the squalid houses of Labrys Town, surrounded by boundary walls and the twists and turns of an endless maze.

He remembered not wanting to turn back from those walks, not caring if he never saw the Labyrinth again. The adolescent Samuel had been jealous of the Aelfir of Sunflower; they were living a life far more wholesome and free than a boy from Labrys Town had ever thought possible. And that jealousy had never entirely left the old bounty hunter.

What event could have turned Sunflower into such a cold and unwelcoming place, Samuel didn't know. It was depressing to see it in such a state. The glorious House that had impressed itself upon the mind of that young magicker might have gone now, but the memory of it had been the spark of warmth that had given Samuel hope through his long years of isolation in the Labyrinth.

Samuel sighed. There was a sense of irony inherent to the situation in which the Relic Guild found itself embroiled. Irony that was personal to him. Only a few days ago, the enigmatic avatar had instigated Samuel's involvement in this whole mess, and the shame of it lingered inside him.

Before Samuel knew that Fabian Moor had returned, before he knew that the Relic Guild was needed – for the first time in forty years – the avatar had visited him, offering a bounty contract that was too good to turn down. The reward of the contract was escape from the

Labyrinth. Samuel could choose any House of the Aelfir he liked, and the avatar would procure his passage to it. Instinctively, Samuel had thought of Sunflower; and for a while, had truly believed he might get to spend the rest of his days among lush fields of crops and forests of tall trees. All he had to do to secure this reward was to kill a young magicker called Clara.

In the neighbouring cell, as if sensing Samuel's lingering shame, Clara moaned in her dreams. She fell silent, and her sleeping breaths mingled with Van Bam's once more.

Samuel had meant to do it. Without a second thought, he would've killed Clara for the chance to return to Sunflower. But the avatar had a strange and unfathomable – not to mention dangerous – way of going about things. The bounty contract it offered had been a ruse, and a part of Samuel had always known that. The avatar had been manipulating events, and it had never intended to let an old bounty hunter kill an innocent changeling. The bounty contract had ensured Samuel's interest; it had been a means to call him back to the Relic Guild, to remind him of his duty and the promises he had once made to protect the denizens of Labrys Town.

Although Samuel had been duped, he could offer no excuses for his actions – he was glad he didn't have Clara's death burning a hole into his conscience. And he wondered if the avatar knew that its promise to him had been kept? Had it known that Samuel would return to Sunflower?

'But not like this,' he whispered.

The view outside was a shattered dream, a broken memory of all that Samuel had once thought of as good and ...

His magic stirred.

It was a pulse of preparation, not a sharp flare of warning. Samuel's prescient awareness was telling him that the Relic Guild's situation was about to change. And dangerously.

He kicked Van Bam's bunk. 'Wake up,' he hissed.

Instantly alert, Van Bam sat up and turned to Samuel. 'What is it?'

'Someone's coming.'

Outside the jailhouse door there was a muffled thump followed by a groan. Van Bam jumped to his feet as the door opened, and two people entered.

The first was short and slight of build. The second, tall and broad, was dragging the limp, unconscious body of the policeman who had stood guard outside. Both of them wore tops with hoods of charmed material that shrouded their faces with impenetrable shadow.

The taller figure dumped the unconscious policeman, and Samuel immediately noted the strange rifle hanging from his shoulder. The barrel was unusually thick, more like metal tubing. And between the barrel and the stock was a drum, giving the weapon a clunky, awkward look. A spell sphere launcher, Samuel realised with surprise. He hadn't seen one since before the Genii War.

The shorter figure paused to look into Clara's cell before moving to the next cell along.

'Your names are Van Bam and Samuel.' A woman's voice, low and secretive. She carried no obvious weapons, but a cloth satchel hung from her shoulder. 'We're here to rescue you, and we don't have much time.'

'And you are ...?' said Van Bam.

'Explanations later. You're in more danger than you realise.'

The illusionist looked at Samuel.

Samuel shrugged. 'I'm not sensing any threat. But she is desperate.'

'Of course I'm bloody desperate,' the woman hissed. 'You have no idea what's heading your way.'

'You should listen to her,' said the woman's companion. His voice was deep. He had moved to the table beneath the window and was checking the items resting there. He came over to the cell and passed Van Bam his green glass cane through the bars. 'And you'll need these,' he said, offering Samuel two power stones. 'Yours have lost their charge.'

Again, the illusionist looked at the old bounty hunter, seeking advice from his prescient awareness. Again, Samuel felt no danger and shrugged.

'How do you know us?' Van Bam said.

'Interesting story,' the woman replied. 'I'll tell you about it later.'

Samuel detected a hint of amusement in her voice.

'I'll have to shoot the lock open,' said the man. 'These are too complicated to pick quickly.' He adjusted the spell sphere launcher and reached for the pistol holstered at his hip. 'Stand back,' he said to the agents.

'Look in my utility belt,' Samuel said before the Aelf could draw the pistol. 'You'll find a phial of acid.'

'That'll do the trick,' the man said, and he strode back to the table.

'When these cells are open, we have to move fast,' said the woman. She was gripping the bars, her voice earnest. 'Do as we say, when we say it. You have to trust us.'

Van Bam cocked his head to one side, a strange expression on his face. 'I know your voice.'

The woman paused for a moment. She then reached up and pulled back her hood. She revealed the face of an Aelf in her mid-fifties. Her hair was shoulder length and curly, black but laced with grey strands. Her large eyes were a soft shade of green, her small mouth and nose softened the usually triangular-shaped face of the Aelfir into a more subtle heart shape.

'Namji?' Van Bam whispered with incredulity.

'Hello, Van Bam.' She didn't quite smile as she studied his face. 'What happened to your eyes?'

'That, too, is an interesting story.'

Samuel watched the interchange with no small degree of confusion, his mind latching on to old memories. 'Namji?' he demanded of Van Bam. 'From Mirage?'

'Indeed,' the illusionist confirmed humourlessly, his metal eyes still fixed on the woman.

'And this ugly brute is Glogelder,' Namji said as the man returned with the phial from Samuel's utility belt.

He also swept back his hood. He was younger than Namji – mid-twenties, Samuel guessed. His eyes were such dark brown they were almost black. His nose had been broken – more than once – and his pointed ears had seen their fair share of beatings. There was not one strand of hair on his head, no shade of stubble on his face, and nothing that even hinted at eyebrows. But the scars of old gashes and wounds pocked his face and scalp like craters on a battered moon.

Glogelder chuckled thickly. 'Pleased to meet you,' he said, as he dripped acid into the cell door's lock.

Whilst metal hissed and melted, Samuel glared at the Aelfirian rescuers. 'Who are you?' he demanded.

Namji shrugged. 'We're the Relic Guild,' she said happily.

Samuel aimed his ever increasing bemusement at Van Bam. 'You know what?' he said in a surrendering sort of tone. 'I'm just about ready to punch someone in the face.'

The Resident was feeding.

A long appendage extruded from Tabet's navel, a pale tentacle that reached down onto the floor, where it stretched and widened into a fleshy sack that held a denizen. The sack squeezed and shuddered as it crushed and chewed away the life of the human male inside; breaking bones, pushing blood along with liquefied skin, muscle and organs up the appendage into Tabet's body. Hanging upon her web of leathery tentacles, the Resident was frozen in a posture of ecstasy. Her arms and legs were splayed, her eyes closed, and her was mouth open as if preparing to issue a cry of pleasure.

Below Tabet, watching her feed, Fabian Moor and Viktor Gadreel stood alongside each other. An air of impatience surrounded the Genii. Tabet had summoned them to the chamber because she had finished processing the memories that had been harvested from the empath Marney and stored within the flower. But the Resident had been weakened by her work, and needed sustenance before she could reveal what she had found.

Moor's hands were balled into fists at his side. He had waited decades to discover where the Timewatcher had hidden Oldest Place, but these final few moments of the long wait were by far the most frustrating to endure. He willed Tabet to eat faster.

'Asajad should be here,' Viktor Gadreel rumbled. 'We should be together for this moment.'

'Mo Asajad is busy controlling the denizens,' Moor replied

offhandedly. 'Her absence makes no difference to the outcome.'

Moor suppressed a smile. If Asajad had heard his words, they would have cut her to the bone. *Good*, he thought; she needed to learn her place within this small band of Genii. She needed to respect that it was Fabian Moor whom Lord Spiral trusted the most, not Mo Asajad. That she had not been summoned to this moment where the Genii would gain the information that would set their lord and master free ... well, perhaps she would learn a little humility and finally begin to temper her challenging ways.

It was then that Moor noticed Gadreel was no longer watching Hagi Tabet. His one eye stared at the floor, ignoring the Resident, and the fleshy sack that devoured a human. His big face was creased with concern.

'Viktor,' said Moor. 'You are offended by Asajad's absence?'

'No,' Gadreel grunted.

Moor raised an eyebrow. There was an almost embarrassed air surrounding Gadreel's reply. His hulking body seemed ill at ease.

'Then what is it that troubles you?' Moor asked.

'Oldest Place.'

'Oh?'

Gadreel drew a breath. 'You said that it is an eternal prison, a House of suffering, where Lord Spiral endures never-ending tortures.'

'Indeed.'

'You said that the Timewatcher ensured our Lord would have no defence against his punishment.'

'Viktor,' Moor said intolerantly, 'tell me what is on your mind.'

Gadreel gritted his teeth, perhaps in anger, perhaps steeling himself. 'Fabian, for forty years Lord Spiral has suffered the Timewatcher's retribution. What if the ceaseless cruelty of Oldest Place was too much for him? What ... what if he is dead?'

'Have you lost your sense of reason, Lord Gadreel?' Moor admonished, his voice laced with disappointment. 'Do you really have so little faith in our lord and master?'

'It is a valid concern,' Gadreel growled.

'No, it is a visceral and self-pitying whim that is clearly beneath you,' Moor snapped. 'Consider what you already know. The Timewatcher created Oldest Place as an eternal prison. For its sole prisoner to suffer *eternally*, I rather think he would have to be kept alive, don't you?' He looked up at Hagi Tabet, still on her web deep in the ecstasy of feeding. 'The Timewatcher might have surrounded Lord Spiral with tortures, but She would have ensured that while in Oldest Place, he would be protected from other harms. At least physically.'

'Then what of his mind?' Gadreel said. 'What would protect him from insanity?'

Moor thought of his own forty years in isolation, and the long wait that had at times threatened to drive him mad. Many things had kept him sane – desire, ambition, *vengeance* – and he was in no doubt that those things would keep the Lord of the Genii sane too.

'You worry needlessly, without thought or logic,' Moor said. 'And perhaps that is why Lord Spiral trusted *me* with command, and not *you*.'

The sting of these words forced the aggression back into Gadreel's body language, dispelling his uncertainty.

Moor added, 'Stop fretting like a *human*, and tell me, Lord Gadreel, how are you progressing with enticing Hamir out of his hiding place?'

Gadreel grunted. 'The necromancer has sealed the door to that room with magic I cannot yet fathom,' he said angrily. 'But give me time, Fabian, and I—'

He broke off with a noise of disgust.

The fleshy sack on the floor was now as baggy and limp as a deflated balloon. The greasy lips of its mouth opened, belched rancid air, and then squeezed out a pile of broken bones smeared in pink jelly. The sack then shrank as Hagi Tabet sucked the tentacular appendage back into her body, leaving an angry red bud the size of a fist at her navel. Tabet relaxed. She gave a satisfied sigh, but did not open her eyes.

Two of the Resident's servants materialised in the room, and Moor was almost too embarrassed to gaze upon them.

It was a strange quirk of the Nightshade to project into being eerie phantoms that represented an inner aspect of whoever held the Residency. Their function was to take care of mundane chores, but the monstrosities that appeared in the room now also showed how damaged Hagi Tabet's inner being was.

Raw and pink skin hung from their withered bodies in folds. Their spherical heads drooped from the end of long, weak necks. Features were smeared across their faces, and they stared with watery, lidless eyes that bulged from sockets as pink orbs. The aspects began gathering up the pile of sticky bones with large, fat-fingered hands on the end of stick-thin limbs. Moor regarded them as disgusting creations, and he decided that Lady Tabet should feel ashamed of herself.

His patience frayed, Moor glared up at the Resident.

'Hagi!' he shouted.

Tabet's eyelids fluttered open. She took a moment, as if struggling to remember where she was. She looked at the aspects clearing away the remnants of her meal, and then at her fellow Genii. Finally, her eyes met Moor's, and her expression became accusing, bordering on rage.

'You were wrong!' Tabet spat at him.

Moor shared a quick, confused glance with Gadreel, before replying, 'Explain yourself.'

'The empath,' Tabet said, as though the word was a bad taste in her mouth. 'That filthy, pathetic bitch of a human … you were wrong about her, my *dear Lord Moor*.' Her teeth were gritted.

'Hagi, stop delaying and tell us how to free Lord Spiral from his prison,' Gadreel said. His simmering frustration seemed ready to boil over. 'Where is Oldest Place?'

'I cannot tell you,' Tabet said in a deathly tone. 'For the empath did not know.'

Gadreel looked at Moor, his one eye shining vindictively. 'What's the meaning of this, Fabian?'

A moment of stunned silence had fallen upon Moor, and he did not answer Gadreel. 'Impossible,' he whispered to Tabet. 'You are mistaken.'

Tabet's gaze was as cold as it was accusing. 'Fabian – the full extent of the empath's memories were laid before me.' She prodded her temple with a finger. 'I can see them as clearly as I see you. The flower gave me every detail of a life belonging to a woman called Marney, and – believe me – she did *not* know the location of Oldest Place.'

For the first time in an age, Moor found himself gripped by doubt. His mouth worked silently, his words frozen in his throat.

'Look again, Hagi!' he said finally, hating the desperate tone in his voice.

'I have,' she replied. 'Many times.'

'But ... but how could I be wrong?'

'Wrong?' Gadreel rumbled. 'You assured us the human knew, Fabian.'

'She did,' Moor replied flatly. 'I *know* she did.'

Hagi Tabet sighed. 'She most certainly did not.'

'Perhaps your tree creature did not function as you hoped it would,' Gadreel said accusingly. 'Perhaps it did not *harvest* the full extent of the human's memories.'

'The tree functioned perfectly,' Moor said through clenched teeth. 'The empath was drained of all she knew.'

'Perhaps we should retrieve her body and try again.'

Moor did not care for the disbelief and disappointment in Gadreel's thick tones. 'The empath is dead!' he snapped at his fellow Genii. 'Do you understand? Dead and *rotting*! We have already taken *everything* she had! Hagi—'

'No, Fabian,' the Resident said. 'Please don't try again to tell me I am mistaken. I searched through the empath's memories a hundred times. At no point in her life did Marney discover the location of Oldest Place. At no point did she hold the key to Lord Spiral's freedom.'

'You said yourself that Marney had shattered her timeline,' Moor said threateningly. 'You said she had hidden memories within memories.' His shock, his frustration, was quickly turning to seething, white hot rage. 'Search them again, Hagi.'

'No.' Tabet turned her pale and watery eyes away from Moor, as if she was embarrassed to be associated with him. 'You have made a mistake, Fabian. Accept it.'

'Accept what?' Gadreel rumbled. 'That we have failed? That Lord Spiral was wrong to trust us?'

Giving a bellow of outrage, he lashed out with a tree-trunk leg and kicked one of Tabet's aspects into the other. With a sickening thud, the grotesque creations tumbled across the room in a mash of loose pink flesh, scattering human bones as they went. The aspects faded and disappeared.

Gadreel rounded on Moor, jabbing a thick finger at him. 'You dared to admonish me for lacking *logic* and *thought*, when all the while it was you, Fabian Moor, whom Lord Spiral was wrong to trust!'

'Hold your tongue,' Moor growled.

Gadreel sneered and issued a bitter laugh. 'You are not fit to order me, you cretin!' The look in his one eye was steely. 'Lord Spiral gave you command, entrusted his freedom to you, and you have failed him and us and the future by placing your faith in a lowly human—'

Moor snapped.

His hand flashed out and gripped his fellow Genii by the throat.

Physically, Viktor Gadreel was an obese brute, easily as strong as three humans. But his thaumaturgy was not as honed and powerful as Moor's – nor was his mind. Always choosing muscle over magic first, Gadreel tried to crash a massive fist into Moor's face. But with a burst of thaumaturgy, Moor lifted Gadreel's bulk off the floor whilst his hand tightened around his throat.

Gadreel began fighting for air, unable to break Moor's grip. Only then did he try to summon his thaumaturgy, but Moor dampened it with his own.

'I told you to *hold your tongue*!'

And with another thaumaturgic burst, Moor sent Gadreel flying from his hand to crash into the wall, where he fell into a heap on the floor, unconscious among sticky, pale bones.

Hagi Tabet watched the proceedings with the simple glee of a child watching a puppet show. 'This is not Viktor's fault, Fabian,' she admonished. Her words were chiding, but her tone was airy and vague. 'He was not the one who placed all hope upon the knowledge of a human empath. *He* did not fail.'

Moor turned his cold gaze to the Resident hanging from her leathery web. 'I want you to consider the answer to an important question, Hagi. And I want you to consider *very* carefully. Will you do that for me?'

She gave a witless smile, as Moor continued.

'If we cannot find where the Timewatcher hid Oldest Place, if we cannot free Lord Spiral, then what purpose do the Genii serve?'

Tabet's response was a giggle.

'I'm sure I don't know why that is funny, Hagi, but if we have no purpose, then surely the only alternative left to the Genii is simple survival?'

Tabet stopped laughing.

'Viktor, Asajad and I may scatter to the winds if we choose,' Moor said. 'But what of you? Where will you go? Without your symbiosis with the Nightshade, you will die. How long do you think the humans will tolerate you without the protection of your colleagues? Who will *feed* you?'

Tabet gave an odd smile, and Moor pulled a thoughtful expression.

'Perhaps the kindest thing would be to take a knife and cut you down from your web,' he said. 'Perhaps I should slice your throat and drink the thaumaturgy straight from your blood and put you out of your misery.'

Tabet's odd smile disappeared, but her tone of voice remained airy. 'That doesn't seem like a very pleasant alternative, does it, Fabian?'

'No.' Moor reined in his anger. 'Now tell me again, Lady Tabet, are you really so sure the Genii have failed?'

Two tears ran in straight lines down Tabet's cheeks. 'I could have been mistaken.'

'I'm relieved to hear it,' Moor said hollowly. 'Search Marney's memories again – another hundred times if you have to, a thousand times, a thousand-thousand. Go through them slowly, methodically. Pull apart every second of her life, and find what she has hidden.' Moor shook his head. 'I was not wrong, Hagi. That empath knew the location of Oldest Place. I have never been more certain of anything in my life. Do you understand me?'

'Most assuredly, Lord Moor.'

'Then get on with it.' Moor looked to the crumpled and unconscious bulk of Viktor Gadreel on the floor. 'And when this fool wakes up, tell him to open the door to that damn room, and drag the necromancer to my feet.'

CHAPTER NINE

FRIENDLY ENEMY

Sunflower's strange sun hung before the stars, apparently never altering its position in an alien sky. The orb of purple burned with cold fire, and Samuel's breath rose in clouds, as the Relic Guild followed their Aelfirian rescuers, who had adopted the same moniker as the humans they were rescuing.

The long, wide street outside the police station was utterly deserted. Not one Aelf was present to witness the group's passing, and the windows on the faces of the terraced buildings remained lightless. Samuel wondered if most of the populace were now at the huge warehouse, sending Labrys Town its shipment of all-important cargo.

'Lucky for us, Marca believes he's a lot cleverer than he actually is,' said Namji. 'He's too sure of himself. He thinks he's one step ahead of us.'

Jogging alongside Namji, spell sphere launcher in hand, Glogelder made a grunting noise that might have been a scoff. 'But Marca's going to learn a harsh lesson tonight – if he hasn't already.'

Both the Aelfir had covered their faces with the charmed hoods of their jumpers. They led the group along by the guardrail that marked the edge of Sunflower, and over which the gaping abyss of space waited to swallow any who might fall. Samuel was pleased to feel his rifle in his hands again and his utility belt around his waist, though he missed the weight of his lost revolver in the holster strapped to his thigh. Along with new power stones, Glogelder had also given Samuel fresh ammunition.

Van Bam carried his green glass cane in his right hand, while his left arm was wrapped around Clara's legs. The changeling was a limp weight on the illusionist's shoulder. Despite several attempts, she couldn't be woken. But Namji, who apparently had skill as a magic-user, assured the group that Clara had entered a healing sleep and would only wake up when she was ready. Samuel didn't really understand what that meant, but Van Bam had said Gideon concurred with her prognosis, and that was as much as the old bounty hunter needed to know.

So the changeling slept, feather-light and limp on Van Bam's shoulder, wrapped up in the thick blue cloak given to her by Councillor Tal.

'Tell me,' Van Bam said. 'Why do we have enemies within this Panopticon of Houses?'

Namji gave a derisive laugh. 'There's a long explanation to that one,' she said. 'But for now you can be sure that your enemies have more power than your friends.'

'That's an understatement,' said Glogelder in his rough, guttural voice. 'Some people in the Panopticon really hate the Relic Guild.'

Samuel wondered if he was talking about the human Relic Guild or the Aelfirian.

'You have to understand,' Namji continued. 'The Labyrinth might consider Sunflower an important House – the *most* important, seeing as it's responsible for keeping the denizens alive – but to … *certain other* Aelfir, it's a scab on a wound that won't heal properly. Sunflower really isn't equipped for this kind of situation. Nobody expected to see humans again.'

'But you did,' Samuel said.

'And also Councillor Tal,' Van Bam added.

'Catch on quick, this lot,' Glogelder said to Namji with a throaty laugh. 'Let's just say we were given a heads up by a *mutual friend* who likes to appear now and then all shiny and blue and full of secrets.'

'The avatar?' Samuel's voice was full of surprise. 'You've seen it?'

Again, Glogelder laughed. 'You could say that.'

'What do you know about it?' Van Bam said.

'Only that it gets around,' Namji replied.

'Do you know where it comes from?' Van Bam pressed. 'Who is controlling it? Who is the avatar's master?'

'We don't know. But as I said, we'll talk about this later. Let's get you out of here first.'

Their breath steaming in the air, the Aelfir continued to lead the three humans along the edge of Sunflower at a light run. Every so often, they passed gates to the bridges that crossed the gulf of space to the floating islands of portals. Each of those portals led to a different sub-House of the Aelfheim Archipelago, every one a bright and golden farming community – or at least they had been. Samuel wondered if all the sub-Houses had suffered the same eerie transformation that had rendered Sunflower a cold and miserable place.

'We've arranged transport,' Namji said.

'Transport to where?' Samuel asked instinctively, suspiciously.

'Anywhere rather than here,' Glogelder replied gruffly. 'We can't afford to stand still for long. From this moment, we're all on the run.'

'He's right – we have to keep moving,' Namji added. 'The Thaumaturgists might have disappeared, but they did leave behind certain … *safeguards* that the Panopticon of Houses won't hesitate to activate.'

'Safeguards?' Van Bam said. 'Against humans?'

'To stop us contacting the Labyrinth, and to deal with you if you should get out,' Namji explained. 'The Thaumaturgists left behind an agent. They call him the Toymaker, and he's an exceedingly efficient tracker.'

'*Tracker*,' Glogelder grunted. 'An assassin and an evil bastard is what he is.'

'One man?' said Samuel. 'I'll take care of him if he comes our way,' he added confidently.

Glogelder chuckled, half in approval, half in pity. 'I don't think anyone's ever laid eyes on the Toymaker,' he said. 'You don't know he's around until his toys come for you – that's what they say. I'm not sure your prescient awareness could stop him.'

Samuel narrowed his eyes. 'How do you know about my magic?'

'More than that,' said Van Bam, 'why would the Aelfir send an assassin to kill us without listening to what we have to say?' His voice was angrier than Samuel was accustomed to. 'I suspect it has to do with more than the fact that we have broken the Timewatcher's law, yes?'

Namji seemed exasperated by the continual questions, but Glogelder was happy to provide answers.

'A lot of Houses blame humans for the way things turned out,' he said. 'They think it's your fault the Timewatcher left. They're important Houses too, lots of influence—'

'The point being,' Namji said testily, 'there are people in the Panopticon of Houses who already hate humans enough. Once they know denizens have escaped the Labyrinth, they won't listen to anything you have to say about Fabian Moor and the Genii. But they *will* send the Toymaker. We have to keep moving.'

As Van Bam shifted Clara's position on his shoulder, Samuel could see the troubled, suspicious expression on his face, could almost hear the pernicious questions of Gideon inside his head. How much more did these Aelfir calling themselves the Relic Guild know? How much had the avatar shared with them?

'Wait,' Namji said.

She came to a halt beside one of the gates cut into the guardrail. There, two police officers were on their knees. Samuel could tell straight away they had been shot by ice-bullets, and recently. Frozen into position with rifles still in their hands, they wouldn't defrost for a long time. Despite the scene before him, Samuel's magic detected no immediate danger.

'As I told you,' Namji said with a dangerous edge to her voice, 'Marca believes in himself too much. We have more friends in Sunflower than he realises. This way – everything has been arranged.'

Leaving the frozen officers, Namji led the way through the gate and onto the wide bridge on the other side. Considering it was comprised of wooden slats held together by rope, the bridge was sturdier than it appeared. To Samuel's surprise, it didn't sway or groan as the group headed across to the floating island at the other end. Held by some feat of magic, the bridge remained as solid as stone, and made for a safe crossing over the endless abyss of star-filled space.

As they neared the end of the bridge, Samuel could see a cargo container positioned before the huge archway of a portal. The container was at least seven foot tall, and nearly as wide and long as the floating platform it sat upon. The double doors at its end were already open; the portal behind it was active and humming, alive with liquid darkness. And lying on the ground before the open doors of the cargo container were the frozen bodies of four more police officers.

The environment pressed in on Samuel's senses with sharp needles; time dulled, and his prescient awareness flared with warning. With his back to them, an Aelf was crouched over one of the frozen bodies, holding a pistol with its power stone primed and glowing.

'Stop,' Samuel ordered.

Namji and Glogelder came to an instant standstill on the bridge, as if they had been heeding Samuel's magic all their lives. They looked back at Samuel, waiting. Leading with his rifle, Samuel stepped ahead of the group, almost to the end of the bridge, taking steady aim at the crouching figure.

'Who is that?' Van Bam said.

'It's all right,' Namji said hurriedly.

The figure turned to the group and rose to his feet. Tall and thin, it was Hillem, Supervisor Marca's idiot lackey.

He smiled and waved. 'I was getting worried,' he said in a clear voice far from that of a simpleton.

'Hillem's an agent of the Relic Guild,' Namji explained. 'He's been undercover in Sunflower for a while now.'

'We've got a problem,' Hillem said. 'I can't find Marca—'

'Shut up,' Samuel spat. He kept his rifle aimed at the tall and thin Aelf.

'Hillem's one of us,' Glogelder stressed. 'Lower your—'

'I said *shut up*!'

Samuel's magic was gaining momentum, the sharp needles in his blood growing hotter, building to an event. But the danger did not come from Hillem, or the revelation that he was not the imbecile that Samuel and Van Bam had been led to believe; the danger was not in the immediate vicinity. But …

Van Bam stepped up behind him. 'What is your magic telling you, Samuel?'

The answer came with a series of shouts filling the air, and Hillem's expression dropped as he stared at the mainland behind the group.

Samuel wheeled around. Glogelder ducked out of his way as Samuel took aim at the other end of the bridge. A door on one of the houses had burst open, and five police officers were running across the street.

'You were supposed to take care of Marca's surprises?' Glogelder shouted at Hillem, hefting his spell sphere launcher.

'That's what I've been trying to tell you,' Hillem snapped back. 'I don't know where Marca is!'

'It's not an ambush,' Samuel said.

The police headed towards the bridge, but their shouts did not carry authority, nor were their weapons aimed at the Relic Guild. Their words were unintelligible, panicked, terrified; the officers were fleeing.

A sixth person emerged, running and shouting in desperation. It was Supervisor Marca. He held a pistol, and turned, power stone flashing as he unloaded into the open doorway, blindly, madly. But he could not halt the progress of a stream of silver that rushed from the house. Marca dropped his weapon and began running again, shouting for help, but he didn't get far.

By the time Samuel could see that the stream of silver was in fact a swarm of small automatons, scuttling on metallic legs, each no bigger than a hand, the first of them had caught up with Marca. They clambered over him, stabbing his head and body with whipping tails that flashed with thaumaturgic light each time they pierced his skin. And by the time Marca fell to the ground, face down and dead, the swarm had caught up with the police officers.

Each of them fell screaming, dying from the sting of thaumaturgy, leaving the band of scuttling automatons to head for the bridge. There had to be at least a hundred of them.

'Shit!' Namji hissed.

'How did he find us this fast?' Glogelder said. There was fear in the big Aelf's voice.

Samuel wasn't listening. As the swarm approached the gate to the bridge, he emptied his rifle's magazine into them. Four shots, each one hitting a hand-sized automaton with a dull ring, punched them all back into the main horde. The power stone on Glogelder's launcher whined. The drum of spell spheres whirred and clicked into place, and the big Aelf fired. The sphere arced over the bridge and exploded in the middle of the swarm. With a roar like thunder, the fiery shockwave sent small machines flying in all directions, and shattered the frozen bodies of the police officers on their knees, whilst setting aflame the rest of the dead.

But the magic had as little effect on them as Samuel's bullets. Before the firestorm had fully died, the automatons had regrouped and were swarming through the gate, small, fast, insectoid. Samuel didn't bother replacing the empty magazine in his rifle, but, when the first of the horde reached the bridge, his prescient awareness knew exactly what to do next.

'Everybody,' he shouted, 'get to the island! Glogelder – blow the bridge!'

Glogelder didn't need to be told twice. As soon as the group joined Hillem on the floating island, the big Aelf turned, aimed the launcher low, and fired a spell sphere.

Whatever magic had made the bridge feel unnaturally rigid disappeared as the sphere smashed halfway along its length and released its fiery spell. Wood shattered and burned, flaming rope snapped, and the two halves of the bridge fell away from each other. Against Samuel's hopes, the scuttling automatons didn't fall into the yawning chasm that suddenly opened between them and their prey; they clung to their side of the bridge that hung limp from the mainland of Sunflower. They clambered up, fleeing the flames and smoke that chased them.

Regrouping on the mainland, the swarm scuttled away, scrambling over the dead bodies of burning police officers and supervisor Marca, back into the house from which they had appeared.

'What was *that*?' Samuel said angrily.

'The Toymaker,' Glogelder replied. He pulled down his hood, revealing his scarred face. 'I told you – you don't see him coming. You only meet his *toys*.'

'And right now he'll be thinking of a way to get to us again,' said Namji. She also pulled down her hood. 'We have to leave.'

The group approached the transformed Hillem, who had stepped away from the frozen bodies on the floor and now stood before the open doors of the cargo container. As Samuel slapped a fresh magazine into his rifle, Hillem holstered his pistol at his hip, quickly embraced Namji, and received a slap on the arm from Glogelder.

'Is she all right?' Hillem asked, nodding at Clara's limp form slung over Van Bam's shoulder.

'She's fine, Hillem,' Namji said. 'Now, please tell me everything's set.

Hillem nodded. 'We're all clear.' He gazed across at the mainland and exhaled heavily. 'For now.'

'Good.' Namji turned to Samuel and Van Bam. 'It's important you keep quiet in there,' she said, jabbing a thumb at the open cargo container. 'Officials can be paid to ask no questions, but if anyone suspects we're transporting humans, no one's going to let us pass. And we need to get through a few checkpoints. It should only take a couple of hours to reach our first stop.'

'Which is where?' Samuel said, sliding his rifle into the holster on his back.

Namji shook her head. 'Hillem's going to travel with you. He'll fill you in. Glogelder, you're with me.' She stood to one side and gestured to the empty container. 'Let's move.'

Van Bam was the first to enter, carrying Clara into the container and laying her gently on the floor. Samuel followed, Hillem at his side.

Namji stood in the doorway with Glogelder standing behind her, towering over her. 'We'll see you on the other side,' she said.

As the two Aelfir made to close the container doors, Van Bam stopped them.

'Wait. The avatar has given you the benefit of peculiar insights that were not shared with us. Did it tell you the reason why the Genii have returned? What they are planning?'

Namji was taken aback by this. 'You … You don't know?'

'Do you think I would ask if I did?' Van Bam sounded angry with her.

Namji shared a glance first with Hillem and then with Glogelder before replying guardedly, 'Isn't it obvious?'

Her voice sounded small and frail. Samuel understood Namji harboured terrible news, and she didn't want to be the one to break it.

'We haven't had time to breathe, let alone think,' Samuel said from between clenched teeth, anxiety boiling in his gut. 'The first warning we got was when Fabian Moor started taking Labrys Town apart. I haven't got much patience left. Just answer the bloody question.'

Namji hesitated.

'Tell them,' Glogelder said. 'They have to know eventually.'

Hillem gave a nod of agreement and averted his gaze.

Namji moistened her lips, and her voice was filled with regret. 'The Genii are planning to take what they've always wanted. The Houses of the Aelfir. But they can't do it on their own. They want to find Oldest Place. They came back to free Spiral.'

THE WAY OF THE BLIND MAZE

From the outside, the mighty citadel of Mirage was hidden from the naked eye, shrouded by a powerful spell of concealment. But within its walls, there were such sights to see.

The bazaars of Mirage were a hive of colourful activity, dusty and stifling, bustling with Aelfir. Pairs of armed militia patrolled every street and narrow alley; the air was filled with the buzzing of voices and the rich scent of spices. Van Bam watched the bustle around him, enjoying the atmosphere as he read the dishonest body language of traders haggling over prices for their wares with customers who knew better than to believe the promises of bargains. There was an everyday sort of urgency about life in Mirage, and the Aelfir seemed too busy to show much interest – or surprise – in the human walking among them.

'What about this one?' Namji said.

The young Aelf was standing at a jewellery stall. She wore a simple, light gown of white cotton, with a loose hood of the same material protecting her head from the sun. Her large green eyes stared shyly out from the hood as she held a pendant up to her throat. She had selected the piece from many items displayed on the stall. The wooden pendant, on a simple leather thong, was decorated with an intricate blue design.

Van Bam stepped back and pretended to consider the pendant's suitability.

Earlier, after entering the citadel, Ambassador Ebril, his daughter, and his entourage, had quickly dispersed, eager to see their families and homes for the first time in two years. Van Bam and Angel had been led by armed guard through the streets of Mirage to the High Governor's house. This grand and serious building, looking much like a small fort situated somewhere at the centre of the citadel, had thick and high walls, and was manned by armed sentries. Van Bam and Angel saw nothing of the plazas and gardens they had been told lay within the walls; they had been escorted directly to a plush guest apartment at the top of a tower accessed by a spiralling staircase. They had passed no one on the way, and Angel had speculated to Van Bam that they were being kept out of sight because the presence of the Relic Guild in this time of war was an embarrassment to High Governor Obanai.

'Well?' Namji said, jiggling the pendant. She obviously had no interest in purchasing the item and was fishing for a compliment.

Van Bam played along. 'I think it suits you perfectly.'

With a pleased smile, Namji placed the pendant back onto the stall. 'Maybe later,' she said to the craggy old vendor, and then, linking her arm in Van Bam's, began leading him through the marketplace.

Van Bam and Angel had scarcely been given time to settle in the guest apartment before Namji had come calling. The young Aelf had said it would be a while before the Relic Guild were officially welcomed by the High Governor, but in the meantime it was customary to show visitors around the bazaars of Mirage. It was an invitation made to Van Bam alone, with Namji taking subtle measures to make it quite clear that it did not extend to Angel.

Namji was young, but she was clever. Back in the Labyrinth, Marney had warned Van Bam that Ebril's daughter was a devious customer; that she had secrets, and was not to be trusted. This private sojourn through the streets of Mirage was the perfect time for the illusionist to try to detect what it was Namji was hiding.

'Forgive me, Van Bam,' Namji said, and she giggled girlishly. 'But compared with the rationing that the war has imposed upon Labrys Town, it must seem now as though the choices of all the Houses have been laid before you.'

There was truth to that, Van Bam conceded.

The stalls of the market traders lined both sides of the street, and voices were raised in argument and laughter, banter and barter. The textile merchants sold cuts of cloth as multi-coloured as the robes worn by prospective customers; butchers sold joints of dried and salted meats, while confectioners offered fruits and sugared nuts and all variety of other delicacies. Spirits and liqueurs were displayed in bottles of every shape and size and colour; wines and ales in dark wood caskets.

Trinkets and jewellery, spices and herbs, perfumes and ointments – yes, compared to Labrys Town, it did indeed seem as though the citizens of Mirage had the choices of all the Aelfirian Houses before them.

'You haven't been to Mirage before, have you?' Namji said.

'I have not,' Van Bam admitted. 'Though Angel has.'

'But what do *you* think, Van Bam? Do we make a good first impression?'

'Mirage is a beautiful House,' Van Bam said, choosing his words and tone carefully. 'I only wish my visit coincided with a happier time.'

Namji ensured her green eyes and shy smile were partially covered by the folds of her hood. 'Me too.'

Ambassador Ebril had clearly trained his daughter well in the art of deception, and the illusionist would have to work hard to decipher this girl who would be so obvious in her affection for him.

Arm in arm, they walked in silence until the street opened into a sizeable plaza devoid of market stalls. There were sentries, though, and many of them; each carried a rifle. Unlike the militia that patrolled the streets of Mirage, these sentries didn't group together, or speak, and they stood to attention with unfaltering concentration.

Portals – the sentries were guarding the portals of Mirage. There were four of them, placed at seemingly random positions around the plaza, but Van Bam knew there had once been others. Their absence felt as obvious to him as missing teeth in a mouth. The absent portals had been removed because they had led to Aelfirian Houses that had sided with Spiral in the war. Those that remained led to Houses that had fought for the Timewatcher.

House Mirage had abstained from fighting in the war, though it retained its loyalty to the Timewatcher. Van Bam supposed that Mirage was shielded from the conflict by the Houses on the other side of the portals in the plaza. One of them led to Ghost Mist Veldt, another led to the Burrows of Underneath: two vast realms, embroiled in huge campaigns, the armies of both sides numbering in the millions. But of the last two portals, one led to the farms and plantations of Green Sky Forest, while the other led to the laboratories and weapons forges of the Floating Stones of Up and Down.

Mirage's part in the war was to act as a supply line, keeping the

Timewatcher's troops fed and stocked up with ammunition. If this House were ever to fall under the Genii's control, it would give Spiral a new line of attack on four very important realms.

Under the watchful eyes of the sentries, Van Bam and Namji skirted the plaza and joined another street where the market stalls began again, and the crowds of Aelfir were thicker than ever.

'Tell me,' Van Bam said as Namji studied the wares on a cloth merchant's stall. 'Why is it that you are not with your family at this time, celebrating your homecoming?'

Namji shrugged as she waved away the attentions of the stall's vendor – an Aelfirian boy younger than her – and ran her hand through a display of silk headscarves hanging from the stall's awning. 'Being part of such a ... *political* family, I'm well used to coming second place to duty.'

'But you must be keen to see your mother, your siblings?'

'I'm an only child, Van Bam. I am especially keen to see my mother again, as I'm sure she is to see me.' Her tone was affectionate. 'I have truly missed her. However, as my ... *father's wife*, my mother is highly involved with affairs of state.'

'Ah,' said Van Bam. 'Then your parents are currently meeting with High Governor Obanai? Your father is being debriefed, as it were?'

Namji gave a coy little look from beneath the hood, and said, 'Yes ... *as it were*,' before returning her attention to the scarves.

Van Bam recognised the provocation in Namji's manner. Those odd pauses in her speech, those fleeting moments of almost amused silence followed by carefully selected words – they were designed to entice Van Bam. She was trying to lead him into asking questions that she could answer with more flirting and evasion. Namji was playing some game, angling for his attention, and it was beginning to irritate the illusionist. He decided to challenge her playful provocation with a touch of discord.

'I am surprised that no one seems interested in your testament, Namji. Is it because of your age, do you think?'

'Excuse me?'

'You spent as much time exiled to the Labyrinth as your father. I am wondering why your account of that time is not considered important.'

Namji stiffened, not from offence but with consideration. 'I'm sure I will be heard in time,' she replied, seeming a little more uncertain than before.

'Yes, perhaps you are right,' Van Bam said consolingly. 'It would seem only prudent to question every member of your father's entourage. After all, this is a terribly worrying time for you and your family. Embarrassing, one might add.'

Namji turned from the scarves with a frown. 'Oh?'

'Ursa,' Van Bam said, studying her face. 'He was part of Mirage's official delegation, your father's trusted records keeper, or so I understand.' He dropped his voice to a whisper only Namji could hear. 'That he harboured loyalties to Spiral and the Genii raises certain ... *suspicions*.'

A little of Namji's charm drained away. The light and easy expression on her face became tinged with worry. The change only lasted a second, but long enough for the illusionist to detect.

'Van Bam,' she said, her voice carrying a tone of wisdom that belied her youth. 'Ursa's actions may raise the direst of suspicions, but, as your Resident has already told you, he did not speak for the rest of us trapped in the Labyrinth with him. And, let me assure you, he did *not* arrange a Genii's passage into Labrys Town on behalf of House Mirage.'

Her body language, her tone of voice, the micro-expressions on her face, they carried absolute sincerity. Yet there was something this girl was hiding.

Namji smiled effortlessly. 'I think you'll find the High Governor as keen to clear his House's name as much as ...'

She broke off as something caught her eye. 'Master Buyaal!' she called excitedly.

Namji grabbed Van Bam's hand and dragged him across the street to a stall that bore the strangest of wares.

Three large and bulbous glass tanks were lined up on the stall, each one half filled with copper-coloured sand. Standing behind the tanks was the vendor, an Aelf around the same age as Van Bam. His head was shaved, his triangular face tattooed with black swirls and symbols; his skin was weathered and his smile easy. His brown eyes narrowed as Namji came before him excitedly.

'Forgive me, young madam,' he said, in an educated voice. 'You seem to know me, but …' He peered closer at the face in the hood. 'Have we met?'

'No, but I remember you very well,' Namji said with a grin. 'Van Bam, let me introduce Buyaal, Master of the Desert. His Spectacular became quite famous in Mirage shortly before I left for the Labyrinth.'

'Ah, a good reputation is everything in my game,' Buyaal said with a bow. His gaze switched to Van Bam, and without hesitation he added, 'It has been a long time since I last laid eyes on a human. Please, allow me to welcome you to Mirage.'

'The pleasure is mine,' Van Bam said, considering it strange that Buyaal had apparently no interest in finding out why a human was visiting his House at this time.

Now here was a man with secrets.

'I can tell you are confused by the wares on my stall,' Buyaal continued, motioning to his tanks.

Van Bam smiled. 'I must confess I am curious as to what you are actually selling.'

With a flourish of his hand and a charming wink that made Namji giggle, Buyaal said, 'What you see before you are the performers in Master Buyaal's Desert Spectacular!'

Van Bam pulled a dubious face. Small air holes had been cut around the top of the glass tanks, but he could see nothing inside which might need to breathe. 'Your performers appear to be absent.'

'Allow me to demonstrate, my friend.'

Dipping out of sight for a moment, Buyaal produced a leather sack from under the stall. He thrust his hand inside and pulled out a grey-skinned lizard around the size of his thumb with a jagged black line running down its back. It wriggled as Buyaal held it by the tail and dropped it into the centre tank through an air hole.

To Van Bam's surprise, the lizard stopped falling halfway down to the sand, gently bobbing as if on thin air. He peered closer to the glass, and only then did he see the intricate lines of web filling the tank, thin as hair, clear as glass but obviously strong.

He jerked back as a puff of sand erupted and a creature jumped up onto the intricate web. A strange merging of scorpion and spider, the creature was bigger than Van Bam's hand. With a pale, sun-bleached body, eight thick and armoured legs, the thing stared at the struggling lizard with the black beads of its many eyes. A long tail arched back over its body, clear venom dripping from the sting at its tip.

Namji gave a little squeal as the creature darted across the web, quick as lightning, and pounced on its prey. The lizard didn't stand a chance. The scorpion-spider stabbed its body with the sting, and all struggle ceased. Without hesitation, the scorpion-spider climbed down to the sand with the lizard impaled upon the sting like a trophy held high for all to see, then descended into whatever feeding nest it had made for itself.

Namji shivered. 'It's called a coppion,' she explained. 'They are found in the desert of Mirage. One sting can be fatal.' She shivered again.

'And it takes nerves of steel to train them as I do,' Buyaal added boastfully.

'I can imagine,' said Van Bam. 'But what is it you have trained these *coppions* to do, Master Buyaal?'

'Tricks and wonders your eyes will not believe!' was the exuberant proclamation.

'Truly?'

'Ah, I see you are having trouble trusting Buyaal's word.' He grinned at Namji. 'Perhaps your friend needs to see my Spectacular for himself?'

'Oh yes, that would be wonderful,' Namji said, and she clapped her hands. 'You still give performances?'

'Well,' Buyaal leant across his stall in a conspiratorial manner, 'the war has been hard on my business, but the desert wind tells me there will be a new performance very soon.' He winked for Namji, and then smiled for Van Bam, motioning once more to the bulbous tanks where his deadly troupe hid. 'As for now, these fine fellows have unfortunately reached retirement age. They are tame and make loyal pets, my friend. It grieves me to part with them, but needs must and they are for sale. Can I interest you in a purchase?'

Van Bam chuckled. 'Another time, perhaps.'

'You are sure? I can remove the stings and poison glands if you wish—'

Buyaal froze as he spotted soldiers pushing through the crowd in the street towards his stall. In front was the captain of the guard who had earlier led Van Bam and Angel into the citadel. His face was flustered, his expression intolerant. Behind him, a group of six armed guards drew to a halt. Buyaal bowed his head and stepped back from his stall as the captain approached.

'Mistress Namji,' the captain said. 'Your father has asked me to remind you that you were told to remain in your chambers.' Although his large eyes stayed on Namji, his voice was directed at Van Bam too. 'You are not supposed to be walking around the city at this time.'

Van Bam turned his frown to the young Aelf.

'I understand, Captain,' Namji said primly. 'Please tell my father that I shall return with our guest shortly.'

Despite the fact that he had just participated unwillingly in a minor affront to the Ambassador of an Aelfirian House, Van Bam had to stifle a smile. Namji was trying to make the captain feel uncomfortable rather than showing any real intent to defy her father further.

The captain turned his authority to Van Bam. 'You and your fellow delegate of the Nightshade are to attend a banquet this evening as honoured guests,' he said in a stony voice. 'I must insist that you return to the High Governor's house to await summons.'

'Of course,' Van Bam said respectfully.

'How splendid,' Namji said dryly, 'A banquet to celebrate the home-coming of us poor exiles.' She sighed. 'Very well, Captain, you may lead the way. And thank you, Van Bam, for such a pleasant afternoon.'

'My pleasure,' Van Bam replied, which clearly pleased Namji. She raised a hand in farewell as the captain and three of his guard led her away.

Van Bam watched after her, realising that Ebril must be well-respected indeed if the captain of the High Governor's guard was willing to tolerate such taunting from an Ambassador's daughter.

As the three remaining armed guards began to escort him back to the High Governor's House, Van Bam spared a last glance at Master Buyaal's stall. The Aelf himself had disappeared, but within the glass tanks, each of the coppions had emerged from the sand. They hung on their webs, their stings held above their bodies, poised to strike.

Wake up!

Denton's voice cut through the darkness like a spear of sunlight slashing across a starless sky.

Put up your defences, the old empath added urgently, anxiously. *Make them as strong as you can.*

Instinctively Marney obeyed, closing down her every emotion, protecting them behind a shield of apathy.

She became aware that her body was being jostled; she felt the pressure of blood in her head. The scents of mud, sweat and spent thaumaturgy filled her nostrils. Orders were barked. Somebody screamed. Intense emotions – fear and panic – tapped at her protective shield with a finger of hopelessness.

At a dull boom, Marney's eyes snapped open. She looked down onto the back of someone's legs, someone who was carrying her over their shoulder, wearing heavy black boots and running through thick mud. She lifted her head to see Denton struggling to keep pace with whoever carried his protégée. He clutched Marney's rucksack in his hand. Beneath the brim of his rumpled hat, the old empath's face was deeply anxious.

Stay on your guard, Marney. Don't let your magic slip. With that warning also came a giant cracking sound, and Denton's concerned face turned sharply to his right.

Marney looked to see what had attracted his attention, what was making such a nerve-shredding din. Not too far away was the edge of a great city. Many of the outer buildings were badly damaged and smoking; but one, a mighty tower, was in the process of collapsing. With a shower of stone and fire, the tower crumbled to the ground. Before a cloud of smoke obscured her view, Marney tried to convince her dulled mind that she had not witnessed many figures failing to escape the screaming avalanche of debris.

Another boom jerked Marney's gaze in the other direction, and she saw pandemonium.

Huge guns with barrels as long and round as lampposts shot missiles into the air, streaking the grey sky with tails of magical light as they sped towards the spires and high-rises of a second smoking city. Before the huge guns, a makeshift defensive wall had been built from hard-packed dirt and stones. Aelfirian soldiers in green uniforms lined up along the wall, firing weapons of all shapes and sizes. The air was filled with the flashes of thaumaturgy, the din of chaos, and the stench of war.

'This way,' said the one carrying Marney. It was a man's voice, raised against the tumult.

Marney was carried down a crude set of stairs cut into the earth and into an empty underground bunker. Descending a second flight of stairs brought the group to a damp and cold room where the roar of violence became blessedly muffled. Marney was dumped into a rickety wooden chair beside the door, and she gained her first look at the Aelf over whose shoulder she had been slung.

He seemed little older than Marney herself. His hair was shaved close to the scalp and his grubby face bore some scars.

'How do you feel?' he asked, his large Aelfirian eyes searching for signs of concussion.

'I'm all right.' Marney blinked the grogginess from her head. She looked from the Aelf to Denton who stood beside him. 'What happened?'

'Bad timing, Marney,' Denton replied, shrugging off his backpack and placing it beside his protégée's on the floor. 'This is Lieutenant Morren. He and his soldiers saved our lives.'

'A stray missile exploded near the portal just as you came through it,' Morren said grimly.

'The blast knocked us all off our feet,' Denton added. 'But you took the worst of it.'

'After that, we were lucky we weren't shot by snipers.' Morren managed a smile for Marney. 'Welcome to the Union of Twins.'

'Lieutenant!' a man's voice interrupted, low and commanding.

Morren snapped to attention. 'Yes, sir.'

'A word, please.'

As Morren left and Denton stepped to one side, Marney gained her first proper look at the room.

It seemed to be a command centre. As in the observation chamber in the Nightshade, the back half of the room was filled with spectral imagery of the outside world. The war being fought at this House played out in eerie silence. Two soldiers lay on reclining chairs, their heads and faces concealed within the black glass bowls of receptor helmets. Marney reasoned the Aelfir of the Union of Twins were using devices similar to the eyes on the streets of Labrys Town.

The Aelf who had summoned Morren stood straight-backed and stiff as he surveyed the silent imagery. Without looking at the empaths, he addressed the lieutenant.

'I assume these are our *visitors*?'

'Yes, sir.' Morren turned to Denton and Marney. 'This is Captain Eddine. Sir, these are—'

'Save the introductions, Lieutenant,' Eddine growled. 'It hardly matters who they are.' He turned his large, grey eyes on the empaths, his expression carved from stone. 'I've enough on my hands already without having to escort a couple of humans safely through this battle.'

'I understand, Captain,' said Denton.

'Do you?'

Denton cleared his throat. 'I appreciate our presence might be most inconvenient, Captain, but let me assure you that we are keen to journey on and be out of your hair. We only need to reach the portal to—'

'Ghost Mist Veldt, yes I know,' Eddine interrupted, thus revealing to Marney the next destination on this unlikely journey to find the Library of Glass and Mirrors. 'I'm afraid what you *need* is easier said than done,' Eddine added, and turned again to the silent imagery of war.

Hazily, Marney seemed to recall that Denton had once told her that Ghost Mist Veldt had a portal that led directly to Mirage, the House to which Van Bam had been sent.

'Show me the enemy position,' Eddine ordered the watchers.

As the image of the battlefield slid to a new viewpoint, Lieutenant Morren stepped away from his captain, indicating furtively that the empaths remain patient and silent. He moved to a small stove in the corner of the room, and poured two tin mugs of coffee from the pot warming there. Marney's hands shook as she accepted a mug. The coffee was bitter, unsweetened, but its heat and strength was a welcome breeze that blew away the last clouds in her mind.

'As you've no doubt guessed,' Morren whispered, 'our fight against Spiral's army is a little relentless.'

The imagery that flowed through the control room zoomed up to display the defensive wall of hard-packed dirt and stone, then over the heads of the soldiers, and finally gave a view of the enemy Eddine's troops were fighting.

The combatants were separated by a wide and wild river, the torrid current frothing the water to a dirty brown. On the far bank was another makeshift defensive wall. All along it, power stones flashed on enemy rifles; from behind them, mighty guns pumped missiles into the air. Yet the distant rumble of concussions was the only sound that reached the command room.

On both sides of the river were the remnants of a demolished bridge that must at one time have been wider than any street in Labrys Town. Now, only the first few metres of either end remained on the banks.

The cities are the twins, Denton said in Marney's mind. *Technically, they're two separate Houses – sworn enemies, at one time. But they made peace and joined together when the Timewatcher created the Labyrinth. That broken bridge was once the only way across the river. It stood as a symbol of unification. But now the Twins are divided again.*

Marney nodded her understanding. *Spiral's army controls one city, the Timewatcher's the other.*

Exactly, Denton replied. *Let's be thankful that we arrived on the right side of the river.*

Although the tone of Denton's voice was calm and exhibited none of his earlier anxiety, his emotions were shielded and his true feelings were hidden from Marney.

Captain Eddine told his watchers to pull back from the enemy position, and to show him his own defences.

The view shifted, slipped along the wall until it reached an area where a high section of the makeshift defences filled a gap between two grassy hillocks. Before it, one of the huge guns had been wheeled into position. Its lamppost-sized barrel was pointed at the enemy. It was an ornately designed weapon, looking almost like an antique; its metal body was fat and inlaid with curving symbols, with a glowing power stone as large as an eye device set into its side. An Aelfirian soldier sat behind the gun's controls, pulling levers and turning wheels, adjusting the height and aim of the long barrel.

On the ground beside the gun was a pallet upon which missiles had been stacked into a pyramid. In the middle of each bullet-shaped missile was glass casing, within which the light of magic glowed and swirled. Just as two more soldiers lifted a missile between them and began loading it into the gun, Captain Eddine gave a sudden growl and addressed his watchers with some urgency.

'Tell those gunners to move position—'

He didn't get the chance to finish the order as an enemy missile cleared the defences and smashed into the pyramid of ammunition.

The explosion blinded Marney. She turned her face from the fierce glare, yelping, dropping her coffee, struggling to keep control of her emotions. She felt Denton's empathy helping her to remain calm. His hand squeezed her shoulder.

When Marney looked back, she was surprised to see that the explosion hadn't devastated the area, but had created a dome of magic like a perverse snow globe containing a firestorm. The magical energy swirled within the dome, pale pink and blistering, raging with the force of a tempest. Silent and fierce, it burned for only a short while, but again Marney had to avert her eyes from the glare. When the storm of magic had subsided, Marney saw that it had reduced the gun to a shapeless mound of molten metal, and had left behind not one trace of the three Aelfirian soldiers.

'Damn it!' Captain Eddine shouted.

The shockwave from the explosion had demolished the section of defensive wall that ran between the two hillocks.

Eddine wheeled around. 'Find an engineering crew and fix that breach,' he barked at Morren. 'Take a squadron of reserves to guard the work. Go! Now, Lieutenant!'

'Wait, sir,' Morren answered. He pointed at the imagery. 'It's Lord Habriel ...'

On the battlefield, a tall, broad man walked into view. He wore purple robes; his back was turned to the spectators in the command centre. The breeze fluttered his unruly black hair.

'Of course it's Habriel,' Eddine said, unimpressed. 'Who else could contain a blast like that?'

'You ... you have a Thaumaturgist fighting for you?' Denton asked. His emotions were closed down, and his voice was barely above a whisper.

Eddine grunted. 'Yes – for all the good he does us.'

Marney could tell the captain believed Denton would be impressed that the Union of Twins had a Thaumaturgist fighting for its army, but he was mistaken. The old empath's emotions might have been locked down and hidden, but Marney easily sensed the anxiety that accompanied his question.

Lord Habriel stared fixedly at the breach in the defensive wall. All the while there was tense silence in the control room. Marney allowed enough of the atmosphere to invade her apathetic shield to register sadness diluting hope within Morren; but within Eddine there was cold misery, hard as ice, and utter acceptance that his life had long ago passed the point of despair.

Unable to stand the silence anymore, Marney rose to her feet. She shared a quick look with Denton, and then gestured to the Thaumaturgist out on the battlefield. 'What's he doing?' she asked the Aelfirian soldiers.

'Waiting,' Eddine stated humourlessly.

Morren was more forthcoming. 'Lord Habriel bolstered the defensive wall with thaumaturgy. Nothing living can cross it. However, the enemy occasionally damages the wall enough to create a gap. Habriel is waiting for what will be sent to take advantage of it.' He looked at the empaths with scared eyes. 'We might have a Thaumaturgist on our side, but the enemy has a Genii.'

As he said this, and as Marney blocked a pulse of fear threatening to invade her emotions, the breach in the defensive wall was assaulted by a strange darkness.

It appeared at first as though a flock of blackbirds had descended from the sky. Fluttering, hopping, they landed and perched, filling the gap. As if waiting for the battle to offer them carrion to fill their hunger, they did not venture beyond the wall. Only on closer scrutiny did Marney realise they weren't birds at all. Without true shape or form, thin enough to be almost two-dimensional, they were more like the shards of a broken shadow. Whatever dire purpose these things had been created for, it was evident that Morren and Eddine had seen them before; Marney could sense their fearful recognition. This was Genii magic.

'Come on,' Eddine urged in a hoarse whisper. '*Do* something!'

The Thaumaturgist Lord Habriel took two steps towards the breach, and the flock of shadow shards shifted, fluttered almost. He splayed his fingers and pointed them at the ground; his skin began glowing with a pale radiance. The air around him wavered as though trapping him within a bubble of something liquid. On the far side of the river, enemy riflemen were trying to take advantage of the situation; they fired through the gap in the wall, but their bullets melted upon hitting the wavering barrier surrounding the Thaumaturgist, sending molten metal splashing and hissing to the muddy ground.

The flock of shadows shifted again, and then sped from the breach to attack the Thaumaturgist. Lord Habriel released the thaumaturgy he had summoned.

The fluid bubble expanded like a shockwave. When it met the broken shadows, the Thaumaturgist's spell altered the Genii magic, and the shards immediately changed. Each shadow glowed with dazzling pearlescent colours; and then, as a single flock, they launched into the air and flew back across the river, speeding back towards their creator as a host of shooting stars.

Lord Habriel gestured at the defensive wall. The air within the breach distorted and churned into swirling energy that sucked up debris from the area like a vortex. When the energy receded, it left behind a new section of solid wall made from all manner of materials.

Morren released a relieved breath. Captain Eddine, still tense, stared at the image of the Thaumaturgist. Marney looked to Denton, and the old empath motioned for silence.

Out on the battlefield, Lord Habriel stiffened as though he sensed he was being watched. He turned and stared directly into the command centre, allowing Marney her first look at his face. She resisted the urge to step back.

She hadn't expected this creature of higher magic to be as young-looking. His face was smooth, his features were sharply defined, without a single line of age or wrinkle of worry. On his forehead, the tattoo of a black diamond stood out on his skin. The expression on Lord Habriel's face was one of curiosity. He stepped forwards.

'Oh shit,' Denton muttered to Marney. 'This isn't good.' He allowed his protégée to feel his fear, and his voice entered her mind. *Whatever happens, keep your mouth shut, your thoughts to yourself, and let me do the talking.*

Habriel kept advancing until it seemed he must surely move out of view. But the projected imagery fizzed with a burst of static, and then the Thaumaturgist slipped from the image of the battlefield into the control room.

Bowing his head, Morren backed away until he was practically hiding behind Marney. Eddine held his ground, though he seemed unwilling to look directly at the creature of higher magic. Denton began crushing his hat in his hands, encouraging Marney to bolster the barrier of apathy around her emotions.

Lord Habriel scoured the room with bright green eyes flecked with copper, paying particular attention to Marney and Denton.

'Captain Eddine,' he said after a while, his voice a slice of tranquillity. 'Would you mind explaining why there are two humans in your control room?'

'I ... I ...' Eddine took a breath. 'I received a message sphere this morning,' he said deferentially. 'I was told these humans would be visiting the Union of Twins, and—'

'Who, Captain?' Habriel interrupted gently. 'Who sent you a message sphere?'

'I don't know. It was sent anonymously.'

'And this didn't strike you as strange?' A light smile quirked the Thaumaturgist's lips. 'You didn't think to inform me?'

'No, my lord, I—'

'Have you at least discovered the reason for their visit, Captain?'

'I haven't had time to ask them anything!' Eddine snapped. His face reddened, but still his eyes were averted. 'And I didn't question the message in that bloody sphere because it came with the mark of the Thaumaturgists,' he added angrily.

Habriel paused. 'Have I offended you?' he said lightly, but he glared until Eddine mumbled an apology for his outburst. 'That's better, Captain.'

Marney had been warned in the past that Thaumaturgists could be arrogant, capricious, hostile. The way Habriel carried himself was poised between benevolence and intolerance, but never far from dangerous. He seemed pleased with having intimidated Eddine into an apology.

'Perhaps I can offer you an explanation, my lord,' Denton ventured, his voice smaller than Marney had ever heard it before.

The old empath stepped forwards, holding out the sigil wallet for the Thaumaturgist. Habriel stared at the wallet for a moment, then finally took it, flipped it open, and touched a finger to the plate of strange metal inside.

A further moment passed, and then the Thaumaturgist raised an eyebrow.

'The Treasured Lady,' Habriel said to himself, and flipped the wallet closed. First looking at Denton, and then at Marney, he added, 'Captain Eddine, I would like you to leave the room.'

'My lord?' Eddine replied with a touch of confusion.

'I wish to be alone with the humans,' Habriel replied. 'Please leave. Take Lieutenant Morren and your watchers with you.'

The imagery of the war fought above the command room blinked out, leaving behind the dull, metallic substance that coated the back wall. The two watchers sat up on their reclining chairs, but they did not remove their receptor helmets.

'As you wish, my lord,' Eddine said grimly. 'Everybody, with me.'

As the four Aelfir obeyed the Thaumaturgist's order, Eddine spared an angry glance for Marney and Denton. Morren's expression was more sympathetic, perhaps apologetic. Once they were alone, Habriel handed the sigil wallet back to Denton. Marney felt scared, and she projected her mental voice to her mentor.

Denton, I—

Quiet! Denton snapped back. *I told you to say nothing!*

Habriel was staring at Marney, not quite amused, but definitely not indifferent.

The old man is quite wise to say this, the Thaumaturgist's tranquil voice said in her mind. *I can easily read your magic, young empath.*

'But I'll hear your secrets only if I choose to,' Habriel said aloud. He took a thoughtful breath. 'So, you are magickers of the Relic Guild, humans of Labrys Town, and you are operating covertly on the orders of Lady Amilee. Where, I wonder, should we begin this discussion?'

With his hands clasped before him, Habriel began pacing. He wasn't pleased.

'Perhaps I should start by reminding you of why we Thaumaturgists wear this diamond symbol upon our foreheads. For us, the diamond represents *possibility*. We ink it into our skin in such a conspicuous place because it is also a symbol of the promise we make to serve the Timewatcher – that we will show Her nothing but unquestioning faith and love. It's a mark of loyalty. *Trust*.'

'My lord,' said Denton, but Habriel cut him off.

'You will speak when I wish you to.' The Thaumaturgist looked up at the ceiling. 'Now, the Genii broke the promises they made to the Timewatcher. They burned the diamond symbol from their skin with acid, and now wear their scars with pride, in open defiance of our Mother. But as you can see –' Habriel tapped a finger against the tattoo on his forehead '– *my* promise, *my* faith and love for the Timewatcher, remains very much intact.'

Marney could sense no emotions coming from the Thaumaturgist, but he was obviously offended. Denton remained pensive, with his emotions closed.

'Lady Amilee,' Habriel continued with a musing air. 'There is now no creature of higher magic whom the Timewatcher trusts more. Yet, it troubles me that the Skywatcher would confide in human magickers, inform the Aelfir of your movements, but not trust *me* – her brother Thaumaturgist – with the details of her plans.'

'Indeed, my lord,' Denton said quietly.

Habriel considered Denton. 'At least you're smart enough to show respect. Now please tell me why this House interests Lady Amilee. What is it in the Union of Twins that she wants?'

'Nothing, my lord.'

'*Nothing*,' Habriel repeated in a dangerous whisper.

Still crushing his hat, Denton looked at his feet. Marney did the same. Only then did she realise just how secret this mission to find the Library of Glass and Mirrors was. Could it be that Lady Amilee had informed no other Thaumaturgist of her plans? Did Lord Habriel know that Fabian Moor was loose in Labrys Town?

'I'm waiting for an explanation,' Habriel said primly.

'We …' Denton stopped crushing his hat, and his hands dropped to his sides in a defeated gesture. 'We are only passing through the Union of Twins. We need to reach the portal that leads to Ghost Mist Veldt.'

'I find this strange,' Habriel said after a moment's consideration. 'If your goal is to reach another Aelfirian House, why circumnavigate through the Union of Twins at all? There is, after all, a doorway to Ghost Mist Veldt in the Great Labyrinth, is there not? Why didn't Lady Amilee send you directly to your true destination?'

'Ghost Mist Veldt isn't our true destination,' Denton replied.

'I am not fond of my questions being answered with evasion, old empath,' Habriel said warningly, and then he shrugged. 'Nonetheless, the same logic applies. Why aren't you taking the direct route?'

Denton cleared his throat. 'With respect, my lord, as a creature of higher magic, you can surely fathom a reason for our *circumnavigation*?'

'*Ah*! Then perhaps I can.' Habriel looked directly at Marney, and he seemed to know that she didn't have the faintest clue as to what Denton was talking about. It amused him. 'Now, old empath, you will tell me where, ultimately, Lady Amilee *is* sending you.'

'Forgive me, my lord, but I cannot.'

Habriel's amused expression became mixed with pity. 'I have heard that you magickers of the Relic Guild are courageous and loyal, but to defy a Thaumaturgist to his face? That is brave of you indeed. Or perhaps stupid.'

Denton didn't quite look at Habriel's face, and raised his hands in a show of helplessness. 'Please, Lord Habriel – Lady Amilee was quite clear with her instructions.'

'Was she now?'

'And I would not betray the trust of a Thaumaturgist who, as you rightly say, is so *highly esteemed* in the eyes of the Timewatcher *Herself*.'

All sign of amusement and pity dropped from the Thaumaturgist's face, and he drew himself up.

Marney couldn't quite believe that her mentor had just made a thinly veiled threat to a creature of higher magic. It felt to her as if the thaumaturgy held within Lord Habriel's body filled the room, pressing against her, holding her ready for a blow.

'My *friends*,' Habriel said almost in a hiss. 'If Lady Amilee has need to keep her secrets, then I must trust her reasoning. But do not think for a moment that I will tolerate your impudence simply because you carry out the behest of a Skywatcher.'

He turned away from the empaths and stepped towards the metallic wall. 'Rather inconveniently, all the portals in the Union of Twins stand on the open ground between the city and the river. The enemy's snipers watch them night and day. It is doubtful that you would reach your destination before being killed.' He faced the magickers with a supercilious expression. 'I suppose I could help you reach the portal to Ghost Mist Veldt, but if Lady Amilee is certain that you must not include me in her plans, it is perhaps best if I do not get involved at all.'

'Please, I beg you, my lord,' Denton said, his head bowed again. 'Whatever slight you feel at Lady Amilee's methods, the mission we are on is important to the war—'

Denton was interrupted as the wailing of a siren filtered down into the underground command room from above. As the Thaumaturgist looked up at the ceiling, listening, Lieutenant Morren rushed into the room.

'Forgive the intrusion, Lord Habriel,' Morren said quickly, a little out of breath, his young face creased with panic. 'It's the Genii, my lord. She's attacking.'

Without a hint of concern on his smooth and unblemished face, Habriel raised an eyebrow at the empaths. 'Perhaps circumstance will favour you.'

He turned to the back wall again and flicked a finger at its dull metal coating. Instantly the images of war filled the control room. Soldiers were running in all directions, and gunners were hastily adjusting the aims of their mighty guns.

'Lieutenant Morren,' the Thaumaturgist said, walking forwards, 'while the soldiers are distracted, please escort our human guests to Ghost Mist Veldt.'

Morren frowned. 'Umm ... yes, my lord.'

But Habriel had already stepped into the imagery, using his thaumaturgy to cross the divide between the control room and the world outside. Once again he stood amidst the chaos of war.

In a foul mood, Samuel made his way through the south side of Labrys Town, heading into a two-square-mile landscape of storage warehouses. It was around midday, he was sure, but he didn't really care. All he knew was that the glare of the sun, high and bright in the clear blue sky, felt like a hammer pounding nails into his temples and eyes. By the time Samuel reached his destination, he was beginning to suspect there would never be an end to this savage hangover.

Ironically, if Gene had still been alive, the elderly apothecary could have eased Samuel's self-induced suffering.

He stood before the plain white shutter door of an abandoned ore warehouse. First ensuring there were no denizens around to witness his presence, Samuel stepped forwards. He shuddered as he passed through the perception spell that had been cast upon the building. It was a curious magical charm, designed to convince most denizens to forget that the warehouse was there. Getting past the spell, Samuel laid a hand upon the shutter door. The magical locking mechanisms recognised the touch of a magicker, and the door rose with a series of metallic clangs as sharp as bullets firing straight into Samuel's brain.

Macy and Bryant turned to look at Samuel as he entered and closed the shutter behind him. Bryant pulled a face that suggested Samuel was something he had trodden in; Macy wore a half-amused but fully knowing smile. Hamir had no interest whatsoever in who had arrived. The necromancer clutched a leather-bound book to his chest, his attention absorbed by the man he was holding prisoner.

Fabian Moor was staring at Samuel. The Genii sat cross-legged on the warehouse floor, upon the symbols Hamir had carved into the stone – strange shapes and swirls from the language of the Thaumaturgists, configured into a rough circle. The symbols glowed with a low purple light, radiating the power that sapped Moor of his higher magic and kept him incarcerated within the circle. The prison was obviously working, as Samuel's prescient awareness detected no danger whatsoever from the Genii.

Moor's eyes lingered on Samuel, full of indifference. His skin was as pale as an albino's, smooth and unblemished, except for the patch of scarring on his forehead that had once been the tattoo of a black diamond.

Samuel met Moor's gaze evenly. 'Has he said anything yet?'

'No,' Hamir answered. 'We are waiting for our Resident before I begin the interrogation,' and he began leafing through the leather-bound book.

Moor blinked – once – and turned his stare to the necromancer.

'But I have heard an interesting story,' Macy said as she walked over to a small table on which two carafes sat. 'There was a drunken idiot in one of the taverns down Green Glass Row last night,' she continued as she filled a cup with water. 'Apparently, he was trying to fight anyone within punching distance.'

'Funny, I heard that same thing,' added Bryant. 'Whoever he was, he was very upset about the death of his friend. He started ranting at any denizen who would listen about –' he looked to Macy '– what was it again? Something to do with magickers?'

'Yep.' Macy carried the cup of water over to Samuel. 'According to witnesses, none of us know how fortunate we are to have the Relic Guild protecting us.'

'Oh, yeah – that's right.' Bryant shook his head. 'I suppose it's lucky for everyone that this lunatic decided to leave his guns at home.'

He gave Samuel a hard stare.

'Here, drink this,' Macy said, offering Samuel the cup. 'You look like shit.'

Samuel looked at the clear water, but didn't take it.

'We're all grieving for Gene, Samuel,' Bryant said. 'But most of us have the good sense to remember our duties too. You're lucky you didn't get locked up. Or shot.'

Silently, Samuel took the cup from Macy.

The memory of the previous night was a little blurred to him now, but Samuel remembered the anger and the shouting, though he couldn't recall returning to his hideout. Or exactly how much he had drunk. He hadn't meant to let the situation get out of control.

Nobody had ever really got to know Gene – he'd kept himself to himself. Samuel had known him better than most, though, certainly better than Macy and Bryant. Samuel had only been a boy when he first joined the Relic Guild; and Gene, as much as Denton, had taken the youngster under his wing, looked out for him. Samuel remembered working as a shop boy at Gene's little apothecary store in the western district, sweeping up and running errands. It had been the first time he had ever known a sense of family.

He met the gazes of the twins and sighed. He wanted to explain to them that he was trying to get over Gene's death; that he thought getting drunk might banish from his mind the memory of the old and harmless apothecary succumbing to the ravages of the Genii virus. But the sound of Gene's desperate and pleading voice kept on rattling round and round in his head. Samuel didn't know how to explain the grief he was experiencing.

Keeping his silence, Samuel lifted the cup to his lips and drained it of water.

'Better?' asked Macy.

Samuel nodded and offered back the empty cup.

Macy didn't take it and snorted. 'I'm not your bloody housemaid,' she said before moving off to leave Samuel feeling foolish.

Bryant sneered at him. 'Really? You set fire to that homeless shelter?'

Macy barked a derogatory laugh. 'Gideon isn't too pleased about that, Samuel.'

Bryant shook his head. 'You burned the whole place down, you arse.'

'Give it a rest,' Samuel grumbled, walking over to the table.

As he drank a second cup of water, Samuel noticed that next to the carafes was a small wooden rack holding a few phials of blood. His stomach flipped. The blood was to feed Fabian Moor, the only source of food the Genii required now. Samuel didn't want to know who had donated the contents of the phials.

In the corner of the warehouse, the automaton spider that had captured Moor lay on its back, legs curled, seemingly dead – its purpose served. The sentient metal that the spider had been created from, along with the leather-bound book that Hamir was reading, had been gifts from Lady Amilee, parts of a secret art that only Hamir could understand. These secret arts had made Moor's capture possible, but they weren't to be used to execute him, as logic might dictate. Lady Amilee wanted the Genii questioned.

Fabian Moor was Spiral's most trusted general. He had been heavily embroiled in the plots and plans of the Genii Lord, and there was undoubtedly much he knew that could benefit the war effort.

'I wonder if he's ever seen the Timewatcher,' Bryant said to no one in particular. He only seemed to realise he had spoken aloud when he noticed his fellow agents looking at him. 'I mean – Moor was a Thaumaturgist once,' he added quickly. 'They all get to see Her, don't they?'

Hamir considered Bryant's question, tugging at the tuft of beard that sprouted from the point of his chin. 'Not all of them,' he said after a moment.

Samuel and the twins waited for him to reveal more, but he simply returned to reading the book.

'Well, thanks for that, Hamir,' said Bryant, rolling his eyes.

The necromancer acted as though no one had spoken, content to ignore all present. Bryant shrugged at his sister, and Macy chuckled. They were all well used to the strange ways of the Resident's aide.

Hamir had always struck Samuel as a contradiction. He might be small and elderly, but his magic was probably more powerful than anyone's in the warehouse – excepting that of Fabian Moor, of course. He was always smartly dressed in a three piece suit and tie, his shoulder-length iron grey hair was swept back from a face that held placid green eyes and a calm expression. He carried himself with an amiable manner, yet he was capable of such terrible, destructive things. His tone of voice remained gentle and welcoming even when he issued cutting comments. It was impossible to fathom what he was thinking or feeling.

Hamir was an oddity, a mystery, and he had served as aide to the Residents of the Nightshade for longer than anyone knew.

Fabian Moor was watching Samuel stare at Hamir. The slightest of smirks had turned the corner of the Genii's mouth. Samuel once again heard Gene's pleas in his mind, and he wished he could put a bullet through Moor's head.

'Shall I tell you what I *am* curious about?' Hamir said, looking up from the book. 'What the Genii was doing at the homeless shelter.' He looked at Samuel. 'Of course, if it hadn't been gutted by fire, I could've investigated the building for myself.'

'Well it was, so you can't,' Samuel replied levelly. 'What's your point, Hamir?'

Hamir blinked, and then addressed the twins. 'Tell me again – what did you see at the shelter? You mentioned shadows?'

Bryant answered. 'It was like he was controlling them.'

'Moor was summoning them, Hamir,' said Macy. 'Those shadows had been fractured, shattered, and they moved towards him like a massive swarm of insects. But they didn't attack us. They didn't try to stop us.'

By this point the Genii had averted his cold gaze from Samuel.

'In fact,' Samuel added, 'I'd say the shadows moved out of our way, and Moor didn't seem interested in doing anything other than harvesting them.'

'And then he stored the swarm in the device he had created,' Hamir said, nodding.

The necromancer stepped away from the incarcerated Genii, placed the book down on the table, and moved to the far wall of the warehouse, where a large rectangular hole was cut into the floor. Using a small control panel on the wall, Hamir raised the elevator platform from the cellar. With a whirring hum, the platform arrived from the lower level and *clicked* into place. Sitting on the platform, contained inside a clear glass box, was the head-sized sphere that Fabian Moor had been using when the Relic Guild had found him. A light purple smoke of protective magic drifted within the box.

Still surrounded by that metal mesh holding the fingernail-sized power stones, the sphere remained full of the murky liquid. When Samuel had first laid eyes on the device, it had seemed powerful, important. But now the Genii's toy appeared inert and useless.

Sitting calm and cross-legged upon the glowing symbols on the floor, Moor gave the device a cursory glance, before resuming watching Samuel with utter dispassion in his eyes.

Samuel's skin itched.

'Have you deactivated it, Hamir?' Bryant said, nodding at the sphere in the glass box. 'Is it harmless now?'

Hamir gave him a withering look. 'To render a device harmless, Bryant, one must first understand what function it was designed to perform.' He shrugged. 'At present I have no idea what this thing is.'

'Maybe we interrupted Moor before he finished making it,' Samuel said.

'It is possible,' Hamir replied.

Moor looked away again, irritation flittering across his otherwise expressionless face, perhaps confirming the suspicion.

Samuel gave a bitter smile. 'It's probably as useless as it looks.'

'Impossible to say for sure.' Hamir considered the device for a long moment. 'I can tell you that the mesh holding the power stones had been infused with thaumaturgy, though the metal itself is just ordinary lead, easy to come by. The glass sphere, however, is a little more specialised. It is Aelfirian, imbued with magic – similar to the glass we use for spell spheres – and not at all easy to come by in Labrys Town at present.'

'Moor must've got it from a magic-user,' Bryant said.

Macy agreed. 'But which one? Most of the magic-users went to ground when the war started.'

'That's exactly what I want you to find out,' said a new voice, hard and spiteful.

Samuel wheeled around to look at the observation eye fixed to the wall behind him. It had activated, and the milky liquid inside the glass hemisphere was roiling. Slowly, the ghostly image of a man materialised from the eye, projected into the warehouse from the Nightshade. His greying hair short but unkempt, he wore a dark green roll-neck jumper.

The skin of his hands was decorated by old scars. Gideon's drawn face and sunken eyes expressed his usual state of borderline anger, and he glared at Samuel.

'Please tell me this penchant for arson is a new hobby and not a career move,' the Resident said caustically, his voice slightly distorted. 'I dread to think what I would do if I lost another of my agents this soon after Gene.'

The twins tensed, and Samuel clenched his teeth.

'Show some respect, Gideon.'

'Why, would that help our situation, Samuel?' Gideon pursed his lips in mock consideration. 'Perhaps you would like to build a shrine to Gene upon the ruins of that homeless shelter you destroyed so wantonly?'

'Perhaps I would,' Samuel growled, trying to swallow his anger before it turned to white hot fury. 'Maybe you should help me. You might learn what compassion feels like.'

'Is that right?' Gideon's expression became dangerous. 'Gene isn't the first magicker to die in service to the Relic Guild, and he won't be the last. If you ever act like this again, Samuel, I'll have the police shoot you on sight. Do you understand me, you idiot?'

Macy interjected before Samuel could unleash a blistering retort. It was not the first time she had headed off a confrontation between the Resident and her fellow agent.

'Has there been any word from Angel and Van Bam?' she asked.

Gideon faced Macy, his teeth bared in an expression somewhere between a grin and a threat. 'No,' he said. 'Not yet.'

'Then what about Denton and Marney?' Bryant said. 'I haven't seen them since ...' He screwed his face up. 'When *was* the last time I saw Denton and Marney?'

Macy shrugged, and Samuel's anger dissipated as he tried to answer the question for himself. Denton should've been in the warehouse. His wisdom would be invaluable when dealing with the Genii. But the last time Samuel had laid eyes on the empaths had been at the Nightshade the day before yesterday.

'Denton and his *pupil* are busy,' Gideon said.

'Why?' Samuel demanded. 'What are they doing?'

Gideon turned sunken eyes to Samuel. 'If you were supposed to know the details, don't you think your Resident would have already told you, Samuel?'

Samuel looked away as his anger threatened to rise again.

'Now, enough about your fellow agents,' Gideon stated. His image fizzed. 'Let's deal with the matter at hand.'

The Resident gazed upon Fabian Moor sitting in his thaumaturgic prison. The Genii was looking back at him with a curious expression.

'So this is Fabian Moor,' Gideon said, his tone unimpressed. 'Has he still not volunteered any information, Hamir?'

'He has refused all invitations of discourse.'

'*Invitations,*' Gideon said with a sneer.

The necromancer stared at the Resident. 'I suspect politeness will mean as little to a creature of higher magic as demands and threats, Gideon. *Talking* to this Genii was always going to prove fruitless, yes?'

'Then I assume that book will help to make him more cooperative?'

'Naturally.' Hamir walked to the table and took the leather-bound book into his arms again. 'Lady Amilee's methods of interrogation are quite clear, and she has left a little room for me to add a few of my own modifications.'

'Excellent,' Gideon said, and he gave Moor a cruel smile. 'Are you listening, Genii? Talk is pointless, the necromancer says. Do you understand what that means?'

For his part, Moor appeared utterly unconcerned. Macy and Bryant looked uncertain, edgy at hearing the casual threats Gideon was aiming at a creature of higher magic. As for Samuel, he was not affronted by the prospect of Hamir torturing Moor for information.

'Now, Hamir,' said Gideon, 'What do you suggest we do about the Genii's little toy?'

The glass sphere apparently remained inactive inside its container upon the elevator platform.

'Until I can fathom what it is for, I rather think I'm stuck with it,' Hamir said. 'It certainly wouldn't be wise to store this device at the Nightshade.'

The Resident thought for a moment. 'You say the sphere is magical glass? Aelfirian?' Hamir nodded, and Gideon added, 'And there is no way Moor could have brought it with him when he arrived in Labrys Town?'

Hamir shook his head. 'Upon reanimation, he would have been as naked as the day he was born.'

Gideon looked at Macy and Bryant. 'I think you're right. We know Moor has been dealing with denizens from the underworld, and one of them must have provided him with Aelfirian glass. I want you two to talk to your contacts. See if you can find out who gave it to Moor.' He jabbed a thumb at Samuel. 'And you might as well take the arsonist with you.'

Macy shot Samuel a warning look, and he bit his tongue.

Gideon turned his malicious regard back to Fabian Moor. 'Hamir, you know which questions to ask this bastard, don't you?'

'Indeed.'

'Then short of killing him, indulge yourself. You all have your orders.'

And with that, the image of Gideon blinked out, and the eye on the warehouse wall deactivated.

In the following silence, the three agents looked at each other, then at Fabian Moor in his prison of glowing thaumaturgic symbols. The Genii was staring at Hamir. It seemed that all were wondering what the necromancer was planning to do with the secret arts hiding in the pages of the leather-bound book. But Hamir, phlegmatic as always, gave nothing away and raised an eyebrow at the magickers of the Relic Guild.

'Please close the door on your way out,' he said.

Van Bam and Angel didn't have to wait long to discover what secrets Namji was keeping.

In the banquet hall in the High Governor's house, a string quartet of beautiful Aelfirian women played lilting music. Van Bam sat cross-legged upon thick cushions at the end of the head table, Ambassador Ebril beside him. Next to the Ambassador sat Mirage's ruler himself,

High Governor Obanai – a stern and serious-looking Aelf – and next to Obanai was his equally serious-looking wife, Governess Vael. Positioned at the other end of the table was Angel, and between the healer and Governess Vael sat Namji.

Angel looked along the table, past the line of Aelfir, and discreetly rolled her eyes at Van Bam.

Namji was not Ambassador Ebril's daughter. The secret that she had been keeping – that everyone around her had been keeping – was that she had been born to a far nobler family. Namji was High Governor Obanai's only child and heir, destined to be known one day as High Governess Namji, the ruler of House Mirage.

'The deceit was necessary,' Ebril had explained to Van Bam earlier. 'It was for Namji's safety.'

And to better prepare her for her birthright, he had added. Posing as Ebril's daughter would allow Namji to experience the grittier side of inter-House relationships undistorted by the privileges and niceties usually bestowed upon the nobility. Van Bam fully understood, agreed, that this ploy would give Namji understanding of a more truthful – perhaps harsher – side of the political life she would one day come to inherit. But the illusionist had also pointed out that, when the war began, the Nightshade should've been made aware that one of its refugees was the future ruler of an Aelfirian House. Namji would have been afforded better protection; possibly a return to her own House might have been arranged much earlier than the two years she'd had to wait. But Ebril had shaken his head at these words.

'On the rare occasions that I received any message from Mirage, I was instructed to maintain the pretence,' Ebril had said with an apologetic air. 'The High Governor and his wife decided that Labrys Town, protected by the Timewatcher as it is, was the best place to shield their daughter from the war.'

To Van Bam, Ebril seemed to be making excuses for his High Governor: a diplomatic answer given by a master diplomat.

Now, sitting near the end of the table, wedged between her mother and Angel, the young Namji had not only lost her secret but also her flirtatious air; she was refusing to make eye contact with Van Bam. Was it merely the official nature of the banquet that made her appear miserable? Her mother, Governess Vael, seemed equally unhappy. Looking much like an older copy of her daughter, she sat with a rigid back, kept all conversation to a minimum, and showed no interest in anyone around her. The reunion between mother and daughter did not appear to be a joyous one.

As for High Governor Obanai, Van Bam suspected he was utterly humourless. He had watched the string quartet showing neither pleasure nor displeasure on his gaunt Aelfirian features. Tall and lean, with a beard neater and less grey than Ebril's, Obanai seemed a little younger than his ambassador. He wore white robes and headscarves inlaid with golden thread. His large eyes were brown and calculating. Thus far, he had addressed the Relic Guild agents directly only once, and that was to offer vague thanks for returning his daughter and ambassador to his House.

Van Bam noticed Angel try and fail again to make conversation with Namji and her mother. Catching Van Bam's eye she gave him a slight shrug. Van Bam returned the gesture. He was beginning to feel the magickers were being kept apart on purpose. With a frown, he surveyed the banquet hall.

Beneath glow spheres that hung from golden chains, the tables had been laid out in a rough semicircle, leaving a clear area of floor in which the musicians played. Around fifty guests attended the banquet, enjoying generous offerings: platters of seasoned meats and herb breads, fruits, nuts and vegetables, jugs filled with wine and ale and water – more food and drink than this gathering could consume at a single banquet.

Around the hall, hanging on the wall spaces between ornate sandstone pillars, tapestries depicted moments from House Mirage's history. And in front of the tapestries, guards stood with rifles hanging from their shoulders, watching the guests.

The Aelfir of Mirage were hard for Van Bam to read. Considering this gathering was to celebrate Ebril and Namji's homecoming, the atmosphere was oddly subdued. There was a low hum of chatter beneath the lilting string music, but the way most of the guests went about their meals with polite conversation, wearing obviously fake smiles, avoiding eye contact with each other, made the illusionist wonder if this room was filled with people who didn't much like each other.

Van Bam glanced quickly at the three armed guards standing behind the High Governor's table, and then at the Aelfir with whom he sat at the table. Just when he decided that this was going to be a long night, he saw Governess Vael break her silence and engage Angel in conversation. And then, as the string quartet finished their piece, acknowledging light applause before beginning a new tune, High Governor Obanai also decided to speak.

'Gentlemen,' he began. His voice was low but perfectly pitched for the ears of the Relic Guild agent and the ambassador. 'Having been informed of Ursa's conduct, and the unfortunate events which led to his demise, I think we can all agree this is a troubling time.'

'Yes, High Governor,' Ebril replied formally. He looked at Van Bam. 'The very idea that a citizen of from Mirage would align with the Genii, and bring the wrath of the Timewatcher upon our House, is as terrifying as it is abhorrent to us.'

Perhaps especially for the ambassador, Van Bam reasoned. Ursa had, after all, been a member of Ebril's entourage.

'High Governor,' the illusionist said, 'The Relic Guild's mission is not to accuse Mirage, but to discover if Ursa was working alone or for someone else in your House.'

'Ah …' Although Obanai still didn't look at Van Bam, a smile had quirked his small lips. 'You search for a rat hiding in this nest of snakes that you see enjoying my food while concealing their disdain behind fake smiles.'

Van Bam looked over the guests. 'Perhaps.'

Obanai scoffed. 'My family has ruled this House for eleven generations, and we have occasionally had to fight to maintain our position. Every single person here belongs to a respected family that would gladly try to supplant me if I turned my back for even a moment. But would any of them betray the Timewatcher to attain the governorship of Mirage?'

His tone of voice was unconvinced, and Van Bam saw doubt creep into his body language. 'I honestly can't decide if your list of suspects is long or short, Master Van Bam.'

'High Governor,' Van Bam said. 'Ambassador Ebril told me that before the war exiled him to the Labyrinth a delicate situation had emerged in Mirage. A conflict that was kept in-House?'

'You were told correctly,' Obanai stated, but offered nothing else.

Ebril cleared his throat and leant into Van Bam. 'Such conflicts are not unusual, but neither are they considered polite dinner conversation.' He gestured meaningfully at the banquet guests.

'Forgive me, gentlemen,' Van Bam said, keeping his voice low, but with a hint of steel. 'I was given no details of Mirage's problems, but it was implied they were directly connected to Ursa and the Genii who is loose in Labrys Town. Therefore, I'm sure you'll agree, the nature of our investigation demands a touch of *urgency*, yes?'

Ebril chuckled politely, almost embarrassed. 'Van Bam—'

'It's all right, Ebril,' said Obanai. 'I've nothing to hide anymore.' He would not look at Van Bam as he spoke. 'But first, I would like to know about this Genii that Ursa brought to Labrys Town – this Fabian Moor. What precautions have been taken to prevent him seizing control of the Nightshade and conquering the Labyrinth?'

'I am afraid that I am forbidden to reveal specific details, High Governor,' Van Bam replied. 'Needless to say, the Relic Guild has taken the matter into hand.'

'Magickers against a Genii?' Obanai said dubiously. 'No, no, no – I suspect Lady Amilee, or another Thaumaturgist, has better prepared the Relic Guild for this occasion?'

It appeared the High Governor was seeking comfort. For a member of his House to have loyalties to Spiral was one thing; to be responsible for the traitor who might ignite events that led to the downfall of the Labyrinth was entirely another. Obanai wanted – *needed* – to know that Ursa's mess was being cleared away.

'As I said,' Van Bam assured him, 'the matter is in hand, High Governor, and – yes – the Relic Guild has been well prepared for dealing with Fabian Moor. Perhaps now you might tell me about this conflict your ambassador spoke of?'

'Of course.' Obanai nodded, his eyes scanning his guests. 'It came to a head before the war began. I believed back then it had been resolved, but this is not the first time it has come back to haunt me. It is a long story, I'm afraid.' He sighed. 'Ebril, perhaps you would care to explain further.'

'As you wish, High Governor.' Ebril cleared his throat again. 'A few months before the war began, there was a rumour of a lone man roaming the desert. He dwelt in the mountains close to the west of the citadel. The people of Mirage began calling him the Hermit.'

'He lived *outside* the citadel?' Van Bam said, sounding surprised. 'I was led to believe that no one could survive the hostility of your desert.'

'True enough,' said Ebril. 'We tried to communicate with the Hermit on several occasions, but he either disappeared from sight, or simply couldn't be found. It was clear that he was surviving by preternatural means.'

'A magic-user?'

'And one of skill. He became quite a legend. In fact, it was said his power was so great that many began speculating that the Hermit was in actuality the Wanderer.'

'The Wanderer?' Van Bam said in surprise. 'You mean Lord Wolfe, the Thaumaturgist?'

'The very same,' said Ebril. 'Though it proved to be wild rumour, and I suppose to speculate on the Hermit's true identity in this way now seems a little in bad taste. I'm sure you will agree.'

Van Bam nodded. Lord Wolfe, known to the Aelfir as the Wanderer, was a Skywatcher who had been killed by the Genii at a House called the Falls of Dust and Silver. Known as a benevolent Thaumaturgist, his name had become legendary because his murder was Spiral's first strike against the Timewatcher, the act that started the war.

'At first it appeared there was nothing the Hermit wanted,' Ebril continued. 'He was content to *roam*, no more than a charming curiosity of the desert. However, shortly before I undertook a diplomatic trip to Labrys Town and was stranded there by the war, the Hermit revealed his true intent—'

'I do not know where he came from,' Obanai interrupted, with no small degree of bitterness in his voice, 'but there is blood on his hands, Master Van Bam. He tried to steal this House from me.'

Obanai fell silent again, clearly simmering, and Ebril took up the story once more.

'As I said, for the longest time the Hermit was no more than a curiosity. But then he decided to stage a coup. With his magic, he coerced some of Mirage's citizens into taking arms against the High Governor's family. The uprising was short lived, but there were a lot of deaths.'

'My people died in the Hermit's name,' Obanai said lowly. 'If only *he* had died with them.'

'He never set foot in the citadel himself, you see,' Ebril explained. 'He cast his magic from the desert, and allowed his followers to perish. At that time, he had only ever been seen from afar. After the failed uprising, he ... *vanished.*'

The ambassador was thoughtful for a moment. 'As I told you, although I could send no message home from the Labyrinth during my exile, I occasionally received reports from Mirage via the Nightshade. They were ciphered, of course, but a few of them mentioned that the Hermit had been spotted again, lingering in the desert, watching the citadel. And then, after hearing of Ursa's crimes, I suspected that not all of the Hermit's followers had died in the uprising.'

'Misdirection,' Obanai snorted. 'The Hermit used the coup to conceal his real goal. '

Van Bam looked from one Aelf to the other.

'Please understand,' Ebril added quickly. 'Challenges to the ruling family are not uncommon in Mirage. It was easy to suppose that the coup was the Hermit's intent. But Ursa's actions point to a more sinister motivation. The Hermit hid him well, Van Bam. Ursa was the son of minor nobility, a trusted member of my entourage who *never* gave me reason to question his loyalty to Mirage and the Timewatcher.'

'The Hermit must have subjugated him,' Obanai growled. 'He sent Ursa to the Great Labyrinth with a mission to bring Fabian Moor to Labrys Town, I'm sure of it. And I would be very surprised if Ursa was the last of the Hermit's followers hiding among *my* people, waiting for orders.'

'Wait a moment,' said Van Bam, looking puzzled. 'If you believe Ursa was acting under the Hermit's orders, and if the Hermit's magic is as powerful as you say, then it was ... higher magic? The Hermit is a Genii?'

'No,' said Obanai. 'But perhaps no less an abomination.'

Ebril added, 'While I was away, there were a few failed attempts to hunt and kill the Hermit. A few of the militia briefly had him in their sights. They report seeing the strangest of men. Ten feet tall, they said. Skin as pale as the desert moon and covered in the telltale scars of a blood-magicker.'

'A blood-magicker?'

For the first time, High Governor Obanai turned to face the illusionist, his Aelfirian eyes serious. 'They say the Hermit is a Nephilim.'

Obanai and Ebril joined the rest of the guests again offering polite applause to the quartet of musicians, who had finished their final piece and were now taking their bows. Van Bam looked down the table at Angel. The healer was looking back at him, her expression alive with bemusement; perhaps she had learned the same information as Van Bam, from Governess Vael.

The Nephilim. Van Bam knew their reputation well. They were a race of nomadic giants who roamed through the realms of the Aelfir as a single clan, without a House to call their own. Their origins were unknown, but they were feared because they were powerful blood-magickers. Such a race would make a fearsome ally for Spiral and the Genii. But only one?

'Forgive me, gentlemen,' Van Bam said. 'I have heard tales of the Nephilim, but I have never known anyone who has actually seen them. Can the word of your soldiers be trusted on this?'

Ebril shrugged. 'It's true to say that the desert sun can play many tricks on the mind of an Aelf.' He joined the crowd in giving the string quartet a second round of applause, as they carried their instruments to the doors on the far side of the banquet hall and left. 'Who knows for certain what those soldiers saw?'

'Whether he is a Nephilim or not,' the High Governor said, his voice hard, 'I believe the Hermit is still out there, hiding in the desert. And I am quite convinced that he is loyal to Spiral, and that Ursa was his servant, Master Van Bam.'

'Perhaps you are right, High Governor.'

'Be assured that my magic-users protect the citadel from the spells of blood-magic. Our walls are guarded night and day, as are the portals of Mirage. We have done all we can to ensure the Hermit cannot reach those portals and mount an attack on our neighbouring Houses. But you must understand that the real threat could come from within our walls, where the Hermit's followers might hide.'

Obanai sighed and his eyes scoured his guests before returning to Van Bam. 'I beseech you, Master Van Bam – you and your colleague – help me to clear my family's name in the eyes of the Timewatcher. Help *us* to uncover the *truth* of the Hermit before this infernal war reaches my House.'

Perhaps the war is already here, Van Bam thought, but said, 'Of course, High Governor. We all serve the Timewatcher.'

'I am relieved to hear you say it,' Obanai said, and with unexpected effortlessness his manner reverted to that of the serious, taciturn ruler of House Mirage. 'You must conduct your investigations in whatever way you see fit,' he continued. 'You will receive the full cooperation of my people. And Ambassador Ebril will remain as your consultant – won't you, old friend?'

'My duty and my pleasure, High Governor,' Ebril replied.

'Tomorrow morning,' Obanai told Van Bam, 'I will arrange for you to send a report to the Labyrinth. You must, of course, tell the Resident of Labrys Town everything. Withhold nothing.'

Van Bam nodded. 'I appreciate your call for candour, High Governor.'

Obanai surveyed his guests again and sighed. 'But for the rest of this night – please, try to enjoy our hospitality.'

At that moment, a slew of excited whispers buzzed through the banquet guests. The doors to the banquet hall had opened, and a huge glass tank was wheeled through it by a broad figure hidden beneath a heavy hooded cloak. The glass tank stood eight feet tall, and at least five feet wide and deep. Inside, the bottom foot or more had been filled with coppery sand. With the tank positioned at the centre of the floor, surrounded by the tables of excited guests, the cloaked figure stepped forward and bowed to the High Governor and his family.

'Do not be afraid.' It was a man's voice, whispery, mysterious, yet loud enough for all to hear. 'They say there is one who cannot be trusted. They say he is the keeper of the desert's secrets, and only he knows how the desert *lies*!'

The cloaked man flashed out a hand. There was a *crack*, and a burst of light. A few gasps came from the audience as a second man appeared, standing inside the tank upon the sand.

A wry smile cut through Van Bam's thoughts of giants roaming a desert plain as he recognised the man in the tank. It was Master Buyaal, the coppion merchant from the bazaar.

Dressed in only a loincloth, his body tanned and oiled, his facial tattoos glistening in the light, Buyaal turned full circle, glaring enigmatically, theatrically at the audience through the glass. When he came to face the head table once more, he opened his arms wide, his fingers stroking the glass walls either side of him.

The cloaked man addressed the hall again. 'There is danger in what you are about to witness,' his whispery voice said. 'Buyaal, Master of the Desert, requests your silence.'

The guests fell into a hush.

As the cloaked man stood to one side and bowed his hooded head, Van Bam looked along the High Governor's table. Considering that earlier Namji had spoken ebulliently about Buyaal's show, she now appeared vastly uninterested – as did her mother and father. Angel seemed curious enough, but the only person at the table who seemed genuinely delighted by the spectacle was Ambassador Ebril.

Grinning broadly, he leant into Van Bam. '*This* should be good,' he whispered.

The hush endured in the hall. Buyaal closed his eyes and gave a single, piercing whistle.

With dusty eruptions, three coppions jumped from the sand beneath Buyaal's feet and scurried up his body. More gasps came from the audience. One of the hand-sized scorpion-spiders sat upon Buyaal's head, while the other two perched on his shoulders. Their stings were raised above their bodies, but they did not strike their master, and seemed quite tame and content. Buyaal opened his eyes and grinned.

A few of the audience member attempted to begin a round of applause, but the cloaked man's voice sliced through the air. '*Silence.*'

Buyaal dropped his arms to his sides and once again closed his eyes. He paused a moment, allowing expectation to rise, and then issued three short whistles. The coppions began crawling over his body, spinning their webs.

Van Bam sat forward and narrowed his eyes. The creatures moved with preternatural speed, scurrying over their master's form, leaving behind thin lines of glistening thread, wrapping Buyaal in a cocoon. The guests watched, awed and silent.

The coppions moved so fast, extruded so much web, that Van Bam grew suspicious. Discreetly, he took his green glass cane under the low table, flicked it gently with his finger, and whispered to his magic. He searched for a concealing charm, illusionist magic that was fooling the audience. But he detected nothing – no spells, no illusions.

The coppions had become blurs of movement as they spun their webs faster and faster. Buyaal's face, his Aelfirian features calm, his large eyes closed, disappeared beneath a glistening white covering. His legs were bound together, his arms wrapped to his sides. In less than a few minutes, Buyaal was hidden in a shroud of thick web that glittered in the light like frosted glass.

With their work done, the coppions jumped back down to the sand and disappeared into their burrows, leaving Buyaal looking much like an ancient mummified corpse.

A long moment passed. The banquet guests began exchanging looks and whispers. A few nervous chuckles filtered through the hall. Ebril's grin split his beard. The illusionist caught Angel's eye, and she pulled a perplexed face.

The hooded man, who had remained still throughout the performance, now raised his head. The hall gasped as his hand flashed out. Inside the tank, Buyaal's cocooned figure burst into quick fire. The flames made short work of the web, incinerating it entirely in a matter of seconds, to leave behind ... *nothing*. Buyaal, Master of the Desert, had disappeared completely.

A few members of the audience rose to their feet, faces stunned, murmuring in consternation.

The cloaked man threw back his hood, revealing his face. Master Buyaal grinned mischievously for his audience. 'You were warned that I cannot be trusted!'

More guests stood up. The applause was thunderous. Buyaal took his bow.

Like the other members of the High Governor's table, Van Bam remained seated, looking from Buyaal to the empty tank and back again. The illusionist knew that this trick would be impossible for anyone but a magic-user. Yet...

Once again Van Bam tapped his glass cane and whispered to his magic. Once again he detected no spells or illusionism around Buyaal and his show.

Ambassador Ebril, clapping his hands, grinned at Van Bam knowingly. 'If you ever do discover how this trick was done,' he said, 'please be sure to explain it to me.'

When the wail of the siren died away, an eerie hush descended over the battlefield.

Along with Lieutenant Morren, Marney and Denton hid behind a thick metal blast shield. Behind them, smoke as thick as fog obscured the city's edge; before them, the Timewatcher's army manned cannons and lined up along the defensive wall with their rifles. Each soldier was alert, ready, waiting to resume fighting. On the opposite side of the raging river, a column of unnatural darkness had twisted up into the grey sky above Spiral's army. And in the silence, the clouds broke, and heavy rain began falling upon the scorched and battered landscape of the Union of Twins.

'We've been fighting this battle for nearly a year,' Morren told the empaths as he watched the sky. He had explained earlier how the twin city had fallen when the Genii seized control of the portals on the other side of the river. 'But we reached a stalemate after only a few weeks of hostilities. We've been fighting to maintain it ever since.'

'Really?' said Denton, raindrops tapping upon his crumpled hat. 'There's no chance of victory?'

'I wouldn't say that, but it's complicated,' Morren replied. 'What the Genii really want is control of our portals, especially the doorway that leads to the Great Labyrinth. Fortunately, that doorway is on this side of the river, in the city. The enemy won't try to cross the river because they know that if our defeat ever seemed likely, we'd destroy the only way they have to access the Labyrinth before they could land. Instead, they continue trying to bombard us into surrender.'

Morren faced the magickers and gave them a wry smile. 'I like to think we're the guardians of the Labyrinth.'

Marney was once again struck by how young the Aelf was, and she wondered if officer fatalities incurred in the war had fast-tracked him into the position of lieutenant.

'What about the Thaumaturgist?' Marney asked. 'Surely he could turn the battle in your favour?'

Morren shook his head. 'Lord Habriel and the enemy's Genii spend most of their time cancelling each other out. They only really help to preserve the impasse—'

The young Aelfirian officer looked at the sky, as worried voices rose among the soldiers. On the opposite side of the river, a figure had levitated into the air and was hovering before the column of darkness that spiralled towards the sky. Marney's gut tightened. The figure was dressed in a black cassock, with long hair flapping in the wind, and the empath knew that if she got close enough, she would see a scar on the figure's forehead where the tattoo of a black diamond had once been.

'But then again,' Morren added, 'the Thaumaturgist and the Genii sometimes like to go toe-to-toe. Get ready.'

A few orders were barked, echoing across the rain-soaked stillness. All along the defensive wall, soldiers looked up at the Genii floating in the sky. Gunners adjusted the aims of the long cannon barrels. Behind the Genii, the spiralling energy began to thicken and spark.

'When the fighting distracts attention,' Morren said seriously, 'that's when I'll lead you to the portal to Ghost Mist Veldt.'

'You don't have to come with us,' Denton replied. 'Just give us directions, and we'll take it from there.'

'We're very good at concealing ourselves,' Marney added. 'The snipers won't see us.'

'I'm sure that's true, but you still can't do this on your own,' Morren said, looking back at the empaths with a frown. 'The portals are protected by energy barriers.' He showed them a pendant hanging from a chain around his neck: a simple metal rectangle inlaid with a small crystal. 'Only captain Eddine and his officers can use these keys. You can't deactivate the barriers without me.' He looked up, blinking against the rain. 'Here we go.'

A second figure levitated into the air almost directly above Marney. Lord Habriel the Thaumaturgist hovered and faced his enemy, serene and beautiful in the standoff, unconcerned by the weather.

Marney held her breath.

In the sky across the river, the Genii threw her arms forward. Behind her, the column shattered and sped towards the Timewatcher's army.

As it had during the earlier attack on the breach in the defensive wall, the higher magic came as a flock of shadow shards. But this time the flock stretched in a wide arc, multiplying, spreading as it came onwards, until it was surely wide enough to encompass every soldier in the Timewatcher's army.

Marney felt an emotional charge in the air, a wave of loathing that preceded the Genii's magic, stronger than the fear and trepidation of the soldiers standing their ground. The feeling grew fiercer as the flock came, and Marney quelled her panic.

I can feel it too, Marney, Denton's voice said in her mind. *Have courage*.

High above, Lord Habriel waited until the flock of hate-filled shadows began crossing the river, and then he retaliated.

The Thaumaturgist's voice whispered across the battlefield. With quick sighs and fleeting hisses, he chanted in a language beyond Marney's comprehension, but it was filled with such compassion, such affection and hope. Marney shivered as Habriel's voice reached a crescendo and he showed the palms of his hands to the oncoming flock.

All along the defensive wall, soldiers jumped back as the thaumaturgy imbued into the hard-packed dirt and stonework rose up like a curtain of liquid air that folded back to cover the Timewatcher's army in a monumental, shimmering dome, crackling with sparks of higher magic. The flock of shadow shards hit the barrier with sharp pings like bullets rebounding off metal. The Genii's spell began to change. Though several of the shards clung to Habriel's barrier like bats, most were instantly repelled, but all of them began shining with a pearlescent gleam.

Still travelling as a huge flock, the multi-hued shards of light raced back to the enemy's side of the river. The emotion they left in their wake filled Marney with more than mere affection.

'Is that what it is?' Marney wondered aloud. 'The Genii attacks with hate, and Habriel fights back with, what – *love*?'

'I suppose it's along those lines,' Denton replied. 'But I don't think it's quite that simple, Marney.'

'No, it really isn't,' Morren said. 'The Genii's spell is designed to turn the Aelfir against the Timewatcher. That's how she subjugated the people of our twin city.'

Marney remembered the words of the Aelfirian guide back in the Trees of the Many Queen, and her fear of subjugation.

'Lord Habriel is trying to win the enemy back,' Morren continued, 'to remind them that they never *chose* to support Spiral. The trouble is, the magic doesn't always work.'

'Doesn't work?' said Denton. 'I can't say I recall many stories concerning thaumaturgic spells with flaws.'

'Well, you haven't seen what I have.' The lieutenant shivered, and his voice became filled with bitterness. 'Whenever the Genii's magic manages to get through the defences, it has different effects on people. I've seen soldiers turn on their comrades. I've seen friends commit suicide. Some simply die or have their minds wiped. Others aren't affected at all. That spell is unpredictable and dangerous, and the battle between Habriel and the Genii is as pointless as the rest of the fighting in the Union of Twins.'

Across the river, the Genii had raised her own wall of liquid air to protect her troops. When Habriel's magic hit it, the colourful flock reverted to dark shards of a shattered shadow, and then raced back towards the Timewatcher's army, once again radiating hatred.

'I've seen this dance more times than I care to remember,' Morren said sadly. 'It could be hours before the spell dissipates. And after that, no one will see Lord Habriel or the Genii for days.'

'Shouldn't we be moving?' said Denton.

Morren raised a hand. 'Not yet.'

As Habriel once again took the Genii's rage and inverted it to compassion, Marney began to find the whole display of higher magic somehow childish. A new series of orders arose among the troops, and Marney flinched as the Timewatcher's army unleashed their arsenal at the Genii. Almost simultaneously, the enemy fired at Lord Habriel.

The air was filled with the roar of thunder, the lightning of power stones, and streaks of thaumaturgy as deadly projectiles sped towards their targets. But every missile, every bullet stopped before getting close, exploding in the air, rendered useless, the debris falling from the sky with the rain to be lost in the raging river, as ineffectual against higher magic as throwing leaves to break a window.

'It's a waste of ammo, but we can't stop trying,' Morren shouted above the tumult. His face was stern but emoted hopelessness. 'If your magic can hide our movements,' he added, 'now's the time to use it. Let's go.'

As the battle between Thaumaturgist and Genii persisted in stalemate, the futile bombardment continued. Lieutenant Morren led Marney and Denton away from the metal blast shield and across the open ground towards the broken edge of the city, away from the river. Marney summoned her empathic magic, creating a cloak of concealment around her that would hide her presence from any enemy watchers or snipers whose attention wasn't attracted to the aerial display. Denton did the same, and extended his magic to also conceal Morren.

Marney's pack felt heavy as the group travelled as fast as they could. The scorched ground was churned and rain-slicked and thickly muddied, dotted with impact craters. Denton struggled most, gripping Marney's arm as she helped him to keep pace with Lieutenant Morren, trying not to slip over in the mud herself. Marney prayed that no stray missile exploded nearby, or stray bullet hit her in the back.

Smoke from the burning city drifted across the open ground like a light mist. The group made progress in silence, Denton breathing hard. Marney flinched with every boom of a great gun or flash of thaumaturgy. When Morren finally drew them to a halt, he took off the chain around his neck and held the metal pendant in his hand.

'Over there,' he said, pointing to the shape of a portal archway in the smoke. He led the empaths to it.

'As soon as I drop the barrier the portal will activate,' the Aelf said as they got closer. 'Don't hang around. Just leave.' He paused with his thumb hovering over the crystal set into the pendant. 'Whatever it is you're doing, I wish you luck.'

'And the same to you, Lieutenant,' Denton replied.

'Thank you,' said Marney.

With a nod, Morren pressed the crystal. There was a low buzz of energy, and the barrier surrounding the portal revealed itself as a dome of translucent blue that momentarily illuminated the smoke with a ghostly effect before deactivating. When the light disappeared, the glassy portal began to swirl within the archway, and the Aelf ushered the empaths towards it. As soon as they were close enough, Morren reactivated the barrier.

Marney turned to see him with a hand raised in farewell. She just had time to realise that with the magical barrier separating them, the Aelf was no longer concealed by Denton's empathy, before Morren's chest exploded with a spray of blood and bone.

He dropped to his knees and fell face down in the mud. The sniper's bullet had torn a ragged, crimson hole in the back of his uniform's jacket.

Marney was shouting Morren's name as Denton took her by the hand and dragged her into the portal.

The guest apartment in the High Governor's house carried the kind of grandeur that Van Bam usually associated with the western district of Labrys Town. The floor of the spacious lounge area had been laid with tiles of cream and red-veined marble. The sandstone walls were decorated with intricate carvings, many of which were inlaid with coloured glass or precious metals. Glow lamps sat in sconces fixed to four pillars in each corner of the room. They were designed to give the illusion of naked flames when they were activated.

Two bedrooms were adjoined to the lounge area, both large enough to be an apartment in its own right. Each room had a set of thick wicker doors leading to a balcony that overlooked the fountains and foliage of the garden plaza at the centre of the High Governor's house.

Everything about the guest apartment spoke of wealth and taste, including a pull cord of white rope which would summon a servant to attend to the needs of houseguests. Angel had already taken full advantage of the rope to procure herself a large jug of berry wine. She was enjoying her second goblet while lounging on the pillows before a low table at the centre of room. Across from the healer, Van Bam sat deep in thought, his wine untouched.

'So,' said Angel. 'What's your opinion about tonight?'

A cool breeze of desert air blew in from the open balcony doors and stroked his face. The banquet had concluded more than an hour before, and Van Bam was still trying to make sense of things.

'I am undecided,' the illusionist admitted. 'How did he do it, Angel?'

Angel paused with her goblet an inch from her lips. 'Do what?'

Van Bam shook his head again. 'For the life of me, I cannot fathom how he did it without magic.'

'Are you *still* thinking about Buyaal's show?' Angel rolled her eyes and took a sip of wine.

'He has to be a magic-user, Angel, but I detected nothing.'

'So?'

Van Bam frowned at her. 'It does not bother you?'

'Not especially. I just enjoyed it for what it was – a bit of entertainment.'

'You are not in the least bit curious?'

'Look, Van Bam, I once saw a street performer levitate two feet off the ground without the use of magic. To this day, I don't know how he did it. But unlike you, I don't need the answers to everything. I enjoy a little mystery now and then.'

'Well, it bothers me,' Van Bam said moodily. 'How *did* Buyaal do it?'

'I don't know, and I don't care.' Angel sighed, and she sipped her wine again. 'Now, switch that big brain of yours over to the important matters. Tell me what you think of this Hermit story.'

Letting go of the riddle of Buyaal and his performance, Van Bam considered for a moment. 'Well, High Governor Obanai and

Ambassador Ebril are entirely convinced that the Hermit is a servant of Spiral, and that Ursa was working for him.'

'Governess Vael said as much herself,' Angel replied. 'At least they got their stories straight before the banquet,' she added dryly.

'Yes. And if the Hermit is a Nephilim – and that is a big *if*, Angel – then that would make him a dangerous magicker indeed.'

'You've got that right,' Angel agreed. 'But even if you believe every legend about the Nephilim, would he be powerful enough to take on a huge citadel by himself?' She swirled her wine, a dubious expression on her face. 'Either way, if I was an Aelfirian ruler, I'd shit a brick if the Nephilim came to my House.'

'The Hermit's identity is based more on rumour than fact,' Van Bam said. 'Whoever he is, when Ebril suspected that he was helping the Genii and placing Mirage in grave danger, why did he not just report it?'

'Loyalty, probably,' Angel replied. 'And concern for the safety of the citadel. In times like these, any suggestion of supporting Spiral could bring the Timewatcher down upon you.' She shrugged. 'Still, Ebril managed to get himself home, didn't he?' She stared down into her drink. 'I don't like Ebril, Van Bam. What do you think of him?'

Van Bam pursed his lips. 'I find him pleasant enough company, but most Aelfirian politicians are taught to mask what they are really thinking and feeling, nearly always via magical training. The ambassador is virtually impossible to read. High Governor Obanai is much the same.'

'So are his wife and daughter,' Angel replied sourly. 'You know, I never would have guessed that Namji was the bloody heir of Mirage. She's a slippery bitch.'

'You are not the first person to call her that.'

'And Governess Vael is as miserable a cow as you're ever likely to meet.' Angel shook her head, perplexed. 'She's Namji's mother, Van Bam – you'd think she'd at least show a modicum of joy at being reunited with her daughter. But it was like Namji and Vael didn't know each other at all, or didn't care to. The ruling family of Mirage is a little too *guarded* for my taste.'

'I would say this House as whole appears defensive. Considering Mirage has remained neutral in the war, it has a surprisingly large militia presence.'

With a disgruntled noise, Angel drained her goblet and then refilled it. 'And I'll tell you something else, if there *are* more of the Hermit's followers hiding among the citizens, I don't know how we're going to find them – not quickly. There's a hundred thousand Aelfir in Mirage, Van Bam. Could be any of them.'

'Yet, apparently, there is only one Nephilim,' Van Bam replied. 'The story cannot be true, Angel. I have been told that the Nephilim travel as a single clan, always – as a *herd,* I believe they call it.'

'Maybe there are more of them hiding in the desert,' Angel said. 'Maybe we should admit that no one knows anything about the Nephilim at all. What concerns me most, Van Bam, is the doorway to the Labyrinth. It's all alone outside the citadel walls, sitting on the Giant's Hand. It's exposed.' She bit her bottom lip and shook her head. 'Obanai doesn't need the Relic Guild's help. There should be a Thaumaturgist here dealing with this.'

Van Bam agreed. 'Until we can uncover the truth, Lady Amilee should at least close Mirage's doorway to the Labyrinth, as she did in the Houses that sided with Spiral.' He nodded to himself. 'First thing tomorrow, we will make a report and send a message sphere to Gideon.'

'I'd rather just go home,' Angel said miserably. 'I really don't like it here.'

Van Bam watched as the healer rose from the table and took her goblet over to the balcony doors. She stood on the threshold, leaning against the jamb, looking up at the night sky.

'Do you know what's funny, though?' she mused. 'I've never heard of the Nephilim taking anyone's side before. They're reviled, yes – I mean, the Aelfir have always feared them, and rightly so. The Nephilim don't believe in the Timewatcher. They worship something else – the *Progenitor*, is it?'

'Yes. I have heard that name before. A patriarch of some sort.'

'That's the one,' Angel said. 'If this war has taught me anything, it's that if you're not following the Timewatcher, you're either stupid or very unpleasant company. You've heard the stories about the Nephilim – about what happened to the Aelfir who tried to drive the *herd* out of their Houses. Bloodshed and carnage. The Nephilim are savages, Van

Bam, but have you ever heard a story of them fighting in someone else's name? Or trying to conquer a House?'

'No,' the illusionist admitted.

Angel shook her head. 'You're right, Van Bam. The Hermit can't be a Nephilim, can he?'

A hint of uncertainty in Angel's voice gave Van Bam pause for thought.

Nobody really knew where the Nephilim came from, but there was a colourful myth that claimed they were created a thousand years ago, far back enough in time for the Labyrinth to have been new, by a mysterious entity known as the Progenitor. Van Bam knew of no other race that believed in this entity, and had always considered the Progenitor an invention by the Aelfir to distance themselves from as fearful a tribe as the giant blood-magickers. The Nephilim had never been considered a race of the Aelfir. They were more like an anomaly, a clandestine tribe of nomads wandering from House to House, without a realm to call their home. Every story painted the Nephilim in the colours of nightmare, for it was said that cutting themselves was their sole method of expressing the power locked within them; that blood-letting was the only way to release their magic.

But for a thousand years, the Nephilim had never shown any interest in trade with the Aelfir, or in sharing cultures, and seemed perfectly content to abstain from contact with anyone outside their own kind. Of course, there were the many tales of troubles, of blood being shed and Aelfir disappearing – all of which was blamed on the Nephilim. But every story also concerned people who went out of their way to pick a fight with the blood-magickers. Given their usual lack of involvement, based purely upon what was known about their actions and conduct, it would seem that the Nephilim were by and large apathetic towards other races – *if* they were left alone.

But as Angel had said, *next to nothing* was known about them.

Van Bam took his goblet from the table and sipped the wine for the first time. It was sweet and warming as it slid down his throat.

'Angel,' he said contemplatively. 'Gene once told me that one of Gideon's ancestors was likely a Nephilim.'

Still standing at the balcony doors, looking up into the night sky, Angel scoffed. 'It wouldn't surprise me if it was true.'

'I cannot help wondering that if Gideon's sociopathic manner is an indication of what it is to be a blood-magicker, then the Nephilim might be as merciless as the Genii.'

'If only it was just his personality,' Angel replied. She turned in the doorway and gave Van Bam a serious look. 'You didn't know Gideon before he was Resident, when he was just an agent of the Relic Guild. I worked the streets of Labrys Town with him, Van Bam. I've seen what he can do with his magic.'

'Yes,' said Van Bam, 'Gene implied that he could be a little … unpredictable.'

'That's one way to say it.' Angel shivered. 'I once saw Gideon rip the skin off a black marketeer, using no more than a cut on his hand and a dirty look. And I *really* wish I could say that's the worst thing I ever saw him do.' She puffed her cheeks. 'Blood-magickers are rare, thank the Timewatcher. And Gideon is the most dangerous magicker I've ever known.'

'He has always been the same?' Van Bam asked. 'There was never a time when he was more amiable?'

'Not as far as I know,' Angel replied. 'Gideon never really learned to temper his blood-magic, but he certainly knew how to revel in the power it gave him. It was already taking its toll on his mind when I met him. But he got worse over the years. It was like he became addicted to himself. And when he cut his skin, you kept well clear. He was nearly impossible to control, Van Bam. I can't tell you how scared I was when he became Resident. Trust me, you do not want to cross Gideon. Ever. You *or* Marney.'

Van Bam placed his goblet back onto the table. He didn't need skills in reading micro-expressions to understand the implication behind Angel's words.

'Tell me,' Van Bam said. 'Earlier we were talking about how Gideon loathed his agents having anything other than platonic relationships. You said that you had personal experience.'

'It was a long time ago, Van Bam.' Angel walked over from the open doors and sat down on the pillows at the table again. 'Macy and me were an item for a while.'

'You were?'

'Ah, it's well in the past now.' Angel sighed, and she topped up her goblet. 'I suppose we were good together. We were young. We both enjoyed life.' She sipped her wine. 'But when Gideon became Resident, he made it very clear I was to stop seeing Macy.' She chuckled sadly. 'As I said, you don't cross Gideon. It didn't occur to me to argue with him.'

'I am sorry, Angel,' Van Bam said. 'No one ever mentioned it to me.'

Angel shrugged. 'I think the others avoided the subject because they thought it was a sore point, but it wasn't really. It wasn't as if Macy and me would've lasted forever. Neither of us are the settling down type, and Bryant gets a bit jealous, anyway. He never takes kindly to his sister's partners. Pain in the arse, to be honest with you. Likes to play gooseberry, that one.'

Angel paused and tapped the rim of the goblet against lips that had turned into a light smile, as though lost to memories of a better time. She snapped out of it.

'My point is, Van Bam – if you and Marney really love each other – as much as it pains me to say this – you might want to stop your relationship while you're still ahead. Before Gideon decides to settle the matter himself.'

It was the honesty in Angel's face that disturbed Van Bam. She was speaking with the experience of a magicker who had served the Relic Guild for over twice as long as he had. He looked out of the open doors. Did his time with Marney really have to come to an end?

'Anyway,' Angel said, 'in the morning we'll send a message sphere to our terrifying Resident, and wait to hear what he wants us to do about the Hermit and anything else that might be going on in this bloody House. For now, I need to sleep.' She swirled the contents of her goblet. 'This wine really is good stuff.'

Rising, she made her way across the lounge, taking her goblet into the bedroom with her. 'Goodnight, Van Bam.'

'Goodnight, Angel,' the illusionist replied, still staring out onto the balcony.

'Oh, and one more thing,' Angel called out, voice muffled behind the closed bedroom door, 'if you figure out how Buyaal did his trick, please don't ruin it for me.'

A wind this bracing was near impossible to walk against. Howling a song more mournful than any Marney had ever heard, it blew with a graveyard chill that cut to the bone, stinging exposed skin with grit and chips of stone. The wind stole the voice from Marney's mouth as she pulled her travelling cloak tighter around her body and turned her back to it.

What's going on? she thought to Denton, wiping grit from her eyes. *Where is everybody?*

I don't know, Denton replied miserably. He was struggling to hold his hat down on his head. *Let me think!*

The ground sloped upwards with a steady gradient and was covered in scree. Marney suspected that she and her mentor stood upon a mountainside, but she couldn't tell for sure. A fog, as thick and white as billowing clouds, shrouded the area, drifting almost lazily, strangely undisturbed by the bracing wind. And within this contradictory weather system of the House called Ghost Mist Veldt, the empaths were entirely lost. The heavy fog had secreted away the portal that had delivered them there from the Union of Twins.

Shivering within her cloak, Marney focused her energy into locking down her panic and confusion. Only then did she sense a presence in the air that made the hairs on the back of her neck stand on end. It was light and inquisitive, bordering on emotion.

Denton, Marney thought quickly, *I can feel magic!*

Of course you can feel bloody magic! Denton replied testily. *Ghost Mist Veldt is riddled with the stuff.* Still pressing a hand to his hat, the old empath looked out from beneath the brim, searching the fog. *I think this House is protecting itself. Something bad must have happened here.*

Marney quelled a pulse of fear. Had the Genii conquered Ghost Mist Veldt?

Where are the soldiers, Denton? Where's the fighting?

I don't know, Marney. A liaison should've been on this mountain to meet us ... wait!

Marney sensed it too. The magic in the air welled up and pressed against her, making her skin tingle, drying the inside of her mouth. The bitter wind moaned savagely, this time displacing a patch of fog, parting it like curtains to reveal two huge boulders. Jammed between the boulders was a stone hut , windowless and crudely built. Its chimney was crooked and looked about ready to collapse. At its centre, a rough wooden door had been set.

Come on, Denton urged.

Struggling, helping each other along, the empaths hurried as best they could down the tunnel that cut through the fog like a pathway in the Nothing of Far and Deep. As soon as she opened the wooden door, the wind snatched it from Marney's hand, slamming it against the hut wall. Together, she and Denton heaved it closed and latched it securely once they were inside.

Denton slumped against the door; Marney sat down on a rusted metal chair at a rickety metal camping table. They both caught their breaths in silence while the wind whistled through gaps in the stonework.

The hut was larger than it appeared from the outside. Fixed to one wall were two bunked cots, devoid of mattresses or blankets. Another cot had been laid in an alcove on the opposite wall that must have been cut into one of the boulders the hut was built between. The cots, table and chairs were the only items of furniture. The floor was bare stone, hard and rough, and at the far end of the room was a fat, black iron stove with a slim chimney that rose all the way up to the ceiling. On one side of the stove was a box for storing wood or coal, but it was empty.

'How about we try to get that stove working?' Denton suggested. 'Warm this place up a bit, and then we can figure out what in the Timewatcher's name is going on here.'

'Be my guest,' Marney said miserably.

Now that she was sheltered from the harsh weather, Marney found her thoughts lingering on a subject much grimmer than the confusing situation she and her mentor had stumbled into in Ghost Mist Veldt.

Denton frowned at her, sensing that she was now struggling with feelings of anger and remorse.

'You're thinking about Lieutenant Morren, aren't you?' he said sympathetically.

Marney looked at the floor. 'He shouldn't have died,' she whispered. 'Not for us.' If she let it, Marney was sure the image of Morren's chest erupting, the memory of him falling to the ground, his young face slack and dead, would haunt her forever. 'The Thaumaturgist could've helped us, he could've spared Morren instead of acting like a spoilt *child*.'

'Lord Habriel is not responsible for Morren's death,' Denton told her kindly but firmly. 'And we cannot change what has happened.'

Marney looked up at him sharply. 'Is that your advice, Denton – *get over it*? Is that what you're telling yourself?'

'Marney ...' Denton sighed. He moved away from the door and took a chair on the other side of the table. 'Please understand that Morren is not the first Aelf to die protecting the Labyrinth from Spiral and the Genii. And he won't be the last.'

'They're not just fighting for the Labyrinth,' Marney retorted. 'They're fighting for themselves too.'

'Ah, but Morren considered himself a guardian of the Labyrinth – and *that*, Marney, is what I keep telling myself. His death, as much as it saddens me, is the inspiration that makes me more determined than ever to succeed in our mission.'

Marney blinked away tears as Denton reached across the table and patted her hand. He sent her a wave of emotions that at once comforted her and helped to bolster her defences against the grief she felt for an Aelf she barely knew, who had given his life to help the Relic Guild.

As for the mission, Marney had come to realise that she was as much in the dark about the details as Lord Habriel had been.

'What is it you haven't told me, Denton?' she demanded. 'Why hasn't Lady Amilee informed the Thaumaturgists about our mission?'

'I'm not entirely sure, to be honest,' Denton admitted, looking troubled. 'For all I know, Lady Amilee hasn't told the Timewatcher Herself what she is doing. Only we might know.'

'But I *don't* know, do I? Not really.'

'Marney, we have been entrusted to find a very dangerous place—'

'Yes, the Library of Glass and Mirrors is a dangerous place. I get it, Denton. But there's more to this than just going to find information on the Icicle Forest, isn't there?' There was an edge of pleading to Marney's voice now. 'When you were talking with Lord Habriel, he made a really good point, Denton. Why are we traipsing across the Houses? Why didn't Amilee send us directly to the library's portal?'

Denton allowed her a small, conceding smile. 'All right,' he said. 'I don't suppose there's any harm telling you a little more.' He took off his hat and placed it on the table. 'Marney, the Library of Glass and Mirrors is not an Aelfirian House. It has no doorway in the Great Labyrinth. The portal to the library is hidden, and to find it we first have to travel what some would call the *Way of the Blind Maze*.'

There was a hint of amusement in his voice, and Marney narrowed her eyes at him. 'You made that up,' she accused. 'You're making fun of me? At a time like this?'

'No, Marney! That's just the name that *I* like to call it. I don't know if it has a proper title. Let me explain. There are many secret realms hiding between the Houses of the Aelfir, each as near impossible to find as the next. Unless, of course, you happen to have knowledge of a peculiar method of travelling.'

'The Way of the Blind Maze,' Marney said.

Denton's smile became a grin.

Marney sighed. 'I assume Lady Amilee has shown you how to navigate it?'

Denton nodded. 'Think of our journey as the combination to a lock, Marney. First and most importantly, you need to know which hidden realm you wish to find – in this case, the Library of Glass and Mirrors. Then, if you travel through particular Aelfirian Houses in a particular order, using particular portals along the way, the entrance to the secret realm will appear to you at a particular location.'

'That's a lot of particulars.'

'Yes. Exactly.'

Marney sighed. 'I don't suppose you could've told me all this at the beginning.'

'I understand your frustration, Marney – and yes, there might just be more to this mission than discovering information on the Icicle Forest

– but I need you to trust me. The less you know, the less dangerous this is for everyone. I really can't be sure what we'll discover at the Library of Glass and Mirrors.' He ruffled the grey hair on his head. 'But if the worst should happen, everything you need to know about the Way of the Blind Maze is in that envelope I gave you. You still have it, I trust?'

Marney patted the leg pocket on her fatigues. 'Safe and sound.' She gave her mentor an appreciative smile. 'I do trust you, Denton. Completely.'

'Glad to hear it,' Denton replied with a wink. 'And when this is over, Marney, we two will find a quiet moment in which to raise a glass to Lieutenant Morren's memory. I promise you.'

Though saddened, Marney accepted this. Honouring Morren's memory was the only thing she could do for him now.

'Of course,' Denton continued, 'You and I are going nowhere if we can't figure out what's happened on this mountain.'

Putting on his hat, Denton arose and walked to the hut door. He continued talking as he peered through the gaps in the wooden slats, trying to see the world outside.

'The magic of Ghost Mist Veldt is a little like the magic of the Nightshade,' he said. 'It's almost sentient, and will protect its House as it deems necessary. But why it needs to protect itself now, I don't know, Marney. However, I'm hoping the magic will recognise us as friends not foes, and show us a way through that fog.'

'Perhaps it already has recognised friends,' Marney replied. 'Maybe Ghost Mist Veldt is protecting *us*.'

'That's a very good point – hold on …' Denton adjusted his position at the door. 'Yes, I think the fog is clearing. Let's take a look.'

Bracing himself, Denton unlatched the door and opened it. A fierce breeze blew into the stone hut, bringing with it the unmistakable, almost emotional, presence of magic. But before either empath could do or say anything, the pressure of the magic grew oppressively heavy, and thick tendrils of fog surged into the room. Denton yelled as the tendrils wrapped around his body and dragged him outside. The door slammed shut behind him.

Marney jumped to her feet, shouting Denton's name. She heard a gasp from behind her, and wheeled around. Marney only had time to acknowledge that four Aelfirian soldiers had magically appeared in the hut with her, before one of them rammed the butt of a rifle into her face.

CHAPTER TEN

REFLECTIONS

Clara dreamed of a graveyard. But it was no ordinary graveyard.

She found herself on an island cemetery of rough, grey stone that drifted through the endless void of space. The only source of light came from the dim and distant glow of stars filling the darkness in clusters of dot-to-dot configurations that seemed to spell out Clara's name, and tell the story of her life. The graves filled the island as far as she could see, simple mounds of small, heaped rocks, similar in size; but instead of a headstone, each grave was marked with a jagged shard of mirror, like a shattered fragment of some monstrous looking-glass.

Clara might have been in human form wandering among the graves, but she was stalking like a wolf, cautious and painfully alert. She wasn't sure why she was there, but the secrets of her magic, an innate memory locked tight within her blood, told her that this island cemetery was the final resting place of every magicker who had ever lived and died in service to the Relic Guild.

And she wasn't alone.

Every now and then, Clara would catch a glimpse of blurred movement in the looking-glass shards. At first, she had spun around, thinking that the movement came from behind her, expecting to find a lurking presence trying to creep up on her. But when she found nothing, she realised the blurs were passing in front of her own reflection. With closer scrutiny, she came to understand that, in the reflections, she was watching a woman who was fleeing through the graveyard by jumping from mirror-headstone to mirror-headstone.

Although Clara saw little of this woman, she soon realised whom she was watching.

The woman's passing was quick and blurred, but it caused a flickering effect that left behind an image of her, imprinted upon the surface of the mirrors. The effect didn't last long, blazing from the shards then quickly fading – like the after-glare of a lightning strike. But enough detail was imparted for Clara's heightened sense of sight to recognise the empath caught in fast, frozen moments.

At times Marney appeared as an older woman of around sixty, at others a young woman, closer to Clara's age, but her dress never changed. Clad in black leggings, jumper and ankle length boots, the empath wore a leather baldric around her torso like a waistcoat. It held a set of slender and sharp silver throwing daggers. Her long, light brown hair pulled back from a handsome face into a tail, revealed eyes wide and full of fear. In every frozen image that Clara saw, Marney was looking back over her shoulder at the nightmare that hunted her.

Clara caught fleeting glimpses of the pursuing demon in the same flickering lightning that exposed the empath, but the changeling could never quite see it clearly.

Marney was losing the race, only just managing to stay one mirror ahead of her demonic pursuer. Clara understood then that her purpose on this drifting island cemetery was to save Marney – just as the empath had once saved her.

As the stars above told the story of Clara's childhood, she struggled to keep track of the random path Marney took through the mirrors, trying to throw off the demon. But the honed instincts of the wolf prevailed, and Clara managed to keep pace with the empath's flight. Eventually, she was led to a structure that stood unique and conspicuous at the centre of this graveyard of dead Relic Guild agents. It was a grand mausoleum of luminous moonstone, its pallid glow seeming bright against the huge shard of obsidian perched upon its roof.

The shard was black and neatly cut into a perfect diamond. Though highly polished, its surface supported no reflection; instead, the obsidian absorbed any light that hit it from the tale-telling stars above. Marney's image appeared in the diamond, three quick frozen ghosts, brightly silver, descending the length of the black glass, falling down into the moonstone mausoleum beneath. The smoky nightmare was not far behind her.

The heavy stone doors parted for Clara like curtains as she ran into the mausoleum. She found a young version of Marney crouched against the far wall of the chamber inside. The chamber was otherwise empty, made from smooth cream stone that was decorated with tiny square maze patterns, hundreds of them, like a room in the Nightshade. The empath was sobbing, covering her face with her hands, fearful eyes peeking through splayed fingers.

Clara rushed to her, but stopped halfway across the mausoleum floor as Marney spoke.

'Please,' she whimpered. 'Not yet.'

At a strange, high-pitched gurgling noise that sounded almost like shattering glass, Clara wheeled around. Where the mausoleum doors had once been, but now was only a smooth, cream-coloured wall covered in tiny maze patterns, stood Marney's nightmare.

A *thing* that carried a human shape but little humanity, withered and spindly, it was wrapped in strips of black cloth from neck to foot. The nightmare-demon's head was bald, its skin decaying and the colour of death. Its eyelids had been sewn closed with twine; its thin, grey lips were fused around a glass tube, and a second tube sprouted from a crude puncture in one temple. Both the glassy lengths connected to a diamond-shaped box of obsidian in the nightmare's gnarly-fingered hands. Upon the box's black stone, symbols glowed with the purple light of thaumaturgy.

'Tell me!' the nightmare hissed, and its voice came from all places at once.

'No,' Marney pleaded. 'The time isn't right.'

Fluid gurgled along the glass tubes. 'Then I'll make it right.' Its omnipresent voice was full of spite and desire; the thaumaturgic symbols on the box flared.

Marney moaned and hunkered down against the wall as the nightmare stepped forwards menacingly. Clara stepped protectively before the empath and raised her hands – palms out – in a warning gesture. The monster halted, seeming to notice the changeling for the first time. Fluid sang along the tubes like stardust telling stories.

It was only then that Clara realised she could see her face in the backs of her hands. Her skin had changed to the smooth, reflective surface of mirrors.

'Whatever you're thinking of doing,' the nightmare said from every-where, 'don't!'

A quirked smile came to Clara's lips. She turned her back on the monstrosity and strode over to Marney. The empath looked up as the changeling approached. An older woman now, her faced lined with age, but the crow's feet surrounded eyes tinged with hope.

'Here,' Clara said kindly. 'Take my hands.'

Marney didn't hesitate. As soon as she slipped her fingers into Clara's cool, mirrored grasp, her physical form turned into wispy incandescence that was drawn into Clara's hands like inhaled smoke – until she was entirely absorbed into the changeling's body.

Have patience, Marney's voice whispered in her mind. *All things are known in the end.*

In control, feeling strong, ready to battle whatever foe was placed in her way, Clara turned to the nightmare.

But the nightmare had no interest in fighting. It shook its head, apparently disappointed with the changeling, and made an angry noise that was more from frustration than rage. 'Brilliant!' it snapped from all places at once.

To Clara's surprise, the nightmare yanked the diamond-shaped box away from its body, shattering the glass tubes that connected it to its temple and mouth. Throwing the box to the floor, where it landed with a stony thud and the symbols lost their thaumaturgic glow, the monster began ripping the stitches from its eyelids with long, gnarled fingers. It spat out broken glass as it glared at Clara with strangely familiar, mad brown eyes.

'I hope you're satisfied, child.' The nightmare's voice was no longer an omnipresent hiss but a laconic drawl that Clara recognised all too clearly. 'Do you have any idea how close I was?'

Clara cocked her head to one side. 'Gideon?'

'Yes, Clara, and thank you so much for making this exercise a com-plete waste of bloody time.'

All anger deflating within her, Clara looked at her hands. They were no longer mirrors but covered in short silver hair.

'Am ... Am I dreaming of you?' she asked Gideon. 'Or are you dreaming of me?' She turned her gaze to where the empath had been a moment before. 'Maybe Marney was dreaming of both of us?' She rubbed her temples, confused. 'Is this even a dream?'

Gideon angrily spat out a final shard of glass and sent it tinkling across the floor. 'For the love of the Timewatcher, child, order your thoughts before your head caves in!'

The image of the withered ghoul wrapped in strips of black cloth morphed and changed into a tall and thin man as human as Clara. His hair was short, streaked with grey. The olive skin of his gaunt face was shaded with stubble, and his sunken eyes were full of menace. He was wearing black trousers and a roll-neck jumper; his hands were covered in scars. This was how the man remembered in Labrys Town as Gideon the Selfless must have appeared in life.

Clara pointed a silver-haired finger at him. 'You were searching my mind for the information Marney planted there,' she accused.

'As always, you're as sharp as a razor, Clara,' he replied cruelly. 'But actually, I *found* where that information was. Unfortunately, you decided to get in my way before Marney could spill the beans.'

Again, Clara stared at the empty space where Marney had cowered against the wall. 'I-I can't explain what happened,' she said. 'I had to protect her. I *needed* to.'

'It doesn't surprise me,' Gideon said, as though his reasoning was to do with Clara being an idiot. 'You women do like to stick together.'

Ignoring the jibe, Clara marshalled her confusion. 'If you wanted Marney to cooperate, why frighten her as a nightmare with tubes in its face and carrying *that* thing?' She gestured to the box of obsidian still lying on the floor.

A laconic, lopsided grin spread across Gideon's face. 'What, you think Marney would've been less frightened had I appeared to her as myself?' He wagged a finger in the air. 'Yet you have a point, child. I certainly didn't conjure the image of such an ugly creature. It must've been a projection from Marney's memory.' His eyes became shrewd as he looked at the diamond-shaped box. 'An aspect of whatever she planted in your head.'

'What does it mean?' Clara whispered.

Gideon gave her a sour look. 'If you hadn't interfered, I might've found out.'

'And if you had told me what you were doing before you did it, I might've been more cooperative.'

'Fair enough.' That unsettling grin returned to Gideon's face. 'Next time we'll search your mind together.'

Clara nodded at him confidently, though she wasn't exactly sure she had just entered into an entirely agreeable pact.

She flinched and darted her gaze around the room as whispering voices suddenly filled her ears. She couldn't understand what the voices were saying, and they soon faded to silence. She looked at Gideon and he was looking back at her curiously.

'What's the last thing you remember, Clara?'

'I ... remember taking human form again.' She shuddered at the memory. 'There was an old Aelf. He gave me a cloak to wear.'

'That'll be Councillor Tal,' Gideon said. 'He seems to be on our side, but it's difficult to tell with Aelfirian politicians.'

'I don't remember anything after that.' Clara shook her head. 'What happened to me, Gideon?'

He smirked. 'You've been unconscious ever since you reverted to human form. But that's another story.'

Again the whispering voices filled Clara's ears and her eyes searched the room that looked like a chamber in the Nightshade. Was she dreaming now?

'Are we still in Sunflower?' she asked. 'Are we still in our cells?'

'No, we're in transit,' Gideon replied, clearly amused. 'Funny story, actually. Van Bam ran into an old friend of his.'

'An old friend? Who?'

'Perhaps I should start from the beginning,' Gideon said happily. He rubbed his hands together. 'Once again, Clara, the Relic Guild is in a whole world of shit ...'

Samuel felt hungry, and his parched throat craved a drink.

If not for the green illumination shed by Van Bam's illusionist's cane, the interior of the cargo container would have been pitch black.

Not that there was much to see inside. A few meat hooks hung from the ceiling, jingling together now and then when the journey got a little bumpy; and at the back of the container, two large trunks rested against the indented metal wall.

Van Bam sat cross-legged on the floor with his glowing cane resting upon his knees. Beside him, Clara lay in her healing slumber, still wrapped in Councillor Tal's cloak. Samuel stood behind Van Bam, leaning against the container wall. Both men faced Hillem, who sat with his back to the wall opposite.

Far from being the fool that he had first appeared to be, Hillem was clearly a fine actor – his performance had duped even Van Bam. He had been maintaining the role of Supervisor Marca's idiot lackey for a long time in Sunflower, waiting for the Relic Guild's arrival, or so he had said.

'The avatar told us you were coming,' he had explained earlier. 'But it couldn't be sure when exactly you'd arrive. Apparently there are variables hard to factor into its predictions.'

Which Samuel had decided was an understatement, but he had continued to listen to Hillem as he had explained how the Aelfirian Relic Guild, working in secret, had known for a little over six months that the human Relic Guild would be coming; and that their arrival would also signify the return of the Genii.

As Hillem talked, it became clear to Samuel that he knew nothing about what had passed in the Labyrinth in the last four decades. It seemed the Aelfir knew as much about what became of the Labyrinth's denizens after the war as the denizens knew about the Aelfir. Although the Timewatcher left the inter-House portals in place, she had removed all the Aelfirian doorways that led to the Labyrinth – with the exception of the doorway in Sunflower, of course. Hillem claimed that the Aelfir had been warned about the Retrospective, the nightmare land of wild demons that existed between Labrys Town and the Houses, and the certain death awaiting anyone who tried to reach the humans.

The young Aelf was in possession of a strange device: a red crystal, flat and round, strapped to his wrist like a watch. Earlier, he had extracted a small needle from the device's surround, which he had used to prick Clara's finger so as to feed a drop of her blood into the crystal.

He had repeated the process with Samuel and Van Bam, explaining, 'Now the crystal recognises you, it won't react to your presence. But if there's anyone close by that it doesn't know, it'll start to glow. It's not much good in crowded places, but for this stage of the journey, it's a handy device to have around.'

This had proved to be true on a couple of occasions when the container stopped at portal checkpoints. The red crystal gave off a low light, shortly before muffled voices came from outside. Hillem had become tense at these moments, motioning with urgency for them to remain silent, only relaxing when the container continued its journey, and the light of the crystal had died.

Samuel's gut instinct was to trust Hillem. Glogelder and Namji, he wasn't as sure of. As for the avatar, did Samuel have any other choice but to trust it?

Of course Fabian Moor had returned to free Spiral – it seemed obvious now. The Genii were creatures of higher magic, yet they were too few to take on the combined strength of the Aelfirian Houses. But with the Lord of the Genii, the most powerful Thaumaturgist that ever existed, at their side again, who knew what they could achieve? All Fabian Moor had to do was find Oldest Place. It almost sounded easy.

Samuel had to believe that whoever had sent the avatar, whoever was its master, it was someone who knew what they were doing.

'Tell me about Councillor Tal,' Van Bam said, after a lull in the conversation. 'What part does he play in all of this?'

Hillem sucked air over his teeth. 'Tal's a tricky one to pin down,' he said. 'The rumour is that during the Genii War he held quite an important position in the Timewatcher's army. But that's really all I know about that side of him. What I do know for sure is that after the war, Tal fought very hard for governorship of the Aelfheim Archipelago, and the export operation to Labrys Town.'

'You trust him?' Samuel asked.

'Without question,' Hillem replied. 'Tal's the Relic Guild's spy within the Panopticon of Houses. Our network isn't as large as we would like, but his involvement has been vital.' He smiled coyly. 'It was actually Tal who prepared the way for your escape. He delayed reporting your arrival to the Panopticon, while I got word to Namji.

Marca was a problem. We knew he was watching you, but he didn't know we were watching him.' He shrugged. 'We had to get you out of Sunflower before the Panopticon knew you were there.'

'But they did know we were there,' Samuel pointed out. 'They sent the Toymaker.'

Hillem's face looked troubled. The shadows cast by the light of the green glass cane gave his Aelfirian features a shade of the demonic. His pointed ears seemed to grow longer.

'Marca was a fool, but he didn't deserve to die,' he said. 'As for the Toymaker – there's a lot of mystery surrounding him, but I'm not sure he's really controlled by the Panopticon. The Thaumaturgists left him behind to guard the last portal to the Labyrinth. They told us that if anyone as much as looks at that portal in the wrong way, the Toymaker will appear.'

'Is this the first time he has appeared?' said Van Bam.

Hillem shook his head. 'About twenty years ago, a freedom group tried to take control of Sunflower. They thought they could rescue the denizens from the Labyrinth somehow. But the Toymaker turned up, killed everyone, and then disappeared. Just like that, or so they say.'

'And no one knows who he is?' said Samuel.

'As I said, there's a lot of mystery,' Hillem replied. 'But it's generally believed that the position the Thaumaturgists gave him wasn't an honour, but a punishment. The Toymaker used to be a Genii.'

'What?' said Samuel.

Hillem shrugged. 'That's the story. They say the Thaumaturgists stripped him of higher magic, used their own thaumaturgy to *force* him into obeying their commands. They punished him by making him enforce the Timewatcher's final prerogative.'

'Which is to stop humans escaping the Labyrinth,' Van Bam said.

'And the Aelfir from breaking in.'

'But the Genii were executed after the war,' Samuel pointed out. 'Their bodies were flung into the Nothing of Far and Deep.'

'What – like Fabian Moor and his cohorts were?' Hillem countered. 'I don't know if the Thaumaturgists punished any other Genii in this way, but I do know the Toymaker has no other choice but to perform his duty. He'll destroy anyone who gets in or out of the Labyrinth.'

Samuel folded his arms across his chest. 'And he's hunting us right now.'

'Which is why we have to keep moving,' Hillem said with a nod.

Samuel's brow furrowed as silence unfolded in the container. Above, the meat hooks hanging from the ceiling chimed together. Van Bam shifted the illuminated cane in his lap, and shadows danced upon the metal walls.

'Then who controls the Panopticon of Houses?' the illusionist asked Hillem. 'Who are these enemies of ours?'

'Look, the Panopticon is supposed to be a democratic union, but ...' Hillem rubbed his face. 'After the Genii War, without the Thaumaturgists looking over our shoulders, there was a very real concern that the Houses would start fighting among themselves again, that we would slip back to the Old Ways.'

The Old Ways, Samuel thought: a millennium ago, when the Houses of the Aelfir had engaged each other in bloody wars that were unending – senseless fighting that never produced a victor or served a purpose. The Timewatcher put a stop to the Old Ways by creating the Labyrinth, the great meeting place that linked together every House of the Aelfir, and where all castes were welcome. She and the Thaumaturgists managed to maintain peaceful unification between the Houses for a thousand years. Spiral destroyed it in two.

Van Bam said, 'The Panopticon was formed to prevent further wars?'

'And it worked at first,' Hillem replied. 'It held the Aelfir together. But now it's a fragile peace, and trouble flares between Houses much more often than it did during the thousand years of unification. Sometimes it's encouraged.' His expression became sour. 'If nothing else, the Thaumaturgists were a great deterrent.'

Samuel considered the Aelf. Hillem was young, in his mid-twenties, yet he spoke about the subject matter with the confidence and familiarity of one who remembered the Genii War.

'What changed?' Samuel asked.

Hillem pursed his lips. 'Without a bigger fish looking over his shoulder, the toughest bully will always get his way, right?' He sighed. 'Unofficially, there's a group called the Sisterhood – though the term is so widely used and accepted that it might as well be official. It's formed from the most influential Houses, the richest and biggest. The Sisterhood rules the Panopticon, and they're not particularly fond of the Labyrinth.'

'So we were told,' said Van Bam. 'Your friend Glogelder explained that certain Aelfirian castes blame us for events following the Genii War. Why?'

'Because that's what happens when people are left to draw their own conclusions,' Hillem replied. 'We were never given a reason why the Timewatcher abandoned us. She just ordered us to continue sending supplies to the denizens of Labrys Town. Some castes considered this duty a punishment – that the Timewatcher was favouring you, when She should've been condemning you most of all. It was because of the Great Labyrinth that the war began.'

'Please believe me,' said Van Bam. 'The past forty years in Labrys Town have hardly been luxurious.'

'I know,' Hillem said quickly. 'But it's more than that, you see. The Sisterhood no longer has faith in the Timewatcher – they don't fear flouting Her final laws. They want nothing more than to cut all ties with humans.'

'Cut *ties*?' Samuel's tone had fallen flat. 'They want to let us die?'

Hillem raised his hand in a placating gesture. 'Fortunately, they can't achieve their ends because the majority of Houses *do* still believe in the Timewatcher, and they definitely fear Her wrath. But you have to understand, the Sisterhood is absolutely convinced that cutting ties with the Labyrinth will end the final stigma of the Timewatcher and Her Thaumaturgists once for all, and show the Aelfir that they no longer need to fear Her.

'Over the years, the Sisterhood has been slowly gaining support. Theirs is a sly, pernicious crusade, and as time goes on, they're convincing more and more Houses to question their faith in the Timewatcher.' Hillem seemed sad. 'It might not happen for another forty years – it might take a hundred – but if no one stops the Sisterhood, one day they'll get their majority, and the Aelfir *will* abandon the denizens of the Labyrinth.'

Van Bam glanced at Samuel before responding to Hillem. 'Surely attitudes would change if this Sisterhood knew that the Genii have returned – that they are planning to free Spiral?'

'Oh, without question,' Hillem said. 'But it's convincing them to believe you that's the problem. And what evidence can you give them? The avatar certainly doesn't seem keen to pay them a visit.

'I don't doubt the Sisterhood knows all about what happened in Sunflower by now, but all they'll do is use it to highlight how dangerous and unworthy humans are.' He made an angry noise. 'I bet not one of them bothers to wonder *why* you are here. And if they do, they'll be too scared of damaging their positions to wonder aloud.'

'Isn't this where Councillor Tal can be useful?' Samuel said.

'Tal is doing all he can,' Hillem assured them. 'But it's not easy for him. Considering that he represents the Aelfheim Archipelago in the Panopticon of Houses, and add in the operation he's in charge of in Sunflower ...' He exhaled heavily. 'Tal isn't the most popular councillor in the Panopticon. He doesn't exactly have a lot of friends there. But he'll get through to the right people eventually, I'm sure.'

'And in the meantime we do what?' Samuel said, irritated. 'Keep running?'

'Samuel has a good point, Hillem,' said Van Bam. 'If everything you say about the Toymaker is true, he will catch up with us eventually.'

'To be honest, I'm not sure what happens next,' Hillem said apologetically. 'Namji is the only one who knows the details. She's our ... Resident, I suppose you would call her. She's a lot closer to the avatar than Glogelder and me. We only get told what we need to know, when we need to know it.'

His large Aelfirian eyes gazed at Clara lying on the floor beside Van Bam. 'All I know for sure right now is that we need to stop the Genii finding Oldest Place.'

'And how do we do that?'

Hillem didn't answer Samuel but raised a hand for silence as the vibrations in the cargo container's walls and floor lessened and then stopped. A gentle bump followed, which Samuel took to mean that the floating platform upon which the container sat had been deactivated, and that they had reached their destination.

Hillem motioned for continued silence as he rose from the floor and crept towards the doors. While watching the inert red crystal strapped to his wrist, the young Aelf listened intently. He flinched as three sharp clangs echoed around the container. But the red crystal did not glow, and Hillem visibly relaxed. In return, he banged twice on the doors, waited for the two clangs that replied, then banged one more time.

Smiling, clearly relieved, Hillem turned to Samuel and Van Bam, opened his mouth to speak, but was rudely interrupted by a series of fresh clangs that came like a loud and clumsy drumbeat.

'Glogelder!' Hillem shouted, and the drumbeat ceased. 'Stop pissing around!'

The container doors opened, and the big form of Glogelder was revealed, his scarred face split by a broad grin. Behind him, an arched portal was set against a redbrick wall.

Glogelder pulled a disgusted expression and waved a hand to clear the air. '*Whoa*! What've you been eating in there?'

Samuel shared a look with Van Bam. The sewers beneath Labrys Town were still heavy upon them.

'Actually, you two *are* a bit ripe,' Hillem said.

'But don't worry,' Glogelder said, wrinkling his nose. 'There's a laundrette and bathhouse here. Got some food for you, too.'

'And where is *here*?' Samuel growled.

'Come on, I'll show you around,' Hillem replied.

'And I'll take care of the little one,' Glogelder said, nodding at Clara's sleeping form. 'Namji's getting a cosy bed made up for her.'

Inside the Retrospective, in a sharp-walled valley, hidden away from the blood and thunder raging across an implausibly huge landscape, Fabian Moor's wrath surpassed anything to be found in that hateful place.

Sweat shining upon his face, body aching and limbs trembling, Moor focused his thaumaturgy upon the valley's dead end wall. He had already split the rock, widened the rent, and through it created a pathway that bridged the land of dead time to a House of the Aelfir.

He was diverting the higher magic of the Nightshade, that power to connect the Retrospective to all realms, and Moor wielded it with the full fury of a Genii, though it threatened to crush him.

At no point in her life did Marney discover the location of Oldest Place … The words of Hagi Tabet rattled in Moor's mind, and failure burned into his core.

Earlier, Moor had summoned wild demons to his side. Five had come to him. Evidently, the Retrospective encouraged its denizens to remain within their social groupings; each of the five demons had been made to a similar design of perversion. They had scurried and clambered down the sharp and jagged valley wall, fighting to be the first to reach the source of the summons, eager in their madness to rip their summoner apart. But Moor had controlled them. While simultaneously wielding the Nightshade's power and maintaining the portal to another world, he had stabbed his thaumaturgy into the demons' beings like a hook into the belly of a fish. He had wrenched at their obedience, forced them to do his bidding.

Moor could see them now, through the rent in the wall, out in a verdant House where the sun shone, golden and warm. The demons ran amok, savage and wild, among a large group of shaven-headed Aelfir who wore the robes of monks. Most of the Aelfir fled, and Moor allowed them to escape. Several lay dead already, their blood and flesh staining the green grass. Moor tempered the violent lusts of the demons. He ordered them to capture one victim each, and to then return.

The first demon returned to the valley, creeping with the twitchy nervousness of a wingless fly. Gangly and thin, fragile-looking but strong, its skin was a grey carapace that glistened with an oily film. With two of its long, knife-like fingers stabbed into the eyes of a monk, it dragged its victim, kicking and screaming, over the threshold. The four other demons, almost identical to the first, followed closely, each consigning an Aelf to the corrosion of the Retrospective.

As soon as the last demon had crossed the threshold, Moor released his grip on the portal with no small amount of relief. The rent in the valley wall sealed, reverting with a snap to sharp and jagged rock, forever closing off the world of sanity to the Aelfirian monks. But Moor did not relinquish his control over the demons, and he forced one last command into their madness.

The monsters shrieked in frenzy and slaughtered their captives with dizzying speed. Stabbing, biting, tearing, they revelled in the meat and blood that showered their hard skins. Before the screams of the monks were cut short by the sudden and final silence of death, their ripped and shredded masses became the raw material that fed the Retrospective.

Blood began to steam; organs and bone began to melt: all organic matter condensing into a soup that would be absorbed into the rock of the valley floor to be later used for spawning new monstrosities to stalk this broken House.

While the process took place, Moor rewarded his minions by allowing them to feed upon the diminishing remains.

Surely he could not be wrong? All these years he had been certain that the empath knew the location of Oldest Place. He had *known* that Marney was the key that would free Lord Spiral from his prison. It was this certainty that had bolstered Moor's resolve through four decades of utter isolation within the tomb of his silver cube. But had he made a mistake? Miscalculated? Forgotten a crucial detail while the Relic Guild meddled in his affairs? Could it be that Fabian Moor, Lord Spiral's most trusted Genii, really had failed his master?

A bellow came from the sky, wrenching Moor's attention away from his feeding minions.

A new and very different kind of wild demon had been attracted to the carnage in the valley. It hovered in the air on wings of smouldering feathers, ash-grey and smoking, burning beneath with a blistering furnace-orange. It was formed more from bone than flesh, with thick skeletal plates covering its chest and abdomen like armour. Easily twice the size of the demons in the valley, its face was an eyeless mask studded with small, barbed horns, its mouth a curved and vicious beak.

Against the backdrop of a bruised sky and spiteful lightning, wings beating and smoking, the new monster descended towards Moor's minions, leading with clawed feet like skeletal hands, its talons clacking together.

Moor tried to hook its obedience with his thaumaturgy; but whether because its madness was too strong, or Moor's exertions had put a dent in his strength, the flying demon was able to deflect the Genii's attempts. Opening its wicked beak wide, its bellow reverberated off the valley walls like a hail of rage. It moved in for the kill.

'No!' Moor shouted.

But the monster had already closed a clawed foot around the head of one of Moor's minions, and ripped it free without effort. The corpse fell to the ground, thrashing and spraying blood.

The four remaining demons panicked before the new monstrosity. Fear of this greater might overcame the thaumaturgy that subjugated their will, and they slipped from Moor's control. One of them tried to escape, but only made it halfway up the valley wall before the flying demon plucked it from the rock, tore its body in two, and then hurled the bloody pieces to smash into two of the remaining three demons.

Though he knew it was useless, Moor tried to reinforce his influence over the last of his minions; he tried to synchronise their actions, get them to attack as a team, and at least put up a fight against the flying demon. But the fallen two were easily slaughtered and reduced to ruined mounds; and by the time Moor accepted the futility of his attempts, the flying demon had wrapped its burning wings around the last minion and was bathing in the flames that consumed its victim, severing the Genii's final connection.

Only when the final threads of his thaumaturgy were cut did Moor realise how much energy he had expended. He slumped to his knees as if a crushing weight had fallen on his shoulders. A gnawing void gripped his insides, a sudden, encompassing hunger that demanded to be fed, and he retched and vomited bile onto the scorched valley floor. The effort of using the Nightshade's higher magic to connect the Retrospective to an Aelfirian House had drained Moor utterly. He could not rise to his feet.

Smoky air buffeted him, and he looked up. The flying demon was drifting towards him now, wings beating slowly, ash and embers swirling up to the poison sky. It bellowed again, covering the Genii with scorching, rancid breath. It rose above him, preparing to descend, to strike. It was enormous, at least twelve feet tall. Moor tried to summon at least a spark of thaumaturgy, but the emptiness and hunger roiling inside him sapped his energy, and he only succeeded in falling back onto his rump.

In that moment, Fabian Moor knew that he had truly failed. That he had condemned himself to death.

The flying demon's final bellow was triumphant. Moor closed his eyes as long talons reached for him …

He heard running footsteps, each one as heavy as a stamp. He felt the air displace, and sensed a large presence jumping over him. Moor opened his eyes just in time to see the Woodsman vaulting high into the air to smash its huge axe into the flying demon's chest.

Shrieking, the demon fell to the valley floor, billowing smoke and ash. The Woodsman stepped upon its body. Rising flames, tall and dancing, burning fiercely, sent Moor scuttling back. The flying demon reached for its attacker with bony hands tipped with knife-sized talons, but the Woodsman had already wrenched the axe free from its foe's chest. Before one of those vicious talons could cause a single scratch, the Woodsman cut first one and then the other of the flying demon's arms away at the elbows. The beast's shriek shocked Moor's ears. And then, undeterred by the red flames raging around it, the Woodsman proceeded to butcher its foe.

Again and again the huge axe rose and fell, the Woodsman's iron hard muscles bulging, the gashes covering its limbs straining their stitching. The flying demon was hewed into a mound of meat and bone, the fire of its burning wings doused by the deluge of blood. With ash drifting on the breeze like gentle snow, the gruesome remains began steaming as the Retrospective accepted the latest offering of raw material. The Woodsman strode away from the carnage, heading back towards Moor.

While its studded kilt, leather jerkin and hood were charred and smoking, the demon appeared unscathed. Covered with gore, the head of its giant axe gleaming and dripping, the Woodsman strode past the Genii. Exhausted, still unable to rise from the valley floor, Moor shifted his position to see the demon stand obediently behind the thin and menacing figure of Mo Asajad.

'Do you have a death wish, Fabian?' Her voice was as cold and hard as her stare. Beside her, an open portal had split the air, giving a view into the Nightshade.

As Asajad walked towards him, Moor glanced briefly at the swiftly diminishing remains of the flying demon.

Exhaustion turned to shame. To exhibit his weakness before anyone was disgraceful enough, but to do so before Lady Asajad, who had always questioned his leadership, was the height of humiliation. Moor succumbed to despair, feeling the indignity of needing a wild demon to save his life. He prepared himself for Asajad's next scathing words.

But to Moor's surprise, when Asajad reached his side there was a tinge of sympathy in her voice.

'You are normally such a cautious creature, Fabian,' she said. 'Might I suggest you remember that in future?'

She offered Moor a fat phial. He stared at the blood that filled it, but he didn't accept the offering at first.

Asajad sighed. 'We are all in the same predicament. Drinking blood is a necessity, not a choice.' She offered the phial again with more insistence. 'I have no wish to see you like this, Fabian. Please, regain your dignity.'

As if urging him to take the advice, hunger churned Moor's gut fiercely, threatening a second bout of vomiting. He snatched the phial from Asajad's hand, popped the cork, and drank the salty contents thirstily.

Immediately, the blood lifted the fatigue. Strength returned to his body. The blood filled the draining emptiness inside him with a heat that reignited the higher magic in his veins. Slowly, Moor got to his feet, unsteady at first, but the blood rapidly made him feel solid and whole again.

'Better?' Asajad asked.

'Not especially,' Moor grumbled. He looked at the empty phial in his hand, and let it drop. It shattered into myriad shards upon the valley floor.

'Fabian, you told me that taming the Woodsman was relatively easy because it has an uncommon intelligence among the wild demons of the Retrospective.' Asajad took in her surroundings with a disgusted look. 'Why, then, are you bothering to attempt the subjugation of demons clearly cursed with a far lesser intelligence?'

Moor glanced back at the Woodsman, standing still and patient, axe in hands, face concealed by the leather hood.

'You know damn well why,' he told Asajad bitterly.

'Do I?' Asajad's tone was scalding. 'Because you also told me that you did not compare your powers with those of Lord Spiral – not even remotely, you said. Yet here you are, out in this vile place, trying to do Lord Spiral's work.'

Moor took a calming, steadying breath. 'What if we have no other choice, Asajad?'

She glared at him for a moment, and the patch of scarring upon her forehead grew paler than her porcelain skin.

'Have you lost your senses?' she snapped. 'The power of the Nightshade is the power of the Timewatcher. You, me, Viktor and Hagi – we can barely control a *fraction* of that power. Among every Thaumaturgist and Genii that ever existed, only Lord Spiral came close to equalling the Timewatcher. Only he could truly wield the First and Greatest Spell. You know that, Fabian. So did you come here to vent your anger, or have you decided to lose all hope?'

Moor looked up at the hateful sky, the poison clouds full of anger and spite. How had he ever believed that he alone could control the Retrospective and conquer the Aelfir?

'I had to try something,' he told Asajad bitterly. 'What if we cannot find Oldest Place? What if Lord Spiral is never free again?'

'Yes,' said Asajad. 'Hagi has been filling me in on the situation.' She looked Moor over and seemed concerned by what she saw. 'Viktor is not best pleased with you, Fabian, and I do not blame him. It is not his fault that you were deceived by the empath, and you should not have treated him as you did. He is owed an apology.'

Moor didn't reply but simply stared at the shards of broken phial at his feet, wishing that he had more blood to consume.

'Oh, poor Fabian,' Asajad's mocking smile came back to her face. 'You know, for what it's worth, I've come to think that you were right about these human magickers. They really aren't to be underestimated. They are ... clever. Perhaps more than you believed.' She laughed into the back of her hand. 'You really didn't see the Relic Guild coming, did you?'

Moor felt a flush of anger. 'First you admonish me, then you speak of *apologies* as if we are squabbling children, and now you mock me? Do you have no comprehension of the predicament we are in, Asajad?'

'Of course.' Asajad's voice was as stony as her expression. 'But *you* have not heard what Hagi has to say.'

Moor frowned at her. 'There is news?'

'*Such* news!' Asajad's eyes flared hungrily. 'The Resident needs to speak with you, Fabian.'

'What?' he demanded.

In reply, Asajad turned and began walking back towards the portal that led to the Nightshade. The Woodsman turned and followed her.

'Go and see Hagi, Fabian,' Asajad called back. 'Before more of these filthy demons are attracted to your despair.'

CHAPTER ELEVEN

SANDALWOOD

Although Clara didn't know where she was, or how she had got there, she doubted she was dreaming. But how could this world in which she found herself possibly be real? Everything was cast in its own shade of grey, as if etched in pencil, but with a degree of clarity and detail that Clara didn't know could exist without colour.

She was heading across a courtyard, wide and spacious. The ground was stained in places with patches as dark as slate against off-white cobbles. Up ahead, the courtyard ended at a line of ugly, squat buildings with grainy brickwork. Clara was moving towards them, though she was not walking. She couldn't feel the ground beneath her feet; only a curious sense of detachment, as if she was floating – dreamlike, but not in a dream.

Clara tried to look at her hands, but her vision would not shift. She tried to look to her left and right, but no matter what she did, her line of sight simply would not stray from the buildings ahead. It was almost as if ...

Samuel appeared to Clara

He stepped in front of her, talking to her, his mouth moving but his words inaudible. In fact, Clara realised, there was no sound of any kind in her strange world. Or scent.

Samuel was cleaner than when she had last seen him; his face was no longer grime-smeared, the skin around his goatee beard was shaved smooth and shiny. His short, grey hair was no longer matted and greasy, and his long coat and clothes had been cleaned of the filth from the sewers beneath Labrys Town. Although Samuel's image was also drawn in shades of grey, there were splashes of subtle colours, hues that pulsed around his head and torso. It struck Clara that these weak colours represented the old bounty hunter's mood. The changeling was relieved to see him, in a distant sort of way.

Samuel? Clara said – or did she think it? Either way, he did not hear her.

Two Aelfir walked alongside Samuel. The first was the lanky idiot Hillem, looking slight beside his broader companion. The second Aelf was a real bruiser, with a scarred face as hairless as his cratered head. Clara knew the bruiser's name was Glogelder, and that Hillem – not stupid after all – had been the Relic Guild's secret ally in Sunflower.

Had Gideon told her these things?

Appearing iron grey to Clara's vision, neither Aelf radiated dull colours as Samuel did.

Glogelder spoke, silently to Clara's ears, and made himself laugh – an inappropriate joke, apparently, as no one else laughed along with him. Clara found herself looking down at the green glass cane in her hands. Only they weren't her hands.

Of course she was in Van Bam's head, seeing how he saw. Why had she ever been confused? Hillem and Glogelder appeared so colourless because they were not magickers; and in this grey world, Van Bam saw colour only in magic.

The group of men reached the end of the courtyard and stopped before a shabby door inlaid with a cracked stained glass window. Clara knew the door led to a chapel of the Timewatcher.

Hillem was speaking now. Although Clara couldn't hear his words, she knew he was telling Samuel and Van Bam about their location. As Hillem's mouth moved, Van Bam looked away from him, and Clara had her first proper look at a place that she suddenly understood was called Nowhere Ascending, a realm that could not truthfully claim to be a House of the Aelfir.

More buildings, grainy and ugly, lined the opposite side of the courtyard. There were thaumaturgically-powered lifting trucks, piles of floating platforms, and two large metal cargo containers. But when Van Bam's sight lifted up and above the buildings, Clara's mind was filled by a vast backdrop so utterly black that it was like staring into a lightless void. The blackness was not still; it rippled with a liquid quality that gave it a graceful sense of flowing, as if the courtyard and its buildings were surrounded by mighty falls of oil.

Van Bam looked directly above. There was no sky. Instead a huge disc blocked the way, far overhead, with a deep grey colour only a shade lighter than the oily falls.

Nowhere Ascending is a portal, a woman's voice said in Clara's mind. *It's used to transport large shipments of cargo.*

The voice didn't surprise Clara, nor did it alarm her. Within her detachment, she realised this woman had been with her from the moment she perceived this place. Hadn't she?

I didn't know portals could be this big, Clara replied.

I suppose portals can be any size, within reason, the woman said. *That huge disc up there is the base of the next level. There are more levels above it – and below us – all rising in unison.*

Where does it lead? Clara asked. *What's at the top?*

A network of other portals. Nowhere Ascending is a trade route that connects many Houses, Clara. Though I don't think you ever really reach the top. You either go somewhere else, or keep rising until you … join the bottom again, I suppose.

The explanation made sense to Clara, though she wasn't sure why. *How many levels are there?*

I have no idea, said the woman. *But I can tell you that this level is an abattoir. It's on its way to pick up a team of butchers and a herd of cattle. For now it's empty, and safe for us to ride unnoticed. Don't worry – we'll be getting off before the butchers arrive and the slaughtering begins.*

A flash of intense colour assaulted Clara's senses as a brief burst of thaumaturgic energy crackled over the surface of the flowing darkness. For but a moment, the grey world was streaked by purple. Van Bam's vision then shifted to look at Samuel, Hillem and Glogelder standing before the shabby chapel of the Timewatcher. Hillem was still talking.

Clara. There was amusement in the woman's voice. *Aren't you curious as to who I am?*

Your name is Namji, Clara replied instinctively, her mind filled with an image of a petite Aelf with a heart-shaped face. And then, because she knew it was true, she added, *I don't like you.*

But you don't know me.

I know you can't be trusted, Clara said. *Why do I know that?*

Namji chuckled. *Well, it probably isn't your own opinion that you're expressing right now.*

Gideon's?

Namji scoffed. *Gideon doesn't care about me one way or another. Or anyone else, I shouldn't wonder.*

Then … do you mean Van Bam? Gideon said someone he knew had rescued us. But Van Bam doesn't trust you?

There was a pause. *It's a little complicated to explain, Clara, but no. I think it might be Marney's opinion you're experiencing.*

Samuel was addressing the group now, with his usual abrupt and borderline angry manner. Glogelder seemed unfazed by the old bounty hunter's approach, but Hillem had raised his hands in a calming gesture.

Let me back this up for you, Clara, said Namji. *I'm guessing you've already figured out where your mind is right now. As for your body, it's safe, recuperating in a healing sleep.*

That's a lie, Clara said, because it was true. *I don't need to heal. You're keeping me unconscious on purpose. You're a magic-user.*

Another pause. *All right, you got me,* Namji admitted. *I wanted to keep you out of the way for a while because I need to talk to you secretly, Clara. Gideon allowed me to use his connection to Van Bam as a conduit that would connect the two of us. Gideon said he'd stay out of our way while we talk, but I don't doubt he's listening.* She chuckled, adding wryly, *And feeding you information.*

Tell me why Marney doesn't like you, Clara said, a tinge of intrigue invading her detachment.

Namji sighed. *I wasn't very kind to her once. A long time ago, Clara, when I wasn't much more than a kid and didn't know better. Lots of things have changed since then.*

Clara knew that was the truth; there was an immaturity about her dislike of this Aelfirian woman that belonged to a time long before she was born.

Glogelder was talking now. Whatever the big and scarred Aelf was saying, he punctuated his words by slapping a clunky weapon hanging from his shoulder, which Clara knew was designed for launching spell spheres. Samuel shook his head, and Glogelder rolled his eyes. Hillem took over, pointing at the empty holster strapped to Samuel's leg as he spoke. Samuel nodded thoughtfully. Hillem then looked directly at Clara as he continued speaking; only he wasn't looking at her.

Did Van Bam know the changeling was in his head?

Gideon told me that he filled you in on the situation, said Namji. *You know why the Genii have returned, don't you?*

To find Oldest Place and release Spiral. Clara didn't say this, but assumed her silence would provide affirmation enough for the Aelf.

Namji continued. *And you know about Hillem, Glogelder and me, and our relationship with the avatar, right?*

Why do you call yourselves the Relic Guild? Clara asked.

Imitation is a sincere form of flattery, Namji replied offhandedly. *Now, I need you to focus, Clara. The avatar told me that Marney hid a secret message in your mind. Gideon says you've been trying to find it.*

Is that why you're here? Clara said. *Are you going to force the message out of me?*

No. I'm here to tell you that you have to stop searching for it. Namji's voice had become hard. *Marney planted information in your head, Clara – information that comes with a set of very specific instructions that must not be revealed, not until the time is right. Do you understand?*

With Glogelder beside him, Hillem raised a hand in farewell. Samuel was mouthing 'See you later,' and then he and the two Aelfir walked away, leaving Van Bam on his own.

Clara grew suspicious. *The avatar told you what the message is*, she said to Namji. *You know, don't you?*

The avatar never gave me any details of the instructions, Namji replied, *but, yes, it told me what the message is about.*

Van Bam looked up as more flashes of purple energy danced upon the surface of the gigantic, liquid portal that formed Nowhere Ascending. His vision then shifted back to the cracked stained glass window of the chapel of the Timewatcher.

Namji's voice became solemn. *I'm sorry to be the one to tell you this, Clara, but right now you might just be the most dangerous human that ever existed …*

'Hello, Fabian.'

His strength returned, his hope rekindled, Moor looked up at Hagi Tabet, hanging on her web of leather tentacles in the Nightshade. The Resident's voice retained its airy, disassociated quality, but she appeared calmer, saner than she had since her reanimation, and, perhaps, a little smug.

'Lady Asajad claims you have news for me,' Moor said.

'Indeed.' Tabet's eyes filled with water. 'It would seem that you were right about the empath all along.'

Moor's hands shook and he clenched them into fists. 'Tell me she knew where the Timewatcher hid Oldest Place, Hagi.'

Tabet answered with a triumphant expression. Moor's relief almost forced a laugh from his mouth.

'Where is it?' he demanded.

Tabet averted her watery gaze and idly fondled the pink, fist-sized bud at her navel. 'I do not know,' she whispered. 'Marney hid her secret in a place I cannot see.'

Moor glared up at her. 'Hagi ...' His voice was full of warning. 'I do not have the patience to play a game of riddles with you. Did the empath know how to reach Oldest Place or not?'

'The answer is not as simple as you would like, Fabian.' Tabet smiled at him almost lovingly. 'At one time, Marney most certainly knew the location of Oldest Place. But she stopped remembering it.'

'That makes no sense,' Moor said hotly. 'You have *all* her experiences, Hagi. Everything she ever knew is yours to see.'

'Yes, including the moment in which the empath purposely removed all knowledge of Oldest Place from her mind,' Tabet replied. 'I have found the residue of a memory, Fabian. Marney transferred the location of Lord Spiral's prison from her mind to the mind of someone else.'

'*Transferred* it? To whom?'

'Another magicker.' Tabet's eyes moved from side to side, clearly recalling the memories stolen from an empath. 'It occurred during the minutes before you captured her, Fabian. With a kiss, Marney planted the information inside the mind of a girl. Her name is Clara.'

The name struck a chord with Moor and he clenched his teeth. 'The changeling?' he said, voice rising in pitch. 'The *whore*?'

'Marney used the changeling as a vessel to prevent you gaining the means to release Lord Spiral. I think she knew you were coming for her, Fabian, though I cannot tell how she knew.'

Moor's mind raced. The changeling called Clara had been the bait Moor used to capture Marney. Clara was nothing, no one, a piece of meat to attract an animal. Who could have warned the empath? Who could have frightened her into trusting someone expendable with something so important?

'Tell me where the changeling is now, Hagi,' he growled. 'Where is she hiding?'

Tabet seemed to have genuine sympathy in her rheumy eyes as she stared down at Moor. 'Fabian, you were right in your beliefs concerning the empath, but you were wrong to suppose the Relic Guild are still in Labrys Town. They have escaped.'

'Impossible,' Moor said adamantly. 'There are no doorways left to the humans!'

'Be assured that I am not mistaken on this,' Tabet said calmly. 'I do not know how they achieved it, but the magickers escaped the Labyrinth, and they took Clara with them. And the location of Oldest Place is with the changeling.'

An icy pang of panic gripped Moor's insides. 'How can you be sure of this, Hagi? What did you see?'

'I saw what we need to know,' the Resident stated. 'I did as you asked, Fabian. I studied every second of the empath's life, and I found a discrepancy. A shattered memory, the fragments of which Marney had scattered throughout her life experiences. But I pieced them together, and I saw things that have not yet come to pass.'

Moor sobered instantly. 'What?'

'Marney had gained a glimpse of the near future.'

'No more games, Hagi,' Moor said, struggling to keep his voice below a shout. 'Speak plainly. What has the empath seen?'

'She saw where Clara is going to be. And soon, Fabian.' The madness returned to Tabet's eyes, and a tear ran down her cheek as she swayed on her web. 'Oh my,' she sighed excitedly. 'They don't know it themselves yet, but the magickers of the Relic Guild are heading for a place that we, the last of the Genii, know all too well.'

The churches and chapels of the Timewatcher were ubiquitous throughout all the realms. It often seemed that a place of prayer was within walking distance wherever the location, in whichever House. It therefore came as no surprise to Van Bam that a chapel should be found in the gaps between the Houses; even here, in this mammoth portal called Nowhere Ascending, on this rising level that had been designed for death.

The chapel was dusty and grimy, unused for some time. There were two rows of bench seats, and Van Bam sat in the front row on the right side, facing a tapestry on the wall. In a state of disrepair, it depicted the Timewatcher as a soft cloud with a sun at its centre, spreading rays of light. Before the tapestry was an altar; upon it sat a small copper bowl half-filled with sand; and, stuck into the sand, an incense stick burned.

Van Bam mulled over the words of Hillem as he watched lazy tendrils of smoke coiling into the air, and he wondered how long it would be before the Aelfir's faith in the Timewatcher died completely.

He breathed the earthy scent of the incense smoke, and sighed. 'May the Timewatcher welcome your spirit to Mother Earth,' he whispered, and was thankful that Gideon had no caustic opinion to offer.

Alone with his thoughts, Van Bam considered the facts which the Aelfirian Relic Guild had recently brought to light.

The avatar had been more forthcoming with the information it had shared with Namji and her colleagues. The revelation that the Genii had returned to free Spiral from Oldest Place was in itself disturbing enough; but Gideon had earlier told Van Bam just how much more the avatar had shared with Namji.

The connection between Clara and Marney was now clear, and it made the illusionist comprehend what a truly dangerous situation the Relic Guild had been delivered to.

Van Bam looked at the green glass cane in his hands. So many questions, so many riddles – did nothing have a straight answer anymore?

'Many Aelfir believe that smoke will guide a spirit to Mother Earth and the loving arms of the Timewatcher.'

Startled, Van Bam turned to see Namji making her way down the aisle.

'Do you still have faith, Van Bam?' she asked. 'After all this time?'

'Occasionally, faith is all that keeps me sane in my old age,' Van Bam replied. With a small smile, he faced the tapestry again. 'And in *your* old age, it seems you have improved your skills as a magic-user.'

Without replying, Namji sat next to Van Bam and sniffed the smoky air. 'Sandalwood,' she said with a tone of approval.

The smile fell from Van Bam's face. 'It was Marney's favourite scent,' he said.

'Oh …' Namji joined the illusionist in watching the smoke rise. 'I'm sorry, Van Bam.' She spoke with an odd mixture of sympathy and apology. 'The avatar warned me that Marney might not be coming with you.'

A moment of silence passed.

'The truth is,' said Van Bam, 'it has been many years since Marney and I were close – not since I became Resident. But …'

'But good memories have a habit of lingering?' Namji suggested.

'Yes, I suppose you could say that.'

Instinctively, Van Bam paused, allowing for a gap in which Gideon's voice could offer an abrasive remark concerning the illusionist's sadness over the death of his old lover. But again the ghost of the ex-Resident remained silent.

Van Bam faced Namji. She was staring at the image of the Timewatcher on the wall.

'Over the years, I occasionally wondered what happened to you,' he told her. 'To be honest, I believed you were dead. When the Genii War ended, and we heard of the Timewatcher's retribution, I naturally assumed that Mirage and all its citizens had been sentenced to the Retrospective along with the other enemy Houses.'

Namji was quiet for a moment. 'I went into hiding, and waited the war out,' she said, voice low. 'I didn't get a chance to escape Mirage until the Last Storm happened.'

The Last Storm: the day the Genii War ended. The day the Time-watcher's armies launched a massive, synchronised offensive against every House and stronghold under Spiral's control, and the Genii were defeated.

'As far as I know,' Namji continued, 'I was the only Aelf who got out of Mirage.' She sighed and looked at Van Bam, her large Aelfirian eyes scouring his face. 'It's disturbing, don't you think? Spiral subjugated a lot of the Aelfir, forced them into serving him and the Genii. But that wasn't a consideration for the Timewatcher. She showed little mercy at the end of the war.'

Her eyes dropped, contemplating the horrific past as though for the first time in years. Namji might have been showing the signs of age – the wrinkles around her eyes; her hair still black but streaked with grey – but to Van Bam, her delicate face still seemed as young as the last time he had seen her.

'The Thaumaturgists didn't discriminate,' Namji said. 'Every Aelf who served Spiral, whether by choice or subjugation, was sentenced to the Retrospective. I shudder to think of how many innocent people were punished, Van Bam. I suppose I was one of the lucky ones.'

The shades of her emotions waxed and waned with sadness, anger, guilt.

'Piecing your life back together must have been hard, Namji.'

She managed a smile and patted Van Bam's hand. 'Oh, it hasn't been such a bad life – though I never found a place that felt like home again.' She snorted a laugh. 'I considered getting into politics. After all, at that point I'd spent most of my life being trained to govern people. But I was never quite sure if I'd managed to escape Mirage unnoticed. What if someone discovered that I had not gone to the Retrospective with the rest of my people? I decided to keep a low profile. I travelled around. And, yes, I improved my skills with magic along the way.'

'The life of a wanderer, eh?' Van Bam said kindly. 'And things re-mained this way until you met the avatar?'

'Pretty much.' Namji patted Van Bam's hand again. 'I always

wondered what became of you and Angel, though. I have to admit, I didn't believe you had made it back to the Labyrinth alive.'

Van Bam felt a chill of remorse. He watched the tendrils of scented smoke coiling up towards the ceiling, guiding lost souls to Mother Earth.

'Namji,' he said, voice sombre, 'Angel never made it home from Mirage.'

Namji looked at him sharply. 'Oh.' Her shoulders slumped. 'Damn.'

'It was a long time ago.' Van Bam leaned against the backrest on the bench, his head filled with memories of a distant past. Once again, Gideon had no comment to make. 'So much lost, so many friends dead, so much doubt. I wonder if there was a true victor in the Genii War. It has been such a long time since anyone required the services of the Relic Guild.'

The smile returned to Namji's face. 'But now you're needed more than ever.'

'Ah, but some agents are more important than others, yes?' Van Bam raised an eyebrow at the Aelf. 'I assume you have a good reason for keeping Clara unconscious.'

Namji gave a sheepish chuckle. 'You always were a little difficult to fool, Van Bam.'

'Oh, I seem to remember that you knew how to give me a run for my money,' Van Bam replied. 'But, actually, Gideon told me. I trust your *meeting* with Clara went well?'

Namji stared at him. 'Gideon said he wouldn't tell you what I was doing.'

'Gideon is not always a man of his word.'

'You know everything?'

'I know that Marney hid the location of Oldest Place in Clara's mind to stop Fabian Moor finding it.'

Namji sighed. 'I came here to explain the situation to you, Van Bam. Gideon might've jumped ahead of me, but I have my reasons for caution. Councillor Tal knows, but I haven't told Hillem and Glogelder.' Van Bam could tell by her emotional shades that it was the truth. 'Have you told Samuel?'

'Not yet.'

Namji was thoughtful for a moment, clearly pondering how best to express it. 'Considering how dangerous the information is, I thought it safer for Clara to keep her unconscious – at least for now.'

'How did Clara take the news?'

'Surprisingly well. But it's Samuel that worries me most, Van Bam. I get the impression that sometimes his magic can encourage him to be a little *merciless*.'

It was an understandable concern, Van Bam reckoned. If Samuel ever reached a situation where he believed all other options had been exhausted, then his magic might indeed encourage him to make decisions that were as emotionless as the bullets in his gun. But ...

Van Bam shook his head. 'Samuel is not such a slave to his magic that he would kill Clara just because the information she carries is so entirely dangerous. Besides, the Genii are creatures of higher magic. I am not convinced they would necessarily need Clara alive to extract the information in her head.'

'Not a cheery thought, but I suppose you're right,' Namji conceded grimly.

'I had assumed that Fabian Moor had used Marney as a means to enter the Nightshade. But now ...' Van Bam tried to push away images of Moor exacting his fury upon Marney once he had discovered she no longer carried the information he craved. 'Explain this to me, Namji,' he said in a low voice. 'How is it that Marney knew how to find Oldest Place to begin with? We have had no contact with the outside worlds for decades. How did Fabian Moor know she *knew*?'

'I can't answer that,' Namji replied. 'The avatar never told me.'

Van Bam huffed his frustration. 'Clara is carrying the location of Oldest Place. And as long as we keep her safe, Fabian Moor will be unable to free his lord and master. But I doubt our purpose now is to keep running from the Genii forever.'

'No.'

'Then what are we to do with the information?'

'All right. Just ... hear me out first, Van Bam.' Namji rose from the bench and faced the illusionist, wringing her hands together, her petite face filled with concern. 'There are always gaps in whatever information the avatar gives me,' she explained. 'Details, specifics – things that get omitted, every time it appears to me. But I do know that it's been influencing all of us, leading us towards a particular place and time.'

'Yes,' Van Bam said. 'The avatar is a portent – a future-guide. Samuel and I deduced as much ourselves. But future-guides are conjurations, and they are always controlled by a master. Do you have *any* idea who is controlling the avatar?'

Namji shook her head helplessly. 'Someone who very much doesn't want to be seen yet.'

'Then what is this *cultivated future* that we are being guided towards? An event of some kind, or a person who can use the information in Clara's mind to our advantage? The avatar's master, perhaps?'

'An artefact,' Namji said.

'The avatar is leading us to an *artefact*?'

'Look, Van Bam, what Marney transferred into Clara's head is both a map and a *key*. Knowing the location of Oldest Place will activate a relic, a device the avatar calls Known Things.'

'Known Things?' Van Bam repeated. 'I have never heard of an artefact with that name.'

'The avatar was in no way precise, but as far as I can tell, it has a mechanism that only Clara can unlock, with the information that Marney gave her.'

'And what will we discover once Clara has unlocked it?'

Namji paused. 'A secret, Van Bam, some kind of method. Known Things will show us how to kill Spiral.'

Van Bam stared at Namji for several seconds. 'Excuse me?'

Namji raised a hand. 'I know it seems unlikely, but the avatar was adamant.'

'*Kill* Spiral?' Van Bam stressed. 'Only the Timewatcher is powerful enough to achieve that, Namji.'

'What, like only the Timewatcher knows where she hid Oldest Place?'

'*That* is entirely different,' Van Bam said, more angrily than he intended. 'I have encountered *many* relics in my time, and more than a few were indeed powerful weapons. But this Known Things is so potent that it can destroy the highest of all Thaumaturgists?'

Namji raised her hands. 'I don't know how it works, Van Bam, and

I don't know what it is,' she said, her tone placatory. 'I only know as much as I've been told.'

Van Bam rubbed his face with a hand. He looked up to the cobwebs on the chapel's ceiling, heavy and black with dust, and gathered his thoughts. 'Then the location of Oldest Place is either the key to Spiral's freedom, or to his demise?'

'If we can keep Clara away from the Genii, it'll be the latter,' Namji said, her expression assured. 'Feels like I've been waiting an awfully long time to tell you all this.'

'I have to admit, a part of me wishes you had kept it to yourself,' Van Bam replied, but he knew that as extraordinary as Namji's revelation was, it felt like the first advantage the Relic Guild had gained since Fabian Moor's return. 'Known Things,' he whispered. 'Where might we find this relic?'

'I wasn't told the name of the House – or if it is a House where it's kept,' Namji said. 'But I know we are heading for the portal that'll take us to it. That's where the avatar has been leading us, Van Bam. We have to deliver Clara to Known Things.'

'Then I would suggest it is time to bring the others into the discussion, and make our plans.'

'Agreed.' Namji's large eyes were intense, her shades of grey determined. She glanced at the old tapestry of the Timewatcher, at the burning incense stick, and then offered the illusionist her hand. 'No more time to grieve for the dead, Van Bam. The living need the Relic Guild.'

CHAPTER TWELVE

CHASING GHOSTS

Labrys Town was reeling. The deliveries of cargo were not arriving, and news of Captain Jeter's execution had spread throughout the districts.

Little more than a day had passed since Lady Asajad had meted out justice on Jeter in Watcher's Gallery, with the help of the Woodsman. The Resident, Hagi Tabet, had issued no statement on the cargo crisis, and the populace was frightened. The town had changed; the denizens could feel it in the air, in the stone beneath their feet. The Nightshade no longer seemed like their protector, but more a predator, watching and waiting, poised to hunt.

Sergeant Ennis empathised with his fellow denizens, but he had other concerns to focus on.

In the southern district of Labrys Town, Ennis stood in the dingy cellar of a disused ore warehouse, gathering evidence.

The cellar had been gutted by fire. The walls and ceiling were charred and blackened. The acrid stench of smoke clung to the air, along with the greasy reek of roasted flesh. A few piles of ash lay here and there on the floor; but the largest and thickest pile covered the elevator platform that rose to the main warehouse above. The ash was the remnants of the police officers who had been sent to this place to deal with the Relic Guild. Their very bones had been incinerated, and Ennis knew that only magical fire could achieve that at the speed he had been informed it happened.

Magic ...

Wrinkling his nose against the stink, ignoring a bitter after-scent that dislodged an uncomfortable feeling in his gut, Ennis moved to a puddle of metal that had melted at the centre of the floor. Dull grey and without one blemish upon its smooth surface, the metal had hardened to form a rough diamond shape.

Ennis stared at it.

A few nights ago, following a report that the Relic Guild were hiding in this warehouse, eighteen police officers had been sent to execute them. Only one of those officers made it out alive. The fire had fused her uniform to her skin. She had died in hospital before Ennis got the chance to question her but had lived just long enough, been coherent long enough, to give a statement to a fellow officer before she died. The account had been sketchy, confused; but reading through it, Ennis had pieced together the story of what had happened in the warehouse.

The magickers of the Relic Guild had built some contraption in the cellar. Like a metal spear, the report said, stuck into the floor, with a star for a head that blazed with purple light. The star had shot rays of fire around the cellar, smashing glow lamps, scorching brickwork, destroying the wall that partitioned the cellar and stairwell, burning the staircase – making each step perilous. The fire prevented the police from reaching the Relic Guild, it incinerated anyone it touched – and in an instant, the report claimed.

Ennis gazed upon the diamond-shaped puddle of metal, the melted vestige of the spear-like contraption. The police officers had never stood a chance against the Relic Guild's magic. Did any denizen in Labrys Town?

Ennis couldn't recall an occasion in the Labyrinth's history when the Resident had turned against his people. The Relic Guild were supposed to be the protectors of the denizens – putting aside that the Relic Guild had not officially existed since the end of the Genii War. Ennis had never met Van Bam, had never particularly wanted to, always preferring to keep a low profile. However, Van Bam had governed his people well during his tenure. Why choose now, after forty years of faithful service, to become the enemy?

A conversion to demon-worship, was the official line; the Resident had fallen in love with the madness of the Retrospective, tempted into chaos by a whore named Peppercorn Clara, along with the bounty hunter they called Old Man Sam. And the threat of this trio was growing.

Hiding somewhere in Labrys Town, the Relic Guild haunted the denizens like nightmares, parasites lurking in the shadows to feast on the blood that fuelled their magic. The police watched the streets at all times without ever catching a glimpse of their prey; yet reports of missing people were becoming commonplace, and the threat of the magical virus that turned a person into a ravenous beast loomed over the town as if the sky itself might come crashing down.

To break the boundary walls; to expose Labrys Town to the Great Labyrinth; to let the Retrospective escape its confines and devour the town and its denizens; to sacrifice everything to a House of dead time and the hatred of wild demons – that was what the Relic Guild wanted, Lady Asajad claimed. But Resident Hagi Tabet would keep her people safe.

Her people ...

Ennis gazed around at the burnt walls and piles of ash. Perhaps here, in the cellar of this warehouse, the Relic Guild had been attempting to fulfil their goals. Was the contraption, now melted and useless on the floor, a device that was harvesting the Labyrinth's energy? The Nightshade provided power to all the districts, infused the air with ambient thaumaturgy that was as vital to the denizens' survival as the cargo that was usually delivered every day. Had the Relic Guild found a way to focus that energy through their device, converting it into a magical battering ram that could smash down the boundary walls? Perhaps the police had sabotaged the Relic Guild's efforts and saved the town at the cost of their lives, while the magickers escaped.

It was like he was chasing ghosts.

The sergeant's eyes were drawn to the back wall of the cellar.

An area of brickwork, slightly less blackened and charred than the rest, stood out. Stepping up to it, he brushed away thick soot, and uncovered a portion of the wall that had been smoothed to hard stone. There were no bricks, no mortar lines, just a strangely flat section. Clearing away more soot, he revealed an area roughly three-foot wide and rising at least six foot from the floor. Brushing his hands off, Ennis stepped back and stared at it. He had uncovered the shape of a doorway.

In her report, the sole officer who had survived the fight with the Relic Guild said that the confrontation had ended with the contraption exploding, filling the cellar with wild fire. She had only made it out because she had been in the middle of a cluster of other officers who took the brunt of the blast. But she was adamant that an instant before the explosion, the Relic Guild had disappeared – vanished into thin air, she said. Ennis had reasoned that they could've escaped by magical means, casting an illusion or barrier that protected them from the explosion; but as he stared at the smooth, door-shaped section of the wall, his mind was filled with doubt.

Rapping his knuckles upon the smoothed stone, he found it solid, entirely a part of the wall.

Doorway . . .

Moving back to the puddle of metal on the floor, Ennis bent down and ran a hand over its smooth grey surface. Curiously, its texture wasn't as hard as he expected; it felt somewhere between solid and liquid. Cold. He rubbed his thumb across his fingers, expecting them to be wet, but there was no moisture on his fingertips. He picked at the bottom point of the metal, and was surprised when it bent upwards without much resistance. He pushed it back down. Again – little resistance. The metal was malleable to his touch.

Ennis paused, considered, and then dug his fingers further underneath the cold metal, raising a larger point. He worked it up and down until it snapped free. The shard was thick, as large as his hand, but weighed next to nothing. It looked like a spearhead, a rough diamond shape like the metal puddle it had come from.

Ennis stared at it.

Diamond . . .

Raised voices from above disturbed him – happy, joking sounds Ennis hadn't heard for a while.

Wrapping the metal shard in a handkerchief and stuffing it into his coat pocket, he crossed the ash-covered floor, and carefully made his way up the charred and perilous staircase to the warehouse above.

He paused to stare at markings on the floor that he hadn't noticed on his way in. Strange symbols had been engraved into the stone – a long time ago, judging by the amount of dirt that was compacted into them – and they were laid out in a circle pattern. Ennis then acknowlededged the two patrolmen standing guard at the warehouse's open shutter door. The black glass bowls of their receptor helmets bobbed in return, and the sergeant stepped out into a morning sun shining in a clear blue sky.

Five cargo trams were lined up along the street that ran before a block of terraced warehouses. A host of warehouse workers were hurrying to unload the cargo. Ennis reasoned that the supplies had thankfully started arriving through the portal outside the Nightshade.

'Hey,' Ennis called to a nearby supervisor, who was ticking items off a checklist on a clipboard. 'When did the deliveries restart?'

'Late last night, as far as I know.'

'What was the hold up?'

The supervisor shrugged and continued ticking off items.

The atmosphere had definitely changed – laughter filled the air.

Walking along the line of cargo trams, Ennis came upon four warehouse workers, joking amongst themselves as they hefted wooden crates between them. They weren't offloading the cargo as the others were, but loading the lead tram with a delivery for another part of town. The driver sat in the driver's compartment, reading a newspaper, entirely happy to let the others do the hard work.

The shard of metal weighed so little in Ennis's pocket that he had to pat it to make sure it was still there. He pulled it out, folded back the handkerchief, and studied it. The cold metal remained dull and grey, like a storm cloud swallowing the light and reflecting not one ray from the sun. Malleable, not quite solid, it wasn't a substance Ennis could easily identify.

But he knew of a man who could.

As the warehouse workers loaded the last of the wooden crates, Ennis slipped the shard back into his pocket, and stepped up to the cargo tram.

The driver, a gruff and tired-looking woman, didn't seem impressed when Ennis knocked on the window. She glanced up from her newspaper with an irritated expression.

'What?' she said, her voice muffled by glass.

Ennis showed her his police badge. 'Where are you delivering to?'

'Central district.'

'Good. You can give me a lift.'

Hillem and Glogelder had decided that it was high time Samuel received a weapons upgrade. While Van Bam prayed in the chapel, and Clara lay sleeping under Namji's care, the two Aelfir took the old bounty hunter to one of the butcher's workshops on the abattoir level of Nowhere Ascending. It was a large room, cold and grey, all metal and stone. The rough floor was stained with old blood, and damp from leaking water pipes that dripped overhead. Meat hooks hung from the ceiling, and four long steel tables, scratched and worn, sat at one end of the room. Here and there, a few metal pails were filled with animal bones.

The grisly surroundings of the butcher's workshop were to double as a makeshift firing range, and Hillem and Glogelder had quickly set about replacing Samuel's lost handgun.

'Try this,' Glogelder said, offering Samuel yet another revolver. He had removed it from one of two large trunks, each filled with an assortment of hoarded weaponry.

Samuel took the gun and weighed it in his hand. It was clunky, much heavier than his old revolver.

'No,' he said, handing it back to Glogelder.

The big Aelf shrugged, laid the revolver on the floor with the rest of Samuel's rejections, and then rummaged through the stockpile in the trunk once more.

Hillem was setting up an area for target practice. He had found an old-fashioned wooden butcher's block, wide and thick, which he had upturned and set against the wall, where a variety of knives and cleavers hung. Against the block, he had placed a rack of metal shelving. Hillem had then collected an assortment of old animal bones, of varying shapes and sizes. He was now in the process of positioning the bones onto the shelves.

Samuel had to admit he was warming to the two Aelfir. The more he knew about them, the more he trusted them.

Like the agents of the human Relic Guild, fate had made Hillem and Glogelder orphans, though they were not magickers, or magic-users like Namji. They had met while spending time together at a juvenile correctional facility. Both of them were serving sentences for thievery. But while Hillem deployed a knack for avoiding violent situations and preferred to use his brain, Glogelder – as his beaten appearance would suggest – never shied from a good fight.

They had formed an unlikely but strong friendship, one always looking out for the other, and they had conspired to escape the correctional facility together. They had been conning and hustling their way across the Houses of the Aelfir since their teens, surviving by scamming the unwary.

'What about this one?' Glogelder said, emerging from the trunk with a hopeful expression and a pistol that was almost as long as the rifle holstered to Samuel's back.

The old bounty hunter pulled a dubious expression and shook his head, without touching the weapon. Glogelder continued the search with a grumble.

'Tell me something,' Samuel said. 'What happened to Sunflower?'

'What do you mean?' Glogelder replied, head in the trunk.

'It used to be full of farmlands and forests.'

Glogelder looked up with a surprised expression. 'Did it?'

'Apparently,' said Hillem. He looked over his shoulder at Samuel. 'The Timewatcher changed it after the war – literally overnight, according to the locals.'

'Hmm,' said Glogelder, returning to his search.

'But why change it to such a cold and hard place?' Samuel asked. *It used to be beautiful*, he added mentally.

'No one's sure,' Hillem replied. 'The older Aelfir reckon it was the result of the Timewatcher's anger, like the aftershock of Her wrath. Others think She did it to remind us that She's still there, watching, making sure Sunflower never stops looking after the denizens in the Labyrinth.' He thought for a moment. 'Personally, I think She did it as a show of power, to instil fear as a legacy.'

'Not that fear of the Timewatcher is anything like it used to be,' Glogelder mumbled.

'True enough,' Hillem agreed, 'but faith remains, at least for the time being.' He resumed setting out bones onto the shelves. 'Now tell me something,' he said to Samuel. 'When Van Bam was Resident, was his aide really a necromancer?'

Samuel was caught off-guard by the question. 'You know about Hamir?'

'The avatar told us all about the Relic Guild,' Hillem replied. 'Though it was a bit vague with us on whether Hamir would be arriving with you.'

'Well, obviously that question got answered,' Samuel said gravely.

'I don't mean any offence, Samuel, but I was surprised to learn that the governor of Labrys Town had someone as … dangerous as a necromancer helping him. Was this Hamir as scary as he sounds?'

Samuel wasn't sure how to answer. 'I've certainly seen him do scary things,' he said. 'But Hamir was … Hamir.' And he was surprised to feel a sense of loss inside him.

Hamir had always been a strange one; more of a solitary animal than Samuel had ever been. Samuel didn't believe for a moment that anyone in the Relic Guild had ever really known Hamir properly; but he did believe that the necromancer had been killed by the Genii.

'I'll tell you this much,' Samuel said to the Aelfir. 'We could do with his help right now.'

Hillem paused to give the old bounty hunter a sympathetic nod, and then continued laying out the bones.

'What's the story between Van Bam and Namji?' Glogelder said from the trunk. 'How do they know each other?'

Another question that Samuel wasn't sure how to answer. 'They met during the Genii War,' he said. 'Beyond that, I really don't know.'

He could have added the reason why – that he and Van Bam hadn't spoken much over the past forty years; that the remnants of the Relic Guild that had survived Fabian Moor had fallen apart after the war, but decided against it.

Having emptied the pail of twenty or more fragments of animal skeletons, Hillem walked over to Samuel.

'I've got something for you,' he said, pulling a slim metal cylinder from his pocket. 'Hold out your hand.'

Samuel did as he was asked. The tall and thin Aelf held the cylinder out, and pressed the top end with his thumb. The cylinder whirred and deposited a glass ball into Samuel's palm. Small, half the size of a human eye, it was filled with a clear, luminescent liquid.

'A spell sphere?' Samuel asked.

Hillem nodded. 'Leftovers from the Genii War. I don't think any-one makes them anymore.' He lightly tapped the sphere in Samuel's palm. The glow of the liquid brightened and then dimmed.

'What spell does it hold?'

'An anti-magic shockwave,' Hillem answered, almost proudly. 'The radius isn't very big, and it won't have any effect on a Genii, but the spell will drain the thaumaturgic charge from power stones, and dispel any lower magic at work in the area.'

The conversation had caught Glogelder's attention, and he looked over at the pair, frowning. 'I didn't know we had those,' he said accus-ingly. 'Why haven't I got any?'

'Because you're an oaf and you'll use one just to see what it does,' Hillem replied smoothly. 'If I'm going to trust anyone to recognise when anti-magic is needed, it'll be a magicker with prescient awareness.'

Glogelder thought for a moment. 'Fair point,' he said, and then continued rummaging through his collected arsenal.

'But these spheres come with a warning,' Hillem added to Samuel seriously. With care, he took the little glass ball from Samuel's palm, and gently pressed it back into the cylinder. 'The anti-magic shockwave is powerful enough to punch a magicker off his feet. The effects aren't long lasting, but if you use one, it *will* drain the magic from you along with whatever you're using it against.' He held the cylinder out to the old bounty hunter. 'There are three spheres inside.'

With an appreciative nod, Samuel took the cylinder and slipped it into a pouch on his utility belt.

'Now then,' said Hillem, 'let's find you a gun.'

He walked over to Glogelder, crouched down before the second trunk, opened the lid, and joined his thicker-set friend in searching through the stockpile.

'Why are you still wearing that thing?' Glogelder said, reaching over and tapping the red crystal of the proximity device strapped to Hillem's wrist. 'Who do you think is going to sneak up on us here?'

'Oh, I don't know –' Hillem slapped his friend's hand away – 'the Toymaker, perhaps?'

'We're in transit, Hillem! No one else is getting on until we stop.'

'Don't be so sure,' Hillem replied, and he pulled a small stub-nosed pistol from the trunk. 'What about this one?'

Glogelder gave a dismissive grunt. 'Wimp's gun.'

'Hey, I used to have one of these!'

'Sort of proves my point, doesn't it?'

'Shut up.'

Samuel couldn't help a slow smile appearing on his face at the Aelfir's banter. They would fit well into the Relic Guild, he decided.

Earlier, Samuel had asked them why they had got involved with Namji. Both of them were in their twenties, not nearly old enough to remember the Genii War; they didn't know what life had been like when the Thaumaturgists had been around and the Labyrinth had been the one realm that connected every House of the Aelfir. Why did they care? Both Hillem and Glogelder had admitted that until recently the humans of the Labyrinth belonged to an old story that neither of them cared about. But then the avatar changed the course of their lives.

Several months earlier, they had been running a scam to alleviate a noblewoman of the highly valuable contents of her vault. It should have been a *sweet con*, Glogelder had said, the big one that made them rich; but Hillem had explained that it had been a setup from the beginning. They found no riches in the vault, only a detachment of police officers waiting to arrest them.

'I always wondered when we'd get caught,' Hillem had admitted, 'but I never considered that our lives were being manipulated for the sake of the future.'

'The avatar was looking for people it could trust, people with nerve, with no ties and not much to lose,' Glogelder had added. 'Turns out, if you want to gain the loyalty of a couple of thieves, all you have to do is catch them when they're desperate.'

It had been while the pair was locked up in a prison cell that the avatar had first appeared to them. It had told the friends in crime tales of Fabian Moor, of the Genii, and what the future would be like if Spiral was freed from Oldest Place. They had come to care about the humans of the Labyrinth who belonged to an old and forgotten story.

Once the avatar had sprung the thieves from prison, they had found a petite Aelfirian woman waiting for them in the free world. Her name was Namji and she had a plan, she said.

While Hillem hid in Sunflower, waiting for the Relic Guild to arrive, Glogelder travelled the Aelfirian Houses, making contact with certain individuals. He was not recruiting other agents for the Aelfirian Relic Guild, Glogelder had said, but finding people who could be called upon when and if they were needed – Councillor Tal being an example.

'Now then – *this* might do the trick,' Hillem said, disturbing Samuel's thoughts.

He had produced a black-metal revolver from the trunk, which he was showing to his friend. Glogelder considered it before nodding approvingly. They both stared at Samuel. The old bounty hunter liked the look of what he saw, and Hillem loaded the gun with smooth metal slugs.

The eight-shot revolver that was handed to Samuel was longer and more streamlined than the one he was used to, but it was a comfortable fit for his hand. Samuel took a power stone from his utility belt and clicked it into the housing behind the revolving chamber. It whined and began to glow as he primed it with his thumb.

'Give it a go,' Hillem said, gesturing to the bones on the shelves of the metal racking.

Samuel took aim at a spine bone. He pulled the trigger and the power stone released a burst of thaumaturgy with a flash and a low, hollow spitting sound. The bone shattered and the bullet *thunked* into the butcher's block behind the shelving. The impact hole dribbled a tendril of smoke.

Samuel looked at the pistol. The balance and weight were good, the sight was true. It felt right.

Taking aim again, he unloaded the chamber – seven bullets, seven bursts of thaumaturgy, seven bone fragments disappeared from the shelves, high and low; and seven splintered holes, hot and smoking, appeared in the butcher's block.

Glogelder's beaten and scarred face had broken into a grin, and he chuckled. 'I suppose that's how a bounty hunter lives to be as old as you, eh?'

Hillem gave a low whistle. 'We were told you were good, but – where did you learn to shoot like that?'

'I thought the avatar told you all about the Relic Guild?' Samuel said evenly.

'Obviously not as much as I thought – *Old Man Sam*.'

Deactivating the power stone, Samuel thrust the revolver into the holster strapped to his left leg. It was a little loose, but nothing padding wouldn't fix.

'Looks like we have a winner,' Glogelder said. He was about to close the lid of the second trunk, when something caught his eye. 'Hang about!' He delved into the trunk and pulled out a rifle, still in its leather back-holster, and held it up like a prize possession. 'I'd forgotten about you, honey,' he said to the rifle, and then looked at Samuel with a wicked glint in his eyes. 'Now *this*, you *really* have to try.'

Samuel shook his head. 'I already have a rifle.'

'*No*,' countered Glogelder, 'what you have on your back is an antique.' He scoffed. 'Honestly, how long have you been using that thing? Thirty years?'

Samuel had no intention of telling the big Aelf that his rifle had been his companion for closer to fifty years. 'What's your point?' he asked dryly.

'It's older than I am,' Glogelder said. 'Whereas this little beauty ...' He slid the rifle from the holster. 'She's ageless.'

It was an impressive piece. Around the same length as the trusty police-issue rifle that Samuel had used all these years, but its design was very different. Obviously made by a proud craftsman, the rifle was ornately fashioned from burnished silver metal. The butt was dark lacquered wood, engraved with decorative, swirling patterns. It had two power stones; one set behind the barrel as usual, the second set halfway along the barrel's length, where a section a few inches long was fatter than the rest. It did indeed resonate a certain agelessness, but aesthetics alone couldn't convince Samuel to part with his own trusty rifle.

'Glogelder's right,' Hillem said. 'That thing is custom-made, Samuel, maybe one of a kind. Just give it a chance before you say no.'

Samuel's opinion of the decorative rifle quickly changed as, with reluctance at first, he accepted it from Glogelder, and found its shape, weight and balance more perfect than any weapon his hands had ever held. It was as if it had been ergonomically designed for him alone. With an unchecked look of surprise, the old bounty hunter turned the rifle over, frowning as he found no compartment into which a magazine of bullets might fit.

'How do you load it?' he asked.

'You don't need to,' Glogelder said with a grin. '*That*, my human friend, is an ice-rifle.'

Samuel had never heard of such a weapon.

'It's a marvellous feat of magical engineering,' Hillem said enthusiastically. 'The fat part of the barrel is a thaumaturgic crystallisation unit.' He stepped up to Samuel and pointed to the power stone behind the rifle's barrel. 'The trigger stone releases a burst of thaumaturgy as usual,' he said, and moved his finger up the barrel to the thicker part. 'But as it passes through the unit, the second stone super-cools the moisture in the air and converts it into darts of ice that are as hard as crystal.' He seemed pleased with his explanation. 'You have to prime both stones for it to work.'

'Go on,' Glogelder said eagerly. 'Give it a go.'

Samuel activated the power stones. They whined and glowed with violet light. For a test shot, he took aim directly at the butcher's block, and pulled the trigger. The spitting sound was a little louder and higher pitched than normal, and there was slightly more kick than he was used to, but the dart of ice the weapon fired stabbed effortlessly through the wood, clanging against the butcher's tools hanging on the wall behind the block, leaving behind a smooth and round hole.

'Those power stones you brought with you from the Labyrinth?' Glogelder said. 'How many shots can they fire in a row before losing charge? Ten? Fifteen if you're lucky?'

Samuel nodded.

The big Aelf pointed at the ice-rifle. 'Those stones can fire fifty or more.'

'Well, that's technically true,' Hillem clarified. 'But the stone in the crystallisation unit uses a higher charge, and it'll drain quicker than the trigger stone. And, of course, the amount of moisture in the atmosphere is a factor.'

'Oh, *sure*,' said Glogelder. 'If you're standing in the middle of a volcano, the gun won't work so well.' He pursed his lips and nodded his head. 'But you should see that darling dance on a rainy day.'

'You said these rifles are rare,' Samuel said, weighing the weapon in his hands. 'How did you find it?'

Glogelder winced. 'Probably better if you don't know.' He scratched his bald head. 'Let's just say I never asked the owner if it was up for sale.'

'But we do have spare power stones for it,' Hillem said. 'And plenty of ammunition for your revolver – regular and magical.'

Samuel took aim at the bones on the shelves. He adjusted his grip and stance to allow for the kickback, and then began shooting. By the time the rifle had sent an ice-dart to split a lamb skull in two, and no other bones remained on the shelves, the old bounty hunter already knew that it was time to say goodbye to the trusty, old rifle on his back.

'Are you having fun, Samuel?' said a voice.

Samuel swung around to see Van Bam had entered the room.

The illusionist studied the ice-rifle and seemed impressed. Beside him stood the diminutive form of Namji. Her expression serious, she looked at Hillem and Glogelder, and gestured towards the door.

'It's nearly time to leave,' she said. 'Let's go and get ready.' She gestured to the trunks of weapons. 'You can come back for these later.'

Samuel nodded his thanks to the Aelfirian men as they followed Namji out of the butcher's workshop. Van Bam waited until they had gone before facing his old friend again. He was clearly troubled.

'What's wrong?' Samuel asked suspiciously.

'An interesting question,' Van Bam said. He sighed. 'Samuel, we need to talk about Clara.'

CHAPTER THIRTEEN

DREAMSCAPE OF THE NECROMANCER

With the icy lash of a salty wind whipping at his face, Hamir wondered if there were certain things in life to which he should have paid better attention.

Standing on a wide ledge cut high into the face of a sheer chalk cliff, he looked down onto a billowing cloudbank. Vast and thickly white, it hid the ocean which undoubtedly lay beneath. In a clear sky of pale blue, a sun blazed to the east, tinting the crests of the cloudbank with golden highlights. It was a beautiful view, but, buffeted by the icy wind, Hamir felt desperately cold. And he had never enjoyed heights.

He shook his head at the view, most unimpressed.

Hamir would have warmed himself, cast a magical barrier to protect his person from the stinging air, but his magic was no longer at his command – or perhaps it was truer to say that the memory of *how* to command his magic was eluding him. The explanation for this was quite simple: the lofty scene before him, however detailed and beautiful, did not really exist and he was not really there. He could not control his environment, nor could he decide his place within it, for Hamir was trapped inside someone else's imagination.

The art of divination: it had never interested Hamir. In the past, just a fleeting mention of this topic had filled him with a deep-rooted boredom. Diviners proclaimed to have irrefutable knowledge of the future, while also harbouring a long line of convenient excuses for when their predictions, invariably, proved to be false. As far as Hamir was concerned, divination carried such a fundamental lack of cohesion and logic that it might as well be named the Art of Random Guessing.

However, although he was loath to admit it, Hamir had known, among the plethora of dullards, a few rare diviners who were most worthy of the title; a small and unique caste only to be found among the

Timewatcher's Thaumaturgists. And they were called the Skywatchers.

Grumbling an expletive that was lost to the wind, Hamir thrust his hands into the pockets of his suit jacket, and bowed his head to the elements.

He remembered many things that most people had forgotten, and he found himself recalling that there had once been a triumvirate of Skywatchers whom the Timewatcher favoured above all other Thaumaturgists. It seemed strange that the Timewatcher Herself, who insisted on equality between all her children – be they human, Aelfir, or creatures of higher magic – should be unable to avoid the touch of hypocrisy, but such was the way of things, Hamir decided. It was fact; none were more favoured to Her than the Trinity of Skywatchers.

In the pantheon of Thaumaturgists, the Trinity were revered by all. The first of them held the title of the Warden. The Warden acted as an extension of the Timewatcher's eyes, and her purpose was to watch all paths and doorways, ensuring that those who would use them adhered to the Timewatcher's protocols of peace and unity. The creatures of higher magic often referred to the Warden as Treasured Lady of the Thaumaturgists, but her true name was Yansas Amilee.

Of course, in time, Lady Amilee had become the patron of the Labyrinth; but now, Hamir reasoned, she had become the imperial pain in his posterior. While he was happy for his body to lie incapacitated but safe in a sleep chamber back in the Tower of the Skywatcher, he didn't much care for the fact that his mind was being held hostage to Amilee's imagination.

It was quite obvious what the Skywatcher expected Hamir to do next. The only way off the cliff was a small cable car docked quite innocently at the ledge's rim. The car's shell was made entirely of clear glass which reflected the sunshine with a hundred majestic rainbow starbursts; but to the necromancer it still looked as mundane as any tram from Labrys Town. Inside the car was a single chair, comfy-looking and upholstered in padded black leather.

The cable was anchored to the hard chalk surface behind Hamir. It ran through the wheel above the car, and then out over the ledge and down to disappear into the cloudbank that covered the ocean below. The glass door on the side of the car was open, and the leather chair waited with an invitation that Hamir was reluctant to accept, despite the harsh urgings of the wintry climate.

Hamir had never appreciated being ordered or directed or otherwise manipulated into doing what he didn't want to do. He rather fancied that he might have one or two choice words for Lady Amilee – should she ever decide to show herself – but he also understood that the Skywatcher had not projected this environment from her imagination purely for its aesthetic value; this was no ordinary dreamscape created within the realm of sleep. This view, this land, was a harbinger, a representation of things that were yet to happen; and Hamir the necromancer, who had never harboured any interest in the art of divination, could scarcely begin to decipher its meaning.

In this place, a hundred years could pass in the blink of an eye while only a fraction of a second passed in the waking world. Yansas Amilee – the Skywatcher, the Warden, Treasured Lady of the Thaumaturgists – she could wait an eternity for Hamir to play her game. Ultimately, the necromancer had no choice.

'Irritating,' he sighed, and entered the glass cable car.

The door slid closed as Hamir sank into the armchair; the car rocked, lurched forward and over the ledge to begin smoothly sliding down the cable at a speed that caused Hamir to catch his breath and dig his fingernails into the chair's armrests. As his carriage was quickly swallowed by thick clouds, he clenched his teeth against the nausea swimming in his stomach, and closed his eyes firmly to order his thoughts as best he could.

The second member of the Trinity of Skywatchers had been Baran Wolfe, Honoured Lord of the Thaumaturgists, who held the proud title of the Wanderer. Lord Wolfe the Wanderer had a reputation as the most benevolent member of the Trinity. His purpose was as an extension of the Timewatcher's compassion and love. After the creation of the Great Labyrinth, he roamed the Houses of the Aelfir, maintaining a harmonious equilibrium. An enigma, a nomadic mystery, no one could predict the movements of the Wanderer, only that he would appear where he was most needed, always at times of trouble. With kindness, he championed the balance of peace between the Houses; and the Aelfir who encountered him were left enriched by the experience.

Perhaps the saddest tale the Thaumaturgists had to tell was of the day Baran Wolfe was murdered by the third and final member of the Trinity of Skywatchers.

Behind Hamir's eyelids, the light dimmed momentarily as if he had travelled through a shadow. Sensing that the cable car had passed a large mass, he opened his eyes but couldn't see what it might have been.

Beyond the car's clear shell, the world was thickly pale and swirling. Through the forward window, past the moisture that ran in jagged, windblown streaks across the glass, something sullied the whiteness – something very dark and very big and approaching very fast

At first Hamir thought it might be a new cliff, that the journey was to be a swift one, and the car would soon be docking at whatever destination Amilee was leading him towards. But all too soon Hamir realised what the shape was, and he rolled his eyes.

A statue – a gigantic, behemoth statue – rising like a mountain of obsidian, carved in the likeness of a Thaumaturgist.

'Superfluous,' Hamir muttered, and he wondered who it was Amilee was trying to impress with this degree of imaginative detail.

In its hands, the colossal monument held a staff, the end of which was a diamond shape, the symbol of thaumaturgy. The edges of the diamond glowed with a purple radiance, and the cable upon which the car travelled ran straight through its centre, anchored into position by this perceived representation of higher magic. The car slid through the diamond without slowing. The cable sloped downwards on the other side until it finally cleared the cloudbank and the journey levelled out over an ocean as clear and blue as sapphire.

Up ahead, another monumental statue of a Thaumaturgist rose from the water. This one only emerged from the shoulders up, its arms raised above its hooded head. In its hands it held another glowing diamond. Unobscured by clouds, the statue's intricate detail could be appreciated.

Hamir pursed his lips and looked behind him as the car sped through the diamond. 'Superfluous *and* pretentious.'

The cable line dipped again, bringing the car to no more than ten feet above the calm and clear blue waters that stretched to the horizon. Hamir leant forward in the chair, peering through the glass directly ahead. There appeared to be an anomaly on the surface of the ocean in the near distance, like a patch of oil. As the car drew nearer to it, Hamir realised that the anomaly was a hole in the water. He was not surprised to see that the hole comprised a perfect diamond shape with its four edges glowing thaumaturgically, holding the ocean back.

The cable disappeared into the hole. The car followed its course, went sliding down, and Hamir was soon descending a tunnel that stabbed diagonally into the ocean like a spear of hollow glass. But the walls of the tunnel were not made of glass; they shone with the radiance of the thaumaturgy that held back the ocean.

Through the tunnel walls, Hamir could see movement in the purple light that weakly illuminated the ever darkening waters. They were only glimpses, brief flashes, but the necromancer saw enough to know that numerous, monstrously sized sea beasts were swimming around the tunnel. He spied amorphous blubber and tooth-filled maws, powerful limbs and bioluminescent tentacles, horned tails and cold dead eyes; but not one of these beasts dared swim close enough to the tunnel for the radiance of higher magic to light them in any grand detail. They were hints, ghosts, a threat in the unknown.

Evidently, Lady Amilee had never acquainted herself with the concept of pragmatism. 'Utterly pointless,' Hamir whispered, shaking his head at the creatures beyond the tunnel.

As the car continued to descend, Hamir's thoughts returned to the Trinity of Skywatchers.

The third and final member was known as the Word. Favoured above Lord Wolfe and Lady Amilee, the Word was First Lord of the Thaumaturgists, the only creature of higher magic who came close to matching the Timewatcher in power and wisdom. By far the most malevolent member of the Trinity, the Word's purpose was to represent the wrath of the Timewatcher. Principally the overseer of the overseers, he policed the Thaumaturgists, ensured his *peers* never strayed from the Timewatcher's directive that called for equality and gentle guidance for the Aelfir and humans.

The reverence held by the Thaumaturgists for the Word was second only to that which they held for the Timewatcher, but many also feared the power that had been entrusted to him. The day he murdered Baran Wolfe the Wanderer came with a great sense of irony; it was the act of betrayal that began the greatest of all wars. The Word's true name was Iblisha Spiral, but from that day forward he was known as the Lord of the Genii.

Hamir didn't notice until the glass cable car began to slow, but the tunnel had levelled out to run horizontally a few feet above the ocean floor, sandy and littered with black boulders. Signs of the great sea beasts were no longer present in the lowest depths, but directly ahead a huge monument appeared out of the gloom. A triangular shadow at first, it quickly revealed itself to be an underwater mountain, unnaturally smooth in its formation. The tunnel led directly to the mountain's base and the mouth of a cave which was, of course, cut into a perfect diamond shape.

As the car entered the cave mouth, there was a low hum and a flash of purple. The waters parted, and then Hamir found himself entering a large cavern that appeared surprisingly dry.

The car docked, the door slid open, and Hamir stepped out.

The cavern was formed from a dull grey substance, not quite stone, not quite metal. Its wall swept round Hamir to form a perfect circle, as smooth as the disc of the floor upon which he stood. He sniffed. This place wasn't just dry, it was dehydrated; there was a fundamental lack of moisture. The air felt as dusty as old bones, and it scratched the back of Hamir's throat as he breathed.

Illumination came from a pale, glowing pillar that rose at the edge of the circular floor, close to the wall. Hamir would easily need twice his arm span to fully embrace its circumference and it rose so high into the gloom above that he decided the interior of the underwater mountain must be entirely hollow.

At first Hamir thought the pillar was glowing moonstone, but as he took a few steps closer to it, he felt a chill that radiated from the structure's light, and realised it was formed from the hardest of ice.

The necromancer stepped back as the pillar reacted to his proximity.

With dull snaps and low groaning, the ice began to fracture into a host of jagged cracks that interconnected and streaked up its length.

The white glow intensified and the necromancer skipped back another step as the pillar shattered with a nerve-shredding noise. The ice collapsed into millions of tiny shards which swirled like a snowstorm, maintaining the shape of the pillar, but glowing now with a broken sort of paleness, flecked with dashes of dancing black. It looked like a column of static, and filled the cavern with a mournful drone.

At the base of the column, the flecks of black merged together and pushed back the shattered ice until it formed a slim doorway. A figure emerged, and Hamir raised an eyebrow.

Tendrils of sky blue wavered around a centre the colour of twilight forming a vaguely human shape. Eyes leaked tears of vaporous black.

'Hello again,' Hamir said to the avatar. 'I surmised you were working for Lady Amilee.'

Sky blue tendrils coiled and snaked, but the avatar didn't reply.

Hamir sighed. 'Is Her Ladyship planning to make an appearance? She must be bored, judging by the pointless detail of this place.'

Again, the avatar did nothing but hover before the column of droning static while shedding its blue radiance upon the metal-rock floor.

Hamir felt his patience fray. 'It's strange – I have found myself pondering the Trinity of Skywatchers for the first time in many, many years. Was I following a natural train of thought, or – here, in this place – did Amilee wish to remind me of the subject?'

Only then did the avatar speak. 'You know,' it said with a masculine and surprisingly affable voice, 'I still can't work out if you are a friend or a foe, Hamir.'

Hamir rocked his head from side to side. Technically, the answer would lie in the middle of the two options, but this really wasn't the time for a philosophical debate. 'In the scheme of things,' he said, gesturing around the cavern, 'does it really matter?'

'Maybe not,' said the avatar. 'How did you get here?'

Again, the philosophical answer was too splintered to address now, and Hamir stuck with the literal. 'I followed the instructions you gave me back at the Nightshade. How else?' A thought came to him. 'Or perhaps you suspect I've turned double agent for the Genii?'

Smoky tears rose lazily as the avatar relapsed into silence.

'Maybe you would answer a question for me,' Hamir said testily. 'Are the agents of the Relic Guild dead or alive?'

Nothing.

Hamir sucked air over his teeth. 'Thus far I have done everything that was expected of me, whether I wanted to or not.'

To emphasise his point, Hamir produced from his inside pocket the phial of changeling blood and showed it to the avatar. Of course, in this imagined world, the phial had changed. It now appeared as a piece of stone that had been carved to resemble what looked suspiciously like the Tower of the Skywatcher. Hamir stuffed it back into his pocket.

'I am tired of playing Amilee's little game,' the necromancer stated. 'I deserve to know exactly what in the Timewatcher's name is going on. Why am I here?'

'Follow me,' the avatar said. It drifted back into the doorway in the pillar of spinning, droning ice chips, and disappeared.

'Infuriating,' Hamir muttered.

The necromancer's skin tingled as he approached the doorway. He looked up the length of the column, narrowing his eyes against its glare. In this dreamscape, Lady Amilee could wait for an eternity for him to follow the avatar. It made no difference if Hamir stepped through the doorway now or in a hundred years, the outcome would always be the same.

Taking a breath, more from exasperation than any need to summon courage, Hamir stepped into the doorway. There was no pain, no sight, no noise, only a quick and curious sensation that told him his being had crumbled to atoms which were then borne on the spinning storm and sent up and up and up …

CHAPTER FOURTEEN

GRACE AND TRUTH

Clara had no memory of waking up. She couldn't remember venturing outside. But there she was: fully awake and running through a thick and lush forest.

From the taste in the air, and the way moisture seemed to be descending, Clara decided it was evening. The falling sunlight filtered lethargically through a verdant canopy.

Exactly when she had changed into the wolf, Clara didn't know; but she was ravenous, and the thrill of the hunt coursed through her veins. The cool moisture in the air dampening her pelt, the scent of foliage rich in her nostrils, the ground coarse and leafy beneath her paws – Clara felt at home, as though she had been born in the forest, spent her life running free and wild, master of her terrain.

She sped between the trees: a huge, sleek, powerful silver-grey phantom. This was her life, here and now – simple, clean, pure – and there was nothing else in the realms she need concern herself with.

Clara headed down into a depression in the forest floor, a bowl-like clearing where mist had formed, thick and wet. She slowed, creeping into the mist with a growl. The hunt was almost over.

The deer was young and fast – strong, but not strong enough. Its energy expended, the animal hid in the mist, its eyes wide with fear, not quite looking at the wolf, body frozen yet trembling. It didn't move as Clara drew near; she tasted its terrified hopelessness. She wished the chase could've lasted longer, but her hunger demanded feeding.

The deer gave a final, desperate scream, barely struggling, and Clara's huge jaws crushed its neck. Hot and sweet blood coated the wolf's muzzle as she bit and tore, sating her hunger with tender flesh, shrouded by mist.

While she fed, Clara acknowledged a presence at the back of her mind, a brooding shadow that belonged to the dead Resident, Gideon. He didn't speak, but Clara knew he was there, vicariously revelling in the rewards of the hunt, the taste of the spoils. Clara didn't care; let him play the voyeur. His ghost wouldn't hinder her enjoyment.

Comforted by the tang of blood in her mouth and the fresh meat filling her belly, Clara sensed that other animals of the forest were hiding from the new master who now ran among them. She had heard them earlier, scurrying from her path as she hunted down the deer. Although such fearful respect pleased the wolf, the prospect of an after-meal fight greatly appealed to her. She hoped that the forest would send a champion to challenge her dominance, a territorial beast big enough to provide a real test of her strength.

A scent that did not belong in the forest suddenly filled Clara's nostrils. The wolf stopped eating, and retreated from the deer carcass. Turning in a slow, full circle, she scanned the encircling mist.

'Clara,' a smooth voice said.

The wolf could smell Van Bam, but not see him. She remained where she was, proud and alert.

'Clara, I know you are there,' Van Bam continued. 'I can see you.'

Of course he could, Clara realised; the illusionist could see things hidden to others, including wolves concealed by thick mist. But still, she didn't move. If she could have, the wolf would've smiled.

'Please,' Van Bam appealed, 'may I speak with you?'

Boosted by the respect in the illusionist's tones, Clara padded up the slope of the depression. When she emerged from the mist, she saw Van Bam up on the ridgeline, leaning against a tree, green glass cane stabbed into the ground. His metallic eyes dull and grey, he smiled at the wolf.

'I had forgotten how big you are,' he said.

Clara stopped short of him, resisting the urge to race forward and bowl him over. She didn't like that Van Bam stood above her, higher than her.

'Clara, we need to talk.'

There was an unspoken command behind Van Bam words, a demand. Clara showed him her teeth.

Van Bam chuckled kindly. 'You cannot fool me,' he said. 'I know you have gained mastery over your magic. This is a good thing – to be celebrated. But for now, I need to speak with my *agent*.'

He was telling her to change back into human form, but Clara had no intention of obeying. She turned, intending to run through the mists into the forests, to spend the rest of her life among the trees, free and wild.

'I understand your reluctance,' Van Bam said, and by the tone of his voice, Clara knew that he really did understand. 'Gideon warned me that you were proud and stubborn as the wolf – perhaps a little blinkered too?' He chuckled again. 'But I suspect you are also carrying a shadow of self-doubt, yes?'

Clara turned back to him, but still didn't approach.

'If you would let me,' said Van Bam. 'I would banish the final uncertainty inside you with a little reassurance.'

Without waiting for consent, Van Bam tapped his cane against the forest floor, whispering words too quick for Clara to catch. With a brief flare of green light, a glassy chime rippled through the trees, borne upon the droplets of moisture in the atmosphere, resonating in the air. It brushed against the wolf's thick pelt, burrowed into it and tingled upon her skin, like the breath of a magicker whispering to the blood of a kindred spirit. The sensation was enticing, beckoning with the promise of acceptance.

The wolf wanted to back away, but every muscle in her body tensed, hard, ridged, and held her still. Then they relaxed with a sudden, lurching sensation, as if she might vault into the air and soar above the treetops. Instead, the wolf stumbled forward and stood in the forest as a young woman called Clara. Whole and human; a smooth transition from one animal to another, the gentle calling of her magic ringing in her ears.

She looked at Van Bam, up on the ridgeline. 'No pain,' she whispered.

'Acceptance does not always have to hurt, Clara.'

Clara laughed in surprise and delight.

But her feet didn't feel right.

She scratched them against the dirt, as though there was something stuck to her soles that refused to dislodge. When she looked, she found hard, calloused skin had formed there, like the pads of a wolf. And then Clara realised with astonishment that she did not stand naked before the illusionist.

She was dressed in a simple pair of trousers and a long-sleeved hooded top. The material was grey and strange to the touch; as thin and light as silk but with the brushed feel of suede or hair.

'Where did *these* come from?' she asked with a bemused grin.

'A gift from Namji,' Van Bam replied, as Clara made her way up the slope. He looked quizzical. 'I believe she recently introduced herself to you.'

Clara confirmed with a nod. She could recall the voice of the Aelfirian magic-user in her head while she had been viewing the world through Van Bam's eyes.

'Your new clothes are imbued with a surprisingly strong spell,' Van Bam continued as Clara joined him. 'When you change, the wolf will *absorb* the clothes, but – as you have just discovered – they will reappear when you take human form again, thus avoiding embarrassing situations.' He smiled, looking her over, nodding approvingly. 'It is good to see that being a changeling is finally agreeing with you, Clara.'

Once more whispering to his magic, Van Bam conjured the illusion of a mirror in which Clara could study her reflection. She immediately saw the change in the woman who stared back at her.

Clara's posture was straighter, her shoulders a little broader. Was she taller? The streaks of red dye had gone from her hair, but its natural blonde colour was now tinted with silver-grey. And her face ... it was still *her* face in the mirror, but Clara's features were not those of the awkward young girl she had last seen. She seemed older, more mature, gazing upon her reflection with eyes carrying a hint of sunshine yellow.

'How do you feel?' Van Bam asked.

Clara scratched the thick skin that had grown under her feet against the ground again. 'Good,' she said, if a little uncertainly. 'Like I'm supposed to be in this body. Like I've ... grown to fit my skin. Does that make sense?'

'Perfectly,' Van Bam replied, clearly pleased.

He dispelled the mirror, and Clara looked around at the forest.

'Where are we?' she asked.

'Fittingly, this House is called the Face of Grace and Truth. It is a wildlife reserve, which means there are no Aelfir here to witness our passage. Word of our escape from the Labyrinth is out, and we are wanted people.'

Clara nodded. 'So Gideon has told me.'

Van Bam pursed his lips. 'Clara, when was the last time Gideon spoke to you?'

'Not for a while now.'

'He has not spoken to me for a while, either. It is unlike him to be so quiet.'

Clara could feel the dead Resident's presence in her mind, but it was an uninterested kind of presence, as if he had found a secluded table in a library where he wouldn't be disturbed by anything going on around him. She knew he wouldn't reply if she called to him.

'I still don't understand how I'm hearing Gideon's voice,' Clara admitted. 'He said that the two of you believe it was caused by the avatar.'

'That is so,' Van Bam replied. 'I do not know how the avatar did it, or why ... Perhaps it knew that Gideon would help temper the wolf's wilder side.'

Clara gave a smile. 'Well, something certainly worked.'

'How much can you recall, Clara?' Van Bam asked. 'With Gideon being reluctant to speak, I am uncertain as to exactly what you remember from the time you spent unconscious.'

Clara's eyes narrowed as she recalled her strange experiences and related them to Van Bam.

She spoke of what Gideon had told her, of the rescue from Sunflower, of Hillem and Glogelder, and the attack of the assassin known as the Toymaker. She remembered being told of the Panopticon of Houses, a not-so-democratic union set up to govern the Aelfir after the Genii War; and of the secret band of hierarchs called the Sisterhood, who had little love for the Labyrinth and its denizens.

She recalled why the Genii had returned, that they hoped to find Oldest Place and free Spiral. Lastly, most importantly, Clara told Van Bam of her strange conversation with Namji, and of finally learning what had been imparted to her by Marney with the empathetic kiss.

'We really are in trouble, aren't we?' Clara said.

Van Bam shrugged. 'Samuel and I have been in worse situations.'

'Really?'

'No, Clara, not even close.'

Clara chuckled as the illusionist smiled and continued.

'It is impossible to guess if Fabian Moor knows that Marney gave you the location of Oldest Place.' His expression was sympathetic. 'I do not suppose that you ever wished to be the custodian of such a secret.'

Clara could still feel Marney's presence, lingering inside her. But it felt different now, more dormant than it had been before, as if it was sleeping – or perhaps hiding from Gideon – and the changeling had no wish to wake it up again. The box of secrets the empath had planted in Clara's mind, so great a mystery for so long, a mystery she had at one time been desperate to unravel, now felt as if it was filled with poison.

'But the information was never meant for us,' Clara said. 'Marney used me as a courier, a messenger. I'm supposed to deliver the location of Oldest Place to a device called ... *Known Things*? Do we know what that is, Van Bam?'

'A relic of some kind,' Van Bam replied. 'Perhaps a weapon, perhaps a set of instructions. I do not know. Either way, activating Known Things will supposedly rid the realms of Spiral and the last of the Genii forever.'

'And only I can activate it,' Clara said. 'The knowledge in my head is a key.'

A breeze blew through the forest, whispering through the trees. Clara wrapped her arms around her body, her hands feeling the soft texture of her new clothes, her mind going over all she had learned while unconscious.

'What am I supposed to do?' she wondered. 'How do you think Known Things works? How will it take the information from me?'

'At present, I suspect the answers are only known only by the avatar,' Van Bam replied. 'But Samuel and I will stand beside you all the way, Clara. Our new Aelfirian friends, also.'

Clara was reassured to hear that she wasn't alone, but she wasn't entirely convinced. 'How much do you trust Namji?' she asked, remembering her inexplicable yet instant dislike of the Aelfirian woman.

Van Bam chuckled. 'There was a time when I would have told you *not very much*. But that was decades ago. Now, I am very glad to have Namji on our side. I would say the same for Hillem and Glogelder.'

Something curious crept into Clara's mind, like a crackling sensation scratching across the inside of her skull: Gideon's amusement. She waited for him to speak, but he remained silent. A fresh breeze chilled the changeling.

'Clara,' Van Bam said sternly. 'Soon, we will be leaving this House. At our next destination is the portal that will deliver us to Known Things. Are you ready to face the uncertainty ahead?

Clara nodded, and Van Bam smiled.

'But before we leave,' he said, 'Namji has asked for a meeting, to discuss what happens next. Now, you can either accompany me to this meeting, Clara ... or you can stay here for a while and test your *new clothes*.'

There was a sudden lift in Clara's spirit as she remembered the speed and strength of the wolf, the feel of the forest as she sped through it. She looked around at the trees, heard their call, tasted it on the fading sunlight. She rubbed a hand over the material of her new magical clothes – a second skin. Pulling up the hood, she looked at Van Bam, grinning.

'Go – celebrate your magic while the moment allows,' Van Bam told her. 'Gideon will keep you abreast of any important details – once he decides to start speaking again, that is. And, of course, if the wolf is not too stubborn to listen.' With a twirl of his green glass cane, the illusionist walked away. 'Try not to stray too far, Clara. I will let you know when it is time to return.'

Clara watched him until he disappeared into the trees.

Despite the situation, despite the weight of responsibility that Marney had planted in her mind, Clara flushed with exhilaration. She gritted her teeth, and ran down the slope into the bowl in the forest floor, the magic in her blood singing with the sweet voice of power and grace. She willed the animal to come, welcomed the bestial strength and courage, accepting the wolf as an extension of herself, and asking it to accept her.

And with a forwards lurch, without pain or fear, Clara ran on four strong legs and disappeared into the thick and wet mist.

Samuel was thinking about death.

On the outskirts of a clearing, he sat on the rough ground, resting against a tree. With his new revolver holstered at his thigh, and the ornate ice-rifle lying across his lap, the old bounty hunter watched the Aelfirian Relic Guild make preparations to leave the forest House of the Face of Grace and Truth.

Beyond the clearing, Glogelder hid the two trunks, still filled with hoarded weaponry, inside the treeline, grumbling all the while that he didn't like leaving behind his stockpile. Namji and Hillem ignored his complaints as they constructed a contraption out of clear crystals, thin copper wires, and a metal rod, which Samuel understood would eventually form a communications device.

At the centre of the clearing was a tall, wide archway made from roots and vines, twisting and tightly interlaced: a portal, ancient and inactive, but soon to be the pathway that led the group to their next destination – perhaps their ultimate destination. The archway had no symbol that might tell Samuel which House the portal led to, and, as usual, Namji had not been forthcoming with the information.

The old bounty hunter's gaze settled on a stream that skirted the glade before veering off to run through the forest. Its burbling was as peaceful as everything else in the Face of Grace and Truth, though the tranquillity in this House meant little to Samuel.

He was thinking about death.

Before the Genii War, the Face of Grace and Truth had held a different name. The Trees of the Many Queen, it had been called. Home to a race of proud and secretive Aelfir, the Trees of the Many Queen had been imbued with strong and ancient magic. Legend said that the forest was sentient; that the roots of every tree absorbed the souls of the dead, and those souls protected the House. Welcoming to friends, dangerous to enemies, the forest magic of the Trees of the Many Queen had been destroyed by the Genii. The reserved but valiant Aelfir who had lived here had resisted subjugation, and fought Spiral's army to the death. Not one of them had survived.

Hillem had told Samuel that after the war the Timewatcher had preserved the Trees of the Many Queen, perhaps in memory of the Aelfir who had remained loyal to Her until the bitter end. She had instructed that this forest House be left to nature's wild laws, a realm where animals roamed free of Aelfirian interference, and it became known as the Face of Grace and Truth.

A message in the name? Samuel wondered.

He also wondered about the sentient magic that the Genii had destroyed. If the trees were no longer able to absorb their souls, what had happened to the spirits of the Aelfir who died defending their House? What happened to the souls of the dead from *any* House now?

There was a place, a vast phenomenon far out in the void of space known as the Higher Thaumaturgic Cluster. And at the heart of this place was the ineffable world of Mother Earth, the home of the Timewatcher. Not for the first time in the last four decades, Samuel asked himself a question: did the Timewatcher still welcome the souls of the dead into her House with a loving embrace?

He had no answer, but sometimes he didn't believe that any soul could reach Mother Earth now. The Timewatcher had disappeared. She had turned Her back on Her children, abandoned humans and Aelfir alike; why would She do that, but leave the doors to Her House open? Would the Timewatcher care if She knew that a handful of Genii had survived the war? That they were planning to free Spiral from the eternal prison She Herself had created for him?

She should care, Samuel decided. If Spiral and his Genii overcame the paltry resistance offered by the Relic Guild, their goal would be to subjugate every House of the Aelfir. They would raise an army so large that the Timewatcher and all Her Thaumaturgists would be unable to prevent it marching on the Higher Thaumaturgic Cluster, and the ineffable House called Mother Earth. Nothing and no one would be safe.

Namji paused in her work to offer Samuel a slight smile. He stared at her until she looked away to continue helping Hillem construct the communications device.

With a sigh, Samuel ran his hand over the decorative metal of the ice-rifle, and the pattern carved into the wooden butt. At least he now understood why he had never felt comfortable around Clara.

Samuel's magical gift was to be warned of danger, at all times; a prescient awareness that watched his back. His magic steered his thoughts and dictated his actions, but only when trouble was imminent. When he was starting on a path to danger, Samuel's magic became a bad feeling in his gut, as if all hope had been stripped from the future. With the mystery of Clara's connection to Marney finally explained, the old bounty hunter supposed the changeling had been leading him to a troubled future from the moment he had first laid eyes on her. She had always been a bad feeling.

'Do you know what I'm wondering?' Glogelder's voice came from the edge of the clearing. 'How does Known Things work? If it's able to kill Spiral, doesn't it need to go to Oldest Place? I mean – we'll have to take it there, because that's where Spiral is, right?'

Namji and Hillem stopped working and looked at each other. It was a question they hadn't considered before. And neither had Samuel.

Glogelder pulled a duffle bag from one of the trunks and flapped it open angrily. 'And where do you think Oldest Place is, anyway?' By the tone of his voice, it was clear his uncertainty was making him edgy. 'I've heard a lot of theories from a lot of people in my time. Nobody really knows what they're talking about, do they? But what if one of them got it right? After all, Oldest Place has to be somewhere.'

'The people of Labrys Town also have theories,' Van Bam said as he emerged from the treeline and walked over to stand beside Samuel.

The Aelfir looked at them.

'The most common belief is that Oldest Place is the lowest age of the Retrospective,' Van Bam continued. 'They say that, buried beneath a land of fire and poison, Spiral, Lord of the Genii, sits in Oldest Place, feeding upon the souls of the dead that the wild demons capture for him.'

The stillness was only broken by a breeze rustling leaves, and the burbling of the stream.

'That sounds like a myth to me,' Hillem said, his smile uneasy.

'To me, also,' Van Bam replied. 'But the truth will not be revealed until Clara reaches Known Things. Please, do not let me disturb you from your work.'

Taking the hint, the three Aelfir returned to their efforts.

Van Bam turned his metallic eyes to Samuel sitting with his back to the tree, and said, 'I trust your mood has improved?'

Samuel didn't answer. Earlier, when the illusionist had told him what it was Marney had planted in Clara's mind, his reaction had not been particularly helpful.

'Where's Clara now?' Samuel asked tersely.

'Enjoying her magic for a while,' Van Bam replied. 'She will join us when we are ready to leave.'

Samuel shook his head. 'How did Marney find out, Van Bam?' He couldn't keep the irritation from his voice. 'Has she known since the end of the war where the Timewatcher hid Oldest Place? Has she been sitting on it all this time? And who told her? The Timewatcher Herself?'

'I do not know.' Van Bam's voice carried the sad inflection of one as tired of unanswered questions as Samuel. 'But I can guess who encouraged her to give the information to Clara. I suspect Marney had been dealing with the avatar long before the two of us.'

'Like this lot,' Samuel said, nodding to the Aelfir in the clearing. 'But they don't know who's controlling the avatar. Who's the master? Who's dangling the carrot in front of us?'

'I am hoping that all our answers will come at our next destination.'

'That's not the first time you've hoped for that.' Samuel made an angry noise. 'You know, I always used to resent the idea that I would die in the Labyrinth – if not from bounty hunting, then from old age and uselessness. But now … How do you destroy the most powerful Thaumaturgist that ever existed, Van Bam?'

Samuel looked at the portal in the clearing and shook his head with vexation. 'We used to spend our lives hunting down all kinds of dangerous artefacts and relics, but this device, this *Known Things*? How could Marney know about it when we didn't?' He swore softly. 'If it's that powerful, the Timewatcher should've used it to kill Spiral at the end of the war. Not put him in a prison.'

'Samuel,' Van Bam said in a consoling sort of way. 'I would not like to guess at the Timewatcher's reasons, and I do not much like how we have been manipulated, either. But if the future to which the avatar is leading us arrives at a place where Spiral, Fabian Moor, and the last of the Genii, are finally vanquished for good, then I am being led willingly. I know you feel the same, old friend.'

The illusionist offered the old bounty hunter his hand. With a wry smile, Samuel accepted, and Van Bam helped him to his feet.

'I never thought I'd say this,' Samuel said, 'but I wish Hamir was with us. He always seemed to know things we didn't, had secrets up his sleeve that he could whip out at the right moment.'

'I have to agree with you. As indecipherable as Hamir was, I think our chances would greatly improve if he were here.'

'Do you know what really pisses me off, Van Bam? If we're successful, what's the best we can hope for?'

'To return home, I suppose.'

'Exactly.' Samuel gestured to the Aelfir. 'You heard what Hillem said. The Sisterhood isn't exactly a big supporter of the Labyrinth. Eventually, they're going to stop sending supplies, and the denizens will die out anyway. Makes me wonder what the point of it all is.'

Van Bam smiled. 'Samuel, we are old men, long in the tooth, and perhaps we have seen too much in our time. But I keep my faith, even now, and I choose to believe that in the end the Aelfir, including the members of the Sisterhood, will remember their compassion for humans.' He shrugged. 'And who knows, when we return home, perhaps our efforts will become legend, a tale that is told in the Labyrinth for generations to come.'

'Need to avoid being killed first,' Samuel said, sliding the ice-rifle into the holster on his back. 'Personally, I don't give a toss if I never see Labrys Town again.'

Van Bam chuckled and clapped his old friend on the shoulder.

'That should do it,' Hillem announced.

Having completed the construction of the communications device, he and Namji stepped back. Glogelder walked into the clearing, his spell sphere launcher hanging from his shoulder, a duffle bag filled with spare weapons and ammunition in his hand.

Namji shooed the Aelfirian men away, and they came to stand alongside Samuel and Van Bam. Glogelder dumped the duffle bag on the floor with a clunk and acknowledged Samuel. Hillem busied himself fastening the buckle on a holster belt. Two pistols hung at his waist.

Namji stood before the group, gathering her thoughts before addressing them. A cloth satchel hung diagonally from her shoulder, no doubt filled with the paraphernalia of a magic-user. She gestured to the stone archway behind her. 'This portal will take us to a House called the Sisterhood of Bells.'

Van Bam looked questioningly at Samuel.

Samuel shrugged. 'The name seems familiar, but I don't think I ever went there.'

'It's now the Aelfirian capital,' Hillem explained. 'It's where the Panopticon of Houses is based.'

'Then can one assume,' said Van Bam, 'it is also the home of the hierarchy within the Panopticon – the Sisterhood?' Namji nodded, and Van Bam continued. 'I cannot imagine that this House will be the most welcoming for us to visit at this time.'

'Oh, I don't know,' Glogelder said happily. 'Hiding under the noses of the enemy – nobody will suspect we're there.'

'Don't be so bloody sure,' Samuel growled. 'You're saying that to reach Known Things we have to go to the one place that we should be staying very clear of?'

'This portal isn't used anymore,' Namji said, nodding at the archway. 'It leads to a secluded area. No one will see us arrive.'

'You sure of that?'

'I don't make the rules, Samuel. I just follow the avatar's instructions.'

'Don't we all?' Samuel grumbled, and Glogelder chuckled.

'But we have contacts in the Sisterhood of Bells,' Namji assured them. 'We have friends waiting there.'

'That's right,' said Glogelder. 'I sent a message sphere to a contact earlier on. I've told her to meet us.'

'And speaking of message spheres –' Namji began. From her satchel she produced a ball of blue glass. 'This came through the portal a short while ago. It's a message from Councillor Tal. I waited until we were all together before hearing it.' She looked at Van Bam. 'I assume Gideon will keep Clara informed.'

The illusionist nodded, and Glogelder whistled lowly at the mention of the changeling's name.

'I saw the wolf before she ran off into the forest,' he said to Samuel. 'She's a big girl.'

'Hillem,' said Namji.

Hillem stepped forward and took the message sphere from Namji. He carried it to the communications device.

Four fist-sized crystals, clear and roughly cut, sat on the clearing floor, each a corner of a square. At the centre of the crystals, a metal rod had been stabbed into the ground. It rose three feet, and supported a metal bowl. Thin copper wires ran from the bowl, down into the tops of each crystal. The crystals themselves were further connected by four more wires, running along the ground, to complete the shape of the square. The device had the appearance of a pyramid's skeleton.

Hillem placed the message sphere in the bowl atop the metal rod. He placed a cap for the bowl on top of the blue glass ball, concealing it within what was now a sphere of metal, topped with a small power stone. Hillem pressed the stone and it began glowing. He and Namji then moved back to observe with the others.

Hissing, like wind rustling leaves, was followed by the muffled cracking of glass. Blue smoke leaked from the join between bowl and cap, but only momentarily, before it was sucked back into the metal sphere. The copper wires began to glow with heat, and the crystals on the floor were illuminated with the pale violet light of ambient thaumaturgy. A hum filled the forest air. The space within the pyramid frame became thick, grainy, turning dark blue. A face began to form in it.

Slowly, the head and shoulders of an elderly Aelf materialised. Councillor Tal's image was detailed in varying shades of blue, as if he was forming from mist. The councillor looked harassed, apprehensive. His large Aelfirian eyes shifted left and right as though checking no one was observing him, and then he looked directly out at the group.

'My friends, I pray to the Timewatcher this message finds you alive and well,' he said, his voice slightly distorted. 'News of the Toymaker's attack in Sunflower has reached the Panopticon, but they say no human casualties were found. I hope this is true.

'I have been called to the Sisterhood of Bells to report on what happened in Sunflower. The whole place is up in arms—'

Tal broke off to look around, as if distracted by a sound. '*Everything* is being blamed upon the humans,' he continued hurriedly, urgently. 'The Sisterhood is using your breakout to its advantage. Its members are drumming up support in the Panopticon, and once again raising the question of why the Aelfir continue to send aid to the Labyrinth. They are saying that *you* killed the police officers in Sunflower, not the Toymaker. They are saying that you are planning to release *all* humans into the Houses of the Aelfir.' He rubbed his forehead. 'And this time a lot of former Labyrinth sympathisers are inclining to the Sisterhood. Especially in light of another *incident*—'

Councillor Tal's voice ground to a halt, his image fizzed and died, leaving behind only grainy air. Namji gave Hillem a reproachful look.

'I know, I know – it's a bit improvised,' Hillem admitted, stepping forwards. 'Give me a second.'

He began fiddling with the wires where they were connected to the crystals. He winced a couple of times as he burnt his fingers on the heated copper, and when he adjusted the third crystal, Councillor Tal's misty blue image returned.

Momentarily frozen into an unflattering expression, Tal's face crackled, blurred, reformed, and he started speaking mid-sentence.

'... happened in Hammer Light of Outside. The monks there say their House was attacked by an evil presence. Information is sketchy at this time, but by all accounts, a portal ripped open in mid-air. Monsters came through it, demons of some kind. They killed many monks, and dragged a few more back through the—' another burst of static disrupted Tal's next words. '... Witnesses say the portal led to a hostile House – they describe it as a nightmare realm that carried the stench of corruption and death.'

Samuel shared a meaningful look with Van Bam.

Councillor Tal made an angry noise. 'The Sisterhood has been shameless in its crusade,' he said bitterly. 'The Panopticon of Houses has sent an official statement to every realm. It claims that the attack on Hammer Light of Outside was the result of your escape – that by breaking out you have caused cracks to appear in the barrier between the Houses and the Labyrinth. It claims that the Retrospective has followed you here, and it is trying to drag you back to where you belong.

'All magic-users agree – magic-users in the Sisterhood's employ, no doubt – that the only way to seal the breach and prevent the Retrospective attacking other Houses is to execute you, and throw your corpses into the portal to the Labyrinth in Sunflower.'

Again, Tal looked around nervously. His face became bigger as he leaned forward and dropped the volume of his voice.

'I am doing all I can to help you, but it isn't easy. I've never been popular around here, and it's become a lot worse. There is much to this situation that I don't yet understand, but the Sisterhood has created hysteria within the Panopticon. All the Houses are on alert. *Everyone* is looking for you, not just the Toymaker. You *must* keep moving and reach Known Things before ...' Tal broke off as voices came towards him. 'I have to go—'

And the councillor vanished.

The grainy, blue air within the communication device faded and died. The crystals lost their thaumaturgic light, and the glow of heat drained from the thin copper wires. In the following silence, Samuel felt a chill.

'Hammer Light of Outside,' said Van Bam. 'I know that House. It is a spiritual retreat.'

'The Retrospective?' Hillem said. 'Could the demons have really come from there?'

'I ... I am not certain,' Van Bam replied.

'Yes, you are,' Samuel said sharply. 'It was the Retrospective.'

Another quick, charged silence.

'How is that possible?' Namji said.

'I have no idea,' Samuel said, staring at Van Bam. 'But a place of nightmare? Wild demons? The stench of corruption? What else could it be?'

'I do not know,' Van Bam said. 'The Retrospective is trapped within the Great Labyrinth, Samuel. It cannot move beyond—'

'Wait!' It was Hillem who had intervened, and he had lost all interest in the conversation taking place around him. 'Namji,' he said agitatedly. 'There are other portals in the Face of Grace and Truth, right? That isn't the only one, is it?

Namji looked at the archway, and then shrugged, confused. 'I don't think so. Why?'

Hillem showed the group the proximity device strapped to his wrist. The red crystal was glowing. 'Someone's here.'

And Samuel sensed it too; his prescient awareness flared as a bad feeling in his gut. He drew the ice-rifle, and glared at Van Bam.

'Clara …'

By the time Clara took a rest from exploring the forest, stopping beside a stream to lap at the cool, clean water, the sky was dimming towards twilight and the shadows of trees were stretching across the ground. And it was while she slaked her thirst that Gideon decided to break his silence along with the serenity. He carried a warning from Van Bam.

Clara—

I know, she said. The wolf had already detected the change in the atmosphere – something bad.

Looking up from the stream, Clara scanned the trees surrounding her. She could feel that a menace had come to the forest, a nonhuman menace, magical, unnatural. She heard rustles in the undergrowth, tapping against the bark of trees.

Clara, said Gideon, as small points of dull violet light appeared in the forest, *do you remember what I told you about the Toymaker?*

The wolf's hackles raised. *You never see him, only his toys.*

I think it's time you returned to Van Bam and the others.

Clara growled. *Too late, Gideon.*

Slowly, they came from all directions, tightening the circle around the wolf: hand-sized, insect-like automatons. They crept though the brush and over the trunks of trees on thin legs of silver. With metallic tails tipped with pale light hanging above their bodies, the Toymaker's toys closed in, massing for an attack.

The wolf stepped into the stream water and bared her teeth.

If the Toymaker himself was anywhere close by, Clara could not detect his scent. His toys were odourless too, but their presence buzzed in the air with the hum of magic.

See the lights on the tips of their tails? said Gideon. *Each one is a thaumaturgic sting, Clara. I'd imagine one strike is enough to kill a man. How many do you suppose to kill an oversized wolf?*

With cool water reaching halfway up her legs, Clara turned full circle in the stream, her yellow eyes scanning the environment, her brain trying to calculate how many of the Toymaker's minions surrounded her. A hundred? More?

I can't run, Gideon, Clara replied, tense and anxious. *They'll swarm me if I try.*

They'll swarm you whether you run, fight, or stay still. I think it would preferable if we were facing wild demons from the Retrospective. Am I right?

Where are Van Bam and Samuel?

Hold on ... Whilst Gideon fell silent for a moment, the small, insectoid automatons crept closer. *Van Bam says help is on its way, Clara.*

The first of the automatons approached the edge of the stream. The wolf lowered her front quarters and showed it her teeth.

Don't do anything rash, Gideon said, his voice sober. *If you fight, you die, and that wouldn't be good for any of us, would it, Clara? Hold your nerve. Help is coming.*

With their tails shining with deadly light, the horde of hand-sized attackers amassed at the stream's edges on both sides of the wolf. A stillness unfolded, in which they seemed to be preparing for a synchronised attack.

Gideon ...

Hold your nerve, Gideon repeated. *Stand your ground.*

A breeze blew through the forest.

The Toymaker's toys skittered, and then froze as one.

The wolf smelled a new presence.

There was a blur of movement approaching Clara, following the line of the stream. It disturbed the gentle waters like a stone skimming upon the surface as it sped closer. There was a rush of air that crackled with energy. The diminutive automatons moved a little way back from the stream's edge, as if uncertain. And then the small form of an Aelfirian woman materialised at the wolf's side, reeking of magic, holding a spell sphere.

Ah, the cavalry, Gideon chuckled.

Namji shouted in defiance as she raised the sphere above her head and crushed it in her hands. With the tinkle of glass, the spell was released. Fizzing, the magic descended to protect Clara and Namji within an umbrella of wavering energy. With obvious effort Namji uttered a word too fleeting for Clara to catch, and the magical energy shot outwards, slamming into the malevolent toys, sending them rolling and tumbling back into the trees.

Namji collapsed at Clara's side, only managing to keep her head above water by gripping the wolf's pelt.

'They won't stay down for long,' she told Clara. Her voice was hoarse. Casting the spell that had given Namji preternatural speed had clearly exhausted her. 'We need to run, Clara. Can you carry me?'

Clara allowed Namji to climb onto her.

'Follow the stream,' the Aelf said, lying flat against the wolf's back, digging her fingers into the thick hair. 'Go back the way I came.'

Van Bam says the portal is activated and waiting, Gideon said, his tone excited. *But if you want to live long enough to deliver your message to Known Things, then you'll have to be quick, child.* Run!

As Clara bounded out of the water and ran at fast as she could alongside the stream, the Toymaker's minions recovered from Namji's magic, and gave chase.

The insectoid automatons moved with frightening speed. Their motion as quick as fleas, they pursued Clara and Namji, jumping from tree trunk to tree trunk, scurrying on metal legs, following the line of the stream. The wolf could scarcely keep ahead of them.

Hold tight, Clara thought to Namji, which made Gideon cluck his tongue.

You're adorable, the ghost said dryly. *Do you think Namji would be clinging desperately to your back if she had the strength left to cast a telepathy spell? Just focus on getting out of here, you idiot.*

Nonetheless, as if hearing Clara's mental address, Namji's grip tightened and her legs clamped hard against the wolf's sides. The Aelf weighed so little that Clara was able to push her legs to full speed, focusing on the way ahead, not daring to look back – a silver-grey streak rushing through the forest.

She could hear the Toymaker's minions rustling, clicking and clattering behind her – *just* behind her. The glow of their tails shone weak light on the ever deepening shadows in the forest. Clara knew that if her step faltered for a fleeting instant, the horde would swarm her, and her passenger, pierce their skins with those glowing stings, a hundred times over, injecting into their bloodstreams their special brand of poison designed by thaumaturgy.

Stick to the stream, Gideon said. *It will lead you straight to the portal.*

Namji gave a cry of despair.

Two of the automatons had come abreast with the wolf. They jumped from the branches of a tree, flying towards their targets. They were supernaturally fast, but the wolf's reflexes, and the magic that fuelled them, were equal to the attack. Clara ducked and vaulted the stream to the other side. She didn't slow, she didn't falter. Namji, not expecting the sudden change in course, slipped on her back, almost falling. Thankfully, the Aelfirian magic-user righted herself, but it was too late anyway.

On the opposite side of the stream, one of the Toymaker's toys had pre-empted the wolf's manoeuvre and had managed to get ahead of her. It now scuttled head on towards Clara, metal legs a blur of movement; and Clara was left with no time to stop or change directions. All she could do was charge through her foe and hope for the best. The hand-sized automaton vaulted into the air, the light of its tail lashing for the wolf ... but then disappeared from Clara's path, as a projectile hit it with a glassy clang.

Namji cried out again as Clara ran through tiny and sharp shards of shattered ice hanging in the air. A figure stood further ahead, aiming a rifle.

'Keep running, Clara!' Samuel bellowed.

The old bounty hunter continued shooting. Power stones flashing, the rifle sent dart after dart of hard ice into the forest with a low spitting sound. The projectiles whistled over Clara's head, clanging and shattering as they hit their targets. Samuel's sure, cold accuracy never missed.

Beside him, Glogelder aimed his spell sphere launcher. The big Aelf's teeth were clenched as he pulled the trigger and sent a sphere hurtling through the trees. It exploded behind Clara, but she outran the fiery blast. She risked a glance back, saw the flames chasing her, and a few automatons who had not been knocked aside by the detonation. They were close.

With Samuel still peppering the forest with lethal projectiles, and Glogelder readying a second spell sphere, Clara carried Namji past the two men and into a clearing, where an archway of roots and vines was filled with the oily swirl of a portal. Hillem stood on one side of the archway, Van Bam on the other.

'Don't stop!' Hillem shouted, gesturing for Clara to head straight into the portal.

Van Bam stepped forwards as Clara neared, dropping to one knee and stabbing his green glass cane into the ground. With Namji clinging desperately to her back, Clara just had time to see a spray of green illusionist magic shooting into the forest before the portal swallowed her, and the world turned black.

THE REASON OF TRAITORS

Van Bam woke up with a start. It was the dead of night and his heart was racing. He wondered for a moment if troubled dreams had disturbed his sleep. But no; it was a bad feeling, a feeling bordering on panic that suggested something was very wrong.

He sat up, instinctively retrieving his green glass cane from the bedside table. Although the desert breeze coming in through the wicker balcony doors had cooled the room, a thin layer of sweat had formed on Van Bam's smoothly shaven head. He wiped it away. High Governor Obanai's house seemed calm and quiet under the desert moon. Yet something was amiss in House Mirage.

The events during the High Governor's banquet were still fresh in Van Bam's mind. The troubles faced by the ruling family, and the secrets they chose to keep, jockeyed with the stories of a giant blood-magicker haunting the desert of Mirage. And the performance of Buyaal, the self-proclaimed Master of the Desert, still bothered the illusionist.

Van Bam was convinced he had missed an important element within the information he and Angel had gathered at the banquet — some small detail he had seen, maybe a word he had overheard, forming a link in a chain. Perhaps that was what had disturbed his slumber. Had his unconscious mind sifted through the information while he slept and found the link that connected events?

Van Bam gazed around in the gloom. The darkness wasn't quite right. He sensed a lie in the room, an omission. Here and now, a truth was concealing itself from the illusionist.

Van Bam flicked his cane, releasing a small glassy chime, and whispered to his magic.

He detected the anomaly almost immediately. A patch of air dangled over the bed like an invisible cloud of *not-truth*. Van Bam reined in the urge to panic caused by his realisation that it dangled no more than a foot from his nose.

Low, hushed voices came from beyond the bedroom door.

Keeping his body still and his expression natural, Van Bam whispered to his magic a second time. Holding his cane in both hands, he twisted and pulled his hands apart. The green glass had become malleable, and Van Bam kept twisting and pulling until the cane separated into two halves, and the illusionist held a short, wicked spike in either hand.

Voices came through the door again. Hurried. Urgent.

Van Bam took a breath. The anomaly in the air before him shifted. The illusionist thrust up with one of the glass spikes, stabbing – into a solid body.

Jumping from the bed, Van Bam held the spike at arm's length as a struggling, squealing mass slowly materialised, losing the spell of invisibility that had concealed it. Impaled upon the green glass was one of the strange creatures native to the desert of Mirage, part scorpion, part spider – a coppion. Its legs stopped wriggling as it died; its tail ceased thrashing and hung limp, leaking clear venom. A pale corpse on the end of the spike.

A cry of pain came from beyond the bedroom door. It was followed by the tell-tale spitting of a gun. Angel shouted.

'Van Bam!'

The illusionist whipped the dead coppion onto the bed, ran to the door, flung it open, and entered the lounge, a green glass spike in each hand. He surveyed the situation.

Angel was there, dressed in a nightshirt. And she wasn't alone in the lounge area. Namji, the newly revealed heir of House Mirage, stood close behind the healer, wearing fatigues and heavy boots. At first, Van Bam thought Namji was the aggressor; she had an arm wrapped around Angel, and in her free hand she held a small pistol, power stone primed and glowing. But the fear in the Aelf's eyes told Van Bam a different story. The aim of her weapon seemed to encompass the entire room. The two women were moving slowly through the lounge in unison.

'Van Bam,' Angel hissed.

'I know,' he replied. 'Coppions. I have already killed one.'

'So did we. Bastard stung me.'

Van Bam looked through the open door to Angel's bedroom. There, on the floor, lay a dead coppion, a few of its legs missing, its body mutilated by a bullet. Van Bam noticed then that Angel's arm was glowing with the pale radiance of healing magic. There was a puncture wound on the back of her hand, oozing with clear liquid streaked with blood.

'I think there's another one in the room,' Namji warned, the pistol shaking in her hand.

'Keep still,' Van Bam ordered, and both women froze.

Van Bam knocked the spikes of green glass together lightly, summoning his magic for the third time. The chime reverberated around the room, searching for lies. There was a small patch of illusion on the wall behind Angel and Namji.

'Both of you, walk towards me. *Slowly.*'

The women separated, and did as he asked. The anomaly reacted and began creeping down the wall. By the time Angel and Namji had walked past Van Bam, the concealed coppion had reached the floor, and then it scuttled across the room towards them, moving fast. As it jumped into the air, Van Bam stepped forward and stabbed out with a glass spike. He grunted as he lanced the coppion mid-flight. It thrashed in its death throes. With a *clink* of glass on tile, Van Bam jabbed the point of the spike against the floor. The invisibility spell left the coppion, and there it was, wriggling madly, impaled through the body. Van Bam finished it off with the other spike.

Angel rounded on Namji. 'What in the bloody Timewatcher's name is going on?' she demanded.

'Buyaal,' Van Bam answered for her. He kicked the dead coppion away. 'I understand now how he *performed* his show. He was using illusionist magic more powerful than mine. That is why I could not detect it – he was able to hide it from me. It was *blood-magic.* Buyaal must be working for the Hermit.'

'It's not what you think,' Namji said, her voice distraught. 'Buyaal isn't the enemy. I-I came to warn you ...'

She trailed off at the sound of someone clucking their tongue.

At the far end of the room the balcony doors opened, and blue-grey moonlight flooded the lounge. A figure stood on the threshold, tall, burly, head wrapped up in scarves, his Aelfirian face boasting a huge, grey beard.

'Ebril,' Van Bam whispered.

The ambassador's grin was as broad as it was malevolent.

'I have to admit, Master Van Bam, you are disappointingly slow piecing all of this together.'

Although it was Ebril's voice, the words were not spoken by the Aelf at the balcony doors. Van Bam looked to see a perfect duplicate of the ambassador standing in the main entrance to the guest apartment. 'I had believed your mind was far quicker than this.'

'Shit,' said Angel.

Behind Van Bam a third Ebril had emerged from the illusionist's bedroom. A fourth image stepped from Angel's bedroom, and said, 'Now, what am I to do with the three of you?'

Angel swore again. 'What's going on, Van Bam?'

'Illusions.'

'I can bloody see *that*! Which one is real?'

Clearly terrified and on the verge of tears, Namji's hand shook more than ever as she aimed the pistol at one Ebril then the next. 'I-I don't know what to do,' she whimpered.

Each Ebril seemed amused.

Angel made an angry noise. 'Give it to me,' she said and snatched the pistol from Namji's grip. The healer's aim was solid. 'Just tell me which one is real, Van Bam.'

Each image of Ambassador Ebril was a perfect duplicate of the man Van Bam knew. Except the eyes – they were orbs of black. Confused and angry, Van Bam knew that his magic was not strong enough to tell which Ebril was the real Aelf, or indeed if they were all illusion.

'It was you all the time,' Van Bam said through clenched teeth. 'Ursa was working under your orders. *You* were responsible for bringing Fabian Moor to Labrys Town.'

'And thank you for allowing me to bring news of Lord Moor's success back to Mirage,' said the Ebril in the doorway to Angel's bedroom. He smiled. 'Lord Spiral was planning his uprising long before the Timewatcher suspected anything.'

The ambassador by the main entrance shrugged. 'House Mirage

already belonged to the Genii by the time the war began.'

'Ursa and I hid ourselves well in the entourage that was sent to the Labyrinth,' said the Aelf by the balcony door.

Behind Van Bam, the fourth Ebril added, 'All we had to do was wait. No one suspected us. Not even your precious Lady Amilee.'

Angel aimed the pistol at the Aelf near the balcony doors. 'High Governor Obanai and his House sided with Spiral?' she said angrily. 'And no one knew?'

'I suppose you could say that,' Ebril replied. 'Including the other members of my entourage, of course. Their cluelessness helped to conceal Ursa and me. But most of those who returned to Mirage with me were quickly converted. In fact, only one has resisted subjugation.'

'My father trusted you,' the High Governor's daughter hissed. 'And you betrayed him.'

'You suggest I am a traitor?' the Ebril behind Van Bam said. 'It was your father who swore his House's allegiance to the Genii.'

'*I* trusted you!'

'Grow up, Namji. This is your last chance. Join your father, or die – here and now – with these *humans*.'

Namji's lip trembled and she looked more terrified than ever.

Slowly, silently, Van Bam reconnected the two spikes into one cane of green glass. He gave Angel a nod.

'Yeah,' the healer growled. 'Bollocks to this,' and she pulled the trigger.

The power stone flashed, and the pistol spat. The Ebril standing on the threshold to the balcony swirled like smoke as the bullet passed through him, and then he reformed into the perfect image of the ambassador. He was smiling.

As Angel took aim at the next Ebril, Van Bam whispered to his magic, thinking to summon a diversion – anything to confuse the situation and allow his fellow agent a clear shot at each of Ebril's duplicates. But the words refused to pass Van Bam's lips. A sour energy rippled across the room, making the illusionist feel as though he were being forced to swallow his own magic. Angel yelped and dropped the pistol as if the metal was red hot. The power stone cracked and fizzed as it hit the ground. The pistol shattered.

Angel groaned and sank to one knee, clutching the hand bearing the coppion sting. Her skin flared with healing magic and more poison oozed from the wound.

Helping the healer to her feet, Namji looked at Van Bam, and then each image of Ebril. Her fear turned to defiance.

'I will never willingly join Spiral,' she whispered, her young face steely. 'I'd rather die than turn against the Timewatcher.'

'Well, I suppose you had to learn how to stand on your own two feet eventually,' said the Ebril standing in the apartment's main doorway. 'I very much doubt your family will mourn your passing. Personally, I'll be glad to see the back of you—'

Ebril's head was suddenly yanked back, exposing his throat. A shadow had moved up behind him. Moonlight glinted from a blade. A knife sliced into Ebril's skin, severing arteries. Blood erupted down clean white robes, and Ebril dropped to his knees and fell face down upon the tiled floor without a sound. Instantly the three illusions swirled into smoke and disappeared.

Van Bam had just time enough to share a surprised look with Angel before Buyaal, Master of the Desert, stepped out of the shadows and into the room.

He marched straight up to Namji and gripped her shoulders, looking intensely into her face. 'Are you all right?'

Namji looked at the corpse of Ebril and nodded.

'There is an explanation here,' Van Bam said warningly. 'And I *will* hear it!' He stabbed his cane against the tiles with a discordant chime.

'I understand your anger, but now is not the time,' Buyaal said, his expression stern, his facial tattoos eerie in the moonlight. 'We have to leave. In case you haven't guessed, there is a Genii controlling Mirage.'

'*That's* who the Hermit is?' said Angel. She winced and groaned again, using her healing magic to ease the pain in her hand. 'He's a Genii?'

'You have been told many lies since you first set foot in this House, but the Hermit is no enemy,' Buyaal replied. He switched his gaze to Van Bam. '*I* am one of the Hermit's followers. *He* is leading the resistance in Mirage. There is much you do not know, but for now you *have* to trust me.'

'Then get us outside the citadel walls,' Van Bam said forcefully. 'We need to use the doorway back to the Great Labyrinth.'

'Impossible,' Buyaal said earnestly. 'Just about every soldier in Mirage will be guarding the Giant's Hand, and so will the Genii.'

'Then what do you suggest, Buyaal?'

'I will take you to the Hermit. But first get dressed, both of you. The desert nights are cold.'

Van Bam could read the truth on Buyaal's face, an open honesty, pleading and anxious. The illusionist nodded to Angel.

A few moments later, when the Relic Guild agents had hastily dressed and returned to the lounge, Van Bam saw Buyaal holding a spell sphere. Namji stood very close to him, her expression blank, her large Aelfirian eyes staring at Ebril, lying dead in his own blood.

Buyaal said, 'My first duty is to save the heir of Mirage, but the Hermit also needs to speak with the Relic Guild. If you would live longer than this night, you will allow me to lead you to him.'

He smashed the spell sphere against the wall. The intense reek of magic was followed by a moaning wind. A huge circle had been neatly cut into the wall, and through it Van Bam could see the dunes and the shifting sands of the desert, grey under the moon. In the near distance were the silhouettes of mountains.

'A portal?' the illusionist said.

'A gift from the Hermit,' Buyaal explained. 'It's only short range, but it should give us a head start before the Genii realises that Ebril failed to kill you.'

Blood-magic? Van Bam wondered. He had thought only higher magic could create portals.

'This spell won't last forever,' Buyaal said with a smile, though his micro-expressions betrayed his urgency.

Namji moved alongside Van Bam and squeezed his hand. 'You can trust Buyaal. He saved my life. Saved all our lives.'

'Well,' Angel said, clutching her hand. 'I don't know about you, Van Bam, but I'm buggered if I'm staying here.' She gave her fellow agent a shrug.

Van Bam nodded. 'Then lead the way, Master Buyaal.'

Marney felt nothing.

In Ghost Mist Veldt, on a mountainside where the war against the Genii was hidden by sentient magic, she had been captured by deserters from Spiral's army. She didn't know where they had come from; they had simply materialised in the stone hut. And their appearance had coincided with Denton's disappearance. Marney was not holding out for her mentor's return.

The Aelfirian soldiers had relieved Marney of her possessions, stripped her down to her vest and undergarments, kept her on her knees on the hard floor of the stone hut, with her hands bound together behind her back and tied to her ankles. Marney's face ached from bruising. She could feel dried blood in her nostrils, taste it at the back of her throat. Her clothes had been used as fuel to keep the pot-bellied stove burning with such a low heat it barely lifted the chill in the hut. The wind whistled through cracks in the stonework.

Cold and shivering, with her emotions locked inside her, deadened beneath a magical seal, Marney embraced a state of apathy in which she could coolly remember the teachings of her missing mentor.

Know your enemy first, Denton had once told her. *Try not to act before you understand who you are dealing with.*

There were four Aelfirian soldiers keeping Marney captive, but only three were currently inside the stone hut with her. One male and two females. Each of them seemed to have succumbed to a desperation that had sunk far below mere hopelessness. Marney had been listening to them talk, reading their emotions, as they rifled through her possessions which were laid out on the rickety metal camping table. Less than an hour ago, Marney had been at that very table, talking to Denton, before the magic of Ghost Mist Veldt had snatched him away.

'Rations!' the man called out. A young Aelf by the name of Nurmar, he was short and scrawny, barely fitting his ragtag uniform. Nurmar had upended the contents of Marney's backpack onto the table, and had found the sealed nutrition cakes she had brought with her. 'Am I glad to see *these*—'

One of the women, Jantal, snatched the ration from his hand and placed it down with the others. 'We divide these up fairly,' she said, voice full of warning. She slid the pile of nutrition cakes to one end of the table. 'Got a problem with that?'

Nurmar shook his head and resumed searching.

Jantal was an intolerant Aelf, at least a decade older than Nurmar, and she demanded obedience with threats that she issued in a free and easy manner. Within this small group of soldiers, Jantal was second in command to an Aelf called Matthaus, the only deserter currently absent. He had left the hut a while ago, taking with him the envelope containing Denton's secret instructions on how to find the Library of Glass and Mirrors.

The fourth soldier was a large Aelf with a haunted look on her face. Red, they called her – probably a nickname, but nothing to do with the colour of her hair, which was short and black. She didn't help her fellow deserters, only watched as Jantal and Nurmar rummaged through Marney's belongings. Marney could sense that Red's emotions had all but flat-lined. Her mind was war-damaged.

Marney's eyes drifted to three rifles leaning against the hut wall. *Know your enemy first*, Denton had impressed on her.

Nurmar had several weeks' worth of beard on his face. Judging by the dark circles around all their eyes, and the feral quality in their expressions, these soldiers had been living on the edge for all that time. But one advantage the empath had over her captors was that they did not seem to realise their captive was a magicker.

'What's this?' Nurmar said. He had found Marney's tin of sandalwood bath salts and had it open in his hands. 'Looks like salt or sugar.'

Jantal leaned in for a look. She dipped a finger into the bath salts, and then touched it to her tongue. She pulled a face and spat on the floor.

'If we can't eat it, don't waste time on it!' she shouted and smacked the tin from Nurmar's hands, as if the bitter taste of the scented salts was his fault.

The contents of the tin cascaded across the stone floor.

Marney felt nothing.

Unperturbed by Jantal's outburst, Nurmar continued his search, muttering, 'Where did a bloody human come from, anyway? Isn't she supposed to be confined to the Labyrinth?'

'I don't know,' Jantal replied. She was holding up Marney's baldric of throwing daggers. 'But we can be sure she wasn't sent here to help us. And I don't suppose it could hurt to try to make her talk again.'

'No, it couldn't,' said Nurmar.

Jantal turned a cruel sneer to Marney. 'There used to be more of us, you know. But they didn't make it, and we … ah, well, food isn't easy to come by in this place.' She slid one of the daggers from the baldric. 'And your rations won't last us very long.'

Marney responded with a slow blink.

As Nurmar grinned, a strange glint in his Aelfirian eyes, Jantal snorted and offered the slender silver blade to Red. The large Aelf stared at the weapon, but made no move to take it.

'Go on,' Jantal urged. 'You know what to do with it.'

Without a word, Red took the dagger and walked towards Marney, her steps slow, her eyes averted. Jantal walked alongside her, but Nurmar remained close behind, rubbing his hands together, shifty and nervous, like a schoolchild egging on a bully. They reached their captive.

Marney felt nothing.

'She's a tough little bitch,' Jantal said, stepping beside Marney and facing her colleagues. 'But I think we can break her.'

Nurmar chuckled. Marney tried to catch Red's eye, but the Aelf wouldn't look at her.

Jantal gazed down at the kneeling empath. 'One more time – why are you here? Who sent you?'

Marney met her gaze, but said nothing.

Jantal sighed. 'I'd start talking if you don't like pain.'

The threat was ineffectual. Marney had fathomed this woman – nothing like as ruthless as she wanted people to believe. Jantal had her fears, and Marney knew what they were.

'You're going to die here,' Marney told her, voice as stony as the hut, 'and no one will remember you.'

Jantal's features twitched and her jaw clenched. She stared at Marney briefly, before she turned angrily to Red.

'Hurt her,' she ordered, grabbing Marney's hair and forcing her to face the large Aelf. 'Take out an eye.'

Red went down on her knees before Marney. Very slowly, she moved the point of the throwing dagger towards the empath's face.

Ignoring the rough hold of Jantal, and the childlike excitement of Nurmar, Marney calmly summoned her empathic magic. She sent out a searching tendril, probing into Red's emotions, hunting for the place inside her where pain and trauma had taken a toll on her mind. As she found it, wrapped her magic around it, Marney felt herself guided by the teachings of Denton.

Once you understand your enemies, you will know how to turn their emotions against them.

Marney's empathy gripped what remained of Red's emotions, and she injected her voice into her magic.

Look at me.

For the first time, Red's big eyes met the empath's. Pale, watery. Although she kept the blade slowly moving towards Marney's face, there was doubt in Red's mind, a question: had she chosen the wrong side in this war?

Of course you did, Marney thought to her. *You already know that.*

A subtle pulse of agreement tingled along Marney's magic.

But what could she do about that now? Red asked. She had made her decisions, and now she had to live with the regret, with the hurt.

Yes, you've done terrible things in Spiral's name, Marney told the Aelf, watching dispassionately as the dagger inched closer and closer. *But that doesn't mean you have no choices left.*

It had been a long time since Red had believed in choices, salvation, a way out. Marney felt another flare of emotion: primal despair, as if from an infant clinging to her mother, desperate for reassurance, answers …

Isn't it obvious? Marney said soothingly as the tip of the dagger came to rest on her cheek and slid up towards her left eye. *You know what you have to do, Red. You've always known, haven't you?*

The dagger stayed still. Red narrowed her eyes and nodded.

'Yes,' she whispered.

'What are you doing, Red?' Jantal said. 'What are you waiting for?'

The large Aelf smiled at Marney, and Marney smiled back.

Jantal and Nurmar jumped clear with shocked cries as Red stabbed the dagger into her own throat. She stabbed again. And again. Over and over, never making a sound, ignoring the shouts of her fellow deserters begging her to stop. By the time Red died, and her corpse toppled sideways, her blood had spewed over Marney's face, drenching her vest and naked thighs.

Marney felt nothing.

Nurmar choked as he tried to speak. Jantal turned wide and fearful eyes to the empath.

'What did you do, you *bitch*!'

You know what I did, Marney thought to her. *You know it makes sense.*

Jantal flinched. 'Yes … Yes, I reckon it does.'

There's no need to be jealous of Red, Marney continued. *She found a way out, sure – but she left the door open.*

Jantal nodded. 'I suppose you're right.'

'Who are you talking to?' Nurmar said shakily.

Pick up the dagger, Marney told Jantal. *It's for the best.*

Submissively, Jantal bent down and pulled the blade from Red's throat. It came free with a *slurp*, and she studied the red-smeared silver in her hand.

'Jantal,' Nurmar hissed. 'What are you doing?'

'Shut up!' Jantal spat. 'Just … *shut up!*'

Stick Nurmar first, Marney directed. *He's a liability, and you never liked him anyway.*

Jantal clenched her teeth and turned dangerous eyes on her colleague. 'Come here, you bastard,' she growled.

Nurmar yelped and tried to make a dash for the rifles leaning against the wall. But Jantal reached him first and kicked his legs from under him. As Nurmar crashed to the floor, Jantal was on him. She kicked him onto his back and gripped the collar of his uniform in her fist.

'No!' Nurmar screeched as Jantal raised the dagger and prepared to stab it into his face.

The hut door flew open with a howl of wind, disturbing Jantal, disrupting Marney's magical hold. An older Aelfirian soldier ran in, clutching several sheets of paper in one hand, and a spell sphere in the other.

'She's a magicker,' shouted Matthaus, the leader of the deserters. 'Get away from her!'

Jantal released Nurmar. She looked at the blade in her hand and dropped it. 'Shit …'

Nurmar scrambled away.

Before Marney could react, Matthaus stepped forwards and threw the spell sphere at the floor. It smashed two feet from the empath, and released a shock wave. It hit Marney with a droning vibration. She felt as though the spirit had been sucked from her body.

She must have passed out. The next thing Marney knew, she was still bound and on her knees, but Red's body had been removed, though a thick, sticky puddle of her blood remained. The empath felt acutely frightened.

Her magic was gone.

'What are you?' said a calm, amiable voice. 'Telepath? Empath?'

Matthaus sat at the camping table, watching Marney. He was a gaunt and grizzled Aelf, a greying veteran with a thick white beard. He still held the sheets of paper, and Marney realised they were the contents of Denton's envelope of instructions. He also had another spell sphere close at hand on the table.

Marney became aware that she was covered in blood. She could smell it, taste it on her lips. She retched.

Matthaus seemed to recognise the sudden fear that Marney had been exposed to without her magic. 'Empath, I'd say.'

The door to the hut opened. Jantal and Nurmar walked in, looking scared and angry. Nurmar carried a long, sharp knife.

'We were going to get Red … *ready*,' Nurmar said, 'but her body disappeared. Just like that.' He clicked his fingers.

'Doesn't surprise me,' Matthaus replied. He smiled at Marney. 'Things like to appear and disappear in this House, as I'm sure you've fathomed. But,' he said to his colleagues, 'it might not matter now.' He held up Denton's instructions.

'What does it say?' Jantal asked after giving Marney a threatening glare.

'I'm not sure,' Matthaus said. 'It's written in code. But I've gleaned enough to know who she is, and that she didn't come to Ghost Mist Veldt alone.'

'Another human?' said Jantal.

'And almost certainly a magicker. His name is Denton. Her name's Marney.' Matthaus sat back and rubbed his beard. 'If I had to guess, I'd say they're agents of the Relic Guild.'

'The Relic Guild?' Nurmar sounded shaken. 'What do we do?'

Matthaus placed the coded instructions down on the table and sighed. 'First, I need you two to find where the other magicker is hiding.'

'Easier said than done in this place,' Jantal complained. 'Doesn't help that our rifles are useless. The anti-magic drained the power stones. They won't charge up again for a couple of hours.'

'Then take this,' Matthaus replied, handing Jantal the spell sphere. 'Use it wisely. It's the last one we've got. Now go and find this *Denton*, nullify him, and bring him back here.'

Although the order was spoken calmly and quietly, it held gravitas, and Jantal and Nurmar accepted their leader's instructions without question. Once they had left the hut, Matthaus leant forwards in his chair, resting his elbows upon his knees, whilst his large Aelfirian eyes studied his empathic hostage.

'There's a water spring not far from here,' he told her. 'Seems to be the only constant thing outside this hut. Some days, cold water is all we get to put in our bellies.'

Marney was shivering, not just from the chill, and tears came to her eyes.

'It's the magic of Ghost Mist Veldt, you see – protecting its House. Oh, it occasionally gives us a treat or two. One day we might find wood to burn. On another day, maybe an animal to kill and eat. But this House has trapped us in a bubble of magic that we can't escape. And until now, Marney, no one has found us.'

He sat back again. 'I don't blame you for killing Red,' he said wistfully. 'I don't blame anyone for anything, not anymore.'

'Please,' said Marney. Her teeth were chattering. 'Let me go.'

'Go where? You're stuck in this hut with the rest of us. At least for the time being.'

Matthaus took the instructions from the table, and stared at them for a moment.

'Shall I tell you what I did when I first joined the army, Marney? I was a hierophant. I deciphered codes.' He held the pages up. 'And I won't decide what to do with you until I understand what all this means.'

Angel groaned and fell to her knees in the sand. Van Bam was quickly at her side. Angel's skin glowed with magic, as yet more poison seeped from the wound on her hand.

'This coppion sting is freakishly strong,' she said through clenched teeth. 'I can't get a handle on it. I could really use a magical apothecary.' She managed a weak smile for Van Bam. 'Where's Gene when you need him?'

The moon was bright and silver over the desert of Mirage, casting long shadows across the grey sands. Namji and Buyaal were properly attired for the trek, and did not feel the chill of the desert night as Van Bam and Angel did. The dress of the Relic Guild agents was better suited to the heat of the blistering days. Van Bam had cast the illusion of warmth to combat the chill, but Angel still shivered from the effects of the venom.

Namji came over to her. 'Perhaps you should rest for a while,' she said.

'No. We keep moving,' Buyaal said edgily. He was looking to the first outcrops of rock that heralded the western mountain range, a short distance away. 'The Hermit can help her, and we're almost there.'

'I'm okay,' Angel protested, 'I can walk,' but when she tried to stand, she almost fell again and had to grab on to Van Bam for support. 'Or maybe not.'

Van Bam put one of Angel's arms over his shoulder, Namji doing the same on the other side; together they helped the healer to trudge through the sand and follow Buyaal into the rocks. The western mountains rose high above the group, black and formidable.

Van Bam looked back to the east, where they had travelled from, his eyes scouring the shadowy expanse of the desert. He decided that even if the citadel of Mirage wasn't invisible from the outside, its high walls and turrets would still be lost in the gloom. The horizon was thinly lined with the first pinkish evidence of dawn's approach.

As the group began following a path that cut into the base of the mountain, Van Bam grew uneasy. They had been fleeing for two hours or more, yet there was no sign of pursuit. Someone must have been alerted to their escape by now, and the illusionist aired his concerns to his companions.

'Don't be too quick to assume we're not being pursued,' advised Buyaal. 'There is a Genii controlling Mirage, Master Van Bam, and higher magic does not have to be seen or felt to be present.'

As he led the way, Buyaal held a hand out before him, as if feeling the air. Feeling for some magic, Van Bam decided, that would allow the Hermit's friends to find him.

'I still do not understand,' Van Bam said. 'How could an Aelfirian House fall into Spiral's hands without Lady Amilee noticing?'

'Yeah, I'd like an answer to that too,' Angel added weakly.

'I wish I knew,' Namji replied. 'I only learned of the betrayal shortly before the banquet. I wanted to tell you, but ... but I had to pretend I was on board, for my own safety.'

'Have you met the Genii?' Van Bam asked.

Namji shook her head. 'But my mother and father are completely loyal to him. As for Ebril ... you heard what he said back at the citadel.' She broke off as her voice cracked.

'I tell you what I don't understand,' Angel said. 'What are they waiting for?' Van Bam could see the sheen of sweat on her face glistening with reflected moonlight. 'This war has been going on for two years, yet Mirage hasn't been involved in the fighting. In fact, they've been helping as a supply line for the Timewatcher's armies. What are they doing?'

'An excellent point,' said Van Bam. 'Mirage's militia could have attacked Green Sky Forest and the Floating Stones of Up and Down, and destroyed that supply line at any time. Why have they held back? Why the pretence?'

'Because the Genii has been biding his time,' Buyaal explained. 'He has been waiting for confirmation that Fabian Moor was successful in reaching Labrys Town – which you gave him when you allowed Ebril and his entourage to return home.'

Van Bam thought for a moment. 'And now the Genii has confirmation, what is his plan for Mirage?'

'Isn't it obvious?' Buyaal looked back as he led the way. 'Outside the citadel of Mirage, on the Giant's Hand, sits a doorway to the Great Labyrinth. Creatures of higher magic cannot use it, but Aelfirian soldiers …?'

Angel swore.

'He plans to invade the Labyrinth,' Van Bam whispered.

'The doorway in Mirage is the first portal to the Great Labyrinth that Spiral's army has secured in this war,' Buyaal said. 'The Genii has an army at his disposal, Master Van Bam. At any moment, he could send it to Labrys Town to serve Fabian Moor. And seeing as Lady Amilee has already failed to see so much, I doubt anyone will notice until it is too late.'

Van Bam shared a look with Angel. She was clearly as startled by Buyaal's words as he had been. And she was getting weaker.

'We must get word to Lady Amilee,' Van Bam said, 'The Nightshade has to be warned.'

'No, you need to speak with the Hermit,' Buyaal insisted.

Van Bam made an angry noise. 'Who is the Hermit?' he demanded. 'What part does he play in this?'

'Right now, he is the only person who can help you,' Buyaal said sternly. 'The Hermit saved a hundred or more citizens from subjugation. Most of them live out here in the mountains, protected by him. A few of us – like me – hide in the city, gathering intelligence. We are the resistance, freedom fighters, and perhaps the last hope Mirage – and Labrys Town – has.'

'You are a hundred Aelfir against the rest of Mirage?' Van Bam said. He hadn't meant a scornful tone to enter his voice, but it was there nonetheless. 'What does your resistance hope to achieve against such odds?'

Buyaal sighed. 'I don't know.' He looked back at the illusionist, as though searching for an answer. 'Maybe the Hermit will tell you why he hasn't put any plans into action yet. Only he can answer your questions. Come. Not far now.'

With his hand still feeling the air, Buyaal set off along the mountain path. As Namji gave Van Bam a perplexed look, the illusionist adjusted Angel's arm around his shoulder, and the three carried on following.

It wasn't long before the path led into a narrow valley with high walls. Soon after, Buyaal took them out the other side, and down into a wide crater. It was then that Angel groaned and pushed Van Bam and Namji away from her. Falling to her hands and knees, she vomited dark liquid onto the ground. Van Bam tried to persuade himself it was the wine Angel had consumed earlier and not blood. He crouched down beside her.

'What is it?' Namji said, her young face creased with concern. 'Why can't she overcome the poison?'

Van Bam could feel the heat radiating from Angel's skin through her cotton shirt. He pressed two fingers to the side of her neck. Her pulse was fluttering, erratic. The wound on the back of her hand was swollen and angry.

'Hold on,' the illusionist told the healer. 'We will reach help soon.'

Angel nodded. 'Just let me sit for a while.'

Van Bam helped the healer into a sitting position. Once again, Angel's skin glowed with the light of her magic, but this time it paled and flickered out. And it was not blood-streaked venom that oozed from the sting wound; the substance that emerged almost looked like smoke. It ballooned from the hole in Angel's hand like a bubble blown from a child's toy. But the bubble didn't pop or float away; it shrank and disappeared as if it had been drawn back into Angel's veins.

Angel slumped. She closed her eyes and fell sideways, unconscious.

'Angel!' Van Bam caught her and laid her gently upon the ground. 'Angel, can you hear me?'

'It doesn't make sense,' Namji said, also crouching beside the healer.

'Coppion venom can be deadly, but it is simple to cure. Especially for a magical healer. What do we do?'

The young Aelf harboured no deviousness; the fearful, confused expression that her face now held was undoubtedly genuine.

'Buyaal,' Van Bam called urgently. 'We need stronger magic to help Angel. How close are we to the Hermit?'

'Oh, fairly close, I should think.'

Buyaal's reply raised the hairs on the back of Van Bam's neck. There had been a cold and hard quality to it that bordered on wicked amusement. The self-proclaimed Master of the Desert had absolutely no interest in the ailing healer. He stood with his back to the group, facing an uneven path that led up to the wall of the crater, where the warm glow of firelight flickered in the mouth of a cave.

Buyaal dropped his hand to his side. 'So there you are,' he said.

'Buyaal?' Van Bam was ignored.

'I know you're there.' Buyaal was calling to the cave. 'You must have known I would find a way to locate you eventually. And you just couldn't resist a bird with a broken wing, could you?' He glanced back at the unconscious form of Angel. His face was amused. 'You're pathetic,' he told the cave, 'even for an *abomination*.'

Van Bam gripped his cane tightly. Namji looked at him, confused and clearly looking for answers that he did not have.

'Well?' Buyaal shouted. 'Have you nothing to say for yourself?'

'You have the nerve to call *me* an abomination?' The voice that replied was borne on the desert breeze. Male, strong and clear, its tone was pitying, not aggressive. 'I was not the one who turned his back on his Mother.'

Buyaal barked a laugh. 'No, the Timewatcher turned Her back on *you*! But come – what is the point of hiding further?'

As Van Bam watched, a sense of dread sinking inside him, the silhouette of a person appeared in the cave mouth. Stooping to step out into the open, the creature that emerged was a giant. Ten feet tall at the very least, long hair falling about his shoulders.

Van Bam could not make out any features, but he could see something dripping from the giant's clenched fist.

'*I* am the one who is hiding, *Lord* Buyaal?'

The giant thrust out his hand, palm first, long fingers splayed. From a cut on his palm, he sent a small shower of blood into the air. The wind picked up and swirled around Van Bam, Namji and Angel. The illusionist covered his eyes from the sudden storm of dust and sand. The wind died quickly to leave behind a wavering barrier of energy around the two magickers and the Aelf. Glowing with a pale violet radiance, the magical barrier separated them from Buyaal.

His face angry, his teeth clenched, Buyaal turned on the giant. He whispered in a quick, sibilant language, and his skin began to glow with magic. With a yell of rage, he released the magic. But the giant had erected a barrier around himself, and when the energy hit it there was a dull clanging and the crackle of lightning. The impact was enough to knock the giant to the ground, but the magic rebounded and punched Buyaal off his feet too.

Quickly rising, Buyaal staggered, breathing heavily, and glared at Van Bam. The illusionist now saw the Aelf's true image.

Buyaal wore the long black cassock of a priest. His Aelfirian face looked more human – was at once beautiful and terrible. His tattoos had disappeared, but a patch of scarring on his forehead was bright and pale under the moonlight.

'Genii,' Namji hissed, and Van Bam made to stab his cane into the ground.

'Do nothing, Van Bam,' the giant ordered. 'You are well protected, and he's much more powerful than you, anyway.'

The giant's voice, as he slowly got to his feet, carried a distinct lack of worry or urgency. Protected by his barrier, he stood his ground, as if simply waiting for the Genii to make his next move. Blood dripped from his hand, sizzling with energy as it slapped to the rock.

Buyaal seemed unsteady on his feet, dazed. His skin glowed with magic again, and then he slashed his hand through the air. A black, vertical line was left behind, a rent in reality, which the newly revealed Genii stretched open with his hands to expose the glassy surface of a portal. The giant did nothing as Buyaal fled into it and disappeared, the rent sealing behind him.

Magic flared in the giant's hand and healed the cut on his palm. He walked forwards, and the barrier of energy surrounding him and the group disappeared.

Van Bam stood protectively before Namji and Angel's unconscious body. He raised his green glass cane.

'You have nothing to fear,' the giant reassured him. 'Well, at least not from me.'

As the giant came close and looked down at the illusionist, Van Bam illuminated his cane, casting light on the giant's features. His gaunt face, at least four feet above Van Bam's, was more human than Aelfirian; his pale skin was smooth and stubble free, contrasting with the dirty tangles of his long hair. His body beneath a habit of itchy-looking brown material appeared wiry. His arms were criss-crossed with a plethora of scars.

And his eyes ... his eyes were orbs of pure blue that shone in the light of the cane.

The giant frowned at Namji, who couldn't quite meet his dazzling eyes. She looked close to tears.

'Don't torture yourself, Namji,' the giant said kindly. 'Many people have been fooled by Buyaal. It is not your fault that you didn't recognise him for what he was when he first came to Mirage.' His face was sympathetic. 'And I am sorry for your loss.'

'Are ...' Van Bam paused to clear his throat as the giant gazed down at him. 'Are you the Hermit?'

'My *name* is Gulduur Bellow.' The reply came with an admonishing expression. 'And I doubt the stories you've heard about me are particularly truthful.'

'You are a Nephilim.'

'And you are a human. Are there any other obvious facts you'd like us to swap?'

Van Bam kept his mouth shut.

After giving Angel a lingering glance, the giant – the *Nephilim* called Gulduur Bellow – walked past Van Bam and Namji to stare down the narrow valley between the rocks which led back to the desert.

'Buyaal has been trying to find me for a long time,' Bellow said, looking up at the sky. 'Though I don't think he really understood what he was searching for. Not until now.'

Van Bam looked around. 'Where is the resistance? Where are your freedom fighters?'

'Freedom fighters?' The giant looked back at Van Bam. 'What *has* that Genii been telling you? I'm all alone up here.' He shook his huge head and turned his brilliant blue eyes to the sky again. 'But lucky for you I was here. If I hadn't intervened when I did, Buyaal would have started killing you, one by one, and not quickly or without pain.'

The Nephilim returned to the group. 'We have a lot to discuss, Van Bam. But first, your friend Angel needs attention. The coppion venom in her veins has been enhanced by Genii magic. With your permission, I'd like to heal her.'

Van Bam's mouth worked silently as he stared at the giant blood-magicker without replying.

'Please understand,' said Bellow, 'I'm going to heal Angel whether you give permission or just stare at me dumbly.'

'Yes. Yes of course,' Van Bam blurted.

'Good decision.'

Gulduur Bellow bent down and picked Angel up. She seemed as small as a child in his arms.

'I would like you to assist me,' he said to Namji, clearly not giving her a choice. Open-mouthed, she nodded. 'As for you, Van Bam,' he continued, carrying Angel towards his cave, 'please wait here. I'll let you know when your friend is better, and it is time for us to talk.'

'Wake up, Tommy.'

Small eyes blinked open, confused, frightened, as they found the shadowy figure standing over the bed. The man called Tommy panicked. In a flurry of motion, he tried to disentangle himself from sheets, and reach for a weapon concealed in his bedside cabinet. But the shadowy figure punched him hard in the face, knocking his head back down onto the pillow. His nose bleeding, Tommy froze as he stared down the barrel of a revolver which had appeared before his face. A power stone whined into life with a violet glow, illuminating the strong hand that aimed the gun.

'If you think you can reach a weapon before I can put a bullet through your skull,' said the shadowy figure, 'think again.'

'W-What are you doing? Who are you?'

'I'm one of the Resident's men, Tommy. The Nightshade has been watching you.'

'You're … you're …' With the back of his shaking hand, Tommy wiped blood from his nose. 'The Relic Guild,' he finished fearfully.

Samuel switched on the glow lamp on the bedside cabinet. Tommy blinked in the sudden bright light, the blood from his nose smeared across his lean face and hand. Through the wayward strands of hair hanging before his eyes, he stared up at the Relic Guild agent, whose identity was concealed behind the magical shadows cast by the brim of his hat.

'W-what do you want?'

He sounded as scared as Samuel wanted him to be.

'That's an interesting question, Tommy.'

Information supplied by Macy and Bryant had led Samuel to this place. The bedroom was part of the living quarters above a junkshop situated in an unremarkable area of the eastern district. The man in the bed was known as Long Tommy. Around Samuel's age, he had many talents that made him popular in the underworld, perhaps most especially a talent for covering his tracks and avoiding the law. But not this time.

'Here's the deal,' Samuel said. 'In my pocket, I have an envelope filled with money. The Resident wants you to have it in exchange for information. But the thing is, Tommy, *I* don't want to give it to you. You're a magic-user. I should be taking you to the Nightshade.'

'No,' Tommy said quickly. 'You've got it wrong. I don't touch magic.'

There was some truth to that. Macy and Bryant had discovered that Long Tommy had retired his services when war broke out. With the doorways of the Great Labyrinth closed to all, there currently wasn't much call for magic-users among the treasure hunters and other criminals of the underworld. Plus, since the war had started, the

Resident's punishment for the abuse of magic in Labrys Town had become rather more severe. Samuel couldn't decide if it was smarts or cowardice that had inspired Tommy's retirement.

'Just because you stopped using magic two years ago doesn't exonerate you,' Samuel said. 'Besides, I heard that you recently came out of retirement. A one-time job for a special client. Or was I told wrong?'

The man in the bed made to object again, but Samuel stopped him by pushing the revolver closer to his face.

'Think very carefully before you lie to me, Tommy.'

Tommy wiped more blood from his nose, his shoulders slumped, and then the fear on his face became tinged with anger. 'It wasn't a paying job,' he said. 'He didn't give me a choice.'

'Oh, I know that,' Samuel said. 'And when you say *he*, you mean Fabian Moor, don't you?'

Tommy nodded and averted his gaze.

When Moor had first arrived in Labrys Town, Gideon had warned the denizens of his presence using a cover story. Gideon told the populace that treasure hunters trying to leave the Labyrinth had unwittingly set a wild demon loose upon the town. In the meantime, in the underworld, Moor had been introducing himself to many seedy characters, and making the criminals very nervous by asking the wrong kind of questions about the Nightshade and the Relic Guild.

Samuel didn't know how many of those criminals had worked out that Moor was a Genii, but the underworld was as afraid of him as they were of the Relic Guild. Most of the people who had dealt with Moor had gone missing, undoubtedly used to feed the Genii's thirst for blood. According to Macy and Bryant, now that word of the *wild demon*'s capture had spread, the underworld was practically in a state of celebration about it.

'Tommy, the Relic Guild is in possession of a strange magical device. What it is, we don't yet understand. The only thing we know for sure is that you helped Fabian Moor make it.'

'I didn't help him,' Tommy squealed desperately. 'He didn't need me to. I promise, he forced his way into my workshop and started using the parts I had lying around.'

'Yes, parts like a sphere of Aelfirian glass,' Samuel said. 'You know the sort I mean, Tommy. Special glass, designed to hold spells.'

'Listen to me,' Tommy pleaded. 'I couldn't stop him. He made me give him the glass, and the lead—'

'Lead?' said Samuel.

Tommy licked blood from lips. 'I had some that I'd *prepared* for making magical bullets,' he explained guiltily, and was quick to add, 'I wasn't planning to use it. The lead was just left-over stock, that's all.'

'Just like the glass,' said Samuel, his tone unconvinced. 'Moor used the lead to cover the sphere in that mesh?'

Tommy nodded, his brow creased with worry. 'I've known a couple of metallurgists in my time, but I've never met anyone who could do what Moor did to that lead. He changed its state, made it not quite solid, not quite liquid. I've never seen anyone use that kind of magic before.'

'Well, Fabian Moor is extra specially talented,' Samuel replied. 'So, he took Aelfirian glass, surrounded it in magical metal, and then set power stones into it. Why? What's the device for?'

'I don't know.'

Samuel scoffed. 'If you're going to lie to me, you'll have to do better than that. I know you're scared of Moor, but the Relic Guild has him, and he's not getting free any time soon. It's me you should be scared of now. What's the device for, Tommy?'

Tommy swallowed blood, his expression disgusted. 'Transportation,' he muttered.

'Transportation? As in a portal?'

'No. I think it might be some kind of shadow carriage.'

'You'll have to do better than *I think*, Tommy.'

'Look, Moor wasn't exactly chatty about what he was making,' Tommy explained miserably. 'But he said the shadow carriages of Labrys Town were too well-guarded, and he needed to move something to and from the portals without detection.'

'Move what?'

'I have no idea.'

'Then … is he trying to smuggle something into Labrys Town, or out into the Great Labyrinth?'

'I don't know, maybe both.' Tommy sighed. 'When Moor had

finished making the device, all he said was that nobody would see his next move coming.' He opened his hands in a helpless gesture. 'And that's *really* all I know. I swear. He left, saying that he'd need my help again soon, but I never saw him after that.'

Samuel believed him. So what was the Genii trying to transport?

'You're a lucky man, Tommy. Not many people walk away from a meeting with Fabian Moor ... or the Relic Guild.' Samuel deactivated the revolver's power stone, and slid the weapon into the holster strapped to his thigh. 'The Resident has taken a shine to you.'

As Tommy's expression registered the implications of these words with fear, Samuel produced from his coat pocket a brown envelope fat with Labyrinth pounds. He threw it on the bed.

'I tried telling Gideon that you weren't worth it, Tommy, but he's convinced you can be of use to the Relic Guild in the future. And Gideon's not exactly a man you want to argue with. You know a lot of people in the underworld, and you must hear all kinds of things that the Nightshade would be interested in. Understand?'

Tommy stared at the envelope. He seemed relieved that he was about to survive an encounter with an agent of the Relic Guild, but also mortified that he had just become an informant for the Resident. He looked up at Samuel, found no choices in the magicker's shadowed face, and nodded unhappily.

'I'll be keeping an eye on you, Tommy,' Samuel said as he was leaving. 'If you ever mention the name Fabian Moor to anyone, I'll pay you another visit.'

'I've lost track of time, you know,' Matthaus said suddenly. It was the first time in a couple of hours he had broken from studying Denton's secret instructions.

Marney could no longer feel her legs. Beaten, aching and exhausted, she knelt on the hard floor, inadequately dressed, hands and feet bound behind her, shivering from cold and fear, covered in dried blood.

Sitting at the camping table, the grizzled, veteran Aelf laid down the contents of Denton's envelope and looked up at the stone hut's ceiling.

'We've been trapped here for at least six weeks. Probably more. It's hard to tell. Most days we're lucky if we catch a glimpse of the sun. At night, *things* start roaming the mountainside ... monsters.' He shook his head. 'I don't think they're real, but they *are* personal. The ghosts of our sins, Red called them, back when she was sane. Before you killed her.'

Matthaus's large, shrewd eyes met Marney's.

Desperately, Marney tried to ignore the voice in her head that told her there was no way she was getting out of this mess alive. Her empathic magic was gone, drained from her body by the anti-magic spell, and it had left her emotionally raw and exposed. Was her magic dead, gone for good? Or just temporarily anaesthetised?

'Let me tell you the irony of our situation,' Matthaus said. 'Me, Jantal and Nurmar – we're mercenaries. When we first signed up for the war, we were contracted to fight for a House that was on the Timewatcher's side. Oh, I know what you're thinking, Marney – sides don't matter to a mercenary. But I think this was something of an exception, don't you?'

Marney nodded, dislodging a tear from her eye. She tried to smile for Matthaus, thinking that if she could get him to like her enough, he wouldn't allow her to be served up as a meal for his band of deserters.

'For whatever reason,' Matthaus continued, 'the House we were fighting for switched allegiances. And let me tell you, Marney, when your paymasters start serving Spiral and the Genii, they don't exactly give you a fair opportunity to review your contract of employment.'

'I-I know,' Marney said breathlessly. She swallowed, willing her voice to stop shaking. 'I've seen how the Genii try to subjugate the Aelfir.'

'Have you, now?'

'Yes. I-It's a terrible thing.'

Matthaus pressed his lips together, clearly suspicious.

His fellow deserters had yet to return from searching for Denton. Marney prayed the strange, sentient magic of this House would protect her mentor, perhaps show him a way to save her. It was hard to distance herself from the voice in her head that was telling her she would never see Denton again.

Matthaus sighed. 'When you're told to serve or die, that's not much of a choice. But as soon our army came to fight in Ghost Mist Veldt, I saw a chance to escape, and a few of the other mercenaries came with me.' He whispered a curse. 'But apparently, Ghost Mist Veldt can't see us as anything other than enemies. Its magic trapped us as soon as we left the Genii's protection, and it has been picking us off one by one ever since.' He looked at Marney again and his anger evaporated. 'But then you come along.'

Matthaus tapped the secret instructions with the tips of his fingers. 'Having spent a few years deciphering codes for the army, I picked up a trick or two. For example, knowing the origins of a code can give you a handy place to start.'

He plucked from the table a slim leather wallet which had been in the envelope with the coded instructions. Flipping it open, he showed Marney the plate of plain grey metal inside.

'This is a sigil wallet,' Matthaus told her. 'If the right person touches the metal plate, a symbol or a crest will appear, letting that person know they're in … good company, I suppose. Of course, it won't work for me, see?' To demonstrate, he pressed a finger to the metal plate, and it remained smooth and grey. 'However, I do know that this metal was made by someone with magic a little *higher* than the average user.'

Matthaus closed the wallet and threw it down. 'You're working for a Thaumaturgist, Marney. And considering you're a magicker from the Labyrinth, I'm willing to guess it's Lady Amilee. You're on a secret mission for the Skywatcher. Try telling me I'm wrong.'

Marney said nothing. She licked her dry lips, swallowed the taste of blood in her mouth, and desperately prayed for her magic to return. Only emptiness and fear answered.

'Now then,' said Matthaus. He took up the instructions and showed them to his captive. Four pages; and Marney could see they were covered in Denton's handwriting. 'This code isn't too hard, but it's clever,' he said. 'See, I've deciphered enough to know where you're going, but I can't work out the instructions on how you're going to get there.'

'Please,' Marney begged. 'I don't know what's in that letter.'

'Oh, I think you do,' Matthaus replied, flapping the pages. 'If there wasn't a Thaumaturgist involved, I'd write this off as a lie, a piece of shit – a *joke*! You're searching for a House that's not supposed to exist. Say its name for me, Marney.'

Marney clamped her mouth shut and looked away from him.

'Say its name,' Matthaus said, casually leaning over the table and sliding a throwing dagger from Marney's baldric, 'or I'll finish what Red started.'

Marney closed her eyes, swallowed. 'The Library of Glass and Mirrors,' she whispered.

'The Library of Glass and Mirrors,' Matthaus repeated with a pleased air. 'Incredible.'

Throwing the dagger onto the table, he sat back and studied the instructions again. 'I might not be able to decipher how you intend to get there, Marney, but I do know you're looking for information on a secret plot of Spiral's. The Ice House, is it? Or forest? Maybe *icicles* – hard to say. But I'm on the right track, aren't I?'

Marney nodded, sending more tears down her cheeks.

'Good, now help me out with the rest,' Matthaus said. 'See, I'm confused, Marney.' He leafed through the pages, his expression full of thoughtful concentration. 'Two phrases keep repeating throughout the letter. One seems to pertain to knowledge – *things that are known*, it says. Or maybe it's just … *known things*. Obviously, that's referring to the information on Spiral you're going to the Library to find – not sure how it fits in with this Ice Forest, but it definitely connects to the other phrase, which is a bit more enigmatic.'

He held two of the pages side by side. '*Doubt and wonder*,' he said. 'Several times it gets repeated. But I can't work out if it's referring to a House or something *within* a House. Every time it gets mentioned, though, there's an overtone of faith or worship. Is it a church? Maybe grander – a cathedral? *Doubt and wonder* …' He huffed and dropped the pages to his lap. 'Tie this together for me, Marney. What does it all mean?'

Hopelessly, genuinely perplexed, Marney shook her head. 'I-I don't know.'

'You're brave, but you're lying. Don't think for a moment that I won't hurt you, Marney.'

'The Icicle Forest,' Marney whimpered. 'We're going to the Library of Glass and Mirrors to find information on the Icicle Forest. I-It's supposed to be a secret Genii stronghold. But I don't know anything about *doubt and wonder*, or cathedrals – I-I swear.'

Matthaus sucked air over his teeth. 'You either tell me the truth, or I'll cut off your leg and make you watch while Jantal and Nurmar sit at this table and eat it.'

'Please …' Marney's tears flowed free and hot then; sobbing, overwhelming and primal, shook her body. 'I don't know – I'm not meant to read that letter unless Denton dies. Please …'

Matthaus stared at her for a long moment, his large grey eyes as dispassionate as slate. Finally he sighed, and it seemed as though he was beset by a sudden tiredness that cut straight to his old bones.

'I'm too exhausted to play games with you, Marney,' he said. 'You've called my bluff, and I just haven't got the energy to torture more information out of you. I don't suppose there's a lot of point anyway, beyond sating my own curiosity. See, you've already given me a way out of this mess.'

Lifting the coded instructions from his lap, and dropping them onto the table, Matthaus tapped the sigil wallet. 'The thaumaturgy in this metal should attract the attention of this House's magic, if it hasn't already. I reckon Ghost Mist Veldt will alert someone who'll come and take me away from this poxy place.'

'Take the envelope and do what you want with it,' Marney said, her words interspersed with hiccups. 'Just … just let me go.'

'No, I can't do that.' Matthaus's expression was almost sad. 'It doesn't matter which side finds me, you see. If it's the Timewatcher's army, the Thaumaturgists will be grateful that these instructions didn't fall into the Genii's hands. If it's Spiral's army, the Genii will be *very* interested in what the Thaumaturgists are up to. Either way, it's winwin for me. I'd rather go back to fighting for Spiral than stay here.

'But here's the rub for you. I don't need your help, and you're too dangerous to keep around.' Matthaus sat forward on his chair. 'I have no anti-magic spheres left. In a few hours, your magic is going to come back.' He looked at the patch of dried blood on the floor. 'The last thing I want is an empath in my head.'

Marney also looked at the patch of Red's blood that stained the floor; that had stained her vest, and dried to peeling flakes on her thighs. The voice in her head told her that the blood of the first person she had ever killed would be the last thing she ever saw.

Matthaus drew the pistol holstered at his hip. 'Your magic might still be missing, but my power stone has regained its charge.' To prove his point, he thumbed the stone behind the chamber, and it whined into life with a violet glow. 'I'm sorry, Marney, but I really can't think of a good reason to let you live,' and he took aim at her.

Marney heaved bile onto the floor, anticipating the bullet that would tear her life away.

But the shot never came.

The pistol was still aimed at the empath, but the grizzled Aelf had turned to the door. Marney became aware of shale crunching beneath boots.

'Jantal?' Matthaus called. 'Nurmar?'

When the footsteps stopped and no one answered, Marney's captor rose to his feet and aimed the pistol at the door. He looked back at the empath and raised a finger to his lips. The crunching of shale resumed.

Silence again, hard and icy, only broken by the moan of the wind, and then the door slowly opened with a chilly gust.

Marney managed to hold back a fresh flood of sobs as she saw the old man standing on the threshold, tall and burly, wearing a rumpled wide-brimmed hat.

'Human,' said Matthaus. 'You must be Denton.'

With a strange sort of smile that seemed to confirm the words while admonishing the Aelf who had spoken them, Denton stepped into the hut and closed the door. He looked at Marney, and never before had she seen such a complete lack of compassion on her mentor's face.

'Are you all right?' he asked her.

Marney shook her head.

A dark glint came to Denton's eye, and just for that moment Marney was glad she had no magic that would allow her to experience the old magicker's feelings.

'I'm assuming you're Matthaus,' Denton said, undeterred by the pistol aimed at him. 'I'm afraid your colleagues – Jantal and Nurmar, is it? – were reluctant in negotiating a peaceful resolution.'

'They're dead?'

'Yes,' Denton replied, matter-of-factly. 'They were shot by the Timewatcher's soldiers who came with me and are outside, waiting.'

'Then … I'm surrounded.'

'The demise of your colleagues obviously doesn't cause you grief,' Denton said. 'Do you imagine their deaths help your predicament in some way?'

'It certainly makes the way forward a bit simpler.' With almost a laugh, Matthaus deactivated the pistol's power stone, and laid the weapon down on the table. 'I surrender,' he said happily.

'Well now, let's not be hasty.' The old empath was looking at the items on the table. 'I see you've opened the envelope that I gave my companion here. Did you have any luck deciphering my code?'

Matthaus shrugged. 'Parts of it.'

'Commendable,' Denton said, though he didn't appear particularly impressed. 'It's written in an emotive script, you see – an old empath's trick that only another empath should be able to decipher. Or a *hierophant*?'

'Guilty as charged,' Matthaus replied, bowing his head almost proudly.

'Yes … but I have to wonder, Matthaus, did you manage to decipher too much?'

Denton looked at Marney again, his eyebrow raised questioningly. Marney nodded back at him.

'That's a shame, don't you think?' Denton said to Matthaus. 'In fact, I'm quite positive you agree.'

The Aelf reacted by raising his hand before his face, as if trying to block the empathic magic that Marney knew had latched onto his emotions.

'I understand,' said Matthaus. 'I was never meant to look at the contents of that envelope. I'm sorry.'

'Oh, don't be so hard on yourself,' Denton replied, though there wasn't much kindness in his voice. 'You were looking for a way out of this situation. You were desperate. But …?'

'But I saw things that no one was supposed to see.'

'I suspect that you did.' Denton drew a breath. 'However, I'm sure that if you think very hard, Matthaus, you'll know how to rectify your mistake.'

Matthaus raised a finger and wagged it in the air. 'Yes, I have an idea,' he said. He picked up the pistol and primed the power stone again. 'You might want to stand back,' he added before putting the barrel into his mouth and pulling the trigger.

Even as the back of Matthaus's head burst and showered the hut wall with red, Denton was rushing over to Marney.

Marney collapsed into her mentor's arms as he cut her bonds.

'Denton,' she sobbed. 'My magic …'

'Don't worry, it will come back,' he promised, and then he soothed her fear and pain with a wave of empathy, a magical embrace. 'Let's get out of here,' he said, helping Marney to her feet and supporting her. 'I've had enough of this damn House.'

They said that everything was hidden in Mirage.

The sky was steadily turning pink. The warmth of the dawn was creeping in slowly and pushing out the chill of the night, but not a sound was carried on the desert breeze. Standing in a crater within the mountains to the west of Mirage's citadel, Van Bam was trying to make sense of events. How much of what he had been told could he believe? The Hermit, the fall of Mirage, the invasion of Labrys Town – what was truth and what false? The only thing Van Bam knew for certain was that he was looking forward to feeling the sun on his skin again.

What in the Timewatcher's name was going on?

He looked up the path that led to the cave, where golden light flickered and shadows danced. A diminutive figure had appeared there but did not venture out into the open.

Van Bam judged that a couple of hours had passed since Namji had followed Gulduur Bellow into the cave, where she and the Nephilim laboured to rid Angel of the Genii-tainted poison that ran through her veins. Now, as Namji emerged from the cave, Van Bam was relieved to have something immediate to focus on rather than running the strange situation in House Mirage over and over in his head.

Namji walked down the slope towards the illusionist, wearing a lost expression upon her Aelfirian face. Only then did Van Bam fully appreciate how hard the fall of Mirage must be for the young Aelf. Who knew how many of her countrymen and women – the people she loved – had betrayed the Timewatcher and given allegiance to the Lord of the Genii?

Van Bam walked up the path to greet her.

'How is Angel?' he asked as they met. 'Are *you* all right?'

'I …' Namji shrugged, and smiled wanly. 'Angel's fine, Van Bam.' She glanced back towards the cave. 'The Nephilim wants to see you now.'

'He can wait a moment,' Van Bam replied. 'If you need to talk—'

'No. I want to be alone for a while.' Namji reached out and squeezed his arm. 'It's okay. Just … go and see him.'

Van Bam watched as Namji continued down the path, her arms wrapped around herself. There was no deceit in her body language; she genuinely desired solitude. The illusionist headed up to the cave. He discovered that it led into a tunnel that sloped downwards, cutting into the mountain.

The flickering light came from fire burning in hollows carved into the walls. Soft, yellow tongues spilled out of the recesses and licked upwards, blackening the stone. As he headed down, Van Bam was well aware he was walking into the lair of a blood-magicker, a creature that fables described as a savage, a monster. A small sense of dread bloomed in his gut as he wondered what manner of habitat a Nephilim might fashion for himself.

The tunnel continued to slope downwards, steeper and steeper, until it levelled out abruptly. Van Bam found himself stepping into a grand cavern that bore no resemblance to the nest of bones and skin that he had begun to imagine.

Whether created by magic or natural formation, the illusionist couldn't tell, but there was energy in the cavern. It laced the air with a tingling sensation that raised the hairs on his arms. The walls and high ceiling were decorated with tiny twinkling lights and streaks of colours. At first, Van Bam wondered if he was seeing a projection of the night sky, but he quickly realised that the rock was inlaid with thousands of jewels and veins of precious metals. They reflected the light of the magical fires that burned at each corner of a huge flat-topped boulder at the centre of the cavern. And there, upon the boulder's plateau, surrounded by the magical flames, the ailing healer lay, watched over by the giant form of the Nephilim.

Gulduur Bellow's pure blue eyes shone like the jewels around him. He raised a huge, long-fingered hand, beckoning Van Bam to him.

As the illusionist made his way across, he could hear the gentle trickling of water. Steps had been carved into the side of the boulder; his footsteps whispered around the cavern as he climbed up.

Bellow smiled welcomingly when Van Bam reached the plateau. The giant sat cross-legged, dwarfing the body of Angel as she lay unconscious. Although he was seated, his face was still level with the illusionist's. Again, Van Bam was struck by how human the Nephilim appeared, despite his incongruous size. His facial features exhibited no evidence of an Aelfirian heritage at all.

'Please, sit,' said Bellow, his voice calm and affable.

With his green glass cane lying across his lap, Van Bam sat opposite Bellow. On the ground between them was a stone jug and two bowls. The Nephilim lifted the jug and filled the bowls with clear water.

'It has been a long time since I had guests,' Bellow said. His smile broadened, parting lips and revealing blocky teeth. 'Or a conversation.'

He lifted one bowl, and gestured for Van Bam to take the other. They drank together, surrounded by a thousand stars and the warm glow of magical fire.

The water tasted fresh and sweet – a welcome relief for Van Bam's dusty throat. As he drank, he noticed a third stone bowl near to the giant. It was half-filled with blood.

Even though Bellow carried no obvious wounds, Van Bam was certain that the blood had come from the Nephilim's veins. Hundreds of old and pale scars covered his exposed skin like a latticework of neat slug tracks. One on his forearm seemed fresher than the others.

The giant noticed Van Bam looking. 'It is the curse of my kind,' he explained. 'We can heal our wounds, but the scars never fade.'

Evidently, Bellow had been using the contents of the bowl to heal

Angel; the blood had been used to paint Angel's face, arms, hands and feet with the symbols and glyphs of blood-magic. Van Bam guessed that more decorated her body beneath her desert clothes, which were now a blanket over her. The sheen of sweat on her brow and the pallor of her skin troubled him greatly.

'Don't worry about Angel,' Bellow said in that calming, amiable voice of his. 'I am neutralising the poison, and she gathers strength while she sleeps.'

'You have my gratitude,' Van Bam replied, feeling unsure of himself in the presence of a Nephilim.

'Would you like more water?'

'No, thank you.'

'Then what about some food? You'd be surprised by what I'm able to grow in this cavern.'

'I do not doubt you, but, really, I am fine.'

'Then let's have a conversation, you and I.' Bellow put his water bowl aside and clasped his hands together. 'I'm sure you have questions for me, and I'm keen to allay any fears and misconceptions that you might harbour.' He did seem keen, almost excited by the prospect of this conversation. 'But first, let us agree that you will call me Gulduur. None of this *Hermit* nonsense, now.'

Van Bam managed a smile in return. 'I have many questions, *Gulduur*,' he said. 'Many fears and, apparently, misconceptions too. In all honesty, I am not entirely certain where to begin.'

'Perhaps I can help you there,' Bellow offered. 'We Nephilim enjoy stories, and Namji has been telling me some very interesting tales. Let me promise you this, Van Bam – I have never attacked the citadel of Mirage. I have never attempted to seize control of this House. I have never placed my *agents* among its people, and I certainly wasn't involved in the plot to bring a Genii called Fabian Moor to Labrys Town.'

'Meaning everything I was told about the Hermit's actions was a lie?'

'Not a word of it truth. The story was a ruse to misdirect you, to gain your trust. But I hope by now you are convinced that I'm not a supporter of Spiral and the Genii.'

Van Bam chose his next words carefully. 'Then what of the Time-watcher?'

'What of Her?'

'It is said that you have no faith in Her – that the Nephilim worship a patriarch instead. The Progenitor.'

'Now *that* is a complicated issue,' Bellow declared in surprise, clapping his big hands together. 'For my part, I'm certainly not the Timewatcher's enemy. As for the great creator that my people call the Progenitor – the truth of his tale is buried in the myths and legends that *you* people created to ensure the Nephilim are viewed as nightmares.'

Van Bam felt slight admonishment in Bellow's voice.

Yes, he reasoned; he could accept that the stories of the Nephilim might have been embellished, as all stories were, but the illusionist didn't believe for a moment that the giant before him was harmless. He thought of Buyaal, of the way Bellow had confronted him, confident and fearless. The Genii had all but fled after their brief duel. The blood-magic of the Nephilim was powerful enough to be a danger to creatures of higher magic. And where was Buyaal now? Preparing his army to invade the Labyrinth?

'Tell me what's on your mind,' said Bellow.

'Buyaal,' Van Bam replied. 'You told me that he had been trying to find you for a long time – that he used Angel, Namji and me as bait to lure you out of hiding. Now that he has discovered your hiding place, would it not be wise to move location? Before the Genii returns with an army behind him?'

Bellow chuckled. 'Yes, Buyaal used you to find me, but he was only seeking confirmation of my presence. Up until a few hours ago, he only *suspected* I was here.'

The giant reflected briefly. 'Buyaal doesn't need to come back for me. Now he knows where I am, he also knows what I must do next – and he can guard against *that* from behind the high walls of Mirage.'

'And what is it that you must do next?'

'Send you home to Labrys Town, of course. Ahead of the Genii's invasion force.'

Van Bam had to quash a sudden pang of feeling lost and trapped. 'Then not everything we were told is a lie,' he said bitterly. 'Ebril used Angel and me to bring word of Fabian Moor's success to Buyaal. And now Buyaal will send an army to aid his fellow Genii.'

'Be calm, Van Bam,' Bellow said, and he tapped a long finger against his temple. 'In my mind, I am able to see the stone monument called the Giant's Hand, and the doorway to the Labyrinth that stands upon it. I will *know* when the Genii is ready to use that doorway. We have time to prepare.'

Looking up into the giant's blue eyes, Van Bam found it hard to remain calm. 'I think the story of the Hermit carries a degree of truth, despite what you say,' he said flatly. 'Like Buyaal, you have been in Mirage since before the war began, Gulduur.'

'Yes, that *is* true.'

'Then *why* are you here? I do not believe for a moment that our meeting is due to blind luck. Who are you working for?'

'What an interesting perception you have, Van Bam.' Bellow was quiet for a moment, his expression inscrutable. 'I have been doing what we Nephilim do – watching, searching, listening. Buyaal wormed his way into Mirage's society, posing as one of their own, and he poisoned this House from the inside. But until your arrival, he had no idea why I was here, and that is what worried him – as it should. You are quite right to say that our meeting is not a coincidence.'

Bellow narrowed his sapphire eyes at Van Bam. 'But I can tell by your voice that there is another question hiding behind your question. Or is it an accusation?'

Van Bam took a breath. 'For over two years you have been here, observing what has become of this House.' There was an almost pleading edge to his tone. 'Why did you not send word that Mirage was under Genii occupation? Why not use the doorway to the Labyrinth to warn the Nightshade?'

'As easy as that, eh?' Bellow said with a smile. 'For one, I have not yet told you my story. Two, the Timewatcher made damn sure that no creature of higher magic can use the doorways to the Great Labyrinth.'

Van Bam froze, staring at the giant. He again recalled the brief confrontation between Bellow and Buyaal. 'Your ... your magic is *thaumaturgy*?'

The shade of Bellow's eyes altered subtly, suggesting that he was amused by the illusionist's surprise.

'The Nephilim are creatures of higher magic?'

'Of a kind.' Bellow shook his head at Van Bam's dumbstruck expression. 'I think my story will prove to be an education for you, Van Bam.'

'I ...' The illusionist cleared his throat. 'I had no idea.'

'Myths and legends, my new friend, but rarely the truth is told.' Another smile, this one sad. 'I bet you've never heard a tale of my people that wasn't filled with horror, have you?'

Van Bam felt a sudden flush of shame, and he wished he could have told Bellow he was wrong.

'Please, tell me why you are here,' Van Bam said respectfully. 'Why are you alone? The Nephilim travel as a herd – or is that a lie too?'

'No, that one's the truth.' Bellow shook his head again, and a tangle of hair fell across his face. 'I was separated from my herd – but *that* is another matter entirely. Suffice to say, I am lost and do not know how to find my people.'

With unexpected abruptness, the giant's sadness dissipated, and his big face brightened. 'For now, enough of Buyaal and higher magic. I have a story to tell, Van Bam, and it begins with something I would like to show you.'

Bellow picked up the bowl containing blood. He dipped the tip of his long finger into it, and then began to paint upon the rock floor between him and his guest.

First, the Nephilim created a spiral pattern; from it, he drew a straight line and connected it to a simple square shape, to which he added a triangle, giving it the appearance of a simple house lying on its side. Lastly, Bellow fashioned a second triangle within the square as though giving the first triangle a mirror image.

Bellow set the bowl down, and said, 'If you knew the story of the Progenitor and the origins of my herd, you would better understand the fear and uncertainty with which my people are perceived. To the Thaumaturgists, and most especially the Timewatcher, the Nephilim have always been abominations. We were made outcast by the Timewatcher, left to roam the realms without a home to call our own. However ...'

Bellow pointed to the spiral pattern on one side of his blood painting. '*This* represents the chaos from which the Nephilim came.' He moved his finger along. 'The straight line is the passage of time, an unknown count of years, representing the journey we must endure until we are delivered *here*.' He tapped the square with the mirrored triangles. 'Order and acceptance. The day my people find their true place among the realms.'

Bellow's massive hand encompassed the entire design. 'This is the Nephilim's legend, Van Bam, our prophecy. It is the symbol of the House for which we search, the home we one day hope to find.' The giant sat back, staring at the symbol, and a distant, dreamy edge came to his voice. 'We call it the Sorrow of Future Reason.'

Bellow fell into silent contemplation. Van Bam was reluctant to interrupt his thoughts, but was too intrigued not to.

'Forgive me, but there is much I do not know concerning the Nephilim,' he said. 'Why did the Timewatcher refuse to give you a House of your own?'

'She had Her reasons,' Bellow replied, snapping out of his reverie. 'But I can tell you that the fear so many feel for the Nephilim has its origins in the Timewatcher's treatment of us.' The smile returned to the giant's face. 'I see by your expression that your faith in the Timewatcher is unquestioning. Are you wondering how such a benevolent ruler of higher magic could possibly be wrong about the Nephilim?'

Van Bam looked around the cavern from the plateau of the huge boulder, at the jewels twinkling like stars and the multi-coloured veins of precious metal shining like nebulae beyond the golden flames of magic. Such a beautiful creation.

The illusionist opened his hands to Bellow in a gesture of helplessness. 'There are tales of bloodshed,' he said. 'All myths contain at least a seed of truth, Gulduur.'

'I have to concede that,' Bellow replied. 'There were occasions when my herd was attacked by Aelfirian raiding parties – people too frightened and stupid to try treating with us peacefully, or without the good sense to just leave us alone. But there are tales of communion, too. Rare moments where joy was shared by Nephilim and Aelfir. There was love and union between our races, resulting in offspring. And my people have shared similar interactions with humans. I bet you've never heard *those* tales, have you?'

'Only rumours.'

'My herd has many stories to tell about the creatures of lower magic, Van Bam. But there was only ever one Thaumaturgist that the Nephilim could call a friend. He was a Skywatcher. And he, too, was searching for a House.' Bellow looked at the blood painting, the symbol for the fabled home called the Sorrow of Future Reason. 'His name was Baran Wolfe.'

'*Baran* Wolfe?' said Van Bam. 'Do you mean Lord Wolfe – the Wanderer?'

'That's exactly who I mean,' Bellow replied. 'He came to me shortly after I had been separated from my herd, not long before the Genii took control of Mirage and the war began. Perhaps I was the last person to see Baran Wolfe before he was murdered by a fellow Skywatcher.'

'Yes, at the Falls of Dust and Silver,' Van Bam said, and then he started. 'Wait, no – Lord Wolfe was murdered by Spiral.'

The giant gave him a pitying look. 'Your education really doesn't extend very far beyond the Labyrinth, does it, Van Bam?'

Van Bam blinked. 'Spiral is a *Skywatcher*?'

'The most important Skywatcher,' Bellow assured him. 'Spiral was known as the Word of the Timewatcher. Before he betrayed his Mother, he was the most favoured of Her Thaumaturgists.' The giant turned the blue orbs of his eyes up to the glittering jewels above him. 'In light of what happened, I suppose that position now lies with Lady Amilee.'

With a sigh, Bellow looked down at Angel's inert form, and then at Van Bam. 'The Word had no choice but to kill the Wanderer. Wolfe was on to him, you see. He had been reading the stars, listening to the whispers of the skies, and he had divined that something was very amiss with his fellow Skywatcher, Iblisha Spiral.'

Iblisha, Van Bam wondered. 'Wolfe came to you here, in the desert of Mirage?'

Bellow nodded. 'He had sensed a troubling event brewing, but he was having difficulty divining its meaning from the skies. Though he did not know it when he appeared to me, I think Baran Wolfe had sensed the approach of the war.

'Whatever omen had drawn him to Mirage, it was but one stop on a long journey he was undertaking. There was much he was unable to divine from the skies with clarity. He told me that the future was uncertain, but that all answers lay in a hidden location, a secret House that he was searching for. He referred to this House as a *cathedral*. Does that mean anything to you, Van Bam?'

'A cathedral?' The illusionist shook his head.

'Ah, then perhaps its location remains a secret,' Bellow said.

Van Bam thought of Fabian Moor, and of the Icicle Forest, the mysterious House in which the terracotta jar containing the Genii's essence had been discovered. No one seemed to know much about the Icicle Forest at all, including Lady Amilee; and besides Moor, the only other people known to have been there were dead.

'The Labyrinth is supposed to be the only House inside the Nothing of Far and Deep,' Van Bam said. 'But I have been told that there could be many secret Genii strongholds hiding there.'

'Iblisha Spiral is certainly powerful enough to create such places,' Bellow mused. 'Wherever this cathedral might be hidden, the Wanderer seemed convinced that very important secrets were kept there. Who can say if that is true now?'

The giant was contemplative. 'We spoke as equals, Baran Wolfe and I – as I like to think we are doing now, Van Bam. He told me he needed my help. He *asked* me to remain in Mirage. He asked if I would remain as a *favour*, to him – a Thaumaturgist. Can you imagine?'

Van Bam empathised with Bellow. He recalled the first time he had met Lady Amilee, and remembered how he had felt so utterly awed in her presence that he could barely talk to her. He could appreciate how Bellow must have felt being treated as an equal by Lord Wolfe.

'And why did he wish you to remain?' the illusionist asked.

'He said that he could feel trouble coming to Mirage. He asked me to wait, to hide, to not interfere with anything that I witnessed until the day came when someone arrived who would very much need my help to get home.' Bellow considered the illusionist. 'As you pointed out, Van Bam, I have been here for more than two years, waiting for your arrival.'

'Wolfe asked you to wait for us, for Angel and me?' Van Bam asked, taken aback. 'He knew we would come to Mirage?'

'Not specifically. I think he had a vague idea. Nothing Wolfe had divined from the skies was firm, it was all ... doubt and wonder, he called it. In hindsight, the confusion was Spiral's doing. He was covering his tracks, muddying the waters, you might say. He had made it near impossible for the Wanderer to see what he was doing. Until it was too late, of course.'

The giant snorted a sad laugh. 'Baran Wolfe was grateful for my help. But I think a part of him sensed his end was coming.'

A pained glaze came to the Nephilim's blue eyes. He looked down as Angel murmured in her sleep. She now seemed a little more relaxed beneath the swirls and patterns of blood-magic.

'Before he continued his search for his cathedral, Wolfe said that whoever came to me seeking help, I could trust. They would be worthy, he told me. He also suggested that I might share with them the legend of my people.'

Bellow motioned again to the blood painting on the rock between them. Van Bam stared at the spiralling pattern and the square with mirrored triangles, connected by a straight line.

'Why?'

'When I asked him the same question,' Bellow replied, 'he only said that all things were known in the end.

'But you should know, Van Bam, that no other human has seen this symbol before, and *I* show it to you now as a mark of trust – from one *orphan* to another.' The giant paused, staring at the symbol. 'And I will tell you this – should you ever see the sign of the Sorrow of Future Reason again, you can remember that it will always lead you to friends.'

Angel stirred. A moan escaped her lips, but she didn't open her eyes. Bellow placed a hand upon her forehead.

'Good, the fever has broken,' he said.

The healer's skin had taken on a much healthier colour.

'I have enjoyed our conversation, Van Bam. There is more to my story, but it must be heard later. For now I need to attend our friend Angel, and eradicate the last of the Genii's poison.'

Van Bam's gaze lingered on his fellow agent.

'Please,' Bellow urged. 'Join young Namji outside for a while. I'm sure the two of you will be keen to swap notes.'

The Nephilim's tone left no room for argument. The illusionist got to his feet.

'Before I go,' Van Bam said. 'How big is Buyaal's army?'

'I would guess around ten thousand soldiers.'

'So many? A *tenth* of the population?'

'And that is only those who have been trained,' Bellow said. 'The Genii has subjugated this House, Van Bam. They will fight for Spiral till the death.'

Van Bam thought of Labrys Town, and his gut knotted.

'There is much that should concern you, Van Bam, but have courage.' Bellow tapped a finger against his temple again. 'I will continue my story shortly, and then we will discuss how to get you and Angel home ahead of the Genii's army.'

CHAPTER FIFTEEN

THE SISTERHOOD OF BELLS

The Sisterhood of Bells: a monumental city House that dwarfed great Labrys Town; a melting pot of industry, education, politics, the arts; home to over four million Aelfir.

The mighty River Bells ran through the city, wide and filthy, dissecting the districts with a network of interconnecting waterways. At certain points along the river, proud and giant clock towers reached towards the sky, and these towers were called the Sisters. There were fourteen siblings in all, with clock faces as bright as the twin moons that shone silver-blue above the House. Each Sister took turns to twice ring the hour of the day with a low, wistful song, perhaps reminding the four million citizens that time was always running out.

'See that clock tower there?' Hillem said, pointing. He sat opposite Van Bam, next to the window in a private carriage of the train that carried the group into the city. 'The one with the flag?'

The train sped along its tracks on a viaduct that was higher than many of the buildings. Out of the window, Van Bam could see three Sisters rising from the banks of the River Bells. To his inner vision they were huge and slate-grey against the night sky. The closest of them had a flag flying at its summit, fluttering in the wind above its moon-like clock face. There was a crest on the flag; and although, at that distance, normal eyes would have been unable to see what it depicted, the illusionist could discern the symbol of a triangle within a circle.

'They call that tower Little Sibling,' Hillem continued. 'A long time ago, it was the parliament building for the government in the Sisterhood of Bells. It was also home to the High Court, and there are dungeons beneath it that carry all kinds of grim stories. It's said they're haunted.'

Hillem smiled; the young Aelf clearly enjoyed sharing his knowledge.

'During the Genii War,' he said, 'supporters of Spiral were supposedly tortured for information in those dungeons, but they haven't been used for years now. However, when the war ended, and the Timewatcher departed, Little Sibling became the parliament building for *every* Aelfirian government.'

Van Bam stared at the clock tower. 'It is the headquarters for the Panopticon of Houses.'

'Yes,' said Hillem. 'The Aelfir have been ruled from here for the last forty years.'

Van Bam suddenly thought of Marney. He remembered his old lover's passion for history, especially the histories of the Aelfir. He imagined that she and Hillem would have enjoyed many long conversations. For now, the illusionist seemed to be the only person in the carriage listening to the young Aelf. Hillem suddenly seemed to notice his diminished audience, and lapsed into silence.

Next to Hillem sat Namji. Her satchel on her lap, she stared out of the window, entirely lost to her thoughts. Opposite Namji, next to Van Bam, was the bulky form of Glogelder, arms folded, chin wedged into his chest, snoring. The duffle bag containing an assortment of spare weaponry rested on the floor between his legs. Next to Glogelder, Samuel was running a finger along the decorative metal of his new ice-rifle; and opposite the old bounty hunter sat Clara, watching Samuel toy with the weapon.

Considering she carried such dangerous information in her mind, the changeling looked at ease in the magical grey clothes that Namji had given her, confident, assured. *I've grown to fit my skin*, Clara had said, and Van Bam believed it; she had come a long way from the frightened young woman he had first met. It also pleased Van Bam that she and Samuel were now more comfortable in each other's company.

The illusionist wished he could feel as comfortable with himself.

He had been thinking about Labrys Town, about the people he had governed until the Genii supplanted him. What horrors were the denizens facing now? A million humans inhabited the Labyrinth, and as their Resident, Van Bam had let each and every one of them down. Determination flamed within him. He would not fail his people a second time.

Thus far the journey through the Sisterhood of Bells had gone without problem. Earlier, Van Bam had rendered the entire group invisible to other people. This had enabled them to smuggle themselves easily onto the train. The illusionist had then concealed the door of the carriage from the perceptions of ticket inspectors and other passengers. For now, they were safe and hidden within the den of their enemies.

Even so, although the gentle rocking of the train had lulled Glogelder into an untroubled sleep almost as soon as he had sat down, a tense atmosphere surrounded the rest of the group.

At the Face of Grace and Truth, the Relic Guild had escaped the Toymaker when Van Bam had cast illusions of the group to confuse the assassin's toys. While the hand-sized automatons had chased the doppelgangers into the forest, Hillem had set a spell sphere at the base of the portal to the Sisterhood of Bells. The casting of the magic inside had incorporated a delay, meaning the spell hadn't activated until Van Bam, Samuel, Hillem and Glogelder had followed Clara and Namji into the portal.

Hillem had reminded them that although the spell would have destroyed the portal the moment the group had escaped the Face of Grace and Truth, the Toymaker would have known that it led to the Sisterhood of Bells. It was only a matter of time before he caught up with them again.

Somewhere, out there, right now, the Toymaker and his minions were coming, hunting for the Relic Guild, and they all knew it. And they all understood that their would-be assassin was a former Genii.

In Van Bam's head, Gideon stirred.

Tell me, my idiot, what do you make of our current situation? As always, Gideon's tone was inappropriately amused. *The Relic Guild is public enemy number one in the Sisterhood of Bells. I can't imagine there are many Houses more likely to string you up by your feet and flay you alive. And if everything we've been told about this* Sisterhood *is true, I don't think they'll be reticent about punishing you. If* they *capture you, that is.*

What is your point, Gideon? Van Bam said miserably.

Gideon sighed, his amusement remaining, but laced with a modicum of concern. *I don't suppose execution would be as painful for me as it would be for you, but I do fear for myself. I always assumed that when a Resident died his spirit guide took the final journey to Mother Earth. Now, I'm not so sure.*

This gave Van Bam pause for thought.

Since the day the Timewatcher and Her Thaumaturgists had abandoned the Labyrinth, he had been wondering about Mother Earth and the souls of the dead. When a Resident died, his or her spirit delayed the journey to the paradise of the Timewatcher's House by becoming guide to whoever next attained the Residency. But for whom would Van Bam's spirit be an advisor if he died? The illusionist couldn't conceive Hagi Tabet welcoming his ghost to the Nightshade as her guide. As for what might happen to Gideon's ghost …

I like to think that we will find success, Van Bam said. *I like to hope that we will not discover what waits for us after death for a few years yet.*

Denial! Gideon laughed. *That's the spirit, my idiot.*

I only meant that I am choosing to focus on the present, Gideon. Once we have delivered Clara to whatever Known Things is, then *I will consider the future.*

Very pragmatic. Samuel would be proud of you. Gideon sounded bored. *And in the meantime, here you are in the Sisterhood of Bells, a band of renegades, with every Aelfirian House searching for you, as well as a psychopathic ex-Genii – but it's all right! You* choose *to trust the word of an heir to a House that no longer exists and her criminal henchmen. You have* hope *while you all blindly follow the orders of a blue spectre to a secret portal that will deliver Clara to Known Things. Which, by the way, is a relic that none of us had ever heard of, but that can, apparently, kill the most dangerous and corrupt Thaumaturgist who ever existed. The day is surely saved!*

Feeling tired, Van Bam gazed out of the window, watching the city speeding by. *You still haven't made your point, Gideon.*

This all feels a little convenient to me, my idiot. Aren't you suspicious?

No, Van Bam replied. The truth was, there wasn't a single person in this carriage that he wasn't willing to trust. *I will not be suspicious of my colleagues.*

I'm not asking you to distrust your travelling companions, my idiot. I'm asking you to see the whole picture – past, present and future. Something doesn't sit right to me, and I'm damned if I can see what it is.

Be that as it may, Van Bam said, *for the time being, what else can we do besides put our trust in each other?*

Gideon sighed. *This conversation is as painful as trying to talk to Clara,* he said. *All she wants to do is ask question after question about my past. It's very irritating.*

Van Bam looked at the changeling. *Clara has endured much, Gideon – perhaps more than any of us—*

Oh, for love of the Timewatcher! Isn't anyone here willing to discuss the important things? Gideon made an exasperated noise. *I'll tell you what – the rest of you can continue sitting here in morbid silence, waiting for Hillem to bore you with more of his inane stories, but I have better things to think about. Like the one topic that you and your friends seem reluctant to address. Good talk, my idiot.*

The dead Resident's voice fell stone cold and silent inside within Van Bam's mind. And with that silence, the face of an elderly Aelf bloomed before the illusionist's inner vision, and his thoughts turned to the message that Councillor Tal had sent the group. He recalled the fear in Tal's face as he told of the monks who had been attacked by wild demons at Hammer Light of Outside.

Van Bam gazed around at the group, and finally his metallic eyes settled on Namji, who was still staring out of the window.

'What do the Aelfir know of the Retrospective?' he asked her.

The sudden voice breaking the quiet in the carriage caused Glogelder to snort awake and look around with mild confusion.

'Nasty place,' he said sleepily.

'The Retrospective?' Namji said, turning from the window. 'Not much,' she admitted after a moment. 'Beyond the fact that it was where Spiral's Aelfirian armies were sent. We were told it was like a barrier.' She seemed a little lost, and looked for help from Hillem sitting next to her.

'Well,' Hillem said, 'I read that the Timewatcher used the Retrospective to wrap the Labyrinth in a shell of chaos, like a buffer to separate Aelfir and humans.' He shrugged. 'Death awaits anyone who tries to cross it, and that's about as much as I know.'

'At least you got the last part right,' Samuel said.

'Samuel is correct,' said Van Bam. 'The Retrospective is not a shell wrapped around the Labyrinth. It is a House. Of a kind. Founded upon the corrosion of dead time.'

'Which makes it every inch the place of nightmare that you might imagine,' Clara added.

'Indeed.' Van Bam sighed. 'The doorway to the Retrospective is not a fixed point. It is a free-roaming portal that has been haunting the alleyways of the Great Labyrinth since the end of the Genii War.'

'Then you think Tal was right?' said Namji. 'The Retrospective opened its doorway in Hammer Light of Outside?'

'No doubt about it, if you ask me.' Samuel's statement was met by a nod of agreement from Clara.

Hillem sat forward. 'You think it followed you here? That your escape from the Labyrinth caused a *crack* to appear between the Houses, and the Retrospective is bleeding through it?'

'No,' said Samuel. 'We didn't cause this.'

'Then I don't understand,' Hillem said, looking doubtfully at Van Bam. 'You said its doorway is trapped inside the Great Labyrinth. How can it reach an Aelfirian House?'

'It can't,' Samuel answered, aiming his confusion at the illusionist too. 'The Retrospective was designed as a punishment and a deterrent, not to go off ... *marauding* into other realms'

'True,' Van Bam said. 'But perhaps there is a way it could be manipulated.'

Samuel snorted. 'I knew he was going to say that,' he said to Clara.

Clara nodded. 'You could sort of feel it coming, right?'

Glogelder grinned. Namji and Hillem gave Van Bam their full, serious attention.

'The Nightshade,' Van Bam explained. 'It controls every aspect of the Labyrinth. Before the war against the Genii, the Nightshade provided the energy that sustained the portals behind the host of doorways that stood out in the Great Labyrinth, which bridged us and the Houses of the Aelfir through the Nothing of Far and Deep. After the war, the doorways disappeared, but the power to create their portals never left the Nightshade.'

Namji shared a quick look with Hillem, and said, 'We all know the legend of the First and Greatest Spell, Van Bam. But if the Timewatcher left that kind of power behind, why haven't you used it before? Why let Labrys Town spend forty years in isolation, when the Nightshade could've reached out to us?'

'The First and Greatest Spell was created by the very highest of magic.' Van Bam shook his head and sat back. 'Humans and Aelfir are creatures of lower magic. Thaumaturgy is not a science the likes of us can fully understand, still less wield. Perhaps *that* is the reason why the Timewatcher entrusted the Nightshade to us – our inability to abuse its power. But now ...'

Van Bam left the sentence hanging, suddenly feeling as though he didn't have the energy to finish it.

Gideon's chuckle rattled in his head. *Which of them will catch on first, do you think? I bet you a hundred Labyrinth pounds that it's Hillem.*

'Oh, I see,' said Hillem. 'The Genii control the Nightshade now, and the Timewatcher isn't around to stop them.'

You owe me money, my idiot.

Van Bam ignored the dead Resident. 'Who knows what the Genii are capable of achieving now they have the First and Greatest Spell in their grasp.'

There was a moment of silence, and then Samuel exhaled a heavy breath.

'You think they're using the Retrospective to attack the Aelfir? Letting it seep out of the Great Labyrinth through the Nightshade?'

Van Bam nodded. 'Theoretically, the Nightshade could use the Retrospective as a conduit that reconnects the Labyrinth to every House out there.'

'Shit,' Samuel whispered. 'That's clever.'

'Clever?' said Glogelder. 'Yeah, I suppose it is. But how bad is it really?' He shrugged at the group. 'Sure, the Houses will have to stay on their toes, but you all heard what Tal had to say. A crack opened. A few demons got out.' He looked at Clara, and winked. 'The wolf must enjoy a good fight now and then.'

Clara bared her teeth at him. 'Glogelder, do you have any idea how big the Retrospective is? How many demons there are inside it?'

The big Aelf sank back in his seat and shook his head.

'Nor do we,' Clara growled. 'And that's because the number is so high, no one's thought of a name for it yet.'

'She's right, Glogelder,' Samuel said. 'If that doorway starts opening wider, the Aelfir will have more than a few skirmishes to worry about. The Retrospective was designed to swallow realms as well as people. It'll start eating the Houses one by one. The Retrospective will get bigger and bigger, the number of wild demons will swell. No one will be safe.'

Glogelder appeared suitably daunted by this prospect, and raised an eyebrow at Hillem, seeking confirmation. Hillem nodded back at him.

Gideon laughed again. *I like this Glogelder. He's as stupid as he is brave. I bet he's the first of us to die. Double or quits, my idiot?*

Actually, he has raised a good point, Van Bam replied, and then, aloud, he said, 'The attack on Hammer Light of Outside might tell us something. It has always been said that Spiral was the only Thaumaturgist who could rival the Timewatcher in power. If that is true, then only he among the Genii could fully harness the First and Greatest Spell, and use it to force the Retrospective into doing his bidding.'

'But Spiral isn't free, and we have the location of Oldest Place,' Namji pointed out, motioning to Clara. 'So Fabian Moor must have gained some command of the Nightshade's magic. He opened the Retrospective in Hammer Light of Outside, after all.'

'Yes, but only a crack,' Van Bam countered. 'Perhaps it was an experiment. The Genii must have discovered by now that Marney no longer has the information on Oldest Place. Fabian Moor and his cohorts would have been faced with the prospect that Spiral might never be free. Perhaps he is desperate, attempting to do what only his master could. Or …'

Follow the thought through, my idiot.

'Or perhaps he is searching the Houses.'

'For us,' Hillem said. 'Or more specifically, for the person Marney gave the information to.'

All eyes turned to Clara. The changeling, looking so much wiser and self-assured than she used to, met their gazes with a sheen of yellow in her eyes, the hues of her mood confident.

'If Fabian Moor knows I'm carrying the location of Oldest Place, that still doesn't tell him where we're going,' she said. 'If he's desperate and searching blindly – how many Houses are out there? We could be anywhere.' She pulled an unperturbed face. 'And let's face it, we'll probably get murdered by the Toymaker before the Genii catch up with us, anyway.'

Samuel smiled at the reply, and Glogelder gave a throaty laugh.

'Be that as it may,' said Van Bam sternly, 'unless we get to Known Things, I doubt the attack on Hammer Light of Outside will be the last time the Aelfir sees the Retrospective.'

The train rocked, and Van Bam sensed its speed decreasing. His metallic eyes glared at Namji.

'Perhaps now you can tell us exactly where in the Sisterhood of Bells we are headed?'

'It's a tavern, not far from the station,' Namji replied.

'The portal to Known Things is in a tavern?' asked Samuel.

'Don't be silly,' Glogelder replied. 'My contact's going to meet us there.'

'Everything will make sense soon enough,' Namji promised. 'But first, we need to conceal our weapons.' She looked from Clara to Samuel and finally back to Van Bam. 'And you three can't exactly go walking round the city looking like humans. Invisibility won't work as our contact needs to be able to see us.'

Van Bam agreed. He looked at the weaponry the group carried, and at the faces of Samuel and Clara, as human as his own. There were a lot of specific details to conceal if the group was to blend in with the citizens of this House.

'This will take concentration,' Van Bam said, as the train's brakes began to squeal outside. He lifted his green glass cane in both hands. 'Do not talk to me, and ensure I am not disturbed by outside influences.'

And that includes you, he added to Gideon.

There were a lot of characters with chequered histories in Labrys Town. They walked around wearing their legends like coats with deep pockets filled with shady secrets; especially those who belonged to the older generation, the denizens who had misspent their younger days during a time when the Thaumaturgists and the Aelfir were still around.

By the time Sergeant Ennis arrived in the eastern district, and had walked to a little junkshop situated in a courtyard behind a tavern, it was mid-afternoon. He considered the grimy, cracked windows and the peeling paint on the door of the shop, and had to smile at the fading sign that promised quality merchandise within.

Earlier, after leaving the warehouse in the southern district, Ennis had gone to visit the Merchants' Guild offices at Watcher's Gallery in the central district. He had been attempting to gather information on the magickers of the Relic Guild – thinking that knowing his enemy a little better might help his search. He reasoned that the heads of the Merchants' Guild often visited the Nightshade on affairs of business, and had therefore spent the most time in the company of Van Bam – perhaps the shadiest character of all. As it turned out, the trip to Watcher's Gallery had been a waste of energy.

Ennis had been told that every head in the Merchants' Guild was unavailable, as they had been summoned to an emergency meeting with the new Resident. Those Ennis did get to speak with were lower ranking officials, and what they had told the sergeant was unhelpful, at best drawing a picture of a man that nobody really knew at all. Strange, considering Van Bam had been the governor of this town since long before Ennis was born.

And now, standing before the rundown junkshop, the police sergeant swapped his thoughts from one shady character to another, and decided against drawing his pistol before stepping forwards.

The bell should have rung when Ennis opened the door, but it gave a weak, deadened *clack* instead.

Inside, the merchandise for sale hadn't exactly been placed on display, more *dumped* into any available space. The air was musty and full of dust. The vendor stood behind the small counter, leaning against the top, reading a newspaper. He looked up, his old, craggy face seeming surprised that a customer had walked into his ramshackle shop.

Ennis stared at him.

'Are you after anything in particular, young man?' said the vendor after a while. 'Or are you just here to browse?'

Suspicious...

Ennis smiled at the unvarnished furniture, the cracked ornaments, the faded paintings, and the rest of the assorted goods on sale, and wondered if anyone had ever come to this junkshop to simply *browse.*

'It's a scary time, don't you think?' Ennis said. 'The Relic Guild comes back after all these years, the Resident turns against his people, and they all start spreading this virus.' He shivered. 'And did you hear about what happened at Watcher's Gallery?'

'Jeter's execution?' the shopkeeper said, tapping the open newspaper. 'Funny, I was just reading about that.' He frowned and looked his customer up and down. 'I'm sorry – is there something I can help you with?'

Secrets...

Ennis never stopped gathering information. He spent much of his time observing where others thought there was nothing interesting to observe; listening when people thought they weren't saying anything important. Nothing was mundane to Ennis; he watched the unusual, the peripheral, and his attention was always attracted to the subtle things that most people didn't notice. It was clear to the sergeant that the vendor's appearance of simple old shopkeeper, along with the dusty mounds of rubbish that he advertised as *quality merchandise,* was a disguise, a façade. And that told Ennis he had come to exactly the right place.

'Actually, I'm looking to get something identified,' Ennis said. 'I heard you're the man for the job. Or that you certainly used to be.'

'*Identified*, young man? *Used* to be? I'm not sure I follow you.'

'Before the Genii War,' Ennis explained. 'You were a magic-user, right?'

The shopkeeper stiffened behind the counter. 'I beg your pardon?' His voice had become low.

'You heard me,' Ennis said. 'You used to be a multi-talented man. You were an alchemist, among other things. You remember testing stolen artefacts to identify their magical properties, don't you?'

'An alchemist, eh?' One of the vendor's hands was balled into a fist, resting on the newspaper; but the other remained below the counter, no doubt holding a concealed weapon. 'I don't care for your accusation, young man. The use of magic carries a serious penalty in Labrys Town. A one way trip to the Nightshade.'

'Oh, don't take offence,' Ennis said. 'I hear you were a very good magic-user. The best, in fact – always in demand, always busy. That's why the treasure hunters called you Long Tommy, isn't it? Because you were worth the wait.'

Long Tommy's shoulders slumped, and he removed his empty hand from beneath the counter. He folded up the newspaper neatly and slapped it to one side. 'You're a policeman,' he stated.

Ennis showed him his badge.

'Sergeant Ennis,' Tommy mused. 'Can't say I've heard your name before.'

'I try to keep a low profile,' Ennis replied. 'But I'm not really here, if you follow me.' He gazed around and chuckled. 'If this was an official visit, I'd be seizing the contents of your shop. I dread to think how much of this crap is stolen.'

The old man's face broke into a grin. 'I can't remember the last time someone called me Long Tommy, you know. You've got nothing on me, *Sergeant* Ennis. I served my dues when the law caught up with me before you were born. I got out of the magic game during the war.'

'I'm not here to arrest you, Tommy.'

'What are you, then? Bent copper?' Now it was Tommy's turn to chuckle. 'If you're after money, I don't make a fraction of what I did in the old days.' He winked.

'No, I was being truthful with you,' Ennis said. 'I'm hoping you can tell me what this is.'

From his coat pocket, Ennis removed the diamond-shaped shard of metal he had found in the cellar of the ore warehouse in the southern district. He placed it on the countertop and unwrapped the handkerchief.

Long Tommy considered Ennis suspiciously for a moment, and then looked at the item on his counter. He shrugged. 'It's a piece of metal.'

Ennis rolled his eyes. 'Yes, I know, but what *kind* of metal is it? Look…'

Using the handkerchief, Ennis picked up the shard and folded it in half as easily as folding a sheet of paper. He then dropped it; the metal had straightened flat again by the time it clanged down onto the countertop.

'Bugger me,' said Tommy. Tentatively, he reached out and touched a finger to the metal. He snapped his hand back almost immediately. 'It's cold. *Freezing.*'

Ennis nodded.

Tommy shook his head. 'In a room this warm, it should be sweating.'

'Have you ever come across a metal that acts like this before, Tommy?'

'I've come across all kinds of things in my time.'

'Can you test it for magic?' Ennis asked. 'Do you have your old alchemist's equipment?'

Tommy stared at the policeman.

'Don't worry, I'm not asking you to work for nothing.' Ennis produced fifty Labyrinth pounds and placed them beside the shard of metal.

A strange glint came to the old man's eye as he looked at the money. 'There was a time when I wouldn't bother talking to you for that amount.'

'Tell me what this thing is by tomorrow, and I'll double it.'

'Oh, I see. You think I'm desperate for cash.' Tommy sniffed. 'Let me tell you something, *Sergeant.* Back in the old days, if a magic-user got caught, the worst thing that would've happened to him was a short stay in prison. Unless you were stupid enough to get involved with Aelfirian artefacts – *then* you'd have the Relic Guild on your case. There wasn't much mercy in those bastards.'

Ennis made to speak, but Tommy stopped him.

'Nowadays,' he said forcefully, 'dicking about with magic will earn you the death penalty. A lot of people I've known have disappeared in the Nightshade over the years.' Tommy shook his head, looking around his shop. 'Considering everything that's going on in this town right now, you've got some bloody cheek coming to my shop, strong-arming me back into the life I left, and for what? Pocket money?'

Frightened . . .

'I'm not forcing you to do anything,' Ennis replied levelly. 'I could, if that's what you'd prefer. I could threaten to have this place raided, and you in a cell within the hour, unless you do as I say. But I don't want to, Tommy. I just want you to take my pocket money, keep your mouth shut, and identify this metal for me. Will you do it?'

Tommy's expression was sour. 'No choice, eh?'

'Think of it more as *me* not having a choice,' Ennis replied. 'I don't exactly know a lot of alchemists. I need your help.'

Tommy stared at the shard of metal for a moment. 'I don't suppose you'd like to tell me what this is all about?'

'Probably better if you don't know.'

'Bloody coppers,' Tommy swore. 'You're worse than the criminals.' He scooped up the money and stuffed it into his trouser pocket. 'I'll know what this thing is by tonight. But we meet somewhere else. I don't want you ever coming back to my shop again.'

'Fair enough,' said Ennis. 'When you've got that metal identified, go to the northern district. You'll find me in the Lazy House.'

A ghostly radiance hung over the Sisterhood of Bells like a sickly, bruised halo, just bright enough to obscure the stars that surrounded the twin moons in the sky above the city. The scent of forge smoke laced the air, along with the cleaner presence of thaumaturgy. The drone of four million lives drifted through a landscape of old and dirty buildings, creeping down wide streets and narrow alleys like an ancient voice whispering secrets. The ambience of this monumental city House stroked each of Clara's heightened senses, and the changeling felt the pressure of a territory alien yet familiar.

As Glogelder led the group to meet their contact, Clara was amused by the appearance of the three Relic Guild agents. Van Bam's magic had given each of them the illusion of decidedly less human features. They were still vaguely recognisable as themselves, but their ears were pointed; noses and mouths were small; and their eyes were big and round, achieving the triangular face shape that was a trait of the Aelfir. Clara, Van Bam and Samuel blended in perfectly with the citizens of the Sisterhood of Bells – not humans on the run at all.

The illusionist had further extended his magic to also conceal the weapons they carried. But the concentration required to maintain the spell was taking its toll on Van Bam; his triangular face was covered in a sheen of sweat, his eyes, in this state large and brown, stared fixedly at the ground.

From the train station, the group travelled a short distance along a street bustling with pedestrians, following the line of the railway viaduct. Eventually they reached a tavern situated within one of the viaduct's huge archways. The tavern was a large rundown sort of place, and thankfully light on customers. Of the handful of Aelfir present, one or two looked over as the group entered, but no one spared them more than a cursory glance.

The six Aelfir took their seats at a table against the grimy back wall.

To Clara, the customers felt like regulars as they chatted over their drinks, and played cards and dominoes. Clara certainly sensed no danger coming from them. She glanced at Samuel; the old bounty hunter's prescient awareness was obviously not giving him any warning signals, and he seemed relaxed in his surroundings – at least, as relaxed as Samuel ever seemed.

Settling into her seat at the table, Clara noticed three young women descending a set of stairs from the tavern's upper level. They took up a position at one end of the bar. Each of them wore a flimsy dressing gown, and the sight of them filled the changeling with sadness. The young women were waiting for trade.

Does it bring back memories? Gideon purred in her mind.

The tavern door opened, and a middle-aged Aelf entered, looking shifty and nervous.

'Is that your contact?' Samuel asked quietly.

Glogelder shook his head. 'My contact's a woman.'

But Clara was watching the middle-aged Aelf. He approached one of the women at the end of the bar. He whispered into her ear, and she responded with the same fake smile Clara had used countless times on faceless punters. Her sadness was displaced by a flare of anger, as the young woman took the man by the hand and led him up the stairs to her private chamber.

'When will your contact arrive?' Samuel was saying testily.

'Don't worry yourself,' Glogelder assured him. 'We're a bit early, but she'll be here on time.'

Samuel sat back and folded his arms across his chest, his large blue eyes glowering.

Van Bam remained quiet. His Aelfirian face was a mask of concentration as he gripped tightly, with both hands, his green glass cane, which now appeared as a plain wooden walking stick. Namji and Hillem, sitting next to each other, checked out the tavern with suspicious eyes. Glogelder, Clara noticed, was watching the two remaining whores, but with a very different kind of appraisal in his eyes.

'Well then,' Glogelder said, to no one in particular. 'Seeing as we've got a bit of time to kill –' he wiggled his eyebrows at the group – 'nobody minds if I – uh – *disappear* for a while, do they?'

With Gideon chuckling inside her head, Clara leant forwards, and beckoned Glogelder across the table towards her.

'Have you ever thought about the events that might lead a woman into that profession?'

Glogelder shrugged. 'Not especially. Everyone has to earn a living, right?'

'Right …' Clara gave him a dangerous smile. 'Glogelder, if you try to hire one of those girls, I'll rip your balls off.'

Glogelder wasn't sure how to react at first. He frowned at Hillem, who shook his head, indicating that Clara was not joking. Glogelder then looked at the changeling, anger in his eyes.

'You can't talk to me like that.'

'Can't I?' Clara replied. 'Try stopping me. See how far you get.'

Samuel decided to step in. 'Clara—'

'Oh, I'm sorry, Samuel,' Clara snapped. 'Did I say something to offend you, too?'

'Now is *not* the time,' the old bounty hunter said icily. He jabbed a finger at Glogelder. 'And *you* – just shut up.'

'I agree,' Namji said. First looking around the bar, ensuring that the disagreement hadn't attracted attention, and also giving Van Bam a quick, concerned look, she addressed the table. 'No one's going out of sight, especially you, Glogelder. Stay put and keep it buttoned up. Understand?'

The big Aelf sat back sulkily in his chair and glared at Clara. Before the changeling could tell him where he could stick his dirty look, Namji added, 'Clara, would you help me get some drinks, please?'

Gideon, who had obviously savoured the incident, said, *Namji's right, child. A woman's place is to serve the men. Off you go.*

Shut up! Clara hissed in reply.

Careful, Clara. I'm not afraid of the big bad wolf, remember.

I don't care! Go and annoy Van Bam, you bloody idiot.

The silence that followed Clara's scolding suggested that Gideon was highly amused. At least he said no more.

With a final glare at Glogelder, Clara followed Namji over to the bar. While the Aelf ordered a pitcher of beer from the landlord, the changeling found it hard to keep her eyes off the two young women, standing at the far end of the bar.

'Well then,' said Namji quietly as they waited for the beer. 'Glogelder can be a fathead – no doubt about it – and I really don't want to know what he gets up to in his spare time, but he needs a good slap down every now and then.' She smiled at the changeling. 'But I don't think it's really Glogelder you're pissed off about, is it?'

The Aelf looked at the women standing at the end of the bar, waiting to trade their bodies for money, and then back at Clara.

'Who can say?' Namji said, as if reading Clara's thoughts. 'Maybe those girls deserve better. Or maybe they're happy.'

Clara scoffed. 'What would you know about it?'

'You tell me. Everything? Nothing?'

'You've never known the kind of life that these women have.'

'You're right, I haven't. But I've certainly lived through my fair share of bad times, Clara.'

Namji waited until Clara took her eyes off the whores and looked at her before continuing.

'When I was your age – younger, actually – I was being trained to rule an Aelfirian House. I was spoilt, pampered, and every privilege you can think of was within my reach. But my House ended up in the Retrospective. Everyone I grew up with is dead. Now, I'm the only surviving Aelf from Mirage. The last of my people.' Namji gestured to the women. 'Call it fate, the will of the Timewatcher, circumstance

– whatever you want – but I know what it's like when life makes a fist and punches you in the gut, Clara.'

Clara saw the hurt on Namji's face, and couldn't hold her gaze.

'Before all this began,' Clara told Namji with a heavy voice, 'I worked at a club called the Lazy House. They called me Peppercorn Clara.'

'I remember the Lazy House, and its reputation,' Namji said. 'I spent two years in Labrys Town, you know.' She leant into Clara, keeping her voice low. 'The avatar told me that you had been one of the Lazy House's ... *employees.*'

'I was a *whore*, if that's what you mean.'

'I was being polite, Clara.'

'And I was being blunt.'

'So – what? You're going to stay angry about your past until you've taken it out on us all? How does your regret help the bigger picture?'

Clara's jaw set, and the wolf growled in her chest. Namji was undeterred.

'We all come from somewhere, Clara,' she said, studying the changeling's face, and the illusion that had been cast upon it. 'But, for what it's worth, you're very pretty as an Aelf.' She dropped her voice to a whisper. 'Not so much as a human.'

Namji smiled, and Clara felt the tension within her break. She couldn't help a laugh escaping the grim line of her lips.

Yet the two whores, huddled together, whispering, sharing secrets, reminded Clara of her days at the Lazy House. She thought of Willow, her one true friend. They had looked out for each other, kept each other sane. What was Willow doing now – had she managed to find a new friend who would watch her back?

A cold and sudden pang hit the changeling. Now Labrys Town was under the rule of the Genii, was there any kind of life left for the denizens to lead?

'I've had to fight my way through all sorts of crap to get to this point,' Namji said, her eyes drifting up and into memory. 'But I had some good teachers along the way. One inspired me to live the life of a nomad ...' She gave a laugh. 'But that's the past. It's the immediate future that concerns me now.' Her large green eyes found the changeling's face again. 'If you know what I mean.'

Clara sensed the presence of Marney inside her, aloof, hiding, and her gut twisted. 'Known Things,' she whispered.

Namji checked no one was eavesdropping, and then nodded. 'Known Things. The answer to all our problems.'

'If you trust the avatar.'

'And I do, Clara.'

The landlord returned at that moment, his tray loaded with a pitcher of beer and six glasses. Namji paid him and he wandered off to talk to a regular.

Pausing before she picked up the tray, Namji quietly said, 'I'll tell you what I've learnt over the last forty years – you can't save everyone. And to really change the way things are, you have to be royalty or a politician ... or a Resident.'

She looked over at the table, where the group waited for Glogelder's contact to show up. The eyes on Van Bam's Aelfirian face were closed as he concentrated on maintaining the illusions.

'But you're none of those, Clara,' Namji continued, not unkindly. 'You're a magicker, an agent of the Relic Guild. Your lot is to live on the periphery of life, always watching, always ready to protect the vulnerable from what they can't see, what they don't know about.' She reached out and gently tapped Clara on the temple. 'With the information you have up here, you might just save every living soul across all the Houses. And if you do, the worst part is, no one will ever know what you've done. You'll never be thanked for it. *That* is who you are *now*.'

How very profound, Gideon drawled. *She sounds a little like Van Bam. Irritating, isn't it?*

Clara managed a smile, and felt a sudden appreciation for Namji, a woman she hardly knew.

'What about you, Namji?' she said. 'What's your place now?'

'Oh, life is rarely how I'd like it to be, Clara. I'm just doing what I need to do to stay alive.' Namji lifted the tray from the bar. 'If we're going to stay one step ahead of the Genii – and the Toymaker – we all need to trust each other and work together. Even with Glogelder in the pack.' She chuckled and nodded towards the table. 'Come on, let's join the others.'

After a final, contemplative look at the young women at the end of the bar, Clara's mood became surprisingly light as she followed Namji back to the table. Samuel, carrying his usual stern expression, raised an eyebrow, his large blue eyes questioning. The changeling nodded at the old bounty hunter, letting him know her anger had passed. Hillem cleared his throat and looked meaningfully at Glogelder. When Glogelder shook his head, Hillem kicked him under the table.

'All right!' the big Aelf said, rubbing his leg. He faced Clara, but couldn't bring himself to actually look at her. 'I am very sorry for anything that I might have said that caused you offence,' he said perfunctorily.

'Oh, brilliant,' Hillem said. 'That's the worst bloody apology I've ever heard.'

'What do you want from me?' Glogelder snapped. 'I haven't got anything to apologise for.'

Play nicely, Clara, Gideon purred. *It'll be easier in the long run.*

'Shut up, Glogelder,' Clara said, taking a glass from the tray and sliding it across the table to him. 'And have a beer.'

'Excellent idea,' Namji said.

Glogelder gave a wide grin, took the pitcher and filled his glass. He then filled a second one and passed it to Clara.

'To us,' he said, raising his glass to the changeling.

Clara clinked her own against it. 'You're an arse,' she replied, and took a long draught of dark brown beer.

As Glogelder did the same, Hillem set about pouring beer for everyone else. Samuel drained his glass as though he had been desperate for a drink since the Relic Guild had escaped the Labyrinth. Van Bam didn't touch his, but his eyes were open now, and he stared at it.

It was while the group drank in silence that the tavern door opened and an Aelf walked in. She looked to be around the age of Samuel and Van Bam, wearing a uniform of blue trousers and blazer, white shirt and black tie. Under her arm was a peaked hat. Her expression was pensive as she scanned the tavern and finally settled on the group's table.

'That's my contact,' Glogelder said, wiping beer froth from his top lip. His manner had become serious, professional. 'Her name's Symone.'

'I'm not sensing any danger from her,' Samuel said.

'Nor me,' Clara added.

'Of course you're not,' Glogelder said, catching the woman's eye. 'She's here to help us.'

'Then it looks like we're up,' Namji said to the big Aelf. 'The rest of you wait here.'

Closely followed by Namji, Glogelder approached Symone, and began speaking to her in a hushed voice.

Van Bam seemed in touch with what was happening around him for the first time since entering the tavern, and he looked up, speaking quietly.

'This person will help us find Known Things?'

'Yes,' said Hillem. 'She's going to escort us to the portal. I hope.'

'Who is she?' Samuel asked.

'A night guard.'

Clara frowned. 'Night guard for where?'

Hillem shrugged. 'A museum.'

CHAPTER SIXTEEN

GARDEN OF THE NECROMANCER

Hamir was lost, but he remembered …

The Trinity of Skywatchers had been established to be the overlord of the overlords. Its legitimacy arose from the Timewatcher's prerogatives, and its purpose was to administer Her laws, and to ensure they were upheld by *all* Her children. Iblisha Spiral, Yansas Amilee and Baran Wolfe – the *Word*, the *Warden*, the *Wanderer* – represented the Timewatcher among the Thaumaturgists. The Skywatchers were the governors of higher magic.

Some had called the members of the Trinity the personal diviners of the Timewatcher. They had a duty to monitor the skies, to listen to the language of the stars and decipher its tales of the future, especially those futures that whispered of trouble heading towards the creatures of lower magic. Spiral, Amilee and Wolfe were charged by their Mother to stave off these future troubles, to rectify injustices and *mistakes* by always finding peaceful resolutions for Aelfir and humans – unless the sky told them of crimes committed by their fellow Thaumaturgists.

Hamir remembered …

In the far and distant past, there had been uncommon occasions when the Trinity of Skywatchers convened a court known as the Council of Three. Resented by some, feared by most, the Council of Three always assembled on Mother Earth, and any Thaumaturgist summoned before them could not hope for a happy ending.

It was rare for a creature of higher magic to defy the Timewatcher's word and law, but those who did commit this crime were shown no mercy by the Council. There were moments in Mother Earth's long history when the Word, the Warden and the Wanderer had drained the higher magic from Thaumaturgists, burned the symbol of thaumaturgy from their foreheads, and expelled them from the pantheon. There was no severer punishment, no greater shame, that could be suffered by a creature of higher magic. As the Council of Three, the Trinity of Skywatchers exacted the retribution of the Timewatcher.

Hamir could not fathom where he was, but he wondered …

It was said that no Thaumaturgist could hide from the Trinity; that it was impossible to conduct nefarious plans against the Timewatcher without triggering a summons to the Council of Three. Yet Iblisha Spiral proved to be the exception to the rule. His actions betrayed his Mother, and every living being existing under Her loving Gaze. His was the greatest act of deception ever seen among the Thaumaturgists.

Hamir the necromancer could appreciate the logistical problems that Spiral would have faced in the build up to the war. The Trinity of Skywatchers were masters of precognition, and that made Lady Amilee and Lord Wolfe a little difficult to sneak up on. Spiral would have had no easy time concealing his plans from his fellow Skywatchers. An improbable achievement, one might say – though, as it turned out, not impossible.

Hamir reasoned that it would have taken a great and subtle use of thaumaturgy to pull the wool over the eyes of the Warden and the Wanderer, not to mention the eyes of the Timewatcher Herself. To have achieved his goals, Spiral would have had to fool the very skies above him.

Time, Hamir realised, still not knowing where he was.

Spiral must have hid time itself. Every moment, every thought and action that he planned, Spiral had kept secret from the sky, from the stars, from the whispers of the future. He had found a way to make himself *undivinable*.

Therefore his planning was not subject to chance. Everything was calculated. Baran Wolfe's murder had not been a flashpoint that escalated hostilities; it was a catalyst, a strategic decision that caused the final rent between the Thaumaturgists, and brought them to war against the Genii. As Spiral had hidden his actions so masterfully, by the time Baran Wolfe the Wanderer had realised that the end of his life was a part of Spiral's plans, he must have already been at the wrong end of the Genii Lord's distinct lack of mercy.

Hamir came to know these things as he came to know where he was, and with clarity.

He understood that his physical form lay asleep in a dream chamber high in the Tower of the Skywatcher; and that his mental projection hadn't *arrived* at a new destination, but had been *reassembled*, thought by thought, until the necromancer stood in a small grove of apple trees, still pondering the history of the Thaumaturgists and the Genii War.

Beneath his feet was soft, moss-choked grass. Bees buzzed. Insects crawled over fallen fruit. Clouds drifted across the sky.

Hamir tugged at the tuft of beard on his chin. He knew that he could see beyond the grove, that there was more outside the trees, yet his mind would not let him perceive it.

'A disquieting effect, isn't it?' said the avatar. 'To know something is there, hidden in plain sight. Perplexing, wouldn't you say, Hamir?'

The necromancer shrugged. Of course the avatar was there with him, though he couldn't see it. It always had been, hadn't it? And such an annoying presence.

Hamir said, 'I know things about conjurations – such as yourself – that many people do not.'

'Oh?' said the avatar.

'Yes,' Hamir replied. 'Although it can be said that you future-guides are magical beings, you are never formed from magic alone. There is always a building block from which you are *grown*. You are founded upon the spirit of a real person who once lived and died. So tell me, *avatar*, who did you use to be?'

'Curiosity, Hamir?' the avatar said. 'Since when did you take an interest in anyone other than yourself?'

It was a good point, and Hamir didn't suppose that the answer to his question would alter his situation in any way.

He stepped towards the edge of the grove, and began to see something of the gardens that lay beyond it. The avatar materialised before him, a sky-blue aura surrounding the twilight shape of a person. Tendrils of light waved around the future-guide.

'I've been thinking about Spiral,' Hamir said, though he knew it was truer to say that here in this dreamscape Lady Amilee had been *making* him think about Spiral. 'It seems to me that as brilliantly executed as

Spiral's plans were, his predictions could not have been flawless. He must have allowed for at least an element of variability.'

'And what *element* might that be, Hamir?'

'I was thinking specifically about the war itself. To cultivate events that lead to a war is one thing, but to predict its outcome is entirely another. *That* is where the variables lie. I can't believe that Spiral was ever certain that he and the Genii would beat the Timewatcher and her armies. He must have known there was a good chance he would lose.' Hamir narrowed his eyes in thought. 'Did Spiral see two outcomes, two possible futures? Did he prepare for both?'

The necromancer looked up at the clouds in the sky. 'Of course,' he whispered. It all made sense then, and he chuckled heartily. 'Spiral foresaw the creation of Oldest Place. He knew that if he lost the war, the Timewatcher would incarcerate him in his own prison realm.'

'Very good, Hamir.'

The necromancer didn't much care for the avatar's mocking tone, and he glared at it. 'That's why the Genii returned, isn't it? To free their lord and master from Oldest Place. Fabian Moor and his cronies are Spiral's answer to a variable – his contingency for losing the war.'

'It was Spiral's final deceit,' said the avatar. 'Not only had he fore-seen the creation of Oldest Place, but also that the Timewatcher and the Thaumaturgists would abandon the Labyrinth and all the Houses.'

'Ah. I did not know She had abandoned the Aelfir as well as the humans after the war.' Hamir continued. 'If Spiral knew that this would happen, he also knew there would be no one left to oppose him if he escaped Oldest Place. The Houses would be his to take. Ingenious.'

'It was the plan no one knew Spiral had made,' the avatar said. 'The Timewatcher Herself hadn't realised that he had grown so powerful that he could divine Her future actions.'

'Yet Lady Amilee realised,' Hamir countered, gesturing to the apple trees around him, and whatever else he couldn't see in this dreamscape created by the Skywatcher's imagination. 'She would seem to have divined what the Timewatcher couldn't. Strange.'

The avatar was silent. Tendrils of blue light coiled and snaked grace-fully around its body. Smoky shadows drifted from its eyes to dissipate in the air like mist in sunshine.

'Curious, though,' Hamir said. 'I was led to believe that only the Timewatcher knew where She had hidden Oldest Place. Spiral must have become *such* a powerful Skywatcher to have divined its location before She had created it.'

'He didn't divine its location,' the avatar replied. 'It was the one anomaly in Spiral's plans, the mystery he could not unravel. However, he *did* divine that someone other than the Timewatcher would come to know the whereabouts of Oldest Place.'

'Who?'

'Come forward, Hamir, and you will learn more.'

The blue spectre floated away. Hamir hesitated, and then walked from the grove of apple trees.

The garden beyond the trees spread before him, grew around him, like a bubble expanding, to encompass blooming flowers full of vibrant colours, and an expanse of mossy grass, lush beneath a glorious sun. Hamir squinted. He knew the grand garden continued on for a distance, but there was a boundary that he could not perceive beyond, blocking his vision with the same disquieting effect he had experienced in the apple grove. But what he could see clearly, rising towards the sky behind the avatar, was a column of energy, droning, spinning like a whirlwind of black and white dashed static.

Hamir recognised the column immediately; it was the same energy that had disassembled his awareness back in the underwater cavern, and then reconstructed him, thought by thought, in this garden.

The necromancer shielded his eyes against the sun as he followed the column's length up to where wispy clouds drifted across the sky. And there, high in the air, a figure hovered before the column, borne upon wings of fluid silver, dressed in purple ceremonial robes.

Lady Amilee, the Warden, the last of the Trinity of Skywatchers.

Hamir felt no relief at finally finding his host. He watched as Amilee studied the column of droning static, adjusting her height every now and then, and occasionally reaching out to stroke the energy.

'It is a slipstream,' the avatar said. 'An amalgamation of timelines, possible futures.'

Hamir looked intently at the column, and realised that it was a representation of the sky, of the stars, and the language of the future that whispered to the Skywatcher, condensed into energy within this imagined dreamscape.

'The slipstream is the conduit that allows Amilee to access the real world,' Hamir said. 'It is the seat of power from which she toys with people's lives, manipulates their fates. And where do you fit into this, *spectre*?'

'I am Lady Amilee's avatar. She sends me to adjust events as she needs to. As you say, there are always variables in the art of divination, Hamir.' The avatar drifted closer to the necromancer. 'At one time, the slipstream comprised a multitude of timelines that practically filled this garden. But, over the years, Lady Amilee has chipped away at them, whittled the timelines down, until now only four possible futures remain.'

Hamir considered the avatar's words for a moment, and then he asked, 'And in these futures, the Genii either succeed or fail to free Spiral?'

The avatar didn't answer.

Hamir looked up at Amilee, hovering before the column on her wings of silver. How long had she been here, divining the future, while her body remained in the dream chamber in her tower? Yansas Amilee, the Warden, Treasured Lady of the Thaumaturgists – had she foreseen Spiral's actions, but too late to prevent the war? Would anyone, including the Timewatcher, have listened to her if she had spoken against the most favoured creature of higher magic? Had she bothered trying?

'Tell me.' Hamir turned to the avatar. 'You mentioned that one other knew how to find Oldest Place. I suspect it was the reason why Fabian Moor abducted Marney, yes?'

'If Lady Amilee wishes you to know more details, Hamir, then she will tell you herself.'

'Fair enough.' Hamir looked up again. 'I am here, my lady,' he shouted up to the cloudy sky. 'I came as you commanded!'

The Skywatcher didn't reply. She didn't look down. She adjusted her height to inspect a different section of the swirling, droning slipstream, her silver wings gently, gracefully, maintaining her altitude.

'Lady Amilee!' Hamir tried again, louder this time. 'I have one or two questions for you.' Again, the Thaumaturgist ignored the necromancer.

Was she waiting for Hamir to show proper respect, to address her by her full title, perhaps? If that was the case, after what he had been made to endure on his travels to this realm, Hamir rather thought she was going to have a long wait.

He drew a breath, cupped his hands around his mouth, and barked the Skywatcher's true name. 'Yansas! I've no patience for your ignorance.'

'Save your breath,' said the avatar. 'She won't address you, or your rudeness, because she doesn't want to. And perhaps she has good reason.'

Hamir glared at the avatar. 'Meaning?'

'Hamir the necromancer, the one with the mysterious past, the one nobody gets to know. You of all people should understand why we keep our secrets.'

Hamir shrugged. 'Maybe I keep my secrets because I've nothing interesting to reveal. Why does my past arouse such intrigue in others?'

The avatar chuckled humourlessly. 'Perhaps it's because the scarring on your forehead gives people an insight into your true nature.'

'I see,' Hamir said evenly. 'Then you have been told the history of my relationship with our good Lady up there?'

'I've learned enough to know that no one should ever trust you.'

'You are not the first to believe that.'

'You're a ghoul, Hamir.'

If Hamir had been faced with the avatar in the real world, where his magic was his to command, he could have rendered tortures upon its spirit unlike anything it had experienced in life. But he wasn't in the real world.

With a sigh, the necromancer turned his eyes to the Skywatcher again. 'What happened to her?' he asked, his voice tired. 'I was told recently – by another *ghost* – that Amilee was abandoned by the Timewatcher and the Thaumaturgists too.'

The avatar was silent for a moment, its tendrils of blue light waving about with the slowness of strips of cloth floating underwater. 'That is a story for her Ladyship to tell you herself, should she wish to.'

'*Fine*,' Hamir said with sneer. 'Then at least tell me why I have been brought to this damned place. What part am I to play?'

Before the avatar could answer, Hamir was buffeted by a sudden wind.

Lady Amilee landed gracefully on the grass between Hamir and the blue spectre. Her silver wings gave one last beat, and then fell limp and liquid, disappearing through slits cut into the back of her purple robe. Tall and elegant, her head shaved smooth to the scalp, Lady Amilee didn't acknowledge Hamir's presence in the slightest, and addressed the avatar.

'How have events unfolded?'

'As well as can be expected, my lady,' the avatar replied. 'The Relic Guild escaped the Labyrinth. They have been travelling across the Houses with our Aelfirian agents.'

They survived, Hamir thought with relief. He then pushed aside his uncustomary moment of logic-clouding compassion to listen to Amilee.

'Have they reached the destination?'

'Almost, my lady.'

'And Marney is not with them?'

'No,' said the avatar, and Hamir detected a genuine sadness in its voice. 'The changeling – Clara – now carries the information on Spiral's prison.'

'Interesting,' Amilee said coldly, but she was quiet, thoughtful.

Ah, Hamir realised, *Marney's kiss* … That was what the empath had transferred into Clara's mind: the whereabouts of Oldest Place. But how in the realms had Marney known that information to begin with?

'Tell me,' Amilee asked the avatar, 'How many Genii control the Nightshade? Is it four or five? Is Yves Harrow with them?'

'I cannot say,' the avatar admitted. 'I only know that Fabian Moor is not alone.'

'Damn it,' Amilee whispered.

Hamir took a step forward and cleared his throat. 'If the number of Genii is important to your meddling, my lady, perhaps I can be of help?'

Amilee looked back over her shoulder in the necromancer's general direction. Hamir could see the black diamond tattooed onto her forehead, but her tawny eyes didn't meet his as she waited for him to speak further.

'Three other Genii have joined Fabian Moor in Labrys Town,' Hamir explained. 'Mo Asajad, Viktor Gadreel and Hagi Tabet. I have seen or heard of nothing concerning Yves Harrow.'

Without acknowledging Hamir in any way, Amilee sighed, and gestured with her hand towards the droning column of the slipstream.

With a noise like ice ripping apart, a strip of energy uncoiled from the slipstream, peeling away like a loose thread. A giant snake of static, it hung in the air for a moment before losing cohesion and falling like ashes. The column of the slipstream had become noticeably thinner.

'Hmm,' Hamir muttered. 'Three timelines left?'

Amilee addressed the avatar again. 'The time has arrived. You know what has to be done next.'

'Yes, my lady.'

Hamir frowned.

From the sleeve of her robes, Amilee produced a large, black iron key, old and unwieldy. Stepping forward, she reached out and pushed the key into the twilight blue of the avatar's body. When she removed her hand, it was empty.

'Deliver the magickers to where they need to be,' Amilee ordered the avatar. There was sorrow in her voice. 'Only by activating Known Things can the Relic Guild hope to destroy Spiral.'

Known Things, Hamir pondered, but aloud he voiced a very real concern to the Skywatcher. 'Forgive me for asking, but did I hear right? You expect the Relic Guild to *destroy* Spiral?'

'All things are known in the end,' Amilee whispered, still ignoring Hamir. 'Go,' she told the avatar. 'You know what to do.'

Immediately, the avatar drifted away from the Skywatcher, and approached the slipstream, where an arched doorway had formed.

'What in the Timewatcher's name is going on?' Hamir demanded.

The avatar drifted through the doorway and disappeared. Amilee stared after her future-guide, her back turned to Hamir.

'Lady Amilee, how is it that you believe magickers can stand against creatures of higher—?'

Lady Amilee's silver wings sprang from her robes and fanned out behind her. She vaulted from the ground, soared into the air, circling around the three remaining timelines that comprised the slipstream.

She rose higher and higher, until she seemed no bigger than a bird.

'Please, my lady!' Hamir bellowed. 'What have you done? Why does Clara carry the location of Oldest Place? What is Known Things?'

Hamir quickly jumped back as the Skywatcher hurled an object down at him. It came fast, a dot at first, but quickly being revealed as a ball of blue glass the size of Hamir's head. It landed on the spongy, moss-choked grass, bounced a few times, and rolled to a stop at Hamir's feet. He stared at it. On opposing sides of the ball, the glass had been indented with handprints.

The necromancer picked it up, careful not to let his hands touch the indents. He studied the glowing substance that swirled like smoke inside the blue glass.

He looked up at the Skywatcher as she examined the column of energy high above, then he held the sphere up towards her. 'All right, my lady,' he muttered bitterly. 'Once again, let's do this *your* way.'

His hands were a perfect fit for the indents.

CHAPTER SEVENTEEN

RELICS

A few months previously, the Aelfirian woman called Symone had accrued more gambling debts than she had been able to pay back. On the orders of the avatar, Namji had sent Glogelder to visit Symone with an offer to help her out of her plight. There had been one proviso: in return for paying off the debts, she would – at some point in the near future, and with no questions asked – smuggle a small band of strangers into her place of work: the Museum of Aelfirian Heritage.

As the group progressed down a wide street that ran alongside the River Bells, Van Bam was vaguely aware of Hillem telling Clara all of this. The intense concentration of maintaining the complicated illusions disguising the group made it hard for him to fully comprehend his surroundings. He sensed that the riverside street was busy, filled with Aelfir; he knew that Symone led the group, and that his colleagues had surrounded him, protecting him from disturbances. If Van Bam's magic faltered, revealing the human faces of the magickers for but a moment, the Relic Guild's long journey could well end here, on the streets of the Sisterhood of Bells.

In the distance, Van Bam heard a bell in one of the mighty clock towers chime the hour to the city. Hillem was talking again, this time telling anyone who would listen about the history of their destination. Van Bam found the young Aelf's voice surprisingly soothing. It conjured a focal point for his concentration, and he absorbed the information.

The Museum of Aelfirian Heritage had been built shortly after the Genii War. As a memorial, Hillem said, to the Houses which had survived the war and remained loyal to the Timewatcher. Free to visit, funded by the arts assembly, and a regular location for presentations and lectures given by the wisest academics to be found among the realms, the museum had an ongoing and ambitious project to preserve the histories of every known Aelfirian House.

Finally arriving at the museum building, the group was confronted by a colossal monument. Fifteen storeys high, and even wider than the Nightshade. It was new, cleaner than the old dirty buildings around it; built from white stone, looking entirely modern amidst the ancientness of the Sisterhood of Bells. Within the tall railings of thick black iron, the gardens that surrounded the building were lush and blooming, furnished with both park benches and statues. As the museum was closed for the night, Symone led the group around to the security guards' entrance at the rear.

While the Relic Guild hid in the shadows provided by a small copse of trees, Symone entered the museum and relieved the previous shift. A few moments later, she ushered the group into the building and quickly closed the door behind them.

Now standing in a gloomy, musty hallway, Van Bam asked Symone if there was anyone else in the building. When she confirmed there wasn't, it was with immense relief that he finally dropped the illusions he had been maintaining since leaving the train.

As the Aelfirian masks worn by the three magickers swirled away, revealing their true faces, the museum guard's features fell flat.

'The Panopticon is looking for them,' Symone said, apparently to anyone who wasn't human. She shifted her large Aelfirian eyes to Namji. 'They're in the newspaper, you know. Everyone's talking about them. I could get locked up just for talking to *you*.'

By the shades of her emotions, Van Bam could tell the Symone was ready to bolt.

'Is there a problem?' said Glogelder. He had moved behind Symone, towering over her. 'Funny, because there didn't seem to be a problem when I was paying off your debts.'

Symone looked back at him, and didn't seem much intimidated by his size, or by the spell sphere launcher hanging from his shoulder. She noted the weapons carried by the group: the pistols hanging from Hillem's gun belt, and the butt of the ice-rifle peeking over Samuel's shoulder.

'No one told me I'd be escorting *humans*,' Symone huffed.

'There are a lot of things you haven't been told,' Namji responded coolly. 'Trust me, you don't want to know about those, either.'

Considering Namji's words carefully, Symone cast a shrewd gaze over Van Bam, Clara and Samuel, before concluding that, yes, the less she knew the better.

'You lot are on wanted lists in just about every House,' she told the magickers. 'They're saying you're murderers. They're saying you'll bring the wrath of demons down on all of us unless we give you to the Retrospective.'

'Not everything *they* say is true,' Clara said.

'All the same, can't say I'm exactly pleased to meet you.'

'I understand your concerns,' said Van Bam. 'And we are grateful for your help.'

'Are you really?' Symone sighed. 'If anyone finds out that I helped you, I won't just get locked up. I'll get *strung* up!'

'Just keep your mouth shut and you'll be fine,' Samuel said.

'We'll be out of your way soon enough,' Glogelder said with a grin, 'and then you can get on with forgetting that you ever saw us.'

'Now,' said Namji, 'I believe you know the room we need?'

Symone nodded, and she smiled lightly at the three humans. 'Do *they* know?'

'Just lead the way,' Namji replied sternly.

'As you like.'

Gesturing with her head for the group to follow, Symone set off down the hallway towards the main museum. Glogelder and Namji stuck close to her, but Samuel grabbed Hillem's arm and held him back.

'What did she mean?' the old bounty hunter asked. 'Do we know about what?'

Hillem looked both uncertain and amused. 'It's probably easier if you just see for yourselves,' he said.

Samuel let him go and he headed after his colleagues.

'I'm not sure I like the sound of that,' Clara said.

'I tend to agree,' Van Bam replied.

'Well then,' Samuel grumbled, 'let's go and *see* for *ourselves*.'

In silence, Symone led the group through the museum, darkened and eerily quiet for the night, and they ascended flights of stairs to the upper floors. They passed through a host of rooms, each representing various Aelfirian Houses, many of which Van Bam had visited, many he had only heard of, and others that he hadn't known existed until now. There were scale models and replicas, along with genuine artefacts and relics displayed in glass cabinets or in roped off areas. Every wall, it seemed, was covered in illustrations, and written histories of the Houses.

Van Bam's thoughts drifted to Marney again, and how she would have loved to visit the Museum of Aelfirian Heritage.

Gideon decided to speak to the illusionist just after Symone had led them up to the fifth floor.

I've been thinking, my idiot, he said. *I've worked out what has been bothering me. At least, a part of it.*

Oh?

It's Clara, Gideon explained. *Or more specifically,* me *and Clara. How is it that she and I are communicating? All this while, we have assumed that it was a trick of the avatar's that allowed her to hear my voice. But what proof do we have of that?*

Van Bam thought for a moment. *The evidence may not be conclusive, but it seems too coincidental for it to have not been the avatar's doing, Gideon. You returned to me, and Clara began hearing your voice, at precisely the moment the avatar last appeared to us.*

Then let us consider the coincidence. Unusually, there was no spite in Gideon's thoughtful voice. *That blue spectre is a portent, my idiot – a future-guide. It was created to lead us. We can agree that it has a master?*

Yes – whoever that might be.

Ah, now you're thinking!

You have worked out who the avatar's master is?

I have a theory, Gideon said. *Again, we* assumed *that the avatar's master was a person – hoped that it might be a Thaumaturgist, or someone of equal power. But perhaps there is a reason why our benefactor has remained unseen. What if it is not a person at all? What if it is an object – something magical – that is the master?*

This gave Van Bam pause for thought. *You think Known Things itself created the avatar? You think this relic is sentient?*

I'm sure I don't know, but that's not *what I was thinking. I'm certain the avatar is only leading us to Known Things. But consider the nature of what has happened, and think bigger, my idiot.*

Bigger?

And right under your nose, so to speak.

Van Bam frowned. *Explain.*

Gideon paused. *What if my voice appearing in Clara's head was an accident? Perhaps a residue of the magic that created our friendly future-guide got confused by the power of a changeling's metamorphosis into a wolf. Didn't the avatar's appearance also coincide with Clara's change?*

Yes, I remember all too well, Van Bam replied, recalling the first time he had seen Clara change into the wolf, and the harrowing torture she had suffered.

Then consider this, Gideon continued. *In its confusion, the magic that created the avatar was at that moment attracted to the energy surrounding the changeling, not only returning my presence to your mind, but also spilling me over into Clara's. Imagine that, and then tell me, my idiot – what magic has a penchant for haunting a person's mind with a spirit guide?*

As Van Bam considered Gideon's question, the group reached the fifth floor. Symone led the way down a long and wide corridor, flanked on either side by tall urns, many cracked and broken, all quite ancient, roped off with heavy red cord.

Gideon, Van Bam replied dubiously, *are you suggesting that the avatar's master is the Nightshade?*

I certainly believe it's a possible explanation, Gideon said. *It has to have been an accident, my idiot. Clara was touched by a residue of the Nightshade's magic.*

But our connection to the Nightshade was severed, Van Bam countered. *The Genii controlled it before the avatar appeared to us. And to be honest, it is still a mystery how I was able to hear you again.*

Then what, my idiot? Gideon snapped, clearly frustrated. *Give me one good reason why the avatar's master would wish to torture that child by putting my voice inside her head?*

Van Bam couldn't think of one, but remained unconvinced by Gideon's theory. Before the conversation could continue, the group had halted, and Samuel snorted a mirthless laugh.

'This has to be a joke,' he said.

Symone had brought them to the wide open entrance of a display room. As Van Bam read the name of the room, Gideon chuckled in his head.

'Evidently not,' the illusionist said, coming alongside Samuel.

'Incredible,' Clara whispered.

On a plaque fixed to the wall above the entrance were the words: HUMAN CURIOSITIES.

***

Standing in a corridor of the Nightshade, Fabian Moor was looking through a one-way observation window into a conference room. Inside, the members of Labrys Town's Merchants' Guild had assembled round a long conference table. Men and women, the supposed higher caste of this broken and abandoned society – but *human* one and all – sat in their seats, faces intent, confused and suspicious. They were listening to the words of Mo Asajad. While she spoke, Asajad walked around the table with the slow, calm and deliberate manner she often employed before moving in for the kill.

Moor could almost hear Asajad's sly, supercilious tone, gradually drawing her audience to the understanding that they were cattle in an abattoir. Perhaps they already suspected. Nervous eyes darted to the docile golem dressed in a cassock, standing in the corner of the room, still holding the tray that carried drinks to the Nightshade's guests.

Moor did not pity these people.

His attention was ripped away from the window as a bellow of rage filled the air like the sudden roar of thunder. With a frown, Moor looked to where the corridor doglegged to the right. He heard a dull, meaty thump, and then one of Hagi Tabet's disfigured aspects, in a blur of pink blubber, flew from the corridor beyond to crash against the wall with the sickening crack of bones. The aspect fell in a ruined heap to the floor, faded, and then disappeared. A moment later, the colossal form of Viktor Gadreel rounded the corner and stamped towards his fellow Genii.

'Disgusting,' he growled, his one eye glaring with anger. 'Those damned things are *everywhere*! *Always* in my way.'

Moor made no reply, and he resumed watching Asajad through the window. Gadreel came up alongside him, simmering, his thick arms folded across his wide chest.

'What's she doing?' Gadreel rumbled.

'Establishing a proper hierarchy in this town,' Moor replied. 'She feels these humans have enjoyed privileges they don't deserve for long enough.'

Gadreel huffed an impatient breath. 'Why is she wasting time *talking* to them?'

'You know how Asajad is, Viktor. She does enjoy her theatrics. At least it alleviates her boredom.'

'And you have called me here to witness such *pointlessness*?' Gadreel growled. 'Hamir is still barricaded in that room, Fabian. Perhaps my time would be better spent trying to flush him out.'

Gadreel, his heavy face seething, continued to stare through the observation window, deliberately not facing Moor. His huge hands were now balled fists at his sides, and he ground his teeth together.

'Viktor, do you need to feed?' Moor asked.

Gadreel replied with a dismissive grunt.

In the conference room, Asajad continued circling the table, talking, stalking, hunting.

Clearly, Gadreel's earlier confrontation with Moor still rankled. Moor accepted that he had made a mistake. When Hagi Tabet had revealed that Marney did not have the information on Oldest Place, Moor had vented his frustration and anger upon his fellow Genii. It had been a misguided act.

Moor turned to Gadreel. 'I should not have treated you as I did,' he said, and that was as much of an apology as he would give the brute. 'But it is time to put aside your anger, Viktor. Forget Hamir for now. There have been developments.'

Gadreel faced Moor for the first time. His one eye narrowed as he looked him up and down. 'You have word on our lord?'

Moor nodded. 'It would seem that I miscalculated, Viktor. At one time, Marney most definitely knew where the Timewatcher had hidden Oldest Place, but she removed the information from her mind and hid it shortly before I captured her.'

Gadreel's face twitched, perhaps with hope. 'Do you know *where* the empath hid it?'

'Indeed. In the mind of a young changeling named Clara. A memory transference.'

'Hmm.' A small smile came to Gadreel's fat lips. 'Then, please – tell me you know how to find this changeling.'

'It's a little complicated.'

'Explain.'

'Again, I miscalculated, Viktor. The Relic Guild managed to escape—'

Moor was interrupted by a disturbance in the conference room. Whatever Asajad had just said, it had caused consternation among the members of the Merchants' Guild. Some of them had risen from their seats; others gave each other frightened looks; a few stared at the tall and stick-thin Genii with open terror on their faces.

Asajad was now facing the back wall. She raised her hands and the wall's cream colour, together with the hundreds of square mazes decorating it, became entirely black, reflecting light like the polished shell of a beetle. A crack of illumination appeared in the darkness; it stretched and widened until it formed a doorway into a damned House of dead time. On the threshold stood the ominous figure of the Woodsman, giant axe in hand.

There was collective panic amongst the humans when the Woodsman stepped from the Retrospective and entered the conference room. They rushed as one for the door, pushing and fighting among themselves in their desperation to leave; but the doors within the Nightshade were not easy to open. These humans would not escape unless Mo Asajad allowed them to.

With a casual wave of one hand, Asajad directed the Woodsman towards the stampeding herd of humans; with the other she grabbed the hair of a man seated at the table close to her. Fear, it seemed, had paralysed him. He began crying when Asajad forced him out of his seat, and down onto his knees at her side.

As the Woodsman raised the axe, sliced it into the herd, and sent a gout of blood splashing across the conference table, Lady Asajad hauled the man to his feet by his hair, pulled back his head, and sank her long teeth into his throat.

Uninterested in the spectacle, Moor dulled the observation window until it became a rectangle of impenetrable black glass in the wall. He continued briefing Gadreel.

'There can be no doubt that the magickers of the Relic Guild have escaped the Labyrinth. I do not know how they achieved this, Viktor, but it matters little now. Hagi has found an anomaly within the empath's memories. It was fractured, scattered – but Hagi has pieced it together. We know where the Relic Guild are going to be. And soon.'

'This is good news,' Gadreel said, the usual rumble of his voice closer to an impatient whisper. 'And where are they going to be, Fabian?'

'Now that is the question. And I think you'll like the answer.' Moor didn't try to stop the smile coming to his face. 'Come. I'll explain on our way to see Lady Tabet. I have a mission for you, Viktor.'

'*This* is how the Aelfir remember us?' Samuel said, angrily jabbing a thumb at the sign that read HUMAN CURIOSITIES. 'We're a bloody attraction in a museum?'

Glogelder grinned, Hillem shrugged, and Namji turned to Symone the night guard.

'We'll take it from here,' she said. 'You don't have to stick around.'

'Fair enough,' Symone replied. 'Just so you know, two others share this shift with me. I've told them to make themselves scarce while I can make a bit of pocket money with a private tour of the museum. But I can't promise they won't turn up.'

'We won't be here long,' Namji assured her.

Accepting this, Symone took a final look at the humans, and then headed off. 'If you need me, I'll be in the guards' lounge, down on the fourth floor,' she called back. 'But I'd rather I never saw you again.'

When Symone had gone, Namji turned to Hillem and Glogelder. 'You two guard the door,' she said. 'That woman worries me. I don't trust her, and I don't want her spying on us.' She looked at the magickers with an apologetic expression. 'Come on.'

Clara appeared intrigued and eager to see what was inside the display room. Samuel, less keen, rolled his eyes at Van Bam before following Namji and the changeling inside.

The room wasn't particularly big; its very smallness seemed a sad memorial to the people and the House which had at one time been essential to the Aelfir. On the walls were artists' impressions of humans, and scenes of everyday life in Labrys Town – oddly simplistic in style, as though drawn for young children – along with written descriptions of how the town's society had functioned, and its system of government.

Clara stopped to read a disappointingly small section concerning the Relic Guild; Samuel's interest was drawn to a scale model of Labrys Town, which was surrounded by the narrow alleyways of the Great Labyrinth. To catch the eye, the description beside the model began with bold letters: NO ONE KNEW HOW BIG THE GREAT LABYRINTH WAS …

Oh, my idiot, look at this, Gideon said, highly amused.

The ghost directed Van Bam's attention to the information Clara was reading. It informed visitors that no one was certain what became of the humans, and that the last known Resident of Labrys Town was Gideon the Selfless.

You never made it into the Aelfir's history books, Gideon said without a single shred of sympathy in his pernicious voice. *But I have to say I'm glad that tales of my legacy are still being told among the Houses.*

Van Bam ignored this and looked to Namji. She had moved to the corner of the room where a stone dais had been placed, with steps leading up to its display piece.

It was a doorway, like the hundreds, thousands that had once been spread throughout the Great Labyrinth. It was housed in a heavy wooden frame. The plaque on a stand beside the doorway listed it as a replica, for display purposes only, but …

'Samuel, Clara,' the illusionist called, pointing at the doorway with his green glass cane. 'Look at this.'

'What about it?' Samuel said.

'It is real.'

Samuel stared at his fellow magicker for an instant, and then left the model of Labrys Town to march up the steps leading to the doorway. 'Are you sure?'

'Most definitely,' Van Bam replied, joining the old bounty hunter. To his inner vision, the wood of this simple, innocuous-looking door held the fading echoes of magic. Colourful. Unmistakable. 'This is a real doorway.'

'How, Van Bam?'

'I do not know.'

The frame of the doorway was thick, lacquered wood. The entire surface had been intricately carved with a host of House symbols. The weak pulse of magic was ingrained into every aspect of this display piece.

'Maybe it was salvaged after the war,' Clara offered from behind her fellow agents.

Samuel shook his head. 'There wasn't supposed to be anything left to salvage. The Timewatcher removed *all* the doorways. She just ... took them away.'

Van Bam had to wonder: how many Aelfir had visited this room over the years, never realising they were gazing upon a genuine doorway.

'It doesn't matter how it got here,' Namji said. The petite Aelf was standing halfway up the stone steps. 'This doorway is what the avatar has been leading us towards.'

'Known Things is on the other side?' asked Clara, her voice small, afraid.

'Yes,' Namji replied. 'The avatar didn't tell me exactly where the doorway leads – only that we have to go through it to reach Known Things. And that only a human magicker can open it.'

Samuel and Van Bam exchanged looks, then the old bounty hunter grabbed the handle and yanked the door open.

Nothing.

All that greeted the group were the two walls meeting to form a corner behind the display. Samuel closed the door and opened it again. Nothing.

Well, that was a bit of a let-down, Gideon said.

'I don't understand,' said Namji. She looked perplexed. 'The avatar

was adamant that the touch of a human magicker would activate the
doorway.'

Samuel tried and failed again. Van Bam saw the hues of frustrated
anger bloom in him.

'Wasn't there some procedure you used with doorways?' Hillem
suggested, stepping away from the entrance. 'Didn't you have to select
a House symbol, and then draw it into something?'

'You need to know the symbol of the House you wanted to travel to
first,' Samuel replied, jabbing an agitated hand at the host of symbols
carved into the doorframe.

Oh ... my idiot, Gideon hissed excitedly, *I've thought of a reason why
the avatar's master might want Clara to hear my voice.*

Why?

I can see something very interesting.

'The process you're talking about only summons a shadow carriage,'
Samuel was explaining to Hillem, his tone berating. 'And all that does
is take you to the correct doorway.'

What am I missing, Gideon?

Look at the doorframe.

'I was only making a suggestion,' Hillem said defensively.

'And I'm telling you we're *already* at the doorway,' Samuel snapped.

'What's going on?' Glogelder asked from the entrance.

'Arguing won't solve anything,' Namji intervened.

Look harder, my idiot. Before Samuel starts shooting people.

'Listen to what I'm saying,' Samuel said, his voice rising. 'The portals
behind the doorways were never inactive. To use them, you only had
to open the door and step through.' To emphasise the fact that what
should be happening very much wasn't, Samuel opened the door and
slammed it shut again. 'The avatar must have told you something else,
Namji.'

'It didn't,' she said.

'Then how do we get it to work?'

'I don't know, Samuel! I thought it would activate when you
touched it.'

'What have we missed?' Samuel said to himself, and he made an
angry noise. 'What do we do, Van Bam?'

But Van Bam wasn't listening to him. He had discovered what it was that Gideon found interesting.

Among the House symbols carved into the doorframe, one stood out to him. It was situated at the centre of the crossbeam, and it wrenched an old memory from the illusionist's mind.

'Impossible,' he whispered.

Yet there it is, said Gideon, clearly pleased. *Do excuse me, my idiot. I need to have a quick chat with Clara.*

'Van Bam?' said Samuel.

The symbol comprised a spiralling pattern with a straight line that connected it to a square shape with a triangle on its right side. The last time Van Bam had seen that symbol, it had been drawn in blood.

'Just ... *impossible.*'

'What's impossible?' Samuel pressed.

Namji and Hillem had also become intrigued by the illusionist's reaction.

'This,' Van Bam said. He stepped forwards, reached up, and tapped the symbol with his cane. 'It should not be there, Samuel.'

The old bounty hunter studied it for himself. 'I've never seen a House symbol like that before.'

'I have,' Namji said, climbing the steps and standing beside Van Bam. 'Why do I recognise it?'

Van Bam raised an eyebrow. 'I suspect it was shown to you a long time ago, while we took refuge in the mountains close to your old home.'

Namji's eyes widened, and her features fell slack. 'The Sorrow of Future Reason,' she whispered.

'The Sorrow of Future Reason?' Hillem said. 'That's not a House I've heard of.'

'What's going on?' said Glogelder.

'That's a good question,' Samuel growled.

'You would not have heard of this place, because it does not exist,' Van Bam said. 'That symbol is for the House of the Nephilim.'

'The Nephilim?' Samuel was almost shouting.

Hillem shared his surprise. 'There hasn't been a reported sighting of the Nephilim for decades. Not since before the Genii War.'

'Be that as it may,' said Van Bam. 'Namji and I met a Nephilim in Mirage, *during* the war.'

Samuel frowned at the illusionist, suspicious. 'You did?'

'His name was Gulduur Bellow,' Namji answered, a strange expression on her face. She turned to Van Bam. 'I don't know what happened to him,' she said. 'He never came back, and I waited out the rest of the war alone in his cavern.'

'Wait a minute,' Samuel said. By his emotional shades and colours, it was obvious his confusion was pushing him towards a second bout of anger. 'Are you saying this doorway is supposed to lead to the House of the Nephilim? The Sorrow of ...?'

'Future Reason,' Namji finished.

'Whatever!' Samuel snapped. '*That's* where Known Things is kept?'

'I do not know,' said Van Bam.

'Just for once, I'd like a straight answer in all of this,' Samuel whispered dangerously, and his hands clenched. 'The Nephilim don't have a House, Van Bam,' he said with strained patience. 'They're nomads.'

'Samuel, this symbol is part of a legend.' Van Bam tapped it again with his cane. 'It is that of the House that the Nephilim have been roaming the realms seeking for a thousand years. And forty years ago, I was told by a Nephilim named Gulduur Bellow that if I ever saw the sign for the Sorrow of Future Reason again, I was to remember that it would lead me to friends.'

'Friends?' Samuel said. 'The Nephilim are blood-magickers, Van Bam. You *do* remember the stories, don't you?'

'Doesn't everyone?' said Hillem. 'Nothing good came from the Nephilim, did it?'

Namji shook her head. 'Not everything you've heard is true.'

'And I think this House Symbol was left here as a mark of trust,' Van Bam added.

'I'm sick of this game,' Samuel muttered.

'Can someone fill me in?' said Glogelder. 'What's going on?'

Gideon, Van Bam thought. When the dead Resident didn't reply, the illusionist looked at Clara.

The changeling wasn't paying attention to the conversation; she was quietly studying the host of symbols carved into the heavy doorframe, her eyes narrowed. Van Bam could tell by her expression that she was conversing with Gideon.

With a sigh, Samuel faced the doorway again. 'Whatever all this means, it still doesn't tell us how to activate the bloody portal.' He looked back at Van Bam. 'If that symbol was left as a mark of trust, maybe *you* should try opening the door—'

'Samuel, can I borrow your knife?'

The old bounty hunter frowned at Clara's request. She was still studying the symbols on the frame, but she held out her hand, ready to receive the knife.

'Why?' Samuel asked.

'Gideon has an idea.'

Samuel pulled a sour expression and glared at Van Bam. 'What's he up to?'

Why all the suspicion, my idiot? Gideon drawled. *Surely, as soon as you saw the Nephilim's symbol, you would've guessed I'd feel the calling of my ancestry.*

Blood-magic, Van Bam realised.

And blood doesn't get much more powerful in a magicker than that of a changeling, does it? All Clara needs is a little guidance from me, and ... well, the touch that doorway requires might just have to come from the Nephilim's legacy.

'Samuel,' Van Bam snapped. 'Give Clara your knife.'

Samuel opened his coat, and drew the long wicked blade from the holster strapped to his ribs. He paused, looked distrustful, but handed the knife to the changeling, hilt first.

Clara accepted the weapon almost absentmindedly, and only looked away from the doorway to concentrate on poking the palm of her hand with the blade's tip.

'What's she doing?' Glogelder called from the room's entrance.

Namji and Hillem shushed him in unison.

Clara winced as she cut her palm. She gave the knife back to Samuel, and cupped her hand to let her blood pool.

You might want to give Miss Clara a little room, my idiot, Gideon said, chuckling. *I can't guarantee this won't backfire on her.*

'Samuel.' Van Bam beckoned the old bounty hunter to join him further down the steps with Namji. Hillem moved up alongside them.

'Please, someone tell me what's going on,' Glogelder said.

No one answered him.

Clara stood directly before the closed door, scrutinising the symbol for the Sorrow of Future Reason. She was still for a moment, undoubtedly speaking with Gideon.

'I'll need lifting,' she said eventually.

With a quick glance at Van Bam, Samuel stepped forward. He wrapped his arms around Clara's midriff and hoisted her into the air.

'Hold me still,' Clara said, focusing on the carving.

And she began speaking in a language that was too deep and whispery to understand, using a voice that was hard to believe emanated from so small a woman. The voice of blood-magic, Van Bam remembered, taught to Clara by Gideon, a magicker who had been born with the taint of the Nephilim in his blood, a curse that had practically driven him mad.

Using her cupped hand as the ink well and the index finger of her other hand as the quill, Clara began painting the carving of the Nephilim symbol with her blood, chanting all the while. She began by tracing the blood around the spiralling pattern; by the time she was halfway along the straight line that connected to the square with the mirrored triangles, Van Bam began to see the magic imbued in the wood of the door flaring into life.

Clara stopped chanting the incantations of blood-magic at the same time as she finished painting the symbol. She told Samuel to let her down. She seemed energised by her first foray into such an alien power.

'Blood-magic,' she whispered.

I won't deny it, Gideon said a little breathlessly. *After all these years, it felt good to use my magic again.*

'Here,' Namji said, and she passed Clara a cloth from her satchel.

'Is that it?' Samuel said. 'Will it work now?'

Clara shrugged as she wiped away the blood and bound her hand. 'Gideon seems to think so.'

And why wouldn't I? Gideon said. *Look at the colour, my idiot.*

The doorway was alive, filling Van Bam's inner vision with the purple radiance of thaumaturgy.

'It is active,' the illusionist announced.

Samuel grabbed the handle of the doorway, yanked it open, and this time a lonely wind moaned around this room dedicated to the memory of humans. The doorway framed a thick, churning whiteness.

'The Nothing of Far and Deep,' Van Bam said, exhilarated.

'Bloody Timewatcher,' Glogelder muttered, stepping into the room and coming up alongside Hillem.

Hillem exhaled heavily. 'I've always wondered what it looked like.'

They were too young to have ever seen the Nothing of Far and Deep before, or remember a time when all pathways to and from the Labyrinth had led through it. But where did this doorway lead? Surely not back to Labrys Town?

Namji, however, remembered the Nothing of Far and Deep, and she was clearly relieved to see it again. 'I think it might be time to leave,' she said.

Van Bam stood to one side, holding the door open. 'I believe you know the drill, Samuel.'

The old bounty hunter drew the ice-rifle from the holster on his back. 'Really?' he asked. 'The Nephilim?'

'We will talk about it later,' Van Bam promised his old friend.

'Yeah.' Samuel gave a quirked smile as he primed the rifle's power stones. 'Seems like you and me have a lot to catch up on. I'll see you on the other side.' Taking a deep breath he stepped into the dense whiteness.

Clara faced the doorway with fear in her yellow eyes. 'You still promise to stay by my side?' she said with a nervous smile.

'Every step of the way,' Van Bam said.

Clara nodded. 'This had better be worth it,' she mumbled before she followed the old bounty hunter and disappeared.

Namji and Hillem came forwards, but Glogelder seemed reluctant.

'Will it hurt?' he asked suspiciously.

'That depends on what we find on the other side,' Van Bam told him with a chuckle.

'Fair enough.' Glogelder slipped his spell sphere launcher from his shoulder, and took his place behind Hillem. 'After you,' he said, and shoved his friend forwards. Hillem's yelp of surprise was cut short as he disappeared into the Nothing of Far and Deep.

With a grin, Glogelder jumped in after him.

'Been a long time since I last did this,' Namji said to Van Bam.

'A lifetime ago,' the illusionist replied.

'To old times,' she said, taking a breath and stepping forwards.

Now alone in the room of Human Curiosities, Van Bam's eye was caught by movement. Symone the night guard had appeared in the entrance. She leaned against the jamb, holding a hot drink and smiling wryly. She blew away the steam and raised a hand in farewell. Van Bam returned the gesture.

Don't dawdle, my idiot, said Gideon. *I'm already bored.*

ORIGINS

'I hardly recognised them, Van Bam,' Namji was saying. 'I might as well have been meeting them for the first time.'

She was talking about her parents, distressed that they had swapped their loyalty to the Timewatcher for obedience to Spiral.

'They had turned into … *caricatures* of themselves,' Namji continued bitterly. 'It was as if their personalities had been cut out and replaced with a shadow of who they used to be.' She sniffed and wiped a tear from her eye. 'My mother and father were such loving parents – patient, kind. But in the end, I'm not sure they really knew who I was.'

'You acted bravely in the face of such adversity, Namji,' said Van Bam, though his mind was very much on other things.

They were resting at the bottom of the path that led up to Gulduur Bellow's cave. The morning sky was a cloudless pale pink, promising another day of blistering heat in the desert of Mirage. But the shadows cast by the crater walls were cold, and Van Bam had used his magic to summon a fire. He and Namji sat on opposite sides of the rich, golden flames, keeping warm.

It wasn't that Van Bam didn't feel sympathy for Namji's situation, but as terrible as the fate of Mirage was, the implications it wrought were far more terrifying. Lord Buyaal was planning to send an invasion force of Aelfirian soldiers to the Labyrinth, where they would aid Fabian Moor in conquering Labrys Town. There was still so much that confused Van Bam, and as sad as he felt for Namji, he wished it was Angel sitting with him now. But Angel had yet to emerge from the Nephilim's cavern.

Frustratingly, it was impossible for Van Bam to know what the state of play was back home. The Labrys Town Police Force consisted of around three thousand officers, and Buyaal's invasion force was at least ten thousand trained soldiers strong, or so Bellow had said. But even with so large an army, Fabian Moor still could not fully control the Labyrinth without first gaining power over the Nightshade. Yet the invasion was going ahead, nonetheless. What did that mean?

Had the Relic Guild failed? Had Fabian Moor already found a way to conquer the Nightshade and the denizens? Or perhaps Van Bam and Angel's arrival in Mirage had panicked Buyaal into action. If the magickers didn't send a report to the Nightshade by the end of the day at the latest, Gideon would get suspicious, questions would be asked. Maybe Buyaal had been motivated to send his troops before anyone noticed. And if that was true, would Fabian Moor then use his army to hold the denizens hostage? Ransom them in return for the Nightshade?

Van Bam's frustrations increased as grisly thoughts plagued him. He doubted that the Timewatcher would consider the lives of one million humans a fair exchange for control of the Nightshade, and the billions of Aelfir it would give the Genii access to. The illusionist gripped his green glass cane tightly, swallowing an impulse to shout a curse at the sky.

Whatever the situation back home, Moor and Buyaal had obviously devised a method of transporting a huge army through the endless alleyways of the Great Labyrinth to Labrys Town. The invasion was happening, and only the Nephilim Gulduur Bellow could get Van Bam and Angel home ahead of it. But when? How?

'Van Bam?'

The illusionist looked at Namji through the golden flames of the fire, and only then did he realise she had been speaking to him.

'Forgive me,' he said. 'What did you say?'

'I was asking what you thought would happen to Mirage now,' Namji said, her face downcast. 'I can't believe my mother and father joined Spiral willingly. Buyaal must have subjugated them, and the citizens.' Her voice betrayed how much she was searching for hope. 'The Timewatcher would recognise that Mirage isn't a true enemy – She would *know*, wouldn't She?'

Van Bam paused. 'I will not lie to you, Namji. I have no idea what happens next.

Namji wiped away tears, and fell silent.

Once again, Van Bam was struck by how young Namji was. Stripped of pretence, no longer in a position to play her flirtatious games, she appeared no more than a child to the illusionist. She had spent her life being trained to govern her people – the heir to House Mirage. But now her feelings were all too clear: Namji, daughter of High Governor Obanai, was starkly, fearfully aware that she had not only lost her family and friends, but also her future.

'Namji,' Van Bam said gently. 'I am truly sorry for what has happened to your family and your people. I cannot begin to imagine the sense of loss you are feeling.' He gave her a kind smile. 'You must be devastated.'

Namji wiped more tears from her eyes 'It's how this could happen without anyone noticing that I don't understand, Van Bam.' She snorted and shook her head. 'I *knew* Buyaal – I watched his spectacular before the war exiled me to the Labyrinth. I can't believe I was so excited to see him at the bazaar. He was just a *performer*!'

'Buyaal is a creature of higher magic, and he is clever,' Van Bam said consolingly. 'He burrowed his way into Mirage's society perfectly, and no one suspected what he really was until he had gained control.' Van Bam thought for a second. 'I believe he was some kind of advance scout for Spiral, working under clandestine orders – much like Fabian Moor, I suppose.'

'By the time the war started, Buyaal had already subjugated Mirage.'

'And no doubt with the help of the dutiful soldiers he had already planted among your people. Like Ursa, for example.

'And Ebril,' Namji whispered, staring into the fire.

Van Bam warmed his hands at the flames and sighed. 'You are not the only one who was fooled by your father's ambassador, Namji. Ebril managed to dupe the Relic Guild too, along with Lady Amilee. By no means an easy feat.'

'You know, I'd actually come to think of Ebril as my surrogate father,' Namji said. 'He looked after me during my exile. Made me feel as though I was with family. But now? Now I have nothing and no one.'

'You have Angel and me,' Van Bam assured her. 'We will not abandon you, Namji. We will take you home with us to Labrys Town.'

Sadly, appreciatively, Namji tried to rally. 'We have to make it to the Giant's Hand first,' she said. 'We need to reach the doorway to the Great Labyrinth before Buyaal sends his army through it.' She stared into the flames again. 'The Giant's Hand is in plain view of the citadel, Van Bam. I can't see how we'll get to it without Buyaal noticing.'

'Well, I am hoping our new friend Gulduur Bellow has a good plan.' Van Bam looked up the path to the cave at the top, his thoughts returning to the first time he saw the Nephilim. 'Namji, do you recall how Buyaal reacted when Bellow confronted him? The Genii fled after their skirmish. It seemed as though Buyaal was frightened.'

'That's true,' Namji said. Her large eyes stared at Van Bam through the dancing flames. 'It's not just Bellow's size and appearance that's frightening – it's his power. I've had a little magical training, enough to mask facial expressions, and giveaway tones of voice. I can hide my thoughts from most telepaths – I know what magic feels like, Van Bam. But when I watched Bellow healing Angel with his blood-magic, I can't begin to describe the energy that filled the cavern.' Her young face was awed. 'I've never experienced that kind of power before.'

'The magic in Bellow's blood is thaumaturgy,' Van Bam said. 'I do not believe that anyone has realised just how powerful the Nephilim are.'

Namji gave hopeful, if uncertain smile. 'I suppose we might stand a chance with an ally like that—'

She broke off, stretching to see over the illusionist's head. Her face filled with surprise.

'Angel!' she called.

The healer had emerged from the flickering light of the cave. She stood at the top of the path, smiling lopsidedly at the pair. She was holding a small wicker basket.

Closely followed by Namji, Van Bam hurried to greet his fellow magicker. She was still covered in the symbols and glyphs of blood-magic that the Nephilim had painted upon her body.

'How are you feeling?' Van Bam asked.

Angel seemed almost amused. 'If you ignore the fact that I'm covered in someone else's blood, pretty good. You?'

Van Bam smiled. 'Oh, I have known more straightforward days.'

Namji stepped forward. 'It's good to see you back on your feet,' the Aelf said. 'Are you healed?'

'Never felt fitter.' Angel considered Namji for a moment. 'How are you holding up? Or is that a stupid question?'

'I—' Namji stopped as tears threatened to fill her eyes again.

'It's all right,' Angel soothed. 'We'll talk in a while. As for now, I have figs!'

The healer held the basket out for her colleagues to see the round, green fruits it held. 'I have no idea where they came from,' she said. 'I haven't seen a single tree since I came to this bloody desert. But apparently our host knows where to find figs. And speaking of our *host*—' Angel turned a meaningful glare to Van Bam. 'He's a bloody Nephilim!'

'I was as surprised as you, Angel.'

'Well, I suppose it's nice to know that not everything we were told was horseshit. Bit of a shock to wake up to, though.'

'It has been a strange time indeed,' Van Bam said, looking into the tunnel mouth that led to the Nephilim's cavern. 'Has Bellow informed you of the situation?'

'He's told me enough,' Angel replied. 'He explained that Buyaal wants to send Fabian Moor a little help.'

Van Bam nodded. 'Where is Bellow now?'

'I left him sitting on his boulder,' Angel said. 'He's making plans to get us home.'

'Did he tell you what these plans are?'

'Sort of.' Angel shrugged. 'He says it's probably better if he tells you himself. He wants to see you.'

Van Bam hesitated, looking Angel over. 'Are you sure you are—?'

'I'm fine, Van Bam,' the healer interrupted. 'Stop worrying.' She held out the basket to the illusionist. 'Here, take a fig, and then off you go.'

Van Bam took one from the basket, but simply stared at it.

'Go and see Bellow,' Angel said forcefully. 'I want to talk to Namji, anyway.' She smiled sympathetically at the young Aelf. 'Come on, woman. Let's leave the boys to it.'

As they headed down the path, Van Bam heard Namji say, 'What's going on?' To which Angel replied, 'Probably something homo-erotic, and I'd rather I didn't know more than that.'

Suddenly buoyed to have Angel back to full strength, and with her usual humour intact, Van Bam smiled and entered the cave, eating the fig as he headed down the tunnel to Bellow's lair. The fruit was ripe – juicy and sweet.

Once more entering the Nephilim's bejewelled cavern, Van Bam climbed the steps to the plateau of the huge boulder. Gulduur Bellow was sitting as he had before: dressed in a brown habit and cross-legged by the golden flames of a magical fire. Before him sat an empty stone bowl. On one side of it was a knife with a curved blade – big for a human, small for a Nephilim. On the other side of the bowl lay a long, thin stick, its tip sharpened to a point – a wooden scriber.

Van Bam noted that the symbol for the House the Nephilim were searching for, the Sorrow of Future Reason, had disappeared from the ground.

'Ah, my friend,' Bellow greeted. He had tied his unruly hair back into a tail. 'You have seen Angel?'

'Yes. And my thanks for healing her.

'My pleasure. Now come – sit. Your journey home will begin before long.' The giant tapped his temple suggestively. 'Buyaal will make his move very soon.'

Van Bam remained standing and felt a fluttering in his gut.

'Don't worry yourself,' Bellow said. 'There is time enough to hear the rest of my story. Though, if you don't mind, there is something I would like to ask you first. Please, sit.'

Van Bam did so, and the giant towered over him. Bellow was clearly excited by the prospect of another conversation.

The giant said, 'Earlier, you and I were discussing myths and legends. Did you know that the denizens of the Labyrinth also have stories told about *them*, Van Bam? And they have reached my ears.' Bellow's blue eyes considered the illusionist for a moment. 'I have heard a tale that the Resident of Labrys Town is himself a blood-magicker.'

'Ah … yes. That is true.' Van Bam tried to stop an apologetic lilt creeping into his voice. 'His name is Gideon, and it is widely accepted that one of his ancestors was a Nephilim.'

'*Gideon*,' Bellow whispered. He clasped his massive hands together and held them to his chest. 'That one carrying the blood of my herd should find himself such a *worthy* home ... It pleases me. It pleases me very much, Van Bam.'

Van Bam smiled with his lips clamped firmly together, fearing that the giant would ask more; fearing that he would have to explain how the power in the blood of the Nephilim herd had turned Gideon into a borderline psychopath.

'Perhaps I could ask you a question in return,' Van Bam said. 'It concerns your people.'

'You must feel free to ask me anything,' Bellow replied with a smile that revealed tombstone teeth.

Van Bam hesitated, licked his lips. 'The blood-magic of the Nephilim,' he said. 'Is it potent enough to match the power of the Thaumaturgists?'

'How interesting.' Bellow's smile faltered and he narrowed his eyes at the illusionist. 'Once again, I detect an accusation behind your question, Van Bam. I think what you're really asking is could a Nephilim defeat a Thaumaturgist – or a *Genii* – in combat?'

'I do not mean to cause offence,' Van Bam said quickly. 'But after you repelled Buyaal's attack, he seemed frightened of you.'

'So you're wondering why *I* didn't take the fight to *him*. Kill the Genii, perhaps? End the threat that Buyaal poses to the Labyrinth?'

Van Bam averted his eyes. 'It had crossed my mind – yes.'

'Then you should learn to speak your mind, Van Bam.' The giant's smile returned. 'I think Buyaal was more shocked than frightened. I did not retaliate because I do not know if I could defeat him, and I'm sure that he is just as uncertain. We both have much to lose.'

'I see,' Van Bam said.

'However, I am convinced that Buyaal sought my hiding place because he had every intention of killing me – along with you, Angel and Namji. But I think that when he was faced with the reality of his intention, he was not quite so sure of himself.'

'Hence his hasty departure,' Van Bam added.

'The truth is, there has never been an occasion when the Nephilim and the Thaumaturgists have fought. I cannot tell you if we could match their power. Though a clue to the answer might be found in the story that I wish to tell you.' Bellow tapped his lips. 'Take off your clothes, please.'

Van Bam froze. 'Excuse me?'

'Your clothes, Van Bam – lay aside your glass cane, and take them off.' The giant picked up the curved knife that lay beside the stone bowl, and then seemed confused by the fact that the illusionist hadn't moved. 'The magic in your veins needs to be empowered,' Bellow explained, as if it were an obvious thing. He used the knife to point to the bowl and stick as if the gesture answered everything. 'Blood-magic. If you want to get home, you need to be naked, Van Bam.'

'I ... excuse me?'

'Please don't be afraid,' said Bellow, 'but I'm going to need a lot of blood for this.'

And then, with no hesitation, the giant took the knife and sliced into his wrist.

Van Bam watched in alarm as Bellow held his hand over the stone bowl, and the blood ran hot and free from the ends of his long fingers like water pouring from taps. The bowl filled with sickening speed. When he had collected enough, Bellow whispered a word that he seemed to blow upon his wound. His skin sealed, and the cut on his wrist became just one more scar amidst a plethora of others.

'Earlier, you were asking me about the Nephilim's creator – the Progenitor,' the giant said, as he picked up the long wooden scriber. 'I would like you to know the truth of my race's origin, Van Bam. It might hold the answers to your questions. I want you to know that my people and your people are distant cousins.'

Bellow dipped the sharpened point of the scriber into the blood. 'The Nephilim are the Timewatcher's dirty little secret, you see. We were created as hybrids. We are blended, merged – we are part Thaumaturgist, and part *human*.'

The illusionist stared at the giant. 'Excuse me?'

'If you want to hear my story, Van Bam, then please stand up and take off your damn clothes.'

'What was her name?' Denton asked.

'Red,' Marney replied.

As the old empath gave her an understanding smile, Marney dabbed the bruises on her face with a cloth soaked in cold water. The deserters had burned her clothes; she now wore a dark green private's uniform, and a pair of worn but sturdy boots.

The two empaths sat at a table in an officer's tent. It was pitched at the base of the mountain that seemed to serve as the centre point of Ghost Mist Veldt's sprawling and otherwise flat landscape. The tent belonged to a serious and unemotional Aelf called Jolyn, a general in the Timewatcher's army. Its interior had been stripped to a bare minimum. The canvas floor was dusty, and the walls breathed in and out with the wind. But at least it was warm inside.

The table, together with Marney and Denton's chairs, were the only items of furniture in the tent. Upon the table sat a flask of water, some hard bread and dried beef, but neither empath ate or drank. At one end of the table were rolled maps and a pile of letters. Marney could imagine the host of stern-faced, dusty-uniformed Aelfirian officers who had stood around this table, studying maps, planning the war.

'I know what you're going through, Marney,' Denton said. He stared across the table at his protégée, who looked exhausted and miserable. 'I remember the first person I killed, and how it felt. His face still haunts me.'

Marney didn't reply. She had already decided that her dreams would be plagued by the broken Aelf called Red, and probably for the rest of her days. And the dreams would forever remind her how it had felt to control Red's emotions, to make the Aelf believe it was a good idea to slash her own throat. But now was not the time to dwell on that. Since her empathic magic had recovered from the anti-magic spell, Marney had locked down her emotions, taking refuge in a state where she felt nothing.

Unwilling to meet Denton's eyes, she looked at the pile of maps, letters and battle plans on the table. Soon, they would be archived, and the tent would be folded down and packed away. The Timewatcher's army had already won the war in Ghost Mist Veldt. Spiral's troops had been defeated, and that, ironically, had been what caused the trouble for Marney and Denton.

The empaths had arrived at Ghost Mist Veldt shortly after the Timewatcher's army had clinched victory. General Jolyn's troops had been in the process of rounding up the stragglers who had fled the final battlefield rather than surrendering; and they had been doing it with the aid of the strange, sentient magic that suffused this House. The magic had trapped and captured many of the fleeing enemy soldiers, but Matthaus and his cohorts had deserted from Spiral's army weeks before that final battle. They had not learned that the fighting was over.

Jolyn had explained that she was unaware a small band of deserters had been trapped in the stone hut on the mountainside. She felt that in the long run they would have perished, anyway. But then Marney and Denton had stumbled upon them.

It was supposed that the magic of Ghost Mist Veldt had been confused by the arrival of the empaths. Viewing them as an unknown presence, an anomaly, it had tried to snatch them away, but somehow missed one of them, taking only Denton, leaving Marney at the mercy of Matthaus and his fellow deserters. Denton had needed one of Jolyn's skilled magic-users to help him find the stone hut prison again.

Marney thought of Jantal and Nurmar, of their cruel and desperate fight to survive by any means. If she allowed herself to feel her emotions, she was sure she still wouldn't lament their deaths. But when her thoughts switched to Matthaus, the old and grizzled veteran soldier, she didn't want to acknowledge how she might feel about the Denton who had dealt with him: the cold Denton she had never encountered before. Denton the killer.

Perhaps she had let her emotions escape from her apathetic shield, perhaps Denton just knew his protégée too well, but he looked as though he knew exactly what she was thinking.

'Is there something you would like to ask me?' he said.

Marney hesitated, wondering if she was trying to deflect attention away from her own act of murder, but then said, 'How many people have you killed, Denton?'

It was immediately obvious Denton didn't like the question. But he mulled over his answer all the same, taking his rumpled hat from the table, toying with the wide and frayed brim.

'Marney, I would be too ashamed to tell you how many lives I have ended during my service with the Relic Guild. But I'd also feel cruel if I let you believe that Red was a one-off – that you might not have to kill again.'

'I know,' said Marney.

And she did know. In the past, she had lain awake at night worrying about it, wondering when the day would come when her duties with the Relic Guild would include ending a life. Now that day had arrived, she understood that Denton was right: it would likely come again.

'You and I are complicated creatures, Marney,' Denton continued. 'Our empathy keeps record of everything we see, hear, smell, taste and touch – an emotional memory that is locked tight within us forever. It is very difficult for empaths to forget anything. And you *will* remember them, Marney. Every face of every person who dies at your hand will be ingrained into your memory. Unless you care to magically remove them.'

Marney held the cool cloth to the bruise under her eye, her mind, numbed of emotion, finding logic and order in her mentor's words.

'No. We *should* remember them,' Marney said. 'And we should never forget what we've done.'

'I think you're right,' Denton replied. 'But it is just as important that we forgive ourselves for our actions. We kill only when necessary. The last and not the first resort.'

Marney nodded. 'I hate to think that I'd ever reach a place where I could kill without compassion, Denton. I don't want it to be easy for me, not like it is for someone like Samuel.'

'Samuel?' Denton said, clearly surprised.

'I've seen him kill before. He doesn't bat an eyelid.'

Denton was troubled by his protégée's words. 'It is wise to view Samuel as a predator,' he said. 'You could argue that he is a natural born killer. But to believe Samuel kills without compassion? No, no, no, Marney – if that's what you think of your fellow agent, then you haven't taken the time to get to know him at all.'

The look Denton gave Marney was admonishing.

'Hard to believe otherwise,' she said. 'It's not as if Samuel ever likes to explain himself.'

'I'm not saying that he makes relationships easy, Marney. Samuel is a complicated man. He wears his cynicism like a suit of armour, always keeping people at arm's length. But within that hard shell is a person who is very much worth knowing. He was not always the man you know.'

'What happened to him?'

Denton's expression softened. He dropped his hat onto the table and sat back.

'Samuel was a child when he first joined the Relic Guild, Marney. We decided that he was twelve years old, but we've never been sure of his real age. He had been living on the streets in the eastern district, you see. Barely knew how to speak when I found him. He was almost feral.'

Marney tried to imagine Samuel as a child, but couldn't envision anything other than the surly, gun-wielding magicker that he was.

'I don't know how he managed to slip through the net of the child authorities,' Denton continued. 'For all I know, Samuel might have been born on the streets. But if you're going to live in the wilds of a city, and you need to stay one step ahead of the authorities and street gangs, do you know what handy magical talent would be most useful?'

Marney managed a smile. 'Prescient awareness, by any chance?'

'Exactly.' Denton sighed, his eyes sad. 'When I found Samuel he had just murdered a vagrant who had tried to steal his food – scraps from a café dustbin. To this day, I don't know if that man was the first person Samuel ever killed, but I doubt it, Marney.

'Gene was with me when we took him to the Nightshade. We both felt sorry for Samuel – he was such a small and angry little wretch – and we took him under our wings. Gene and I taught him how to speak properly, made him more *civilised,* I suppose. I don't imagine anyone had shown him real kindness before. He wasn't sure how to deal with it, to be honest. Eventually, he worked as a helper in Gene's apothecary shop, and I took him on trips to Aelfirian Houses. Cooling his temper was no easy feat, though – nor was curbing his penchant for biting people.'

Marney couldn't help but chuckle as Denton unconsciously rubbed his hand, obviously remembering a time when the child Samuel had sunk his teeth into it.

'How old was Samuel when he became a full agent?' Marney asked.

'Well, that's where things get a little complicated,' Denton said. 'We weren't sure what to do with him at first. The younger agents were a little dismissive of Samuel. Macy and Bryant had no tolerance for a child. Angel was kind enough to him, but back then she was a little wild herself, and could be a bad influence on anyone. But Gideon seemed to have all the time in the worlds for Samuel. And let me tell you, Marney, the attention Gideon gave the boy was *never* kind in nature.'

Marney narrowed her eyes thoughtfully. 'Is that why they hate each other?' she said. 'Something that happened between them years ago?'

'Oh, I don't think it was anything specific, Marney. More a case of sustained and casual cruelty on Gideon's part. Of course, the Resident back then was Sophia. Like Gene and I, she took a sympathetic view of Samuel. She had been determined to find a use for Samuel's prescient awareness that didn't end in killing. She wanted him to find himself, to develop into a solid, trustworthy man. Gideon didn't like that. He didn't like it at all. He thought Sophia was showing Samuel favouritism. To be honest, I think he might've been jealous.'

'Jealous?' Marney looked disbelieving. 'That would mean Gideon was capable of feeling anything other than spite.'

'A little unfair, but I do see your point,' Denton said. 'However, the trouble with Samuel's magic is that it doesn't extend to other people. For example, he could not sense danger approaching me or you. Samuel can only use his prescient awareness to save his own skin. The instinct his magic gives him isn't primarily to kill, Marney, it's to survive.'

'That doesn't sound true to me,' Marney said. 'Whatever else I might think of Samuel, he's probably the bravest man I know. His magic has saved all of us at one time or another.'

'Yes, you're absolutely right,' Denton said. 'But back then, it was a struggle to find another way for him. Sadly, I think Hamir once summed up Samuel the best. He said that without a weapon, Samuel's magic was of use to no one in the Relic Guild but himself.'

'Then Sophia never found an alternative use for his gift?'

Denton shook his head. 'It became an academic point, anyway.'

Marney understood: 'Sophia died, and Gideon became Resident.'

'And the first thing Gideon did as Resident was put a gun in Samuel's hand.'

Marney was beginning to understand why her fellow Relic Guild agent was such a standoffish sort of character. 'I had no idea,' she said.

Denton groaned as he rubbed at his old knees. He seemed more tired than before. 'I hate to admit it, Marney, but Samuel made more sense after that. He was a natural. That gun and his magic were a perfect marriage, and I've never known him to miss his mark.'

Marney put down the cloth with which she had been soothing her eye. 'I don't think I've ever heard Samuel speak about himself, you know, certainly not about his childhood.'

'And I don't suppose you ever will.' Denton leaned down, undid the string on his backpack, and began rummaging through his belongings. 'Samuel sort of *closed down* after Gideon became Resident. He withdrew. He came from a tough place, Marney, and I hope you will at least bear that in mind when you next consider your fellow magicker.'

With a light smile, Denton sat upright and slapped an envelope down onto the table, causing a puff of air to ruffle the maps and papers.

Marney stared at the envelope. It had been resealed with fresh wax, and contained the coded instructions on how to find the Library of Glass and Mirrors, and what to do once it was reached.

'The worst could still happen, and we need to continue planning for it,' said Denton.

He pushed the envelope towards Marney but she made no attempt to pick it up.

'I don't think you should give this to me, Denton.'

'Marney, I know you have been through an ordeal, but it's highly unlikely that you'll be captured by a hierophant with anti-magic again.'

'No, you don't understand,' Marney replied. 'When I was in that stone hut, I would've done anything to escape. I would've told them everything I knew, Denton. I—'

'Stop it,' the old empath said softly. 'Do you honestly believe that I would have acted any differently in your position? You live and you learn, Marney. But the fact remains –' he pushed the envelope a little closer to her '– if one of us falls, the other must continue to the Library of Glass and Mirrors. Take it.'

Marney reached out. Her hand hovered briefly over the envelope, and then she slid it off the table, and stuffed it into the leg pocket on her fatigues.

But her thoughts remained on the events that had taken place in the stone hut.

'Denton,' she asked in a subdued voice. 'What does *doubt and wonder* mean?'

The old empath levelled a look at her, and Marney knew he had closed down his emotions. 'Pardon me?' he said.

'Matthaus,' Marney explained, suddenly chilled by the steel in her mentor's eye. 'He told me what he'd managed to decipher from your instructions. He said the phrase *doubt and wonder* was mentioned several times, and it was connected to a place of worship – a church or cathedral? He mentioned something about *known things*—'

'Marney, listen to me very carefully.' There was hard frost in Denton's voice. 'I just killed a man for knowing too much. What does that tell you about the information in that envelope?'

Marney swallowed as Denton's empathic magic slithered through her shield of apathy and imparted a sense of dread to her.

Denton continued. 'Whatever Matthaus said to you, keep it to yourself. Unless the worst should happen, it is simply too dangerous for you to know more than you already do. Understand?'

His expression left no room for argument, and Marney nodded.

At that moment, the tent flap swished to one side, and a young private stepped in. He stood to attention, his uniform impeccable, his face freshly shaved. Marney laid a hand upon the envelope in her pocket.

'General Jolyn sent me,' the private said stiffly. 'I'm to escort you out of Ghost Mist Veldt. The portal has been prepared and is ready for use.'

'Ah, then our journey continues,' Denton said, his usual jovial manner returning. 'Please, young man, lead the way.'

As the empaths hoisted their packs and followed the private out of the tent, Denton's voice filled Marney's mind.

You have to trust me, as I trust you, Marney, he said earnestly. *I sincerely hope that you* never *have to know what we're searching for at the Library of Glass and Mirrors.*

The misty, humid hours of Ruby Moon always preceded the rains that fell every night upon Labrys Town. When the clouds broke, torrential downpours washed away the dust and grime and heat of the day, and topped up the reservoirs that kept the denizens supplied with water. But when the rains stopped, a change occurred in the sky above the Labyrinth. Ruby Moon would take a bow, its humid red glow giving way to the cold, clear gleam of its sibling.

The rains had stopped, the clouds had cleared, and Silver Moon's brilliant light shone down from a star-filled sky as Samuel neared Fabian Moor's prison. The streets of the southern district were wet, the atmosphere fresh, the temperature low enough to cause Samuel's breath to fog in the air. Pulling his coat tighter around him, he hurried into the abandoned ore warehouse. The shutter door closed behind him with a series of metallic clangs.

In the dim light of a glow lamp, Samuel took off his Aelfirian hat, stuffed it into his inside pocket, and looked around the warehouse. Hamir was absent. The milky fluid within the eye device fixed to the wall was still, inactive; a reassuring sign that Gideon wasn't watching. Samuel was all alone with the prisoner.

The higher magic radiating from the circle of symbols on the warehouse floor had formed a pillar of purple light. Within it, Fabian Moor floated on his back, naked and debilitated, his skin pale as though he had been leeched of blood. His body, almost folded in two slowly turned in the air, his limbs and long white hair hanging limp. Samuel approached the prison of thaumaturgic light. Moor's chest rose and fell in quick, shallow breaths. His genitals were shrivelled. The skin of his stomach was contorted, twisted, stretched as though he dangled from an invisible meat hook that held him ready for gutting like an animal in a slaughterhouse.

The Genii ceased turning as his upside down face came in line with

Samuel. His mouth was agape as though he slept, but his eyes were open, staring at the Relic Guild agent. Hate bloomed inside Samuel as he came to stand as close to the edge of the symbols carved into the floor as he dared.

'Gene was my friend,' Samuel hissed at Moor. 'But I don't suppose that means anything to you. He was only *human*, after all.'

Samuel wondered for a moment if the Genii really knew he was there. His face was lax, expressing neither pain nor anger. Yet there was something in those dangerous eyes that undoubtedly acknowledged the magicker's presence – and his words.

'See this?' Samuel said, drawing the hunting knife from the sheath strapped to his side. The blade was long and wicked. 'Given the chance, I'd run it across your throat. But maybe that's too quick, too easy for someone like you.'

Still, there was no change in the Genii's expression. Samuel slid the knife back into its sheath.

'The blood of my friend is on your hands,' he growled, 'and the blood of the denizens. I'll make sure you suffer long and hard for what you've done. Do you hear me, you bastard? I'm going to listen to you scream.'

'Save your breath, Samuel,' said the voice of Hamir.

Startled, Samuel looked about the warehouse, but couldn't see the necromancer anywhere.

'Gene's death will mean as little to the Genii as your threats,' Hamir continued. He emerged from the shadowy doorway that led to the stairs down to the cellar. 'And if we were to face harsh truths, Samuel, I think we might find that *you* have killed more denizens in your time than Fabian Moor has.'

Samuel glared as Hamir made his way to a small table upon which the necromancer's paraphernalia was laid out. He carried the big, leather-bound book that contained the secret arts of the Thaumaturgists, clutching it to his chest like a treasured possession.

'Of course,' Hamir added, 'I don't want you to think I'm being callous. I regret Gene's passing as much as you.'

'You could've fooled me,' Samuel muttered.

'Death affects people in different ways, Samuel.' Hamir placed the book down on the table, and selected one of the two remaining phials of blood from a small wooden rack. 'Some people accept death in all its forms. Others cling to the grief and anger, almost as if they would feel lost without it.'

With that strangely amiable manner that never waned, Hamir approached Samuel, phial in hand. 'Am I right?'

Samuel ignored the insinuation in Hamir's words, and gestured to Fabian Moor suspended in the air by his stomach. 'Has he said anything yet?'

'Not a word, but I'm working on it.'

'Don't let me stop you.'

Hamir came to stand alongside Samuel. 'As much as you might want me to satisfy your grim desires, my first duty is to ensure the prisoner stays alive.'

Slowly and carefully, the necromancer fed the phial of blood into the thaumaturgic light. The phial had no cork; both ends were sealed, rounded glass. When he let go, it hovered in the purple glare, and drifted to hang above Fabian Moor's open mouth. The Genii's eyes stared up at it.

'Survival is an interesting instinct, Samuel,' said Hamir. 'Yours is a magical gift, a prescient awareness that gives you no choice but to fight for survival, no matter the odds. But in others, there is always a limit beyond which the survival instinct will give up and accept defeat. The only certain fact I have learned about Fabian Moor, is that he still believes he has something worth surviving for. Observe.'

The end of the phial lowered into Moor's mouth. Automatically, the Genii's lips closed around it and he began to suck in a frantic fashion. But he could not draw the blood through the glass. Aiming a baleful glare at Hamir, Moor took the phial between his teeth and bit, hard.

It cracked and broke.

Blood poured freely, filling Moor's mouth, spilling onto his face and down his cheeks as he choked, trying not to swallow shards of glass. It was a brief meal, little more than a single gulp. With a weak hand, Moor tried wiping the spilled blood into his mouth, slapping his own face in the process, licking his fingers clean. It was an undignified, desperate act that gained him no more than a few extra drops. And then the Genii's arm fell limp again, the last of his strength spent. He worked his tongue around his mouth, and finally spat out a few pieces of glass. The remnants of the phial dissolved into purple light. Fabian Moor closed his eyes, and his blood-smeared lips set into a grim line.

Hamir said, 'If he is willing to bite through glass to ensure his survival, I rather think he has one or two secrets that I might find interesting.'

Samuel grunted. 'Like what it is he wants to move with that device he made.'

'Indeed.'

Samuel looked around for the glass sphere, but couldn't see it in the warehouse.

'I'm keeping it in the cellar,' Hamir explained. 'Out of the way.'

'I take it Gideon told you what I learned from Long Tommy?'

'Yes, he passed on your report.' The necromancer considered the Genii in his prison. 'But if we're going to build on current information, we need to keep up Moor's strength for further interrogation. The supply of blood that Macy and Bryant donated is all but finished.' He motioned to the last phial left in the rack on the table. 'I was hoping you might like to share the load, Samuel.'

Samuel stared at him with disbelief. 'You want my blood to feed *him*?' He jabbed a thumb at Moor.

Hamir blinked. 'Yes.'

'Forget it.' Samuel scowled. 'I want no part in keeping Moor alive. Get it from the hospital, or ask Gideon to donate some.'

'Samuel, feeding Fabian Moor the blood of a magicker has its benefits. The energy it holds means his cravings are sated by consuming far less than he would need from a regular denizen. However, feeding him blood as strong as a *blood*-magicker's?' Hamir clucked his tongue. 'Considering Gideon's ancestry, I think we'd be feeding the Genii the kind of magic that his prison was established to stop him using against us.'

Samuel shrugged. 'Then give him your blood, Hamir.'

The necromancer barked a laugh. 'Now that really *would* be a bad idea. Come, Samuel. It won't take long, and I don't need much. For now.'

Hamir stepped over to the table, pulled out a packing crate from beneath it, and gestured for Samuel to use it as a seat. Samuel's gaze lingered on Moor floating in his prison, eyes closed, face smeared with blood. His expression was almost peaceful, though the contortion at his stomach must have been agony beyond belief.

'Samuel,' Hamir said impatiently, and he gestured to the crate again. 'Remove your coat and roll up your sleeve.'

Reluctantly, Samuel took his seat, and did as the necromancer instructed. He threw his coat on the floor beside the crate, and scrunched the sleeve of his jumper up his right arm.

Hamir unfastened a black medical bag, producing a brown leather roll, which he opened in a perfunctory manner. First, he removed a wax paper packet, which he unfolded to reveal a collection of thin and sharp hypodermic needles. Next, he laid a rubber tourniquet beside the needles, and then removed a little bottle of surgical spirits, along with a few muslin clothes. Last, he pulled a dull metal cylinder from the roll, eight inches long and as fat as Samuel's wrist. The cylinder opened like a book, and Hamir placed it upon the table. Four glass and copper syringes were held securely inside, two in each half.

As Hamir cleaned one of the hypodermic needles with a cloth doused in surgical spirits, Samuel's eyes were again drawn to Fabian Moor, and to the scarring on the Genii's forehead. He looked back at Hamir, and the scarring he wore in exactly the same place. Samuel found himself wondering about the origins of the small, elderly necromancer.

Hamir had always been at the Nightshade, serving as the Resident's aide, but he had never really been considered an agent of the Relic Guild. Samuel didn't know if he was a magicker or a magic-user. Had Hamir been born with the gift of necromancy? Or was it a school of magic in which he had become adept? Either way, Hamir had never tracked down stolen relics or fought treasure hunters as the other agents had. In fact, he rarely left the Nightshade at all. He only came forward to help when the Resident ordered him to, content for the rest of the time to remain as aloof and absent as was humanly possible. Hamir was more like a ghost, haunting the periphery.

There was a kind of acceptance within the Relic Guild that a wall of privacy surrounded Hamir that the agents never tried to breach. Denton, by far the oldest member of the Relic Guild, claimed that Hamir had not changed in the sixty years he had known him. Hamir didn't suffer illnesses, he didn't seem to age, and he certainly didn't talk about himself. No one knew when he had been born. Or what deeds lay in his past. And no one knew how he had acquired that scar on his forehead.

The group liked to swap theories about the Resident's aide from time to time, joke and guess about the secrets he might be hiding. Samuel had never been interested in getting involved – and maybe, after all these years of speculation, people should start accepting that Hamir was just Hamir.

Hamir noticed the magicker staring at him.

'Is there something on your mind, Samuel?'

'What – apart from the Genii we're holding in a thaumaturgic prison, you mean?'

'Hmm.' Hamir tied a tourniquet around Samuel's arm, said, 'Hold still, please,' and slid the needle into a vein without Samuel feeling so much as a slight sting.

'Hamir, do you know where Denton and Marney have gone?'

'No. I'm as much in the dark about their mission as you,' the necromancer admitted. 'And, before you ask, I don't know if there has been word from Van Bam and Angel, either.' He selected one of the glass and copper syringes. 'Now tell me – do you think the information from the magic-user – this Long Tommy – can be believed?'

'He certainly wasn't lying,' Samuel replied, watching as Hamir screwed the syringe onto the needle. 'Whether what he told me is right or not is another matter.'

'Ah. Then let us suppose that the device *is* a shadow carriage.' Hamir began pulling out the plunger, slowly drawing Samuel's blood into the syringe. 'What do you think Moor wants to move with it?'

Samuel narrowed his eyes. He couldn't remember Hamir ever asking for his opinion before. 'Well, if I were to guess, I'd say he's looking to bring more Genii into Labrys Town.'

'You mean other Genii whose essences have been stored in terra-cotta jars?'

Samuel nodded. 'It's the only way they can sneak past the Time-watcher's barrier.'

Hamir didn't seem convinced. 'It is *possible*, I suppose.'

'You *suppose?*' said Samuel. 'Moor told Long Tommy that the portals to the Great Labyrinth were too well guarded. If he was trying to send out treasure hunters to bring back more terracotta jars, it would be too risky for them to use the official shadow carriages in Labrys Town now. It makes sense, Hamir.'

'But would you be as sure if you first considered the bigger picture, Samuel?'

The first syringe filled, Hamir prepared a second and began drawing more blood.

The necromancer continued. 'You assume that Fabian Moor is on the inside looking out – that he has created a portable shadow carriage to send treasure hunters to the doorways of the Great Labyrinth, undetected. But what if he created that device to collect a delivery that is already en route to one of the doorways?'

'Like what?'

'Who can say? A weapon, a message, instructions from Spiral himself? And yes, maybe terracotta jars. Perhaps a detachment of soldiers, for all we know.'

'Soldiers?' Samuel pulled a dubious face.

'I'm merely speculating.'

Samuel shook his head. 'It'd never get past Lady Amilee.'

'Fabian Moor did.'

Hamir began filling a third syringe.

'Consider the possibilities, Samuel. If that device is a shadow carriage, then it was created with thaumaturgy. There's no telling how big a *thing* it could transport from the Great Labyrinth to Labrys Town. In my opinion, I would be highly surprised if there was *no one* out among the Houses standing ready to send aid to Fabian Moor. The Genii obviously has a plan.'

Samuel thought for a moment, and then shook away an icy feeling. 'It doesn't matter now,' he said. 'We have the device, and it's no good to him while he's in there.' He motioned to the Genii floating in the purple light of thaumaturgy. 'Whatever he was up to, we stopped him.'

'I wish I could be as certain,' Hamir countered. 'I have been spending time in the cellar with Moor's little creation. For the life of me, I cannot remove the metal mesh and power stones that surround it. The glass sphere has been toughened by higher magic. And the substance inside it might look as harmless as dirty water, but let us not forget that it was formed from harvested shadows.'

'I cannot tell if that device is useless, or if it will spring into action at any time. That is a very real concern to me, Samuel.'

Hamir placed the third syringe alongside the others in the metal cylinder. 'There ... three should do it.'

'Have you told Gideon about your concerns?' Samuel asked.

'I have indeed. But Gideon says he won't send a report to Lady Amilee based on theories alone. He wants facts. He wants proof. And there is only one way we are going to get that.'

Hamir closed the metal cylinder, then packed his paraphernalia into the black medical bag. He then took the big leather-bound book off the table and walked over to Fabian Moor's prison, stopping at the edge of the thaumaturgic symbols carved into the floor. The Genii's naked body was slowly turning again. His eyes remained closed.

Hamir looked back at Samuel. 'You can leave now. Be sure to eat and rest.'

But Samuel didn't rise from the crate. 'If it's all the same to you, I'll stay put,' he said resolutely.

'An interesting decision,' Hamir said with a frown. 'Are you offering to help me with the interrogation?'

'No.'

'I see.' Hamir raised an eyebrow. 'Samuel, I understand how the death of Gene has affected you, but retribution is such an ugly desire. It can be quite damaging to the mind. I really do not believe that you want to witness what I am about to do.'

'I don't care,' Samuel growled. 'For what this bastard did to Gene, I need to see you hurt him, Hamir. So get on with it.'

The necromancer sighed. The green of his eyes darkened as though ink had been dripped into them. 'As you wish,' he whispered.

Van Bam stood naked before the giant, upon the huge boulder in the cavern of glittering jewels, with his eyes closed. Body tense and teeth clenched, the illusionist tried not to flinch as Bellow used a sharpened wooden scriber to scratch the symbols and glyphs of blood-magic onto his skin.

'The story of the Nephilim begins a thousand years ago,' Gulduur Bellow said as he worked. 'The Timewatcher had completed her grandest creation – the Great Labyrinth – and the Houses of the Aelfir were united. It was the dawn of a new age.'

The illusionist's mind raced. Hybrids, Bellow had said – the Nephilim were hybrids of Thaumaturgists and humans.

'During that time,' the giant continued, 'there was a creature of higher magic, whose true name was never known to my herd, though it is said that the Thaumaturgists still whisper it as a curse. The Nephilim call him the Progenitor.'

Bellow was quiet as he scratched what felt to Van Bam like a triangle upon his chest. Although the illusionist kept his eyes firmly shut, he could feel the giant's huge form looming over him, and he tried not to think about the blood Bellow was using as ink.

'Little is known of the Progenitor. Some say he was a mighty warrior who fought in ancient battles, long before the creation of the Great Labyrinth. Others claim he was a madman who respected only chaos. But what is known for certain is that he formed an unhealthy obsession with the first humans who settled in Labrys Town. And the day the humans met the Progenitor was a day to regret.'

Drawing a straight line and a series of slashes to connect the triangle on Van Bam's chest to the illusionist's abdomen, Bellow began creating a new pattern of swirling shapes. He worked fast, and his use of the scriber was surprisingly delicate.

'The Progenitor went to the humans,' Bellow continued. 'He made them trust him – and why wouldn't they? He was a Thaumaturgist, one of the Timewatcher's favoured children. But once their trust had been gained, the Progenitor betrayed the denizens. He stole one hundred human women from the Labyrinth, and with them he disappeared without a trace.'

Having finished with the abdomen, Bellow was quickly painting script over Van Bam's right hand, and up his arm. His story had gained the illusionist's full attention now.

With his eyes still closed, Van Bam said, 'Why would he abduct denizens?'

'Well now,' said Bellow. 'They say that it was resurrection that intrigued the Progenitor – a fascination with creating life from death. Some say he was a scientist. The one hundred women he had stolen from the Labyrinth – who had trusted him completely – did not realise until it was too late that they were to be the test subjects in the Progenitor's experiments.'

'Experiments?' said Van Bam. Bellow had begun decorating his shoulder with the symbols of blood-magic. A bad feeling rose in the illusionist's gut. 'What did he do to them?'

'He used them to raise the dead,' Bellow stated hollowly. 'They say the Progenitor had collected the souls of one hundred fallen Thaumaturgists. With higher magic, he impregnated each of those human women with one of those souls. He forced death into their wombs, Van Bam, and they gave birth to life.'

Van Bam flinched as Bellow drew a diagonal line from his right shoulder down to his left buttock.

'*That* was how the Nephilim came into existence,' Bellow said.

Appalled, confused, Van Bam opened his eyes to find he looked straight at the giant.

On his knees, with one hand on the ground beside the bowl of blood, the wooden scriber held in the other, Bellow paused in his work to meet Van Bam's stare. The bright blue orbs of his eyes glared, perhaps challenging the illusionist to dare judge him.

'Are you beginning to understand why my people are regarded as abominations?'

'I … I do not know what to say,' Van Bam admitted.

'Then say nothing, and listen.' Bellow dipped the scriber into the blood and proceeded to decorate Van Bam's leg. 'Who can say for sure why the Progenitor forced those women to give birth to the Nephilim? Perhaps he considered himself a *scientist*, after all. Perhaps he created us merely to discover if he could, and *results* mattered to him over the abuse he perpetrated. The Progenitor's reasons are now lost to time.

'However, there is one legend that says the one hundred souls that he had collected had once belonged to creatures of higher magic who were dear to the Progenitor. He sought to bring them back from death, desperately, at any cost, and the creation of the Nephilim was the result of his failed attempt.'

As the giant began scribing upon Van Bam's left foot, there was defiance in his body language, anger and sorrow in his voice.

'The Progenitor's experiments came full circle, Van Bam. He used death to create life, but, in turn, that life brought death. Not one of the Nephilim's mothers survived the birth of their children. We were not born as human babes are. We tore free of their bodies as abominations, part human, part Thaumaturgist, the lowest of all creatures of higher magic.

'From their mothers' abuse and agony, the Nephilim were delivered to the realms. Those poor women never stood a chance. The origin of my people is a horrific legacy.'

Van Bam looked around the cavern, at the jewels and veins of metal shining and glittering like stars and nebulae. He looked at Bellow, still decorating his foot. In the light of the magical fire burning at each corner of the boulder, the scars on his skin were pale. Bellow could obviously see distaste on the illusionist's face.

'Don't look at me,' the giant said, shame and anger filling his voice as it hissed through his clenched teeth. 'Keep your eyes shut while I work.'

Van Bam closed his eyes immediately. 'I do not wish to cause offence,' he said quickly and carefully, 'I only wonder at the cruel methods by which the Nephilim were born. You say the Progenitor was a Thaumaturgist. How could the Timewatcher allow this to happen?'

'She didn't allow it,' Bellow replied, painting a series of circles up the front of Van Bam's left leg. 'The Timewatcher did not know of the Progenitor's actions until after my people were born. And She was horrified at his barbaric treatment of the humans and to discover that their children had arrived with the wisdom and power of the souls that had created them.'

Van Bam winced as the point of the scriber dug into thigh muscle.

'It is said that the Timewatcher, in Her fury, punished the Progenitor in ways that all Thaumaturgists dread.'

Van Bam stayed silent, waiting for Bellow to continue.

'The Timewatcher called the Nephilim perversions of life. We were born with the gift of thaumaturgy in our veins, but cursed to cut our skins to release it. Blood-magickers. Giants. *Fiends!* The Timewatcher turned Her back on the Nephilim, but the Nephilim remembered their *true* mothers, Van Bam, all one hundred of them. Our first memory was of the agony and death we gave them. We cannot – *will* not – forget the price they paid for trusting one of the Timewatcher's favoured children.'

Bellow's strokes were quick, angry, as he moved the scriber over Van Bam's left hip, and began connecting new symbols and glyphs to those he had already drawn on his abdomen. Van Bam dared not open his eyes.

'So the Timewatcher made you outcasts,' the illusionist said, trying hard to keep any trace of an opinion or judgement from his voice. 'The Aelfir shunned you, and you were left to roam the Houses, searching for the Sorrow of Future Reason.'

'The atrocities of the Progenitor were buried, hidden. Over the next thousand years, the myths and legends grew up around the Nephilim like weeds in a garden, while behind the lies the truth was much more terrible.' Bellow ceased drawing upon Van Bam's skin in blood, and snorted a sad laugh. 'What do you think of my story, Van Bam?'

'It … It was certainly enlightening.' Van Bam cleared his throat. 'But given that the Nephilim's *origin* begins in the Labyrinth, I am surprised that I have not heard this tale of the Progenitor before.'

'Details are easily omitted from records,' Bellow replied. 'Truths that the Timewatcher and the Thaumaturgists deemed *embarrassing* were *lost*. And memories fade. But who knows – perhaps in a dusty corner of a library in Labrys Town, an accurate history still exists, hiding in plain sight, waiting to be discovered.'

Bellow sighed, whispered a word that Van Bam didn't catch that might have been a curse, or a plea.

'There was a time,' the giant said, 'when the Nephilim prayed that the Timewatcher would forgive us our existence, and deliver us to the Sorrow of Future Reason. But over the centuries, our search began to feel more like tradition. I think we lost faith in the journey ever ending.

'So imagine our excitement, Van Bam, when, quite unexpectedly, Lord Spiral, the Timewatcher's most favoured son, summoned the Nephilim herd to the Falls of Dust and Silver.'

Van Bam opened his eyes in surprise. He started as he found Gulduur Bellow's huge face no more than a foot away from his own. The giant was bent over, his blue eyes studying Van Bam's features. In one hand he held the bowl of blood, in the other the wooden scriber.

'The Falls of Dust and Silver?' said Van Bam. 'The House where the war began?'

'Precisely,' said Bellow. 'The story of the Nephilim is always growing, my friend.' He used the scriber to stir the blood in the bowl. 'Do you recall that I told you I was lost? That I had been separated from my herd?'

Van Bam nodded.

'It was because of the trick that Spiral played on *my* people.' Bellow tapped the scriber on the edge of the bowl, shaking off excess blood. 'Please keep your eyes closed, Van Bam. The script I am about to paint on your head and face is intrinsic to this spell.'

The illusionist closed his eyes. He felt the delicate touch of the scriber upon his cheek.

'Now,' Bellow continued, 'when my herd answered the summons to the Falls of Dust and Silver, Spiral did indeed tell us that the time had come for the Nephilim to have their home. He told us that the Timewatcher desired peace and unity, true equality for my people. He said that She no longer held us culpable for the actions of the Progenitor.'

He began scribing across Van Bam's chin. 'You have to understand, Van Bam – Spiral was the first Thaumaturgist to treat with the Nephilim since the terrible day of our creation, and we genuinely believed that the Timewatcher had sent him to us. We rejoiced.'

'But you said that Spiral tricked you,' Van Bam said as the scriber moved up his other cheek. 'Why?'

'Spiral regarded the Nephilim as a rogue element in his plans for the war,' Bellow said. 'Earlier, Van Bam, you suggested that the Genii are frightened of the Nephilim, and I think there is truth in that. I think Spiral was too uncertain of our power to attack us directly, and he could not predict which side we would choose to fight for. Perhaps if he had asked us, he might have discovered we would have chosen neither side. But like all Thaumaturgists, like the Aelfir, like *humans*, he decided to treat us with fear and loathing.'

Bellow paused as he painted a series of intricate glyphs up the bridge of Van Bam's nose, and then he continued.

'Spiral had a way of settling the issue. He tricked the Nephilim into gathering at the Falls of Dust and Silver with empty promises and lies. My people walked into a trap, a mighty spell that Spiral had cast. He removed the Nephilim – transported the herd to a location far from the Houses of the Aelfir, I suspect. Perhaps it was one of the Genii Lord's hidden realms that you spoke of, a prison that my people cannot escape from – where they can no longer be a rogue element in Spiral's war plans.'

Van Bam tried not to frown as Bellow swept the scriber across his brow. 'But you escaped,' he said.

'By the skin of my teeth,' the giant replied. 'I alone evaded Spiral's trickery. I fled to the desert of Mirage, where I hoped to understand the reason for Spiral's actions – where I could formulate a plan to find my people and free them.'

'I do not understand,' Van Bam admitted, as the scriber moved over the top of his head. 'How could Spiral remove an entire race without anyone noticing?'

'Van Bam, I am an elder among my people, one of the Progenitor's original children. I have seen the Nephilim herd grow over the years, but after a millennium, we are still less than a thousand. Who among the billions of Aelfir who choose to shun our existence anyway would notice the disappearance of so few?' Bellow had now reached the back of the illusionist's head. 'However, one person *did* notice. He came to me – here, in the desert of Mirage.'

'Lord Wolfe,' Van Bam whispered. 'The Wanderer.'

'Perhaps Baran Wolfe sensed the plight of the Nephilim, and that is what first drew him to Mirage,' Bellow said. 'He was most disturbed to hear what his fellow Skywatcher had done to my herd. Spiral's actions were certainly not carried out in the name of the Timewatcher, Wolfe said. But they did seem to confirm the suspicions he was already having about the First Lord of the Thaumaturgists.'

Bellow snorted bitterly. 'From Mirage, Baran Wolfe travelled straight to the Falls of Dust and Silver to confront Spiral. And we both know what happened next, Van Bam.'

'But why would he confront Spiral?' Van Bam said. 'Why not inform the Timewatcher, or his fellow Thaumaturgists, of his suspicions?'

'I do not know,' Bellow replied sadly. 'But my story convinced Wolfe that everything he had been unable to divine from the skies – including the mysterious cathedral that the skies spoke of but he could not find – was connected to Spiral.'

The giant stopped painting as he reached the nape of Van Bam's neck, and his voice cracked, as though bordering on tears.

'Baran Wolfe the Wanderer … In return for my staying here in Mirage, waiting for you, he promised to come back and help to reunite me with my herd. But now he is dead.'

'I … I am sorry,' was all Van Bam could say.

Bellow drew a breath. 'Keep still, Van Bam. I need to scribe glyphs onto your eyelids.'

The giant continued his gentle work upon the illusionist's skin.

Van Bam wasn't sure what to make of the things Bellow had told him, or its immediate relevance.

As if reading his thoughts, Bellow said, 'It is important to me that you know before we part company the tragedy inherent to my people's story. Open your eyes, my friend.'

The Nephilim towered over the illusionist.

Van Bam studied the patterns of blood-magic on his skin. They covered his left foot and leg, sprawled up to his hip, diagonally across his stomach and chest, up to his shoulder, and down his right arm to his hand. He knew the symbols and glyphs continued in another diagonal line down his back to his buttock where they reconnected to his left leg. For a moment, he wished for a mirror in which he might see the script upon his face and head.

'While my spells remain upon you, your magic will be significantly amplified,' Bellow explained. 'Are you ready to wield such power?'

Van Bam looked up into the giant's face, four foot above him. 'I ... I believe so.'

'Then let us complete my work.'

Bellow bowed towards Van Bam, whispering unintelligible words at him. Van Bam froze, his breath catching, as a wind came from the Nephilim's mouth, and wrapped itself around the illusionist, squeezing, causing every muscle in his body to tense. He felt a burning sensation on his left foot. Where the glyphs and symbols began at his toes, they flared with a violet light that quickly spread up his leg and across his body like a lit fuse. By the time the light had sped along his arm, down his back, and across his face and head, Van Bam felt as though his senses had been finely tuned. He groaned and quivered with energy.

A ringing filled his ears. His cane still rested on the ground where he had placed it, but now the glass flared and dimmed with green light, its song calling to the illusionist. Van Bam reached out a hand, and the cane jumped into his grasp.

Bellow watched on, his huge face almost amused. 'How do you feel?' he asked.

'Powerful,' Van Bam growled.

'Good.' Bellow smiled. 'Now you are ready to go home.'

CHAPTER EIGHTEEN

THE OTHER SIDE OF THE DOOR

Samuel braced himself for the familiar, sudden lurch that always came when stepping through a doorway portal. He expected to be dragged into a spectral pathway that burrowed into the Nothing of Far and Deep, in which he would float, drift, until he was delivered to whatever realm the pathway connected to. But Samuel's expectations were not met. Somehow, the portal turned him around, pushed him back towards the Sisterhood of Bells, and returned him to the room of Human Curiosities in the Museum of Aelfirian Heritage.

Namji, Hillem and Glogelder emerged from the doorway alongside the old bounty hunter. But Van Bam and Clara did not.

In his confusion, Samuel just had time to register the dead body lying on the floor – Symone the night guard – before his prescient awareness went berserk.

In the time it took Glogelder to shout 'The Toymaker!' Samuel's magic had already erupted through his veins, absorbed the atmosphere, and the threat of his environment pierced every part of his being with a thousand fishhooks tearing at his instincts. He knew exactly where each of the Toymaker's *toys* were in the room, and they were everywhere. A hundred glowing dots of thaumaturgic stings surrounded the group like the lights of a distant city. The small, insect-like automatons clung to the ceiling and walls, perched upon museum models and the dead body of Symone. They skittered, trapping the group in the room, preparing to swarm.

Samuel's magic took control of his actions.

He holstered the ice-rifle and pulled out the small metal cylinder that Hillem had given him, releasing a glass sphere of anti-magic into his hand. His prescient awareness flashed a new threat: Glogelder. In his panic, the big Aelf was preparing to fire his spell sphere launcher, which, in such a confined area, would see them all burned to death. Samuel didn't give him the chance.

As the power stone on Glogelder's weapon whined into life, the Toymaker's minions rushed forward, and Samuel smashed the sphere of anti-magic upon the steps that led up to the doorway.

The shockwave moaned across the room, spreading like a ripple in water, and the hand-sized automatons froze in its wake. Deactivated, the lights of their stings died, their tails fell limp. More and more of the Toymaker's minions fell from the ceiling and clattered to the floor. Samuel dropped to his knees, feeling as though the Timewatcher Herself had swooped past, dragging the spirit from his body. He heard Namji shouting his name before he fell forwards and rolled down the steps into nothing.

Samuel didn't know how long he was unconscious, but when he came to, the night air was cold on his face, and he was gently rocking to the sound of lapping water, and the chugging of an engine.

His magic was gone. He could feel no trace of it inside him.

The sonorous chime of a bell reverberated, striking three times before fading to silence.

With a groan, Samuel opened his eyes and tried to sit up. Namji pushed him down again.

'Take it easy,' she said. 'Don't worry, your magic will come back, but it'll be a while yet.'

Her face loomed over Samuel, her green eyes full of concern. Above her, the stars in the night sky struggled to shine through the eerie, bruised glow that hung over the Sisterhood of Bells. The stink of filthy water filled Samuel's nostrils, and the rocking continued.

'Where are we?' Samuel asked, his throat dry.

'On a boat, travelling down the River Bells. We're safe for now.'

A pain flared in Samuel's temples, and he raised a hand to his head. Only then did he realise that he was wearing his hat made of charmed material which concealed his face.

'No, leave it on,' Namji instructed. 'It's better you stay hidden.'

'Van Bam and Clara,' Samuel croaked. He worked saliva around his mouth and swallowed. 'What happened to them?'

'They're missing, Samuel,' Namji said anxiously. 'I don't understand why we were sent back, but Clara and Van Bam didn't come with us. Perhaps the avatar always meant them to go on alone. I just ... don't know.'

'The Toymaker?'

'We never saw him – *as usual*,' she said bitterly. 'But we had to leave the museum before his minions recovered from the anti-magic. The doorway had stopped working, Samuel. Without Clara we couldn't reactivate it. We had to get out of there.'

'Shit,' Samuel whispered.

There was fear inside the old bounty hunter; fear that his magic would never return; fear for Van Bam and Clara. Had the doorway taken them to where Known Things was kept? What was the point in separating them from the rest of the group? Perhaps Samuel and his Aelfirian colleagues had become redundant in the avatar's plans. Were they now expendable?

'We have to leave this House,' Samuel said, trying to order his thoughts. 'If the Toymaker is still here, his toys will wake up soon, and—'

'Samuel, slow down,' said Namji. 'You were unconscious for a couple of hours, and a lot has happened in that time. Believe it or not, we're still one step ahead in the game.'

She helped Samuel to sit up, and he looked past her.

They were on a small and battered trawler that was carrying them gently down the River Bells. Namji and the old bounty hunter sat at the stern, upon a bundle of damp netting. Towards the bow, Hillem and Glogelder stood in the control house, either side of the old Aelfirian man who piloted the boat. His hair was white and wispy, and he wore a thick cloak as he stood straight-backed at the controls.

'Is that Councillor Tal?' Samuel said.

'Lucky for us, Tal was still in the Sisterhood of Bells,' Namji replied. 'I got a message to him and he met us at the docks. Glogelder and Hillem know their way around the seedier parts of cities, and they managed to hire a boat from a river merchant – some old drunkard who could hardly wait to take the money we gave him to the nearest tavern.'

Frowning, Samuel looked out over the water. The River Bells was wide. On either bank, moored barges and boats were shadows; tall buildings were blocky silhouettes. Here and there, warm light spilled from windows. In the near distance, a monumental clock tower – one of the Sisters – rose from the riverside, rising towards the sky, its clock face as bright as a moon.

'Where's Tal taking us?' Samuel asked.

'There's an interesting answer to that.' Namji dipped her hand into her cloth satchel. 'Samuel, is this yours?' She held up a large black iron key before his face.

He shook his head. 'No. Why?'

'When I took your hat from your coat pocket, it was wrapped around this key.'

Samuel took it from Namji. It was heavy, eight inches long at least. At one end of the shaft were three square teeth, and at the other end the bow was cut into a diamond shape.

The symbol of thaumaturgy? Samuel was puzzled. 'How did it get into my pocket?'

'It must've been the avatar. There's more, Samuel. Look on the other side.'

Samuel flipped the key over. On the reverse side of the bow, the metal had been engraved with a triangle surrounded by a circle.

'That's the symbol for Little Sibling,' Namji said.

'Little Sibling?'

Namji nodded. 'That's where we're heading now.'

She turned to gaze up the length of the giant clock tower rising from the riverbank ahead. Samuel remembered that Little Sibling was the headquarters for the Aelfirian governing body.

'Tal's taking us into the Panopticon of Houses?'

'Not *into*, Samuel – *underneath*.' Namji pointed to the black iron key in Samuel's hands. 'Tal says that's an old cell key. He's going to show us a secret entrance to the dungeons beneath Little Sibling.'

'Oh good, more secrets,' Samuel said, turning the key over in his hands. 'So we have to do what – open a cell?'

Namji shrugged. 'That's what we're going to find out.'

At that moment, Glogelder called out from the control house, 'How's he doing?'

'He's awake,' Namji replied.

Hillem and Glogelder left Tal to pilot the trawler, and approached Samuel. Glogelder had a broad grin on his face.

'Reckon you saved our skins back there,' he said, offering his hand.

Samuel pocketed the key and allowed the big Aelf to pull him to his feet.

'But you gave us a bit of a scare,' Hillem added. 'How do you feel?'

'Like I've been beaten up,' said Samuel, and he took a steadying breath. 'Do we have any idea what happened to Van Bam and Clara?'

Both Aelfir appeared as puzzled as Samuel felt, and the old bounty hunter had to quell an uncustomary sense of panic beginning to rise within him.

Glogelder nodded towards Councillor Tal in the control house. 'The old man wants a word with you,' he said.

Confused, frustrated, frightened, Samuel left his Aelfirian colleagues and stepped into the control house, up beside the elderly councillor. He kept his Aelfirian hat on.

'It's good to see you alive, if not entirely well, Samuel.' Tal's large eyes were focused on the black river waters. He used no lamps to light the way; Samuel assumed it was so that no one would see the trawler's passage. Without turning from the window, Tal added, 'I'm sorry to hear that your friends have disappeared. I really can't imagine that anyone would envy you at the moment.'

'Funny,' Samuel said with a small, bitter smile. 'I've been saying the same thing for many years now.'

'I bet you have,' Tal said. 'I don't suppose that you ever knew, Samuel, but in my younger days I once helped the Relic Guild.'

'Did you?'

'Oh, it was nothing really,' Tal said. 'Just a friendly deed for a couple of lost magickers. Though I must confess,' he added conspiratorially, 'I was always a little envious of the Relic Guild agents. Your lives seemed exciting . . . *exotic*!'

'You can swap places with me if you like.'

Tal chuckled. 'A kind offer, but I'm an old man now with far too much experience of trouble.' He sighed. 'Samuel, I want you to know that I've seen first-hand what the Genii are capable of. I know what kind of future those bastards would have given us all if they had won the war.'

The elderly Aelf was clearly agitated. 'You fought for the Timewatcher during the war, didn't you?' Samuel asked.

'Yes, that's right. But not on the frontlines. I was in a special division of the secret service, gathering intelligence. It shames me to admit, Samuel, but I was never better at my job than when interrogating the officers that we caught from Spiral's Aelfirian armies. I am not proud of some of the deeds I conducted in the Timewatcher's name.'

Samuel knew how he felt, and he could see the regret in the councillor's large Aelfirian eyes.

'Hillem told me that you lobbied for governorship of the Aelfheim Archipelago,' Samuel said. 'He said you fought to gain control of the Labyrinth's supply line.'

'Yes, I did.'

'Why?'

'Interesting question,' Tal replied evasively. 'The truth is, Samuel, when the war ended, my soul had been damaged by the things I'd seen and done. I think I fought as hard as I did to get that position at Sunflower because of a need for penance. To do something good. Something right. Looking after the denizens of the Labyrinth, ensuring they received all they needed to survive, seemed a perfect way to make amends.'

'Did it work?'

'Yes. Yes, I think it did. Until now.' Tal drew a deep breath. 'I want you to understand that I will do anything to prevent Spiral's return. Whatever it takes.' He shot the old bounty hunter a quick glance. 'I assume that the key in your pocket was a gift from the avatar?'

Samuel took the key from his pocket, and turned it over in his hands.

Tal said, 'There's something in a cell beneath Little Sibling that the avatar wants you to find. But I really don't want to be with you when you discover it. There are too many of my ghosts in that dungeon. But tell me – do you trust the avatar, Samuel?'

Suddenly weary, Samuel put the key back into his coat pocket. He thought of Van Bam and Clara, missing, lost. Did he trust the avatar? 'I don't see that I have a choice.'

'There are always choices, but so many of us so often make the wrong ones.' The councillor took another breath and gave a resigned sigh. 'Samuel, you should know that I have been removed as governor of the Aelfheim Archipelago.'

'What?'

'It is my punishment for presiding over the *lax security* that let you escape from the Labyrinth, *and* from my custody.' Tal held up a hand to stop Samuel jumping in. 'But my being used as a scapegoat is the least of our problems now. Every Aelfirian ruler has been summoned to Little Sibling. The Panopticon of Houses is gathering to vote on whether it is time to stop sending supplies to the denizens of Labrys Town.'

Samuel's stomach lurched, and his words could not pass beyond his clenched teeth.

'The Sisterhood is orchestrating the whole thing,' Tal continued, his voice grave. 'Its members are vastly influential people, Samuel. They are leaning more heavily than they've ever done on all the Houses in the Panopticon, whether major or minor. The Sisterhood will ensure that the vote does *not* go in the Labyrinth's favour.'

'Don't they realise what it will do?' Samuel said, his voice hoarse.

'They don't care,' Tal replied. 'Your escape from the Labyrinth has given the Sisterhood the excuse it needed. The official reason is the Retrospective. They are now saying the damage is already done. That they no longer believe that throwing your corpses into the portal in Sunflower will seal the cracks that have opened between the Houses and the Labyrinth. They have decided that the only way to ensure the Retrospective and its wild demons can never return, is to destroy the last portal to Labrys Town itself.'

'Madness,' Samuel said bitterly. 'How could they be this blind, Tal? If they knew the truth about the Retrospective, what the Genii are planning to do with it—'

'Samuel, the truth is irrelevant to the Sisterhood.' Tal's voice was sympathetic but laced with the same anger that Samuel felt. 'Oh, I'm sure they genuinely believe that you brought the Retrospective with you, but, ultimately, destroying that portal will give the Sisterhood the same kind of power that I once damaged my soul to stop the Genii gaining.'

The thuds of Samuel's heartbeat were loud in his ears. 'But they already have control over the Panopticon,' he said, voice low. 'How can murdering a million humans give the Sisterhood more power?'

'Faith,' Tal replied. 'In my experience, Samuel, it is the hardest thing to kill.'

'Faith in the Timewatcher,' Samuel whispered.

'The Timewatcher's last order to the Aelfir was to keep the denizens alive – *that* was Her final prerogative. Most Houses still worship the Timewatcher, and fear what She might do should we ever stop sending aid to the denizens. I accept that the Timewatcher abandoned us all, Samuel, and She is *not* coming back, no matter what we do. But the Sisterhood intend to take advantage of her absence.

'Destroying the last portal to Labrys Town will also destroy the stigma of the Timewatcher. To disregard Her final prerogative without retribution will strangle the faith of the Houses until the Great Mother is no more than a vestige of an older time. And then, the Sisterhood will give the Aelfir a new religion.'

'How long have we got?' Samuel said, rubbing his forehead, wishing he could feel the reassuring presence of his magic. 'When will the Panopticon meet? When will they vote on the Labyrinth?'

'Within the next few days.'

'We have to find a way to keep that supply line open,' Samuel said. 'The reserves won't last long, not with a million mouths to feed. The denizens will run out of food in less than a week, Tal.' He swore.

'Samuel, the best thing you can do for the denizens is to continue following the avatar. In the meantime, I'm going to rally every sympathiser you've got left in the Panopticon. With Sunflower taken from me, I've got nothing left to lose. I might be old, but I still remember how to gather intelligence. And how to manipulate people with it.

'I'm going to call in every favour to gather allies, and use every trick

I know, blackmail councillors into supporting me if I have to. When the Houses gather, I will stand up and address the entire Panopticon. By the time I have finished, they will *all* know that the Genii have returned, and the full horror of what they are planning to do.' Tal gritted his teeth. 'Every House ruler *will* understand that the agents of the Relic Guild are risking their lives, as they always have, to protect all of us.'

Tal paused to cut the trawler's engine and steer the boat towards a jetty near the base of Little Sibling.

The elderly Aelf peered at Samuel's shadowed face. 'I've been keeping an eye on the Sisterhood for a very long time. I'm going to call each member out, if necessary, reveal every dirty little secret that I've ever collected on them and publicly shame them into doing what's right.'

Samuel saw fire in the elderly Aelf's face, perhaps catching a glimpse of the dangerous person Tal had been during the war. 'Will it work?' the old bounty hunter said. 'Do you think they'll hear you?'

'I have to pray that someone will,' Tal replied as he brought the trawler to a halt against the jetty with a gentle bump. 'This isn't just about Labrys Town, Samuel. Spiral, the Genii, the Retrospective – *this* threatens everything. But, for what it's worth, I will stand by the denizens of Labrys Town until I am no longer able to stand. You have my word on that.'

And Samuel believed him.

'But for now,' Tal added, 'you need to trust me. I can't pretend to understand the avatar's methods, or why it separated you from Clara and Van Bam, but I do understand that only the Relic Guild can stop Spiral and the Genii. Focus on that, Samuel. Let me worry about everything else.'

Samuel stared out morosely at the dark waters of the River Bells, feeling acutely the absence of his magic.

Namji stuck her head into the control room. 'Are we ready?' she said.

Hillem and Glogelder stood behind her.

With anxiety gnawing at his stomach, Samuel tried to summon his resolve. 'I suppose so,' he said, and gave Tal an appreciative nod.

When Samuel disembarked he leaned back and peered up the

length of the giant clock tower of Little Sibling. He was so close to its huge base that he couldn't see the moon of its clock face. The jetty was broken in places, obviously unused for years, and a little rickety. Dodging the holes in the wooden planks, Tal led the way, holding a glow lamp.

The old riverside path was lined by trees and foliage, overgrown and thick, and it gave no hint of the buildings beyond. The foliage ended where Little Sibling began, and Tal took them down a second path that ran alongside the clock tower's base. The glow lamp swung, and shadows danced in the pale, violet light.

'There aren't many people left alive who remember this path,' the councillor said. 'It hasn't been used since the end of the Genii War. Here we are.'

He came to a halt at the thick metal bars of a gate.

'This is the secret entrance to the old dungeons,' Tal explained. 'It was last used to smuggle war criminals down to the cells – people whom we had decided didn't deserve a fair trial. None of them saw the light of day again.'

As Tal inspected the gate in the light of the glow lamp, Samuel wondered how many of those war criminals had disappeared because of the elderly councillor.

'A few of us were given special power stones that would release the magic on this gate's locking mechanism,' Tal said. 'But even if I still had mine, I don't think it would be much use anymore.' He gave the gate a half-hearted shake. 'The magic probably faded years ago, but the lock and hinges are completely rusted up.' He looked back at Samuel. 'As an agent of the Relic Guild, you must be prepared for such an occasion?'

From a pouch on his utility belt, Samuel removed a phial of acid. Metal hissed and melted as he dripped its contents onto the lock and hinges. After carefully returning the phial to his utility belt, Samuel motioned for Glogelder to help him. Together they pulled the heavy gate from the tunnel entrance, and set it aside.

'And this is where I leave you, I'm afraid,' Tal said, handing the glow lamp to Hillem. 'Just follow the tunnel. It leads straight to the dungeon's entrance.'

'Once again, Councillor, thank you for your help,' said Namji.

'My pleasure,' Tal replied, and then to Samuel: 'Whatever you find down there, whatever happens next – good luck.'

'And to you,' Samuel replied earnestly.

The elderly Aelf offered his hand, and the old bounty hunter shook it. Samuel missed his magic. He missed Van Bam and Clara.

Tal looked slowly from person to person. 'Goodbye, my friends,' he said sadly. 'I hope to see you again.'

CHAPTER NINETEEN

THREE TRUTHS AND AN ECHO

Van Bam remembered the Museum of Aelfirian Heritage. He remembered stepping through the doorway. But he didn't know where he was now.

He couldn't feel his body, couldn't move. Paralysed, he was staring into the face of a man no more than a foot away. The man's features filled Van Bam's vision with a clarity of colours and detail that he had not experienced in forty years – not since before he lost his eyes. And the man was staring back at the illusionist, into him, through him.

Van Bam tried to summon Gideon, but he could not remember how to use his voice, not even in thought. And he knew that none of his colleagues were with him. Somehow he realised that he was not really standing before the man; Van Bam's mind had been hijacked.

The man was a Thaumaturgist; the diamond tattooed onto his forehead was starkly black against a weathered face much older-looking than Van Bam had ever seen on a creature of higher magic. He did not wear the usual elegant purple robe of a Thaumaturgist, but a simple russet habit, cheap and itchy-looking. His hair was unruly and thinning, beard long and grey. His appearance did not seem natural to Van Bam, more the parts of a carefully constructed exterior. It was an inoffensive look, belonging to a pauper, a harmless vagabond. But at that moment, the man looked desolate.

A detached and alien part of Van Bam recognised the raggedy Thaumaturgist, and he knew his name belonged to a dead man, the Skywatcher known as the Wanderer. Lord Baran Wolfe.

Still staring at Van Bam, Lord Wolfe moved back a few paces. The view revealed he was in some kind of amphitheatre, or auditorium. Stone steps, flanked by rows of bench seats, descended to a floor of dusty wooden boards. The ceiling was an artistic mural depicting men and women addressing an audience. Van Bam could see the far end of the auditorium had no wall. Five thick pillars stood before a barren landscape of rocks and mountains beneath a giant sun that drained all colour from the sky. The landscape was pale grey, the colour of skin dust. In the distance, mighty falls spilled from mountain plateaus, but not falls of water: a thick and grainy substance dropped from the mountaintops, sparkling beneath the sun like a hundred thousand stars cascading into deep ravines.

Van Bam knew this House.

Baran Wolfe, the old vagabond Thaumaturgist, stared wearily at the illusionist.

'My dear Lady Amilee,' Wolfe said. 'Not so long ago, you told me that I was a fool. You told me that I was wrong – paranoid, you called me. How I wish I *was* paranoid, my lady. How I wish I was foolish *and* wrong. How I wish you were right.'

Van Bam could only watch and listen. Somehow he knew he was listening to a voice of the past. By a twist of magic, the illusionist had become trapped inside a recording device, hearing a message recorded decades ago.

Wolfe sighed. 'Against your advice, I have been following the clues that I gleaned from my divinations. But as we *discussed*, my lady – the skies have not been quite as forthcoming of late as you believe. But, I have deciphered enough to know three things for certain, three whispers from the skies that speak of truths that have already come to pass. And somehow these three truths have been concealed from us.

'The first speaks of a House that is hidden from our sight within the Nothing of Far and Deep. It is called the Cathedral of Doubt and Wonder, and, no matter what I try, how hard I search, it proves impossible to find. The second is a device that is kept secret at the Cathedral of Doubt and Wonder. I do not know what this device is for, but it is called Known Things, and I am positive that it holds the answers to all the mysteries that have been plaguing my dreams for far too long now.'

Wolfe paused and his face flushed angrily. 'The third truth is by far the most disturbing. I know what you would tell me, my lady, but ...' Wolfe closed his eyes and drew a deep breath, perhaps steeling himself. 'After we *disagreed* at our last meeting, I decided to continue my investigations, regardless of your advice. Much has happened between then and now, and I have finally gained clarity.'

Lord Wolfe's eyes welled with tears. It was the saddest thing Van Bam had ever seen.

'Treasured Lady,' Wolfe continued, 'my fellow Skywatcher, my friend.' He wiped his eyes. 'Every vision the sky has tried to show me, every clue it has tried to whisper, has led me here to this House. And if this message sphere has reached you, then you were wrong, my dear Yansas Amilee, and I was so very, terribly, right. The Trinity of Skywatchers has failed—'

Wolfe stiffened and looked over his shoulder. 'Ah, the time has come.'

Turning away, Wolfe leapt. His silver wings flashed from his robe and stretched wide, sleek and fluid, strong and graceful, each as long as the Skywatcher's arm span. Wolfe glided upon them, over the benches, down towards the wooden floor.

Van Bam felt a lurch, a change inside him, as though his consciousness had become nothing more than a memory of who he used to be; and suddenly, dizzyingly, he was an echo of Van Bam inside the mind of Baran Wolfe the Wanderer, thinking his thoughts, seeing through the Skywatcher's eyes, feeling with his skin, as he came to land, and folded silver wings upon his back.

Clasping his hands before him, Wolfe stared across the floor, facing the five pillars at the open end of the auditorium. The echo of Van Bam knew who Wolfe was waiting for.

And he had arrived.

Borne on wings of silver, a man landed gracefully at the edge of the floor just beyond the great pillars. Against the light, he was nothing more than a tall and broad silhouette. He folded his wings, but remained where he was. When he spoke, his voice was rich, cultured, stronger and more commanding than any voice belonging to a creature of higher magic.

'Baran Wolfe,' he said, 'Honoured Lord of the Thaumaturgists. Welcome to the Falls of Dust and Silver.'

'You have been expecting me, my lord?' Wolfe replied, afraid but calm.

'Since the beginning.'

With a light chuckle, the man stepped past the pillars and into the auditorium, away from the harsh glare of the light. Walking with a slow but confident step, he wore a black, flowing skirt, the hem skimming the floor, swirling with each step, giving fleeting glimpses of bare feet. From the waist up, he was naked, the smooth skin and muscles of his torso decorated with black tattoos: strangely designed symbols, glyphs, shapes that comprised the language of the Thaumaturgists. His head was bald, shaved smooth, but he boasted a thick black beard. His eyes were such a bright and clear violet they practically shone from his lean, chiselled face, utterly devoid of emotion.

Simultaneously beautiful and terrible, Spiral, First Lord of the Thaumaturgists, made his way towards Wolfe.

The echo of Van Bam panicked.

'What have you done to yourself, Iblisha?' Wolfe said, using Spiral's true name. His voice, frail with age, was sad, regretful. 'Where is your mark of higher magic? Your promise to serve the Timewatcher?'

'My dear, dear Baran,' Spiral replied. He gently touched a finger to a wound on his forehead; a fresh burn mark, red and wet, where a black diamond tattoo had once been. 'I made the decision to break my promise some time ago. I am free from the Timewatcher's restraints.'

Wolfe seemed close to tears. 'You betray our Mother. Break the Trinity of Skywatchers. Why, Iblisha?'

'There are many reason I could give,' Spiral replied. 'Perhaps I should start with *power*.'

'Power?' said Wolfe. 'My lord, you are the Timewatcher's favoured son. You are the strongest and wisest among us. How much more power do you need?'

'The kind that comes with freedom, Baran. Don't you ever question the status quo? Don't you believe in change?'

'I believe in the way things are.'

'Then you place your faith in stagnation.'

The violet colour of Spiral's eyes flared and dimmed as he advanced to within several paces of Wolfe. Physically, he was already taller, broader than his fellow Skywatcher; but the depth of higher magic he radiated made him seem larger still. The echo of Van Bam felt his presence weighing down on him, heavy, ancient, like a judge's gavel preparing to strike.

'For a thousand years the Timewatcher has forced us to uphold this ridiculous charade of equality,' Spiral said. 'I tire of pretending to be less than I am, and I say *no more*.'

'What do you hope to achieve?' Wolfe said. 'What will this *power of freedom* gain you?'

'To begin with, I will make the millions – *billions* – of Aelfir out there understand that they have never been my equal.'

An ember of anger bloomed into life within Baran Wolfe. 'You speak as though equality diminishes your strength, Iblisha.' His voice was quiet. 'It does not. It diminishes the need for oppression and war. It creates peace.'

Spiral's amusement was evident. 'Do you know what the greatest trick the Timewatcher ever played is, Baran? She convinced the Aelfir that their lives are wrapped around genuine freedom and choice, that they are masters of their own destinies. I will use *my* freedom to dispel such delusions.'

'You seek to abuse your position,' Wolfe countered.

'With respect, I disagree,' Spiral said dangerously. 'I once begged the Timewatcher to see sense. Rule, I told Her. Rule as any hierarch should. Do away with this façade of gentle benevolence that asks only for love and faith in return for all you give. *Demand* worship and loyalty from the lower creatures, I said. *Teach* the Aelfir their true place. *Force* them down onto their knees while they *pray* to you!'

As Spiral spoke, the passion in his voice had risen like fire. The tattoos of the thaumaturgic language darkened upon his naked torso, as if the ink itself had come from a black void. The echo of Van Bam willed Baran Wolfe to step away from Spiral, to flee from this auditorium in the Falls of Dust and Silver.

'But would She listen to me, Baran?' Spiral took a calming breath. 'The Timewatcher is no ruler, She is a peacekeeper. She has enforced her power, yet does nothing with it, and She has made us vulnerable as a result. I will not wait another thousand years, hoping for change, while playing along with this lie of equality. Baran, before the end, the

Timewatcher's hypocrisy will have the Thaumaturgists bending at the waist to the creatures of lower magic.'

Boldly, defiantly, Wolfe took two steps towards his fellow Skywatcher. 'Does your belief extend to the humans?' he asked.

'*Humans*,' Spiral snorted. 'What is the point of their existence?'

The ember of anger inside Wolfe became a bed of hot coals. 'Did you use the same reasoning to justify the ambushing of the Nephilim herd, my lord?'

Spiral's thick beard parted as he showed Wolfe his clenched teeth; his beauty seemed all the more terrifying. 'What – you believe I should treat those *abominations* as equals, too?' He shook his head, disappointed. 'You speak of lesser beings as though they deserve our compassion, Lord Wolfe, like the old and blind fool you are.

'You think that the humans are competent, perhaps? The Timewatcher did not give them the Great Labyrinth because of their benevolence and wisdom, you know. She did it because of their weakness. She said their inability to wield and abuse the boundless thaumaturgy *She* had imbued into the Labyrinth made them perfect custodians. The humans are nothing but caretakers.'

Spiral took two steps towards Wolfe. 'The Great Labyrinth should have belonged to the Thaumaturgists from the moment it was completed. And once I have rid the Houses of our Mother's hypocrisy, I will take the Labyrinth from the humans, and use it to rule the Aelfir. The Timewatcher has had her day.'

Wolfe took a step back. Sadness doused the rising heat inside him, his disillusion battling against acceptance. 'Iblisha, you will bring us to war.'

'Yes. I have *seen* it.' Spiral's violet eyes flashed with fervour. 'I do not stand alone, Baran.' He gestured around the amphitheatre, to the glittering world outside. 'The Falls of Dust and Silver is not the only Aelfirian House to support me. Many others agree that it is time a new regime ruled the realms. And there are more creatures of higher magic who also believe the time of our Mother is at an end.'

Wolfe licked his lips. 'Other Thaumaturgists have turned against the Timewatcher?' The echo of Van Bam was terrified. 'Who?'

'There are more than you would likely believe, Baran,' said Spiral. 'I have my army, I have my generals, and we are ready to strike.'

'How was this possible?' Wolfe breathed. 'How did you hide this from me, from Lady Amilee, from the Timewatcher Herself?'

Pride came to Spiral's face. 'Yes, I suspect the skies have been a little difficult for you to read of late. I have been planning for this moment for so very long.'

Spiral beckoned to someone behind Wolfe. The Wanderer turned as he heard footsteps. The man approaching wore a black cassock and his long hair, straight and white, fell about his shoulders. Like Spiral, he had a fresh wound on his forehead where he had burned the black diamond of higher magic from his skin with acid.

The echo of Van Bam desperately wanted to flee.

'Lord Moor?' Wolfe said.

Fabian Moor ignored the Skywatcher and walked to Spiral. In his hands, he held a box of black stone, with the polished finish of obsidian, and shaped like a diamond. Spiral took it from him.

'Oh, Fabian,' Wolfe said despairingly. 'What have you done?'

Without replying, his face inscrutable, Moor took up a place behind his new master.

'Look at it, Baran,' Spiral said, holding the diamond-shaped box up proudly. 'I created this device from unused time. It contains a gap, a hole that I punched into the fabric of reality. I have been filling that hole with my plans and actions – every deed, every conversation, every thought. That is why you have not been able to divine me. I hid the truth from the sky.'

'Impossible,' Wolfe whispered. 'The only one who can manipulate the substance of time in this way is … is …'

'Who, Baran? The Timewatcher?'

Fabian Moor's affectation of indifference did not hold as he gave Wolfe a cruel sneer. The echo of Van Bam recoiled, not wishing to witness any more.

'Our great Mother is unaware just how powerful her favoured son has grown,' Spiral said proudly. 'Inside this device is my own personal slipstream, Baran, where my plot to overthrow the Timewatcher hides.' He turned the diamond-shaped box over in his hands, studying it almost lovingly. 'I have called it Known Things.'

'Known Things,' Wolfe repeated, 'where all the answers lie,' and he laughed bitterly. The echo inside him understood the importance of what he was witnessing. 'Then tell me, my Lord Spiral,' said Wolfe, 'what is the Cathedral of Doubt and Wonder?'

Fabian Moor gave Spiral an alarmed look, but Spiral assuaged his concerns with a snorting laugh.

'I have to admit that I'm impressed, Lord Wolfe,' he said. 'I had considered Known Things a perfect creation, but obviously you found a flaw. It is commendable – a testament to your power – that you were able to divine enough to lead you to me here at the Falls of Dust and Silver.

'As to the nature of the Cathedral of Doubt and Wonder ... well, as we've established, the Timewatcher isn't the only creature of higher magic able to manipulate the substance of time. The Cathedral is my war room, my private council chambers, concealed in the Nothing of Far and Deep. It is where I meet with my Genii.'

'Genii?' Wolfe queried.

'Ah, forgive me, Baran. Allow me to explain.' Spiral leant back and called out a further summons. 'You can come forward now!'

From behind Wolfe, three more renegade Thaumaturgists appeared, and joined Fabian Moor behind Spiral. Each wore an identical black cassock, and bore fresh burn wounds on their foreheads.

The first of them was a tall and painfully thin woman, her face small, pale as porcelain, with long hair as black as night. Next to her was another woman, not so tall but broader; her sandy hair was short, and she had the face of a predator, almost feline. The last of them dwarfed even Lord Spiral. He stood next to Fabian Moor, obese and hulking, his head bald, his face cruel.

Wolfe recognised each of the newcomers instantly: Mo Asajad, Hagi Tabet and Viktor Gadreel.

'We are Thaumaturgists no longer,' Spiral told Wolfe. 'We are the Genii.'

Standing defiant, Wolfe made a last appeal, 'Please, Iblisha, I beg you – all of you – it is not too late. End this madness now.'

'*Madness*?' Spiral roared.

His eyes flashing, with Known Things still in his hands, the Lord of the Genii stepped forwards, flexed his back, and his wings sprang out like swords drawn from their sheaths. Wolfe did the same, and the two Skywatchers confronted each other, their fluid, silver wings fanned out behind them. The four Genii watched.

Wolfe tried to summon his thaumaturgy to attack, to escape, to create the chance to warn the realms of the coming storm, but Iblisha Spiral was quicker, and much more powerful. Barely moving, his skin glowing, Spiral batted aside his foe's attack as easily as swatting a fly. And then he wrapped his higher magic around Wolfe, squeezing him, crushing the fight from him. Wolfe's wings fell limp as Spiral drove him to his knees.

'I knew you would come, Baran,' said Spiral, his voice like a thousand arrows raining from the sky. He tapped the diamond-shaped box of unused time in his hands. 'I *saw* it.'

Spiral drew a shuddery breath as he siphoned the thaumaturgy from Wolfe's body, devoured it, added it to his own power.

'Iblisha, please …' Wolfe groaned.

But the plea fell on deaf ears.

By the time Spiral had drained his fellow Skywatcher of higher magic, the echo of Van Bam felt as though his soul had been stolen.

Spiral's eyes were luminous, violet orbs as he looked back at his Genii. 'Viktor, take his wings.'

Gadreel didn't hesitate. The brutish Genii stamped forward and moved in on Wolfe, to carry out his lord's order.

Still trapped in the clutches of Spiral's thaumaturgy, weakened by the loss of his own magic, Wolfe could only issue a series of piteous cries as Viktor Gadreel ripped the silver wings from his back, tearing flesh and muscle, breaking bones.

The echo of Van Bam screamed.

When Gadreel was done, he dropped the wings upon the auditorium floor in front of Wolfe. They had lost all malleability, and thumped to the dusty wooden boards as solid silver, smeared in the blood of the Skywatcher. Gadreel returned with bloodied hands to stand alongside his fellow Genii.

'Had Lady Amilee been in your position,' Spiral said, 'she would have had the good sense to come here with reinforcements' His beautiful, terrible face betrayed no emotion, but a single tear ran down his face into his thick beard. 'But you, my dear Baran, always trusted to logic, assured that reason would prevail – the *compassion* of the Time-watcher.'

Defeated, torn and stripped of power, Wolfe had not the strength to weep.

'But we do not have to walk separate paths, my brother,' Spiral continued. 'I would like you to see what I have done. I would have you serve at my side, just as you and I once served our Mother. I've no need to hide anymore.'

Wolfe and the echo of Van Bam could do nothing but watch, as Spiral held Known Things out at arm's length and once again summoned his higher magic. The black tattoos of the thaumaturgic language moved upon his body, the shapes and symbols losing their forms, becoming straight lines that began sliding over his muscles. Like snakes they slithered up to his shoulders, travelled down his arms, over his hands, and onto the smooth, glassy surface of the obsidian diamond that he held.

The language of the Thaumaturgists reconfigured upon Known Things, and each symbol flared with the purple light of higher magic.

'You came here for answers, Baran, and I will give them to you,' Spiral whispered. Tears were falling freely from his violet eyes. 'You will be my records keeper, and you shall have a title. You will be Voice of Known Things.'

As Spiral approached Wolfe, two gelatinous tubes emerged from the obsidian body of the diamond-shaped box, and the symbols of Thaumaturgy intensified, the purple light blazing like fire. The gelatinous tubes whipped the air, as they advanced on Wolfe's face. The echo of Van Bam sobbed and begged for mercy as Spiral gave Known Things its voice.

Ringing like a wet finger sliding around the rim of a wine glass, one of the gelatinous tubes set as hard as crystal and stabbed into Lord Wolfe's temple, punching through his skull and lancing into his brain. The other tube slid into his mouth, down his throat, into his airway, where it too hardened to glass. Wolfe's eyes closed as fluid ran along the tubes, and he began forgetting everything he had ever been. Known

Things filled his lungs with Spiral's concealed truths, and poured hidden time into his mind.

Mercifully, the echo of Van Bam was thrown from the Skywatcher's body. His vision raced back until he was again observing from the safe confines of the message sphere, secreted in a high corner of the auditorium.

Slumped on the dusty wooden floor, in a pool of his own blood, Baran Wolfe, the Wanderer, Honoured Lord of the Thaumaturgists, was on his knees. Broken and drained of higher magic, eyes closed, the glass umbilici connected him to the black diamond in his hands. Spiral stood over him, tall and powerful. The Genii were lined up behind their lord.

At a flick of Spiral's hand the diamond tattoo on Wolfe's forehead smouldered and burned away, leaving a red and ugly wound.

'Now, tell me your name,' Spiral demanded.

'Voice of Known Things.' The reply seemed to come from all places at once, each word provoking the thaumaturgic symbols on the box to flare.

'And what is your purpose?'

'To speak the truths that the Lord Spiral wishes me to speak.'

'Very good,' said Spiral. 'Hagi.'

Lady Tabet stepped up alongside him. 'Yes, my lord?'

Spiral pointed at the silver wings on the floor, coated in the blood. 'Take those, but do not clean them. Ensure they are delivered to Lady Amilee exactly as they are.'

'With pleasure, my lord.'

Hagi Tabet approached the wings with an outstretched hand. Summoning her thaumaturgy, she lifted them off the floor. With the silver appendages floating before her, Tabet walked past Voice of Known Things, and disappeared from Van Bam's view.

'Lady Asajad,' Spiral said, 'you will remain here. The Falls of Dust and Silver is now yours to command. Go about your duties.'

'As you wish, my lord,' Mo Asajad said. Breathless with excitement she too left the auditorium.

'And you, Viktor,' Spiral continued. 'It is time to alert our fellow Genii. Tell them to burn the mark of the Thaumaturgist from their skins, and rally our Aelfirian allies. Tell them the time has come. Tell them to prepare for war.'

With a savage glint in his eyes, Viktor Gadreel strode away.

Spiral turned to the last remaining Genii.

'Fabian,' he said affectionately.

Lord Moor drew himself up, proud and eager to serve the creature of higher magic before him.

'You have been with me from the beginning,' Spiral said. 'The first to follow me, my most trusted confidant.'

'What would you have me do, my lord?'

'First, you are to take Voice of Known Things back to the Cathedral of Doubt and Wonder. You will find Yves Harrow waiting for you there. He knows what to do with this wretch next.'

Moor nodded. 'And then, my lord?'

'And then you are to wait for me. There is a duty that I trust only you to perform, Fabian. Your part in the coming war might prove the most dangerous of all.'

As Moor strode towards Voice of Known Things, the images darkened until Van Bam knew true blindness for the first time, and the last echo of his consciousness faded to silence.

CHAPTER TWENTY

UNKNOWN THINGS

Clara's mind cleared. She found herself facing Van Bam. The two of them were surrounded by a soft blue glow. The shaken expression on the illusionist's face convinced Clara that he had witnessed the same thing as herself.

'Shit,' Clara said. 'Did we just see the start of the Genii War?'

Van Bam could only nod. He looked as confused as she felt.

Clara shook herself, and rubbed her face. She knew that what she had experienced had been much more than merely *seeing* the start of the Genii War. It was as though her spirit had been dragged back forty years in time, to a place that didn't exist in the present, a House called the Falls of Dust and Silver. Clara had suffered the anxiety, the humiliation, the agony that belonged to Lord Baran Wolfe. She knew, profoundly, how it felt to be betrayed by a fellow Skywatcher.

'Samuel is not with us,' Van Bam said.

Clara looked around. Nor were Namji, Hillem and Glogelder.

The changeling and the illusionist stood in a strange chamber enclosed by blue glass. Clara had no memory of arriving in it. Beyond the transparent walls, thick and luminous mists wrapped the chamber. For some reason, the absence of Samuel and the others didn't strike Clara as odd. Somehow, it made sense that they wouldn't be there.

'I wonder where they are?' Clara said.

'Evidently, they were not meant to come with us,' Van Bam replied. 'We can only hope that this is all part of the plan.'

Lightning flashed, silent but fierce as it cut through the luminous mist outside, clawing upon the surface of the blue glass chamber with spiky fingers of energy – above, below, and all around.

Forget the others for now, Gideon said. *I think we are travelling through the Nothing of Far and Deep.*

Gideon, I—

Stop, Clara, the dead Resident snapped. *You, Van Bam and I have all experienced the same thing, and we're as confused as each other. Don't complicate the issue by speaking mentally. I have no desire to play messenger while the three of us are together like this.*

'I don't understand,' she said aloud. 'The doorway at the museum – it was supposed to take us to Known Things. So where are we?'

'Given what we have just been through,' Van Bam replied, 'I would say that we have been delivered to some kind of information storage device, perhaps a greater version of a message sphere.'

Makes sense, Gideon said to them both. *Our shared experience was as witnesses to events of the past.*

Clara shuddered as she remembered how it felt to have silver wings ripped from her back. 'This thing is carrying us through the Nothing of Far and Deep?'

'So it would seem.'

'To where?' Clara looked at the cloth wrapped around her hand. A circle of blood had soaked through from the cut on her palm. She thought about how it had felt to use blood-magic to open the doorway in the Museum of Aelfirian Heritage, and she remembered what Gideon had told her about his ancestors. 'How do the Nephilim fit into this?'

'I do not know,' Van Bam said. He gripped his cane tightly in both hands, and turned his metallic eyes to the ceiling as more lightning danced upon their blue glass carriage. 'I am struggling to clear my thoughts, to understand what any of this means.'

Let's all of us take a breath, and put this together piece by piece, advised Gideon. The ghost spoke without a shred of his customary spite. *At least we now know what Known Things is.*

A records device that Spiral created from unused time. Clara had no idea what that meant, but she remembered vividly how it felt to be connected to Known Things, if only for a brief moment. It was not an experience she wished to repeat. But did she have a choice? Was that how the location of Oldest Place would be extracted from her?

Gideon continued, *I think the most telling fact is, whom Lord Wolfe recorded that message for.*

'Lady Amilee,' Van Bam whispered.

Clara had heard that name mentioned a hundred times before, but only now, with the residue of Baran Wolfe's suffering still within her, did she truly comprehend what it stood for. Lady Amilee, the Thaumaturgist, the Skywatcher, the patron of the denizens …

'It was Amilee who showed us Wolfe's message,' Clara said. 'She must be the avatar's master.'

Van Bam agreed. 'Then not all of the Thaumaturgists abandoned the Houses. But was Lady Amilee the only one who remained?'

'And why doesn't she show herself?' Clara said.

A good question, Gideon purred. *All we can be certain of is that Amilee wants you to reach Known Things, Clara. And I think, via Lord Wolfe's suffering, she has just told us where we can expect to find it.*

Clara flinched as the wall behind Van Bam shattered into a million pieces of blue glass that swirled away, sucked into the luminous mists. The magickers backed away as a circular tunnel formed in the mist. It stretched away from the open chamber, cutting a pathway through the Nothing of Far and Deep; and at its end, churned the blackness of a portal.

A lonely wind moaned. The portal rushed towards the chamber. Clara and Van Bam steeled themselves.

'Clara,' said Van Bam. His face was calm, but she could smell his fear. 'Perhaps it would be a good idea if you changed into the wolf.'

The Lazy House, nightclub and a whorehouse, was thriving. Firearms were prohibited in the club, and it didn't matter how important or notorious you were, or which particular skillset you specialised in, everyone was neutral within its walls. It formed a common ground for Labrys Town's underworld. The police feared it like criminals feared the Nightshade. But it wasn't the clientele that disturbed officers, it was the vice and corruption so readily available: temptation, abandonment, revelry – the Lazy House catered for all weaknesses.

Muffled music resonated through the stairs with a low, driving throb as Ennis made his way up to the second floor. The small wooden token in his hand, no bigger than a coin, bore the number four. It had cost Ennis twenty Labyrinth pounds, and afforded him one hour to conduct private business in a private room.

Ennis didn't consider himself beyond temptation, but he hadn't come to this place to sample its sins; he was trying to gather information on the magickers of the Relic Guild, and thus far he had discovered nothing of use. As he made his way up the stairs, the heartbeat of the Lazy House thrumming beneath his feet, he felt that nothing he had found out was making much sense.

Ennis was trying to piece together a profile of the Relic Guild. He reasoned that if he understood the magickers a little more, he might gain an insight into their methods that would provide him with a clue to their movements, their haunts, hiding places – anything.

Earlier, after leaving the shard of strange metal at Long Tommy's junkshop, Ennis had visited a couple of bounty hunters he knew. He had questioned them about Old Man Sam, the deadliest bounty hunter in Labrys Town, some would say, and undoubtedly the longest serving. They had known his reputation, but nothing about him at all. Ennis had then tried a few police informants, but they had been as clueless about Sam as the merchants had been about Van Bam.

How Old Man Sam had managed to conceal his true identity for all these years was a mystery. If it wasn't for the stack of fulfilled bounty contracts and dead bodies the old bounty hunter had left behind him, Ennis would have begun to doubt he ever existed at all. He was like a phantom. The only useful information Ennis had uncovered came from the police reports. Old Man Sam had a hideout, a secret apartment hidden in the middle of other apartments in the central district. Ennis had gone there, and found it empty, a sad and dingy home, shot up by some bounty hunters who had tried to fulfil the contract on Old Man Sam's head. Bounty hunters who were never seen again.

With first Van Bam and now Old Man Sam leading Ennis to a dead end, only one member of the Relic Guild remained on his list. And the search to discover more about her had brought the police sergeant to the Lazy House.

Ennis reached the second floor and entered a dimly lit hallway. The growl of the nightclub became a faint hum rising through the thick carpet beneath his feet. Closed doors to private chambers flanked him, dampening the guttural exclamations of sex. The spicy tang of narcotic smoke laced the air. Ennis found the room he wanted. He didn't knock; he didn't need to.

The young woman in the room was sitting on a stool by a vanity table. She was dressed for work. Her hair was long, twisted into fat locks that sprang from her head like a nest of spider legs. Heavy, concealing makeup decorated her face. Her legs were crossed, one thigh displayed. The front of her silk dressing gown formed a low V between her breasts.

'You must be Willow,' Ennis said, closing the door behind him.

She answered with a professional smile. 'I don't recognise your face,' she said, her voice low. 'Is this your first visit to the Lazy House?'

Ennis returned her smile, but didn't answer.

Willow's room seemed spiritless – clean but without character, as if she had strategically removed her personality from view, hidden it in the vanity table, the wardrobe, under the freshly made bed, beneath her makeup.

Secrets...

'Are you shy?' Willow said, looking Ennis up and down. 'Do you need me to come and take that ... *token* from you?'

Ennis looked at the wooden coin in his hand. With a casual flip, he sent it spinning across the room. Willow caught it in a clap, and a touch of steel came to her eyes.

'More confident than you look,' she said.

Ennis shrugged. 'I just want to talk.'

The smile returned to Willow's face far too easily. 'I've known a few talkers in my time' – Her *time*? Ennis wondered. She looked shy of twenty '– but you don't look like one of those to me.'

'Then how *do* I look?'

'Like you're not supposed to be noticed,' Willow said. 'Like people only know you're there if you let them see you.'

Clever...

'I want to talk to you about your friend,' Ennis said.

'My *friend*?' Willow narrowed her eyes. 'You mean one I like, or one who pays me?'

'Your work colleague. Peppercorn Clara. I'm told the two of you were close.'

'Oh, I see.' Willow's expression didn't alter. 'Funny – I never would've pegged you as a policeman.' She looked at the wooden token in her hands. 'Are you here to arrest me? Lead me at gunpoint to the nearest station? Or the Nightshade?'

Unconcerned ...

Ennis said, 'I'm not going to arrest you, and I'm not armed. I just have questions about Peppercorn.'

'I've already told the police everything I know.'

'But you haven't told *me*. Don't worry, this is off the record. No one will know I've been to see you.'

'Well then ...' Willow opened a drawer in the vanity table, and placed the token inside it. 'You want to talk about Clara.'

Dangerous ...

By the time Ennis recognised the sudden whining noise of a power stone being primed, Willow had already removed her hand from the drawer holding a snub-nosed pistol. She aimed it directly at him.

'Get on your knees, please.' Her voice and expression remained exactly as they had been before.

'Wait,' Ennis said, raising his hands. 'What are you doing?'

'I told you to get on your knees.' Willow's hand was steady. 'I won't ask you again, *Sergeant Ennis*.'

'All right,' Ennis said calmly, and he did as Willow ordered. 'Who told you I was coming?'

'Shut up and put your hands on your head.' Once Ennis had complied, Willow called out, 'It's him. You can come in now.'

The door opened, and an old man walked in. He gave Ennis a hard stare.

Long Tommy ...

Ennis's mind raced, but before he could protest, Long Tommy had stepped forwards, and broken a small glass ampoule beneath his nose. It released a powerful vapour that filled Ennis's nostrils, and he gasped it into his lungs. The room span and Ennis fell onto his side.

Blinking convulsively, unable to speak, he looked up at his aggressors, his thoughts scattered.

He saw Tommy offering Willow a fold of money.

'I don't care what you're doing,' Willow said. 'I just don't want it coming back at me. Got it?'

'Get out,' Tommy replied.

Willow snatched the money and walked away, pausing on the threshold to glance down at Ennis.

'Just so you know,' she said, 'Clara always hated that name. Peppercorn. It was a bad joke made up by her clients. She was a good person.'

The door closed, and Long Tommy bent over Ennis. The expression on his old face was a strange mix of pity and rage. The light around him was fading.

'I hear you've been asking about Old Man Sam,' Tommy said. It was as though he spoke down a tunnel. 'There're one or two things I can tell you about that bastard.'

The old man reached down.

Ennis couldn't feel his body and he was rolled over onto his front. His vision was failing, his mind slipping away.

'There's more to you than meets the eye, Sergeant,' Tommy added. "I tested that metal for you, and … we really need a good chat.'

CHAPTER TWENTY ONE

THE ORIGINS OF THE NECROMANCER

An almighty crack of energy brought Hamir's mind back to the lush garden in Lady Amilee's dreamscape.

The big ball of blue glass slipped from the necromancer's hands, bumping gently to the grass, and rolling away to stop several feet from him. He stared at the message sphere, its contents brutally fresh in his thoughts: a device called Known Things, a House called the Falls of Dust and Silver, the pain and torment suffered by Lord Wolfe the Wanderer at the hands of the Genii …

Wrenching, a huge noise like that of a mighty tree splitting in two, pulled Hamir's attention to the spinning, droning column of energy that rose up from the garden, high into a perfect sky. Amilee's slipstream was in the process of shedding yet another timeline. A tendril of static energy uncoiled from the column, peeling away to twist and wave in the air like a streamer. Slowly, it lost cohesion, breaking apart into black and white chips that blew away to nothing on the breeze like ash and smoke from a fire. The slipstream shrank, became thinner, and Hamir knew that only two of the Skywatcher's timelines remained.

The necromancer looked around Amilee's garden, the colours of the flowers in bloom, the small grove of apple trees close by; insects buzzed and flew in drunken lines, the green of the grass was verdant, rich, real … Hamir's mind was alight with what the blue glass sphere had shown him: the beginning of the Genii War, Lord Spiral's first strike against the Timewatcher. But there was a glaring contradiction in what he had seen, a discrepancy that did not sit well alongside the earlier conversation that he had listened to between Amilee and the avatar.

However clever Spiral had been in creating Known Things, however complicated storing a personal timeline within a device constructed from unused time could be, essentially it was only a records device. Yet

Amilee had told the avatar that it contained the means of destroying the Lord of the Genii, a way of *killing* the most powerful Thaumaturgist who ever stood by the Timewatcher's side. It didn't add up.

Spiral was no fool. The way he had planned his uprising with such intricate detail and infinite patience, such ruthless precision – it was a masterstroke, the work of a genius. He didn't make mistakes. He would not have been so absentminded, so *stupid*, as to include among the contents of Known Things the method of his own demise. Unless . . .

Unless Spiral had a blind spot. Unless there had been something he missed in his planning. If Baran Wolfe had proved anything, it was that Known Things was not without its flaws.

And with this thought, Hamir's mind raced to what he knew about Oldest Place, the realm to which the Timewatcher had incarcerated Spiral.

The necromancer felt a presence close behind him.

He wheeled around. Lady Amilee stood on the grass, the blue sphere between her bare feet, the apple trees behind her. Her silver wings folded beneath her purple robes, she stood straight and regal. Her head was smoothly shaved, her skin flawless except for the tattoo of a black diamond on her forehead. Her face was ageless, perfect. But the anger in her tawny eyes was a millennium old.

Never one to be intimidated, Hamir addressed her, 'I have questions for you, my lady. Tell me about Oldest Place. What is Spiral's relationship with it?'

Amilee only glared at the necromancer.

'All right – then I'll tell you what I believe,' Hamir continued in a cold voice. 'Primarily, Oldest Place is a prison House. Whether it is filled with the fire and poison and hate that the myths claim is beside the point. What is true is that the Timewatcher created Oldest Place as an *eternal* prison and that Spiral is its sole prisoner. His punishment is to be tortured by his own actions for . . . *ever*.'

The Skywatcher blinked, once, slowly.

Hamir had spent so many years not being bothered by anything beyond his own interests, but now he felt a slight tightening in his chest, a small icy sensation in his gut.

Irrespective of the toll such torture might take upon Spiral's mind, if the Timewatcher wanted her greatest foe to suffer eternally, then she would have to keep him physically safe. She would have made sure Spiral was well protected in Oldest Place. While he remained imprisoned in his own, private House, surely nothing could harm him. And if that was a fact, then what could Known Things do to him?

While he remained imprisoned ...

'Unthinkable,' Hamir said. He looked at Amilee. 'Considering the design of Spiral's prison, one might suspect that the only way to bring harm to the Genii Lord would be to release him from Oldest Place first.'

Again, Amilee gave no response.

'Please, my lady, feel free to tell me I'm wrong.' Hamir's voice had risen in pitch, as the Skywatcher still declined to answer. 'Tell me that your plan to destroy Spiral does *not* involve the Genii freeing him from Oldest Place.'

'Your mind clearly hasn't dulled over the years, Hamir,' Amilee said finally, her eyes still full of anger. 'But did you ever learn remorse? Regret? Shame?'

Hamir looked sharply to the slipstream as it gave another mighty *crack*, and the column of dancing, droning energy fell apart in a shower of static that dissipated on the wind, disappearing altogether. But what did that mean? Which of the two remaining timelines had been set in motion? Success? Failure? Both?

Staring into Amilee's tawny eyes, Hamir felt a flush of desperation. 'What have you done?' he demanded.

'I seem to remember that I once asked you the same thing,' Amilee replied.

Hamir felt anger rising inside him. 'There are only two people who know the location of Oldest Place. One is the Timewatcher. The other is a changeling. What will happen when Clara reaches Known Things?'

Amilee raised her head defiantly. 'The agents of the Relic Guild have sworn an oath to protect the denizens of Labrys Town above all other things.'

'Evasiveness is as good as an admission of guilt, my lady,' Hamir growled. 'How do you live with yourself?'

'Perhaps you are in a better position to answer that than me,' Amilee said evenly. 'How did you live with yourself after you created those *abominations*? How did you sleep at night with your dreams haunted by the screams of the one hundred women who were unfortunate enough to be the test subjects in your *experiments*?'

Amilee stepped closer to him. She towered over the necromancer, but he did not shy from her.

The Skywatcher continued, 'The Nephilim tell a story about their creator, you know. They have a name for him. They call their father the *Progenitor*. Does that make you proud, *Lord* Hamir?'

'Another deflection, my lady?' Hamir said offhandedly, but he felt a twist inside, a resentment that he had not experienced in centuries, rising within him, forcing his teeth to clench, his blood to boil like molten metal.

'You speak as though I escaped punishment,' Hamir said, his voice low. 'Perhaps you need reminding that for my crimes I was dragged to Mother Earth, forced to kneel before the Council of Three. For creating the Nephilim, Iblisha Spiral, Baran Wolfe and *you* drained the higher magic from my body, leaving me with only the dregs of my former power.' Hamir jabbed a finger against the scar on his forehead. 'You burned the mark of thaumaturgy from my skin, claiming that I was no longer fit to carry it. And then you banished me to the Labyrinth to spend my days in the Nightshade serving ... *lesser minds*. You made me a phantom of the Thaumaturgist I once was.'

'You were lucky,' Amilee countered. 'If the Trinity had been given its way, your sentence for what you did to those women would have been execution. But the Timewatcher wouldn't allow it. She ordered us to spare your life, so spare it we did. You remain an embarrassment to higher magic, Hamir. You're a murderer, as much of a monster as those perversions you created.'

'I took responsibility for my actions!' Hamir snarled. 'Who will take responsibility for *yours*, my lady? The agents of the Relic Guild?'

Amilee stepped back as though Hamir's words had slapped her face. For the first time, her eyes lost their anger, and she could not hold the necromancer's hostile stare.

'I have done what needed to be done,' she said in an uncertain voice. 'The future will now unfold as it has to.'

'Ah, spoken like a true Skywatcher.'

Amilee's eyes found his again. 'Careful, Hamir.'

He barked a bitter laugh to the sky, and shook his head. 'The Word, the Warden and the Wanderer – The Trinity of Skywatchers! What a disappointment each of you must have been to our Mother. Tell me, do *you* feel proud, Yansas Amilee?'

'You have no right to use my true name!' Amilee bellowed.

'And you no longer have the right to judge me,' Hamir shouted back.

Amilee's perfect face was a sudden mask of fury, as her silver wings sprang from her robes, rising above her like scythes.

Unafraid, Hamir stepped towards her. 'A thousand years I served my sentence in the Labyrinth!' he roared. 'The Timewatcher and the Thaumaturgists turned their backs on me *long* before they abandoned the denizens of Labrys Town. And now they have abandoned you!' Hamir pointed an angry, shaking finger at her. 'Yansas Amilee, Warden, Skywatcher, Treasured Lady of the Thaumaturgists – *you* are the embarrassment here!'

Amilee's hand flashed out, gripped the necromancer by the jaw, dragged his face within an inch of her own and she screamed, '*Enough*!' before throwing him to the ground.

Hamir expected the assault to continue, knowing that he was defenceless against it; but to his surprise the heat and anger evaporated from the Skywatcher as quickly as it had bloomed. She stared down at him. Her wings fell limp, tears came to her eyes, and an eerie hush fell upon the garden.

'They didn't abandon me, Hamir,' she whispered. 'I walked away from them.'

Hearing the remorse in her voice, seeing her obvious fatigue, drained Hamir of his own anger. He got to his feet, brushing dirt and grass from his clothes.

'I do not think it is unreasonable of me to expect an explanation at this point, my lady,' he said stiffly.

Amilee looked up at the sky of her dreamscape. 'I tried to tell them that the war was not over, that the threat remained, but none of them would listen to me, including our Mother.'

Hamir frowned. 'The Timewatcher wouldn't listen to *you*?'

'In the end, she stopped caring, Hamir. I told them all they were fools. I refused to return to Mother Earth, and so they left me behind. They are not coming back.'

'You stayed because you knew the truth,' Hamir said, almost with respect. 'You knew that Spiral had planned for losing the war.'

'How different things might have been if I had listened to Lord Wolfe in the beginning,' Amilee replied, her sense of guilt clear. 'But I didn't, and so I have been hiding here since the end of the war, watching, listening, preparing ... regretting. I am the discrepancy in Spiral's plans, Hamir, the anomaly the Genii do not know about.'

'But what of the Relic Guild?' Hamir pleaded. 'Tell me what you have done, Yansas.'

'I have ensured the future will arrive on our terms.' There was concern in Amilee's eyes, but also defiance. 'The timeline I have created is in motion, but it is not *set*. You and I have much to do.' A fleeting sadness clouded Amilee's face. She shook her head. 'Timewatcher spare us all,' she growled. 'I hope you are ready to atone, Hamir. Your past atrocities might just be the saving of everyone.'

HOME

The Giant's Hand.

Beneath a sky that burned with pink fire, it stood as a lone sentinel in the desert of Mirage, exposed to waves of blistering heat rising from a landscape of searing sand and copper dunes. It rose palm up, its ledge thirty feet above the sands. And the stone sentinel was the custodian of treasure.

Standing upon the palm of the Giant's Hand were the red glass bell, hanging from a sturdy structure of stone, and the simple, wooden door in its red glass frame. Guarding these monuments, four Aelfirian soldiers held rifles in their hands, power stones primed and ready.

Somewhere, a Genii was watching.

Protected by the illusion of cool air, Van Bam stood barefoot upon the golden-red sands. Beside him, was Angel, dependable as ever, but tense and edgy. About fifteen paces away from the two magickers, stood Gulduur Bellow – an imposing ten feet tall, thin and wiry beneath his brown habit, the scars on his skin paler than the bleached sky. Thirty yards of shimmering heat separated the group from the Giant's Hand; and the Nephilim had used his blood-magic to render himself and his human companions undetectable to prying eyes or listening ears.

Lord Buyaal could not see or hear them. Not yet.

The only person missing was Namji. Before the group had left the sanctity of the western mountain range, Bellow had summoned Namji into his cavern. That had been the last time the Relic Guild agents had seen her. There had been no farewells, no explanations; Bellow had simply emerged from his lair alone, stating that the young Aelf would not be travelling with the humans. Angel had objected, but Bellow had refused to elaborate on his reasons, only saying that it was necessary.

Van Bam recalled how he had promised to take Namji back to

Labrys Town, but the illusionist was a changed man with bigger things on his mind now.

The invasion of the Labyrinth was imminent.

'We must wait for Buyaal to make his move,' Bellow said, his voice calm and close within the concealing spell he had cast. 'We cannot see into the citadel, but the citadel can see out. If you try to open that doorway now, a thousand rifles will fire upon you. But when the time comes, you remember what to do, Van Bam?'

Watching the four guards up on the Giant's hand, Van Bam nodded.

With his body decorated by the symbols and glyphs of a tainted thaumaturgy, the illusionist could feel the energy of his augmented magic vibrating inside him. The power of blood-magic caused Van Bam's green glass cane to sing with a clear, continuous peal of worry that only he could hear. Its song was like a rope stretching to snapping point, an elevator cable trying to lift too heavy a load. It was far more power than Van Bam should have been wielding, but it made him feel invincible.

Angel was looking at him, her face was creased with concern.

'You *do* know what you're doing, right?'

Van Bam nodded at her, once, with confidence.

'It is Buyaal's uncertainty that will work in our favour,' Bellow said. 'He cannot predict what will happen if the two of us fight. And to be honest, neither can I.' The Nephilim looked up at the pink sky and smacked his lips as though tasting the air. 'While I am keeping the Genii busy, the two of you must act swiftly. Head straight for the Giant's Hand. You must get to that doorway before Buyaal locates you.'

'What are you going to do?' said Angel. 'You can't take on an entire citadel by yourself.'

'Of course I can't.' A wry smile came to Bellow's lips. 'That would be stupid.' He turned his dazzling blue eyes to the magickers, his smile fading. 'I promise you that I will do exactly what is necessary to prevent Buyaal sending an army to Fabian Moor. Before this day is over, I intend to destroy Mirage's doorway to the Great Labyrinth. You have one chance to get home.'

With anxious eyes, Angel looked at Van Bam, and then at the

guards standing upon the Giant's Hand, who would think themselves surrounded by nothing but scorching, barren desert. 'We get ourselves into really dumb situations, you know.'

Van Bam didn't respond.

Angel swore. 'I wish I had a gun. A knife, at least.'

'You do not need a weapon,' Van Bam said, his voice a growl of energy. 'Bellow has given me power enough for us both.'

'Then you'd better use it to watch my back.' Angel's face was stern, almost angry, but her voice was small. 'Because I have to tell you, Van Bam, I can't remember the last time I was this scared.'

'Have faith in me, Angel.' The illusionist longed to use the magic he had been loaned. 'I will not let you down.'

The slightest of breezes disturbed the unremitting heat.

'It has been an honour to meet you both,' Gulduur Bellow said. 'And even more to help you return home.' He tasted the air again. 'But now ... it begins.'

Glassy tinkling came from somewhere, higher in pitch than the singing of Van Bam's cane. Up on the Giant's Hand, one of the Aelfirian soldiers shouldered his rifle, and stepped up to the bell of red glass. He reached up into the bell, and began running his hand around the inside of it, creating an answering call to the tinkling, joining with it, and the sound spread across the desert with an eerie voice like ice dust showering upon the strings of a harp.

Buyaal was making his move.

Van Bam's limbs shook with energy.

To the left, beyond Gulduur Bellow, before the Giant's Hand, the waves of heat began to thicken and rise towards the pink sky as if a great veil of water was being drawn up from golden-red sands. Dunes flattened, shapes began to form, and shadows flittered and whispered among them. Slowly, the veil of water solidified into huge stone blocks the colour of copper, and the south wall of Mirage was revealed.

Stretching far to the left and right of the Giant's Hand, the wall had at its centre – directly opposite the desert sentinel – great wooden gates. As Bellow had forewarned, the citadel's rampart was manned by hundreds of soldiers, all watching the desert with their rifles ready, the violet glow of power stones visible despite the harsh glare of the sun.

'Get ready,' Bellow said. He produced his curved dagger from the sleeve of his habit. 'When the fighting starts, don't wait, don't try to help me. I will give you as much time as I can. But when you see me raise the desert, be mindful that your time has nearly run out.'

Movement caught Van Bam's eye.

From the gates of Mirage, a stone bridge materialised, growing from the citadel, bridging the desert to join with the fingertips of the Giant's Hand. Almost as soon as it had connected, one of the guards opened the doorway to the Great Labyrinth, revealing the thick mists of the Nothing of Far and Deep. Mirage's mighty gates yawned wide, and a procession of soldiers strode out onto the bridge, marching six abreast, clad in light blue uniforms. The old Aelfirian captain who had welcomed the group to Mirage led the invasion force, dressed in crimson robes.

'Goodbye, my friends,' Bellow said, then cut his tongue with the point of the knife. He closed his mouth and collected blood.

'Here we go,' Angel whispered.

Van Bam took her hand in his.

Stillness gripped the desert, disturbed only by marching boots. Not until the soldiers were halfway across the bridge in a procession showing no sign of ending, did the Nephilim act.

Bellow barked a single word, spitting red mist into the air. His voice held such volume and passion that it blistered the desert heat with the rage of blood-magic. An eruption of wispy vapour ballooned before the Nephilim as the magic in his voice travelled faster than the sound of it. The roar of a sonic boom echoed among the dunes, but the spell raced straight towards the bridge, carving a deep furrow in the sand, before hitting its target.

The bridge tore apart with an explosion of stone and bodies, and a great cloud of dust billowed towards the sky. As debris and broken corpses rained to the desert sands, the screams of the dying filled the air, along with cries of alarm from the soldiers lining the south wall. Gulduur Bellow took his knife and sliced it across his palm. The blade disappeared up his sleeve, and the Nephilim smeared his blood over both his hands. His voice hissed sibilantly as he began intoning the spells of blood-magic. His long, quick fingers, red and glistening, began weaving an intricate design of symbols in the air.

'Now,' Van Bam snarled, and he and Angel ran for the Giant's Hand.

The illusionist whispered to his own magic, conjuring a globe of invisibility that continued to conceal the agents as they passed beyond the Nephilim's protection, racing as fast as they could through the sand. The cries of soldiers up on the wall became decisive shouts, orders, commands, and all along the rampart power stones began flashing on a host of rifles spitting bullets down into the desert.

Van Bam, risking a glance back, saw that Bellow had dropped his concealment. The giant blood-magicker was free for all to see. He was weaving his spells in the air, and the bullets were reduced to splashes of molten metal before they came within twenty feet of him.

A second sonic boom cracked across the desert as Bellow's second shriek released the magic he had conjured. The spell overtook Van Bam and Angel, racing away from them to slam into Mirage's entrance with hate and fire. The huge wooden gates erupted into fierce white flames; the stone archway collapsed. Voices screamed in agony, and a few burning soldiers rolled out onto what remained of the bridge to die. It seemed the impact had shaken the entire citadel.

With thick black smoke blooming towards the sky, boiling across Mirage like a storm cloud, Van Bam decided to add a little extra chaos to the confusion. He raised his green glass cane, whispered to the magic vibrating in his veins, and with joy released a little of the heightened power he wielded.

Ten thousand coppions burst from the sands at the base of the citadel. The army of scorpion-spider hybrids scrambled up the south wall, poison stings lashing. All along the rampart, soldiers shouted in panic.

Up on the Giant's Hand, the four guards had taken defensive positions. One of them had closed the doorway to the Great Labyrinth, and stood with his back to it. They were not diverted by the Nephilim attacking the citadel; their rifles tracked across the desert, clearly searching for the humans seeking to use the doorway.

Once Van Bam and Angel had come within ten yards of the Giant's Hand, the illusionist drew the healer to a halt. A strange energy was lacing the air, different from blood-magic but no less powerful. It raised the hairs on the back of Van Bam's neck.

'What is it?' Angel said, her teeth clenched. She shivered and rubbed at the gooseflesh on her arms.

'Buyaal,' Van Bam growled.

Although the Genii himself didn't make an appearance, his thaumaturgy did. The illusion of ten thousand coppions scaling the citadel's wall turned to green mist, swirling away to nothing. The white fire burning the tall gates dampened and died; but the billowing smoke was drawn up into the air, gathered into a single, dense black sphere that hung above Mirage like a hole punched into the pink sky. The sphere burst, and sped towards Gulduur Bellow as a great arc of liquid night, sparking with the power of higher magic as it went.

Bellow dropped to one knee, punching a bloodied fist into the sand. A dome of energy inflated around the Nephilim that hissed and screamed when Buyaal's thaumaturgy hit it. In moments, the darkness had surrounded the dome, creaking and droning as it tried to crush the blood-magicker inside.

'No!' cried Angel. 'What do we do, Van Bam?'

'We go home,' the illusionist replied.

He stabbed his green glass cane into the desert and began whispering to his magic.

The darkness surrounding Bellow had set as hard as stone. The soldiers up on the citadel wall were cheering, believing their foe to be vanquished. But Buyaal's magic was no longer compressing the dome. It had ceased crushing the Nephilim inside, and cracks had begun appearing in its surface. A red glow came from within, its light intensifying through the cracks, and the black dome shook. With a shout of thunder, the spell shattered into shards that slapped to the sand, melting and steaming.

Gulduur Bellow rose to his full height. With fresh blood on his hands, he once more wove symbols and glyphs in the air. Up on the battlements orders were shouted, and the soldiers began firing their rifles again.

This time the hail of bullets stopped, hanging like a swarm of bees trapped in the air. With one graceful motion, Bellow swept an arm before him, sending the bullets hurtling back towards the citadel in a mighty barrage. Chips of stone erupted from the walls with a metallic pinging. Cries came from the soldiers as their own bullets tore into them, knocking them away from their defensive positions.

Bellow yelled at the sky, his voice summoning the wind. The gale was sudden, ferocious, howling, and the Nephilim used it to command the desert itself to rise. The sand of Mirage spiralled up into a series of tornadoes. Each grew fatter, thicker, spinning faster and faster, taller than the south wall. As a searing, shredding storm of sand, the tornadoes attacked the citadel.

'He raised the desert,' Angel shouted above the howling wind. '*Now*, Van Bam!'

With the storm raging around him, Van Bam released the spell he had conjured.

Instead of the usual musical chime followed by a soft flare of green, the cane shuddered in Van Bam's hand as he freed the full might of his augmented magic. The blood symbols on his skin itched and burned, and he gritted his teeth. The colour seemed to bleed from the cane, forming a great circle of poisonous green beneath Van Bam and Angel. The illusionist pulled the cane from the ground and stood upright alongside the healer. They watched as the spell flowed towards the Giant's Hand, its venomous hue snaking through the copper sands like a sea beast cutting through an ocean.

It reached its destination.

A tremor shook the desert.

The four soldiers guarding the doorway to the Great Labyrinth staggered. They cried out in alarm as the Giant's Hand began to curl its fingers. With sharp cracks and the grind of stone on stone, the fingers curved over the soldiers. Panicking, stumbling, they lost their footing tumbled down thirty feet to the desert floor. Their cries ended abruptly as their bodies smashed upon the sharp and broken ruins of the bridge.

The Giant's Hand clenched into a mammoth fist. The red glass monuments shattered; the doorway to the Great Labyrinth was crushed to matchwood. Like a slow punch, the fist rose towards the sky, dragging clear the monstrously sized arm bones that connected to it. Twenty yards beyond it, another arm emerged from the sands, handless, chipped and worn, a great pillar of bone. As hand and stump *boomed* to the ground, another tremor shook House Mirage, and a colossus pulled itself out of the desert.

It heaved its body upright, and a great fall of sand pouring from long buried bones went spinning to join Bellow's tornadoes. The lower jaw of the colossus was missing, and red fire burned in the huge eye sockets of its skull. A few of its ribs had snapped off, and its bare joints ground and knocked together. The colossus fell forward, pulling the rest of its body from the desert. It had no legs, and its spine slid free like a tail. It dragged itself into the storm, towards the citadel.

'Oh Timewatcher, oh shit,' Angel cried above the gale. She had crouched down, covering her head with her hands. Her breath came in short, panicked gasps. 'What's going on, Van Bam?' she shouted. 'The doorway ... how do we get home now?'

Van Bam pulled her upright. He laid a hand upon the side of her face, staring deeply into her eyes. 'Illusions are only as strong as your faith,' he said, his breath blowing upon her face, full of the power of blood-magic. '*Believe* as I do. *See* the truth.'

Angel snapped out of her panic. Taking steadying breaths, she blinked rapidly, and saw that behind the grand illusion of the gargantuan skeleton, the Giant's Hand remained where it had always been, a sentinel of stone, upon which still stood the doorway to the Great Labyrinth.

From the citadel, the Genii was launching a counterattack against the Nephilim. The tornadoes lost all momentum, and tons of copper sand hissed to the ground as though the howling wind had been snatched from the air. Buyaal then sent his higher magic over the citadel wall as a flock of frenzied blackbirds, shrieking chaos as they hurtled towards Bellow.

But with the air no longer filled with the sandstorm, the soldiers manning the ramparts gained their first clear view of the monstrosity dragging itself towards the citadel. The colossus had no voice, but its ancient bones groaned like falling trees as its hand grabbed the top of the wall. Stone crumbling in its grip, soldiers shouting in terror, the mammoth skeleton hefted itself up, preparing to breach the defences, to climb into the city beyond.

With blood-magic prickling his skin, Van Bam drew his fellow magicker into an embrace. 'Believe with me, Angel,' he whispered into her ear. 'We are lighter than the air.'

They levitated fast, up and onto the palm of the Giant's Hand. Van Bam quickly assessed the situation. On the wall of Mirage, the few soldiers who had held their ground fired rifles at the colossus, their bullets smashing uselessly against the hard bone of its skull; but most of the soldiers had abandoned their posts, fleeing in fear. Down on the desert floor, Gulduur Bellow fought with Buyaal's thaumaturgy. The giant was almost performing a graceful dance as his blood-magic flared and burned and he battled the flock of frenzied birds.

The magickers of the Relic Guild owed the Nephilim a debt.

'Van Bam,' said Angel. She was almost smiling. 'Let's go home.'

With pandemonium raging across the desert, the illusionist snatched open the doorway to the Great Labyrinth. The Nothing of Far and Deep moaned at him, calling him home—

Angel yelped.

Van Bam wheeled around. The healer was wincing in pain, her teeth bared. Her head bobbed forwards, as though she had been struck from behind, and then she fell to her knees.

'Angel!'

Van Bam rushed towards her. He stopped when a voice said, 'Sneaky little magickers,' and Lord Buyaal materialised behind the healer.

Dressed in a priest's cassock as dark as his eyes, the Genii had Angel by the hair and was holding her down on her knees.

'I've been waiting for the Nephilim to try to send you home,' Buyaal said dangerously. His free hand was balled into a fist, glowing with higher magic. 'Lord Spiral cannot be stopped. Fabian Moor cannot be stopped. Your journey ends here, *human.*'

Angel whimpered.

Van Bam launched himself at the Genii.

Without thinking twice, he called upon every last shred of power that Gulduur Bellow had injected into his magic, channelled it into the green glass cane, and, with a shout of fury, he struck it down on Buyaal as though he wielded a mighty axe.

Buyaal raised an arm to block the blow. When the cane struck it, there was a discordant roar, a flash of blinding green light, and an explosion of energy punched Van Bam away. It sent him and the cane skidding and tumbling along the Giant's Hand, and the illusionist hurtled headfirst into the Nothing of Far and Deep.

'No!' Buyaal shouted after him.

Drifting down the tunnel that formed the pathway back to the Great Labyrinth, Van Bam turned around to face the way he had come. The portal showed a clear view into House Mirage. Angel, still on her knees, her eyes wide in terror, reached out a hand towards her fellow magicker. Try as he might to utilise the power of any blood-magic that remained to him, Van Bam could not make his way back to her.

Lord Buyaal's face was bestial with rage. 'Your death will come soon enough, magicker!' he screeched through the portal.

'Van Bam!' Angel shouted.

Buyaal silenced the healer by yanking back her head, and running the hand glowing with thaumaturgy across her throat.

There was blood as Angel's torso fell to one side, so much blood. The portal began to darken, and the Genii lifted the healer's head up by the hair like a trophy, taunting the illusionist with it. And then the portal turned to swirling blackness.

Van Bam tried to fight the tide, claw his way back, but he couldn't deny the momentum that rushed him away from Mirage. With a sudden lurch, he reached the end of the tunnel, and was expelled to land in a bone-jarring heap onto the damp cobbles of an alleyway in the Great Labyrinth. The green glass cane rolled away from him. Silver Moon's cold glare shone down on him from a star-filled sky.

Van Bam scrambled to his feet as the doorway on the alley wall slammed shut. He ran to it, but reeled away with his hands raised when the wooden door burst into blazing white fire. At the same moment, Van Bam cried out in pain, and the symbols of blood-magic flared with purple light upon his skin, shining through his clothes. When the light receded, the symbols and their power had gone ... as had the door.

Only the black bricks of the wall greeted the illusionist's eyes.

Van Bam staggered back, falling into a sitting position, staring at the wall. Just as he had promised, Gulduur Bellow had destroyed the doorway to House Mirage.

'Angel,' Van Bam whispered.

And he wept.

CHAPTER TWENTY TWO

DOUBT AND WONDER

I don't much like what they've done with the place, Gideon said.

The blue glass chamber had delivered Van Bam and Clara to a light-less location. The illusionist's inner vision couldn't see any details of the environment. He whispered to his magic, and illuminated his cane. The pale green light pushed back the darkness enough to expose the even stone ground, and the huge silver-grey wolf standing beside Van Bam, her head level with his chest.

Clara looked relaxed enough, but the shades and hues of her mood were tense, alert. Her yellow eyes stared into the gloom.

Gideon said, *She's not sensing anything living, my idiot.*

Behind the magickers, the primordial mists of the Nothing of Far and Deep churned within a doorframe set into a rock wall. The portal might have led back to the strange blue chamber; maybe to nowhere at all. Van Bam doubted it would lead back to the Museum of Aelfirian Heritage, to Samuel, Namji, Hillem and Glogelder. Why had the group been separated? Where were his friends now?

This place feels abandoned to me, Gideon said. *And Clara agrees, my idiot.*

Van Bam felt the same. The air was still, cold and dry. The smell of dust and age was rife with undisturbed years. But beyond his cane's glow the lightless shroud remained, giving no clue about the place they had arrived at. Was this their final destination, or merely another stopping-off place?

Whispering to his magic again, Van Bam enlarged the circle of light radiating from his cane, uncovering a little more detail. He and Clara stood on a promontory to which a bridge was connected. Just the beginnings of the bridge were lit; it was narrow, only wide enough to walk single file. Beneath it was nothing but more darkness.

At least you've found a way forward, Gideon drawled. *Such a shame we don't have a miserable sharpshooter with prescient awareness watching our backs.*

We have everything we need, Van Bam replied. 'Stay behind me, Clara,' he added aloud. 'Let me know if you detect anything.'

The wolf snorted her acquiescence.

Holding the green glass cane like a torch, the illusionist led the way onto the bridge. But the magickers had taken no more than a few steps before a sudden brilliance shone down and illuminated their environment.

Behold, Gideon said, amused, *The Cathedral of Doubt and Wonder.*

A cavern of monumental size, the agents on the narrow bridge miniscule within it. High above, mighty stalactites hung from the ceiling like the inverted towers and steeples of a great city, each one shining with a violet thaumaturgic glare. The massive size of the cavern was dizzying, stretching further than Van Bam's vision could see. The illusionist experienced a moment of vertigo as he realised the bridge arched over a yawning chasm that sunk into unknowable depths.

Interesting, Gideon purred. *Our presence seems to have activated old magic, my idiot.*

Indeed. But have we activated anything else? Van Bam replied, extinguishing the light of his cane. He looked back at the wolf; she was peering over the edge of the bridge, down into the endless dark. *What can Clara feel, Gideon?*

She can sense magic in the air, but still nothing living.

Van Bam's inner sight could see beyond the end of the bridge, to where the narrow path broadened into another promontory on the other side of the chasm. Rubble seemed to be piled there. The cavern wall formed a vast backdrop, faceted, sharp, filling Van Bam's vision with varying shades of grey. To normal eyes the bridge would have led to a dead end, but the illusionist could see the circle behind the pile of rubble: not another portal, but a hole in the wall.

Beneath the thaumaturgic light shed by the giant stalactites, Van Bam steadied the anxiety in his gut, and led the way across the narrow bridge at a slow and careful pace, his courage bolstered by the huge wolf stalking behind him.

My idiot, Gideon said, *now that we know Lady Amilee is the avatar's master, I have a question for you. When you returned from Mirage, all those years ago, whom did you tell about Gulduur Bellow?*

Before he answered, Van Bam had to dispel from his mind an image that had haunted his nightmares for decades; the image of Buyaal holding Angel's severed head like a trophy. *I made my report to you, and then to Lady Amilee,* he said sombrely.

Yes, but you didn't tell me the story of the Sorrow of Future Reason. Not back then. I only know now because I can access your memories. And I can't find a memory of you ever telling the Skywatcher, either.

Van Bam thought for a moment. *It didn't seem relevant at the time. I never told anyone about the Sorrow of Future Reason.*

You never mentioned it to Marney?

No.

Then how did Amilee know to leave the symbol for the Nephilim's House on the doorway in the museum? How did she know what it would mean to you?

It was a good question. Van Bam had wondered occasionally what had become of Gulduur Bellow. After all these years the illusionist had decided he must have died along with Angel during the battle against Lord Buyaal and the army of Mirage. But the symbol for the Sorrow of Future Reason, and the story behind it, he had almost entirely forgotten about until seeing it on that doorframe. Did the symbol's appearance mean Bellow had survived? Had Lady Amilee met with the Nephilim who saved the Labyrinth from invasion? And had he told the Skywatcher what that symbol would mean to Van Bam?

I think you're on the right lines, my idiot. But I suspect Amilee used the symbol for bigger reasons than as a lock on a doorway, or for gaining your trust.

I agree, Van Bam replied. *Much of what Bellow told me is making sense now, yet ...* He looked up to the glowing stalactites, took in the vastness of the cavern. *Why did Amilee use his memory to bring us to the Cathedral of Doubt and Wonder? What has the Nephilim to do with Known Things?*

Even now, for every mystery we solve, another ten replace it. Gideon sighed. *Perhaps we will finally gain proper answers at the end of this bridge.*

As the illusionist and the wolf crested the rise, and began walking down the other side, Clara growled as they came upon old bones, lying in a long line on the bridge. The bones belonged to an incomplete skeleton; the skull and spine of a huge creature that had obviously settled there to die a very long time ago. Van Bam looked up at the stalactites. Or perhaps the creature had been felled by something bigger.

Stop fretting, my idiot. Clara's adamant that you and she are the only living things here.

Finding little comfort in the dead Resident's words, Van Bam frowned at the skeleton. The creature's skull was three times the size of a man's, the jaw elongated, and it blocked the path, leaving only a foot of bridge between it and an endless fall. Van Bam tapped his cane upon the bridge, whispered a word, and summoned his illusionist magic. With a flash of green and a glassy chime that tinkled around the cavern, he conjured a rush of energy that pushed the skull over the edge.

It fell into the chasm, the long spine slithering after it, whipping and rattling. The remnants of the skeleton disappeared into the depths, leaving behind motes in the air that sparkled beneath the thaumaturgic light.

The dust settled, and the Relic Guild agents resumed crossing.

I'll tell you something else that's bothering me about our patron Skywatcher, Gideon said. *Do you remember my theory concerning the avatar's master? I hypothesised that it might be the Nightshade?*

I remember, Van Bam replied, focusing on the bridge, and trying not to think about the impossible depths beckoning just a few feet away on either side of him. *But as you said, we now know the avatar's master to be Lady Amilee.*

Exactly. Which reopens the question of how I formed a connection with the wolf. Why does Clara hear my voice?

Van Bam had no answer. He risked a quick glance back at Clara, a large and sleek silver-grey predator shadowing his footsteps, and he pushed the question to the back of his mind. Reaching the end of the bridge, the magickers stepped onto the promontory.

The hole in the wall was neat and circular, leading to a place that was just as dark as the cavern had been. The rubble piled before it appeared at first to be the result of a minor rock fall. But on closer inspection, Van Bam deduced that the rubble was the broken ruins of a huge stone golem. One of its legs from the knee down still stood upon a foot; its boulder-sized head was intact, lying on the ground, its simple features facing up; but the rest of the golem had been smashed into chunks of rock.

A guardian, I suspect, Gideon said. *But not anymore.*

Van Bam motioned for Clara to follow him quietly. Climbing over the debris, the illusionist led the way through the hole in the cavern wall.

The presence of the magickers once again activated the old, dormant magic in the Cathedral of Doubt and Wonder. A domed ceiling, coated in a metallic substance, glowed into life with warm, golden light, illuminating a circular chamber, spacious, its floor and wall as smooth as if it had been scooped out of the rock.

I hope the significance of this place isn't lost on you, my idiot, Gideon said, his voice barely above a whisper. *Right here, in this chamber, is where Iblisha Spiral, Lord of the Genii, planned his uprising against the Timewatcher. And it would seem he left his favourite toy behind.*

At the centre of the chamber stood a large stone table, thick and round. Most of its grand chairs, made from the same grey and black-veined stone, were upturned and broken, lying as more rubble on the floor. But standing upon the table was a glass tank, six feet high, three feet wide and deep. The glass was coated with the grime of age, but the tank's occupant could be seen clearly enough.

Van Bam felt a tightening in his gut.

A ghoul of a man stood in the tank, withered, obviously dead. His limbs and body were wrapped in strips of black cloth, his skin was preserved, mummified, leathery, a sickly shade of grey-green to Van Bam's mostly-colourless vision. A short length of glass tube protruded from his temple, sharp and jagged where it had snapped off. Even in death, the ghoul in the tank held in his thin and gnarled hands a black stone box shaped like a diamond.

'Known Things,' Van Bam said, a chill running through him.

There it is, said Gideon. *Still clasped in the hands of its Voice.* He snorted a bitter laugh. *So this is what really became of Lord Baran Wolfe the Wanderer. Makes you wonder what other details are missing from the history books, doesn't it, my idiot?*

Clara growled. She stood closer to the table than Van Bam, staring at the creature called Voice of Known Things – who had once been a noble Skywatcher. The hues of the wolf's mood were mixed between fear and anger.

Gideon said, *Clara wants me to tell you that she and I have seen this monstrosity in the tank, along with Known Things, once before. It was while I was searching Clara's mind for the message Marney had planted there. It seems our empathic friend not only knew about Known Things, but she had also seen it and its Voice.*

How? Van Bam replied. *What else did you see, Gideon? Did Marney give Clara more information?*

No. But Clara says that Marney's presence was never more dormant than when she was experiencing the events at the Falls of Dust and Silver. Clara says it was as though Marney was hiding, as if she knew what was coming.

And now that Clara is standing before Known Things and its Voice?

There was a pause before Gideon answered. *Marney's presence is stirring. It's like she's reacting to the proximity of—*

Look! Van Bam interrupted, pointing.

In the glass tank, upon the surface of Known Things, strange shapes and patterns began to glow with the purple light of higher magic: the language of the Thaumaturgists. The light pulsed gently, brightening to shine upon the black cloth wrapped around the corpse of the former Skywatcher, and then dimming – as though it breathed.

The wolf bared her teeth.

Gideon chuckled. *Clara says that Known Things and Marney's secrets are calling out to each other. I can feel it too.*

Van Bam shook his head, his confusion outweighing his apprehension. *How did Marney know, Gideon? When did she discover these secrets?*

I rather think that's beside the point. Hows *and* Whens *are of little importance now. What matters is that Lady Amilee and her avatar have led us to Known Things, and what it wants, my idiot, is the location of Oldest Place. All Clara has to do is join with it, and then we will learn how to destroy Spiral and the Genii.*

Van Bam looked around the chamber, at the golden glow of the domed ceiling, the broken stone chairs on the floor, and then back at the glowing symbols. *Samuel recently told me that nothing was ever that easy for the Relic Guild,* he said, and a shiver ran down his spine.

Easy? Gideon chuckled. *You first have to convince a giant wolf to go anywhere near that device.*

Van Bam turned his metallic eyes to Clara. She faced Voice of Known Things, her body rigid with fear, reluctant to move any closer, glaring at the pulsing shapes and patterns upon the diamond-shaped box.

'Clara—'

He stopped speaking as the wolf's yellow eyes flashed in his direction, and she showed him her teeth with a growl.

You can't be surprised by her reaction, my idiot. All of us experienced what Lord Wolfe went through. We know how it feels to be connected to Known Things. Would you wish to go through that again?

Wait . . .

Clara's growls weren't directed at the illusionist; her eyes weren't focused on him. The wolf was staring beyond Van Bam, and the hues of her body were confused, worried.

Oh no, said Gideon.

Van Bam spun around.

Near the chamber wall, a jagged line had appeared, like a crack in the air. Colours began snapping along the line, red and yellow to Van Bam's magical vision, dancing like a host of tiny flames.

'Back,' Van Bam ordered.

There came a hollow noise like a low inhalation, sucking the air from the chamber. Clara whined, and Van Bam skipped out of the way, as the broken pieces of the stone chairs began moving across the smooth floor, rolling and sliding, knocking and clattering, as they were drawn up to fill the circular hole in the wall, barring the only way out.

No escape, Gideon whispered.

The tiny red and gold flames extinguished, and the rent in the air began to widen. Clara growled. The temperature dropped to a wintery chill. The distant tumult of violence reached Van Bam's ears. A powerful stench filled his nostrils: age, corruption, hopelessness ...

'Clara, to me!' the illusionist shouted.

The wolf was at his side in an instant. Summoning his magic again, Van Bam cast a defensive barrier that covered the magickers in a dome of transparent green energy. The rent had widened enough to form a large rectangle in the air, four feet wide and seven feet tall. Its surface was darker than shadows, and uneven, studded as though black ice protruded from liquid obsidian.

The doorway to the Retrospective, Van Bam said, panic rising inside him. *How did it find us?*

Oh, I could hazard one or two guesses, my idiot, Gideon purred.

The doorway opened, the black studs parting, and the Retrospective released its inmates.

Eight wild demons stepped into the chamber. They crept, stalked, twitching nervously. Each of them was tall, thin, gangly but strong looking. Their skin was a hard grey carapace, glistening with an oily film; the fingers of their hands were like sharp blades of bone. Rheumy, fishlike eyes scoured the chamber; long teeth chattered together in gaping mouths.

The demons grouped before the magical barrier, and Clara barked savagely at them. But the monsters did not attack. They made no sound.

Your magic has little effect on wild demons, Gideon said, peevishly. *And I'm not convinced Clara can take them all. It's time to fight dirty.*

Van Bam prayed to the Timewatcher, begging for salvation.

With the wolf barking beside him, flashing teeth and spraying saliva, the illusionist once again whispered to the gift he had been born with. Channelling his magic, he made the green glass of his cane malleable. He twisted and pulled, separating his cane into two wicked spikes.

Makes you wish Samuel was here, doesn't it? Gideon said excitedly.

What about blood-magic? Van Bam suggested – desperate, distressed. *You have already shown Clara how to use it once.*

Gideon scoffed. *There is no time, and I am not Gulduur Bellow. Clara and I could conjure only a fraction of the Nephilim's power. Besides, I think we have bigger problems than these wild demons now.*

The wolf's barking stopped abruptly as the Retrospective opened its door again, and a ninth figure stepped into the chamber.

A hulking brute, tall and broad, dressed in a black cassock. Obese of body, thick across the shoulders, powerful in the arms. His head was bald, one of his eyes was missing, and his fat lips were twisted into a cruel sneer. Beneath the golden light shed by the domed ceiling, the scarring on his forehead was easy to see, and Van Bam felt an agonising echo of silver wings being ripped from his back.

Viktor Gadreel, Gideon hissed.

'Oh shit,' Van Bam whispered.

The Genii pointed at Clara. 'Little wolf,' he said, his voice a rumble of thunder. 'You have something I want.'

In Van Bam's head, Gideon's voice was a long hopeless sigh.

Good luck, my idiot.

Viktor Gadreel clapped his massive hands together, sending out a burst of thaumaturgy that shattered the protective dome of illusionist magic. Van Bam raised his green glass spikes, and Clara bared her teeth. As one, the eight wild demons began screeching with rage and violence, and they rushed forwards.

The demons moved with inordinate speed. With no time to think, the wolf leapt to meet them.

Don't hold back, Gideon urged. *Do what you were born to do, Clara!*

But before the wolf could unleash her full fury upon the demons, Viktor Gadreel stepped forwards, wrapped his higher magic around her, and hoisted her into the air. Snarling, writhing, Clara tried to break free of the Genii's magical grip, but could do nothing but dangle above the fight, watching as Van Bam was surrounded by the vile, grey monsters.

The illusionist tried again to summon his magic, but Gadreel dispelled it with an almost casual wave of his hand. The demons closed in.

No! Gideon shouted.

Clara's gnashed her teeth, barking and struggling, ineffectual against the power holding her aloft, and Van Bam faced impossible odds alone.

The illusionist gave a shout of defiance, and stabbed one of the green glass spikes through the face of a demon. But as the monster fell, the weapon was wrenched from Van Bam's grip, and he yelled as another demon plunged its knife-like fingers into his back. Turning his face to the domed ceiling, Van Bam ejected a fountain of blood from his mouth, before he was dragged down beneath the horde.

Please, Gideon begged. *Not like this. Not like—*

His voice disappeared with such sudden silence it was as if his presence had been cut out of Clara's mind. The demons screamed in frenzy. As a pack, they tore Van Bam apart.

His blood showered their hard grey shells; his muscle and skin filled their sharp-toothed maws.

Clara howled.

As the demons fed upon Van Bam, sating their furious lusts with his flesh, one of the green glass spikes rolled from out of the pack, across the floor, and stopped at the feet of Viktor Gadreel.

Framed by the doorway to the Retrospective, the Genii stared at the spike, his one eye emotionless, before he bent down and picked it up.

'Now then, little wolf,' he growled, stepping away from the feeding frenzy. 'You have my undivided attention.'

He stood before Clara, his fat, slug-like lips approximating a grotesque smile. Immobile, distraught, desperate, the wolf tried in vain to lunge forward to bite and savage his face. Gadreel rumbled a laugh.

Her eyes beholding the grim spectacle of the shrieking demons, her nostrils cloyed with the heavy scent of Van Bam's blood, Clara could do nothing but yowl as Gadreel slowly pierced her skin, almost gently, with the green glass spike, sliding the weapon into her stomach with surgical precision.

The wolf's voice merged with the screams of the demons.

Summoning another burst of thaumaturgy, the Genii raised Clara higher, and then slammed her down onto the stone table. She landed on her side, blood spraying from her mouth. Gadreel jumped up onto the table beside her, landing with a heavy boom that echoed around the chamber. With one massive fist, he punched the glass tank and shattered it, showering Clara in jagged shards.

The Genii grabbed Known Things and ripped it from the grasp of its Voice. The withered creature that had once been Lord Baran Wolfe collapsed and broke apart.

Holding the diamond-shaped box of black stone aloft, Gadreel intoned the language of the Thaumaturgists, his words growled, guttural. The light of the symbols upon Known Things intensified, glaring with the purple of higher magic. The Genii crouched down beside Clara. He was pleased.

'The time has come, little wolf,' said Gadreel. 'Tell me your secrets. Tell me about Oldest Place.'

With the green spike protruding from her gut and all the strength, all the fight, drained from her, Clara could only whine as two gelatinous tubes slithered out from the sides of Known Things. They whipped in the air as Gadreel moved the device towards the wolf's face. Feeling the silence left behind by Gideon in her mind, and the absence of Van Bam in her heart, Clara knew that she would soon follow them both into death.

To the angry noise of blood-smeared wild demons gorging, Clara gagged, then choked as one of the gelatinous tubes slipped down her throat. Gadreel grinned at her, his eye glinting, as the second tube hardened to glass and stabbed into the changeling's head, cracking open her skull, spearing into her brain.

And while Known Things swallowed the wolf's mind, a presence flared inside her, and a voice whispered through her last thoughts.

Be brave, Clara, Marney said. *All things are known in the end.*

ACKNOWLEDGEMENTS

So many people to thank. As always, Mum and Dad, Dot and Norm. My fierce agent John Berlyne. My marvellous editor Marcus Gipps, along with Gillian and Simon, Genn and Sophie and Paul, and the rest of the amazing Gollancz team. Olivia, my scary copy editor. My fellow writers for your support (and stories, of course), and the reviewers for your kind words. And *always* the readers for whom my work is written.

Someone I should've thanked in the first book is the wonderful writer Conrad Williams, who was my external examiner when *The Relic Guild* was a project for a Master's degree, and who, I later learned, put in a good word with my agent. I still owe you a beer, Conrad.

And lastly, Jack and Marney, my wife and daughter, for your unconditional love and support, and for putting up with me. I can't imagine my life without you.

Chapter 10, scene 3 of this book is dedicated to Team Gollancz, as it was written while I visited their grand towers in 2014.

Turn the page for an excerpt from the thrilling conclusion
to The Relic Guild trilogy:

The Watcher of Dead Time

STRANGE CREATURES

And then, for the greatest time, he played the long game alone.

Fabian Moor had spent half a human lifespan isolated inside a cube of thaumaturgic metal, surrounded by silver light radiating from four close walls. A claustrophobic sanctuary, fifteen feet high and wide and long. Mighty spells had been cast upon it by the greatest of all Thaumaturgists, Iblisha Spiral. The cube had been Moor's haven - or prison; a hub for a universal portal, which he had spent the last forty years using to search through the Nothing of Far and Deep for the House of all Houses.

The Great Labyrinth.

It had not been meant to be this way. Spiral, the Lord of the Genii, had a grand plan that should have seen Moor returning to the Labyrinth at the side of his master. But forty years before, the magickers of the Relic Guild had proved to be a bigger obstacle than anyone had anticipated. However, even with the help of the mighty Skywatcher Lady Amilee, the Relic Guild hadn't been powerful enough to destroy Lord Spiral's plan, or Moor. They had only delayed the inevitable.

At the centre of the silver cube a strange tree-like creature grew from the floor. With a small degree of pride, Moor gazed upon its leathery, brown-green bark. Serpentine roots writhed like a nest of snakes; branches grew from a solid trunk, coiling in the air and sliding over the ceiling. Moor smiled lightly as one of the reptilian branches pointed at him. He touched his index finger to its tip. The tree shuddered from the touch of its creator, but the branch withdrew when Moor held out the terracotta jar in his pale hands, recoiling from the forbidden thaumaturgy it held.

There had been moments when Moor had wondered if he would

ever see this jar again. It was one of four, plain and smooth, its lid sealed with wax, filled with the darkest magic. A lifetime ago, Moor had buried them in the foundations of the Labyrinth, where they had remained, waiting for the day of Moor's return when he could reanimate the essences they preserved.

The last of Lord Spiral's Genii, sleeping the long sleep, and it was almost time to wake them up.

There had been moments when the isolation of the long game had threatened to drive Moor insane. The Nothing of Far and Deep was a vast, thick cloud of primordial mist – unimaginably huge to lesser creatures – and the Labyrinth was the only House dwelling inside it. Or so others believed. It would seem that Moor's task was impossible to achieve, like trying to find a single diamond buried in a desert. But he had prevailed. Compromise, adaption, patience – that was all Moor had required to carry Lord Spiral's ultimate goal across the decades to a time where there was no one waiting to help the people of the Labyrinth.

The Genii War was long over, the Timewatcher and Her Thaumaturgists were gone for good, and the terracotta jar in Moor's hands was the beginning of the future. The days of isolation were at an end, and the silver cube had almost served its purpose. Almost . . .

The serpentine tree stirred and writhed as a presence filtered through the thaumaturgic walls, disturbing the stolid air. A curious sensation washed over Moor. Someone had summoned him - but not with words, more with feelings that rippled through the silver cube, carrying fear.

Turning his back on the tree, Moor laid his hand on the glowing surface of a wall subtly unlike the others. Immediately the thaumaturgic metal's state shifted, changing from solid to pearlescent liquid and finally to clear, shimmering air.

A bedraggled man stood on damp cobbles outside. Behind him, an alleyway of the Great Labyrinth stretched away into shadows. He was small, his clothes and skin grubby, and his feral eyes were fixed on the terracotta jar in Moor's hands. Charlie Hemlock, they called him. It was a good name for the poisonous sort of human he was.

"Hello, Charlie," said Moor.

Hemlock gave a quick nod in return.

Three golems stood in a line behind him. Deformed and withered bodies covered by black cassocks, grotesque faces hidden beneath the wide brims of their hats, these stone servants had lost every aspect of the humans they had once been. Subservient, incapable of speech or thought, they waited for orders. The power stones that energised the pistols in their hands glowed with violet light.

Moor said, "I trust everything has gone to plan, Charlie? Our prey has caught scent of the bait?"

Shifty and nervous, Hemlock wrung his hands together and looked at a young woman lying unconscious at his feet. "It won't be long before Marney comes looking for her." His voice was slightly distorted through the wall of air.

Moor ran his hand over the smooth surface of the terracotta jar. "Perfect."

The unconscious woman, the *bait*, unwashed and dressed in oversized clothes no better than rags, had short blonde hair streaked with red dye. Such a small and innocent looking thing, but deceptive in her appearance. Her name was Clara, her clients called her Peppercorn, and she had been touched by magic.

"Marney will be here soon," Hemlock stressed. Anxiety laced his voice. The prospect obviously disturbed him, as it should. Marney, an empath, one of the last magickers of the Relic Guild . . . and the keeper of secrets. She was dangerous and clever, keeping herself well concealed amongst the denizens of Labrys Town. Moor had found Marney practically impossible to locate, but, with Peppercorn Clara's unwitting assistance, the empath had finally been enticed out of hiding.

"So," Hemlock said, eyeing the serpentine tree behind Moor. "If that's everything, I'll just take my money and be on my way."

"On your way?"

"If it's all the same to you."

Hemlock spoke brightly, casually, belying the fear beneath.

Moor clucked his tongue. "I understand how you feel. I've shown you things that frighten you, and now you're wondering if you have bitten off more than you can chew."

After a quick glance at the golems behind him, and the woman at his feet, Hemlock shrugged at the Genii. Moor resisted the urge to wrap his thaumaturgy around the venal idiot's body and crush the life from him.

"We need to discuss the next phase of the plan, Charlie."

Hemlock licked his lips nervously. "I didn't know there was a next phase."

"Indeed. Step inside, please."

Hemlock didn't move. "Look," he said. "I've done everything you asked of me, but I'm through with this now. I'm in over my head." He frowned at the serpentine tree. "I'll just take my money and leave."

"No, no, no," Moor said. "The part you are about to play is surprisingly important, given that you are a human."

"But-"

Hemlock's words choked off. Moor had used his thaumaturgy to pulse a command to the golems. In unison they aimed their pistols at Hemlock, taking a step towards him. With a yelp, Hemlock skipped away from them, through the veil of shimmering air, into the silver cube. As soon as he had crossed the threshold, Moor commanded the golems to guard Peppercorn Clara, and then returned the wall to its solid state.

His face paling, Hemlock stuck close to the wall. His eyes, wide and panicked, darted from Moor to the jar to the tree creature, and back again.

"Charlie, you are too young to remember the Labyrinth before the Genii and the Thaumaturgists went to war." Moor waited for Hemlock's fear to acknowledge that he was being spoken to. "You think of the Timewatcher as an all-loving mother, yet She abandoned you cold-heartedly. Abandoned us all. This is a dangerous time, for you and me both."

"W-what do you want?"

The Genii turned to the tree. A few more of its leathery branches reached for him. He stroked each of them in turn.

"You know the tale of Oldest Place, yes?" He turned to Hemlock. "The prison House in which the Timewatcher incarcerated the Lord of the Genii?"

Hemlock nodded almost imperceptibly.

"Marney knows the tale, too. Better than most, you might say. She is very important to me, Charlie. And the future. But here-" he held up the terracotta jar "-I want to introduce you to a colleague of mine. Her name is Hagi Tabet."

Confused, afraid, Hemlock said, "What?"

"Lady Tabet is to be the new Resident of Labrys Town." Moor ran his finger around the jar's wax seal. "And I need you to deliver her to the Nightshade."

"What are you talking about?" Hemlock whimpered. "No one can get into the Nightshade. Not even you."

"That's not entirely true, Charlie. I know of a way, you see. Unfortunately, it will cost you your life."

Hemlock's simmering panic boiled over. Pathetically, he reached into the sleeve of his coat for a concealed weapon, but Moor stopped him in his tracks. The Genii bound the human in higher magic, rendered him immobile, strangled the voice from his throat. His eyes staring, body and limbs boneless as a ragdoll, Hemlock's feet slid over the cube's silver floor as thaumaturgy dragged him forwards.

Once he was close enough, Moor switched places with Hemlock, watching as the sinuous, leathery branches of the serpentine tree reached out and captured him. They coiled around his legs, removed his dirty, patched coat, and ripped open his shirt. Popped buttons bounced off silver walls. Hemlock expressed a scream with his eyes as a branch slid around his midriff and two others wrapped around his wrists, holding him prone and defenceless before the Genii.

"Calm yourself," Moor said. "You have a little time to live your life yet."

Holding up the terracotta jar again, Moor removed his hand and left it floating in the air, slowly spinning. Hemlock's eyes welled with tears as Moor laid cold hands upon his chest and summoned his power.

"It's a small mercy, Charlie, but you won't remember what I'm about to do. For now, brace yourself. This is going to cause you agony beyond belief."